Ramayana Stories in Modern South India

COMPILED AND EDITED BY
PAULA RICHMAN

Ramayana Stories in Modern South India

An Anthology

INDIANA UNIVERSITY PRESS
Bloomington and Indianapolis

This book is a publication of

Indiana University Press
601 North Morton Street
Bloomington, IN 47404-3797 USA

http://iupress.indiana.edu

Telephone orders   800-842-6796
Fax orders   812-855-7931
Orders by e-mail   iuporder@indiana.edu

The paper used in this publication meets the minimum requirements of American National Standard for Information Sciences—Permanence of Paper for Printed Library Materials, ANSI Z39.48-1984.

Manufactured in the United States of America

Library of Congress Cataloging-in-Publication Data

Ramayana stories in modern South India : an anthology / compiled and edited by Paula Richman.
    p. cm.
  Includes translations from Tamil, Kannada, Telugu, and Malayalam.
  Includes bibliographical references and index.
  ISBN 978-0-253-34988-0 (cloth : alk. paper) — ISBN 978-0-253-21953-4 (pbk. : alk. paper) 1. Dravidian literature—20th century—Translations into English. 2. Valmiki—Translations into English. 3. Valmiki—Adaptations. I. Richman, Paula.
  PL4608.55.E5 2008
  894.8′08—dc22

                                                   2007026594

1 2 3 4 5   13 12 11 10 09 08

In memory of Nathan Richman

Many know the story. Few know its meaning.

Tamil folk narrative

Contents

EPILOGUE: META-NARRATIVE

A map of South India is provided on page 15.

Preface: Compiling a Ramayana Anthology

Veerappan, the mustachioed bandit based deep in the forests of Karnataka, abducted beloved film actor Rajkumar and held him prisoner for three months in 1998. When Rajkumar was finally released, a well-wisher asked how he felt. He was forced to remain in the forest only three months, he replied, but Lord Rama had to endure fourteen years there. As Rajkumar's reply suggests, Indians continue to turn to the ancient story about Rama and Sita for language to articulate their experiences. The selections in this anthology reveal a plethora of evocative ways in which modern writers have drawn upon the story to express, reflect upon, and interpret their deepest concerns.

The stories within the fluid and heterogeneous Ramayana tradition lend themselves to varied transformations in accord with people's changing concerns. Even Valmiki's *Ramayana*, the earliest extant rendition of the story, depicts controversies in which characters disagree, and modern retellings continue that tradition.[1] To ignore these renditions would be to miss out on major debates in contemporary India, debates that articulate competing perspectives on how to live properly. The selections gathered here plunge you into present-day controversies ranging from what spouses should expect from each other to how full equality can be achieved in ascetic practice. You can learn about how fashion exerts pressure on young women, how writers envision the forest as a refuge from urban ills, how silence may enable domestic abuse to continue, or how modern writers fight against the tendency to demonize groups who differ from themselves.[2]

Since modern tellings from the Ramayana tradition encompass this extraordinary range of topics, readers cannot understand the nature of the tradition if they only know one telling of the story. The broadest understanding results from encounters with multiple tellings; this anthology sets out, side by side, selected modern tellings, translated from the four major literary languages of South India: Tamil, Kannada, Telugu, and Malayalam.[3] Because most scholars study a single Indian literary tradition in isolation (e.g., Tamil literary history separately from Kannada literary history), an incident's wider role may be missed. Yet, when one investigates retellings of the same incident in neighboring languages, previously unobserved patterns emerge.[4] The assumption is *not* that certain characterizations, themes, and incidents are found only in the South.[5] Rather this anthology shows that, in four bordering linguistic regions, certain facets of the Ramayana tradition developed in parallel, pronounced, and recurrent ways.

The selections in this volume were chosen from nearly two hundred re-tellings in South Indian languages. Each text in the anthology was published in its original South Indian language before translation. I have included only texts that succeed as excellent literary works and exhibit some kind of compelling innovation or new perspective.[6] Among these works, I chose only texts whose rhetorical effects in the original language could be approximated in English without losing the spirit of the original.[7] In order to reproduce the effects of the original, translators have targeted as units of meaning phrases and sentences, rather than individual words. Since my goal was to enrich, rather than duplicate, the corpus of translations from South Indian languages into English, I have picked, for the most part, works not published previously in book form.[8]

All the selections in *Telling Ramayana Stories in Modern South India* were written during the last hundred years, dating from the first decade of the twentieth century to the first decade of the twenty-first. The anthology includes work from early literary pioneers in each language (Bharati in Tamil, Puttappa in Kannada, Chalam in Telugu, Asan in Malayalam) to call attention to the roots of today's retellings. The anthology belies the claim that, because of their distance from the past, modern tellings always prove more superficial than older renditions. Indeed, modern retellings are often richly self-reflexive because they build upon, as well as respond to, past renditions, benefiting from the distinctive narrative momentum available to writers who participate in an already established story tradition.[9]

In addition to representing several phases of recent literary history, the collection also showcases socio-economic, gendered, generic, and tonal diversity. The writings of authors born into high, middling, and low castes are included; works of male and female writers appear in this book. The anthology also contains a mix of genres, ranging from short stories, plays, and poetry to folksongs. In addition, selections display varied tones, from tragic to mundane, lofty to slapstick, elevated to colloquial. Since one's position in the social order often shapes one's experience and perspective on the world, while the variety of genres and tones enable a writer to express a range of emotions and ideas, the anthology's diversity broadens understanding of the Ramayana tradition.

Rethinking familiar characters in new ways (part 1), focusing upon characters previously seen as marginal (part 2), and looking anew at so-called demons (part 3) have generated some of the freshest and most original writing in modern South India. The book spotlights characters other than Brahmin and Kshatriya males with established authority, who have already received substantial scholarly attention.[10] Instead, characters who were not the main focus in authoritative tellings are highlighted in this volume: women, lower castes, and the "other."

The narratives in this anthology demonstrate the significance of the corpus of modern South Indian tellings of the story of Rama and Sita, showing what has been missed due to lack of systematic study of these literary works. While many see Rama's story as reinforcing the status quo, especially its caste and gender hierarchy, a number of the selections in this collection reveal the liberatory potential present in the Ramayana tradition. Selections provide new readings, some outside the lens of orthodoxy and/or beyond the limits imposed by those who view the story as rigidly static. Indeed, several pieces that won recognition for their aesthetic sophistication have also been pivotal in debates about social transformations in modern India.

This book has been written for three groups of readers. People studying Indian culture for the first time will benefit from learning about the Ramayana tradition in India because it provides the equivalent of the Bible, Shakespeare, Homer, Roman law, and vernacular folktales in the Anglo-American mainstream tradition, all rolled into one. While providing access, through translation, to one of India's most famous narrative traditions, the book's multiple perspectives and stances help to protect novices from essentializing, Orientalizing, or reifying South Asian culture. For readers of literature in one or more South Indian regional languages, this volume provides access to the story of Rama and Sita as told in other major South Indian languages.[11] Scholars of South Asia can learn how one of Hinduism's two pre-eminent epics has been instantiated in South India during the last one hundred years by talented and innovative writers.

No anthology could ever exhaust the range and variety of tellings of the story of Rama and Sita in South India because authors continue to write retellings of Ramkatha today and will probably do so long into the future. Nor could any volume represent, definitively, the range and variety of modern tellings. Indeed, any selection of tellings from the Ramayana tradition will reflect the affinities of the compiler.[12] Nonetheless, the book's focus on contextualizing Sita, bringing formerly marginalized characters to the center, and re-examining demons provides new perspectives on modern Indian culture. By documenting these three strands of the capacious Ramayana tradition, the anthology shows how retellings of the story of Rama and Sita play a vital role in Indian life today and reveals yet another facet of the gem we call Ramayana tradition.

Notes

1. Goldman (2004).

2. During the period under study here, hundreds of pious reiterations of Ramkatha have been produced based on Valmiki, Kamban, Eluttacchan, or Ranganathan and other pre-twentieth-century South Indian texts. These works are not the subject of this book.

3. South India is not, by any means, the only region of India where Ramkatha has been re-interpreted in significant ways by modern writers (e.g., Mathili Sharan Gupta's *Saket* in modern Hindi). Nonetheless, retellings of Rama's story in North and South India vary dramatically. *Ramcharitmanas* by Tulsidas is widely disseminated throughout the North, where many have Hindi as their mother tongue and others learn it as a second language in school. *Ramcharitmanas* has attained the status of the "classic" Hindi Ramayana, so most North Indian Hindus are familiar with at least certain verses from it. In contrast, no single text functions as the sole "classic" Ramayana in South India. From the twelfth century onward, a diverse Ramayana tradition developed in all four

major languages, serving as the foundation for even greater Ramkatha diversity as the centuries passed.

4. Although "South India" suggests an autonomous, self-contained region, the exact borders of many of today's Indian states are relatively recent, most dating to 1947 or the following decade. State boundaries also remain linguistically fluid, since people living near state lines usually shift back and forth from one language to another. Finally, artistic influences often ignore such boundaries. For example, itinerant Marathi performers traveled far beyond Maharashtra, influencing staging of dramas across South India.

5. For example, according to a story that circulates in Tamil (South India) and Bengali (Eastern India), after Rama killed Ravana, he was exhausted. When one of Ravana's kin (bearing one hundred or one thousand heads, depending upon the rendition) came for revenge, it was Sita who defeated him in battle. See Coburn (1995) and Zvelebil (1987).

6. My decisions about what to include developed out of extensive conversations with the writers and scholars listed in the acknowledgments. I am grateful to them for calling my attention to excellent texts, but I alone am responsible for the final choices.

7. Whenever possible, I sought translators who had an affinity for the material being translated. For example, noted Kannada playwright Girish Karnad and scholar of Kannada theatrical tradition K. Marulasiddappa co-translated Puttappa's *Shudra Tapasvi*.

8. As this book was going off to the publisher, a volume of translations, *Retelling the Ramayana, Voices from Kerala* (2005), appeared in print. It contains Vasanthi Sankaranarayanan's translation of C. N. Sreekantan Nair's play, *Kanchana Sita*. The play provides the basis for the film by Aravindan that Usha Zacharias analyzes (#9) in *Ramayana Stories in Modern South India*. The Kerala volume also contains an essay by K. Satchidanadan that surveys recent Malayalam poems, plays, and short stories based on Ramkatha, as well as translations of several short stories by Sarah Joseph.

9. Some recent examples in English include Jane Smiley's *A Thousand Acres*, a retelling of Shakespeare's *King Lear* from the perspective of Gonerill, and *Wide Sargasso Sea* by Jean Rhys, a retelling of *Jane Eyre* from the perspective of Mr. Rochester's first wife.

10. For citations and assessment of such previous scholarship, see the introductions to the translations of Valmiki's *Ramayana* under the editorship of Goldman (1984–1996).

11. Although many Indians speak more than one Indian language, far fewer read literary works in more than one South Indian language.

12. An anthology of modern tellings of Ramkatha could have been created according to many different criteria. One could assemble retellings of interest mainly for their theological innovations or created an entirely different kind of volume based on excerpts from novels based on Rama's story. A compiler interested primarily in social history could have gathered together stories that provoked public outcry. The heterogeneous Ramayana tradition makes such varied anthologies not only feasible but appropriate.

Acknowledgments

During the ten years of this collaborative project, many people have helped to make this anthology richer, more wide-ranging, and more illuminating than it would have been otherwise. First, I thank authors and literary heirs who gave us permission to translate and publish their works (see list at end of acknowledgments). Second, I am grateful to the extraordinary group of translators who rendered the selections into English with flair and fidelity and then uncomplainingly revised and annotated their translations in response to questions raised by scholars, college students, and Ramkatha aficionados both in India and the United States. Third, I appreciate the suggestions of those whose advice I sought in identifying, choosing, and annotating the selections included in this anthology: K. Marulasiddappa, Lakshmi Holmstrom, Velcheru Narayana Rao, K. Ayyappa Paniker, and Rizio Yohannan Raj.

It was my good fortune to present, discuss, and debate many of the issues raised as I compiled this anthology in public lectures at Dhvanyaloka in Mysore, Bangalore University, the Prakriti Foundation in Chennai, Asmita Collective and the Telugu Akademi in Hyderabad and Secundarabad, Samyukta and the Center for Women's Studies in Thiruvananthapuram, Calicut University in Kozhikode, the History Department of Delhi University, Deshbandhu College, and the Sahitya Akademi in Delhi. In the United States, I presented many of the ideas that appear in the introductory essay and the headnotes to the three sections at the University of Chicago, the University of California at Berkeley, Indiana University, Bucknell University, and the Association for Asian Studies meetings. The comments, queries, and enthusiasm of those who attended these talks pushed me to refine and strengthen my arguments; I thank them for their input.

I am grateful to all the translators and almost all of the living authors whose writings appear in this anthology for conversations that elucidated the texts and provided insights about their stances toward Ramkatha. In addition, for thoughtful discussions about individual Tamil materials, I thank A. R. Venkatachalapathy, Prema Nandakumar, "CREA" S. Ramakrishnan, Dilip Kumar, Theodore Bhaskaran, the late Sankaralingam of the Roja Muttiah Research Library, G. Sundar, Uma Narayanan, Subhasree Krishnaswamy, and V. Geetha. For individual Kannada materials, I thank C. N. Simha, Mrs. Varada Panje, U. K. Jayadev, the late Vajramuni, Girija and A. Madhavan, K. C. Belliappa, M. Chaitanya, the late Nittor Srinivasa Rao, Jayaseetha Premanand, N. Gayathri, Mamta Sagar, Ramesvari Verma, G. S. Shivarudrappa, G. Venkatasubbaiah, and U. R. Anandamurthy. For individual Telugu materials, I thank C. Mrunalini, Aburi Chaya Devi, Bapu, Vijaya Chayanti, "Nasy" Narayanaswami Sankagiri,

Afsar, Kalpana Rentala, and the members of the Detroit Telugu Literary Club. For individual Malayalam materials, I thank Gita Krishnankutty, Thachom Poyil Rajeevan, K. G. Karthikeyan, L. Shammiraj, Sushil Pillai, Akavoor Narayanan, Jayashree Ramakrishanan, G. S. Jayasree, Lalitha Menon, Padma Ramachandran, and Leela Gulati. All of them, and many others, whom limits of space prevent me from listing, deepened my understanding of the multiple ways in which Ramkatha has been explicated and reconceptualized in South India.

The students in three sets of Ramayana seminars at Oberlin College articulated probing questions and expressed excitement about the materials, often making me see selections in new ways over the decade that I compiled this anthology. Much of the yearly travel to India was funded by the five-year Irvin E. Houck Chair; I thank Mrs. Houck for her long-standing support for, and interest in, this project. I am indebted to Katherine Linehan, Laurie McMillin, and Sandra Zagarell; their insightful comments and requests for explanations made the introduction and framing remarks more lucid and informative. The nudges and reminders of Rebecca Tolen kept me on track during the final stages of revision. Krissy Ferris provided eagle-eyed proofreading and suggestions that enhanced the usefulness of annotations and the clarity of the translations. Most of all, I thank Michael H. Fisher, who gave me practical advice, contributed insightful observations, clarified wayward sentences, figured out ingenious ways to solve editing problems, and enhanced my peace of mind throughout the process of compiling this anthology.

Rizio Yohannan Raj's pellucid translation of Kumaran Asan's "Sita Immersed in Reflection" led me to pick Pushpamala N.'s artwork, "The Yogini," for this anthology's cover. Until Asan, few Indian poets considered what it would have meant for Sita to live so long in an ashram dedicated to disciplining mind and body. Asan depicts how Sita mastered equanimity of mind and compassionate action as a yogini. If many Hindu women were told to model themselves after Sita, what does it mean that Sita is not only wife of Lord Rama but also a yogini who reflects deeply on the transient nature of existence while living in Valmiki's ashram? The figure in "The Yogini" is *not* Sita, but Pushmala's artwork deals with how the present is mixed with artifacts of the past. Further, Pushpamala has inserted her own photograph into a much older painting from the court of Bijapur; several writers whose works have been translated in this anthology also imagine themselves in Sita's world and consider how Sita would cope with today's world.

Collaborating with so many people knowledgeable about the Ramayana tradition and South Indian literature has enriched my life and that of the students whom I have taught at Oberlin College. I am grateful to all of them for helping to ensure that the literary works in this volume reached new sets of readers through translation into English. The strengths of this volume derive from the vitality of the Ramayana narrative. The lacunae in the volume result from limits of space, time, funds, and copyright permission, as well as from human finitude and life's contingency.

"Deliverance from the Curse" by Pudumaippittan was first published in Tamil as a short story. The translation by Ms. Lakshmi Holmstrom appeared in *Pudumaippittan Fictions* published by Katha in 2002. "Shurpanakha's Sorrow" by Kavanasarma was first published in Telugu as a short story. The translation by Alladi Uma and M. Sridhar appeared in *Ayoni and Other Stories* published by Katha in 2001. The copyright for these English translations rests with Katha, a registered, nonprofit society devoted to enhancing the pleasures of reading.

Lakshmi Holmstrom's translation from Tamil of S. Sivasekaram's "Ahalya," which first appeared in *Lutesong and Lament,* edited by Chelva Kanaganayakam in 2001, has been reprinted with the kind permission of TSAR Publications, Toronto.

Paula Richman's translation from Tamil of Subramania Bharati's "The Horns of the Horse" first appeared in *Manushi: A Journal about Women and Society,* no. 116. Velcheru Narayana Rao's translation from Telugu of the women's song "Sita Locked Out" first appeared in *Manushi,* no. 139. Both works have been reprinted with the kind permission of *Manushi.*

Sita Enters the Fire. All rights reserved by Sowris Pramoda. Translated and printed with permission.

"Letters from Lady Sita" by Kumudini translated and printed with the kind permission of M. S. Nandakumar, son of Ranganayaki Thatam.

Poem from *Iti Gitike* translated and printed with the kind permission of Vijaya Dabbe.

"Forest" excerpt, by Ambai, translated and printed with the kind permission of C. S. Lakshmi (Ambai) and Oxford University Press, New Delhi.

"Reunion" translated and printed with the kind permission of "Volga" Lalitha Kumari Popuri.

"In the Shadow of Sita" translated and printed with the kind permission of Lalitha Lenin.

Scenes two and three of *Shudra Tapasvi,* a play by "Kuvempu" Kuppalli Venkata Puttappa, translated and printed with the kind permission of Mr. Poorna Chandra Tejasvi, son of Kuvempu.

"Woman of Stone" by K. B. Sreedevi translated and printed with the kind permission of K. B. Sreedevi.

"Ahalya" by N. S. Madhavan translated and printed with the kind permission of N. S. Madhavan.

Mappila Ramayana, recorded and transcribed by M. N. Karassery from T. H. Kunhiraman, translated and printed with the kind permission of M. N. Karassery and T. H. Kunhiraman.

Chitrapata, play by H. S. Venkatesha Murthy, translated and printed with the kind permission of H. S. Venkatesha Murthy. First published by Anika Pustaka in Bangalore in 1999.

"Come Unto Me, Janaki" translated and printed with the kind permission of K. Satchidanandan.

Note on Transliteration, Translation, and Pronunciation

Because this anthology is designed to make modern South Indian retellings of the story of Rama and Sita accessible to English readers both in India and the United States, we have tried to translate Indian terms whenever possible, but have not done so when the Indian term is so dense with meaning that to translate it would be to drain it of complexity. Thus, we have kept, and italicized at first use, terms such as *dharma, tapas,* and *shastra.* Each such term also appears in the glossary.

Since this anthology is aimed at a broad readership, we have eschewed diacritical marks whenever possible and employed the familiar Anglicized spellings of Indian names of characters, places, and concepts in order to avoid littering the reader's page with terms in italics and markings that exoticize the translation. Instead, our method facilitates the process by which non-native readers come into contact with Indian terms regularly and, as a result, incorporate them into their intellectual framework and gain a sense of their meanings in multiple contexts. People in South India deal with such Anglicized spellings all the time without resorting to scholarly transliteration virtually unintelligible to most people. We have, however, been consistent in our use of Anglicized spellings. Hence we use Sita, not Seetha, and Kamban, rather than Kampan. For book titles, we have used instead the transliteration into English that appears on the back of the title pages of books published in Tamil, Kannada, Telugu, and Malayalam, whenever possible.

In addition to authors who wrote under their own names, two other kinds of author's usage appear in this volume. If an author chose a nom de plume, we use it in the table of contents and throughout the anthology, but provide the author's given name in the headnotes preceding the translation of the author's literary work. In contrast, if an author's name has been abbreviated to initials, as is common in South India, we have instead used the full name (e.g., K. V. Puttappa instead of Ku. Vem. Pu. or "Kuvempu"), but indicated the commonly used abbreviation in the headnotes preceding the translation.

For practical reasons, most of the headnotes to individual selections were written by the anthology's editor. In a few cases, the translator also wrote the headnotes; there the initials of the translator appear in brackets at the end of the headnotes (e.g., L. H. for Lakshmi Holmstrom).

Approximate Pronunciations of Names of Ramayana Characters

Note: a double vowel indicates the vowel is long, except for "oo" which is used to indicate a long "u" as in English "balloon."

ROYAL FAMILY IN AYODHYA

Kausalya	Cow-SUL-ya	(sul as in sulk)
Rama	RAA-ma	RAA as in hurrah
Kaikeyi	Kuy-KAY-yee	(kuy rhymes with guy)
Bharata	BA-ra-ta	(Ba as in bargain)
Sumitra	Sue-MEE-traa	
Lakshmana	LUCKSH-ma-na	
Shatrughna	Sha-TRUE-gna	(gna as g'night)
Dasharatha	Dush-a-RUT-ha	(dush rhymes with rush, rut rhymes with mutt)
Shanta	SHAN-taa	
Rishyashringa	RISH-yash-rin-ga	(rish rhymes with swish)

ROYAL FAMILY IN JANAKAPURA

Sita	SEE-taa	
Urmila	OAR-mill-aa	
Janaka	JUN-a-ka	(Jun rhymes with sun)

RAKSHASAS AND OGRES

Shurpanakha	SURE-pun-a-khaa	
Ravana	RAA-va-na	(Raa as in hurrah)
Indrajit	IN-dra-jeet	(jeet rhymes with beet)
Mandodari	MUN-doe-da-ree	(mun rhymes with sun)
Vibhishana	Vi-BEE-sha-na	(vi as in visit)
Maricha	Ma-REE-cha	
Tadaka	TA-da-ka	(Ta as in tug)

ALLIES OF RAMA

Hanuman	Hun-oo-MUN	(Hun and mun rhyme with sun)
Sugriva	Soo-GRIEVE-a	
Vali	VAA-lee	
Angada	ANG-a-da	
Jambuvan	JUM-bu-vun	(Jum as in jump, vun rhymes with sun)
Jatayu	Ja-TA-you	

SAGES AND ASHRAM-DWELLERS

Vasishtha	Va-SEESH-the	(seesh as in seashell)
Vishvamitra	Vish-VAH-mee-tra	
Valmiki	Vul-MEE-key	(vul as in vulture)
Lava	LOVE-a	
Kusha	COO-sha	(coo as in coupe)

PREVIOUSLY MARGINALIZED CHARACTERS

Ahalya	a-HULL-yah	
Gautama	GOW-ta-ma	(gow rhymes with cow)
Sadananda	Sud-AA-nan-da	(sud as in suddenly)
Shambuka	Sham-BOO-ka	(sham rhymes with some)

Ramayana Stories in Modern South India

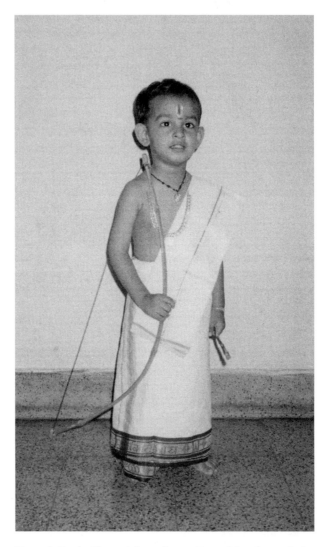

Figure 1. Boy in Chennai dressed up as Rama. Many boys admire Rama's prowess with a bow and play at being Rama, just as other boys play at being soldiers, cowboys, or superheroes. S. Santosh photographed at age seven by C. R. Shyam Sundar. Used with permission.

Introduction: Whose Ramayana Is It?

A striking literary phenomenon has been gradually gathering momentum over the last one hundred years. Although the earliest rendition of the story of Prince Rama and his wife, Sita, dates to before the common era, its incidents have inspired creative writers throughout the twentieth, and into the twenty-first, century.[1] Some of the most talented writers in the four major languages of South India—Tamil, Kannada, Telugu, and Malayalam—have chosen to rewrite stories from the Ramayana tradition. Since speakers of the four languages number more than two hundred million people, these modern South Indian retellings have the potential to reach a huge number of readers.

Ramkatha (Rama's story) is the phrase by which scholars refer to the basic narrative of Rama's marriage, exile, and battle with Ravana. In contrast, when referring in this anthology to specific tellings of Rama's story, the name of the author (such as "Ambai's telling") or the name of the work (such as *Shudra Tapasvi*) is used. If referring to the diverse set of tellings that present the story of Rama in different styles, languages, and media (rather than some abstract summary or single telling), the collective term "the Ramayana tradition" is used.

Ramkatha has already been told hundreds of times in diverse ways. So, why would modern authors want to tell it again? The South Indian writers in this volume did so to express how *they* perceived and interpreted the narrative in light of their own time in history, place in society, literary inclinations, religious commitments, and political views. Each author has recounted the story in a unique way, but when their works are read together, patterns emerge across languages and genres. The modern retellings translated into English in this anthology reveal the range of ways in which thoughtful writers have reinterpreted Rama's story over a century's time in the southern region of India.

This book brings together, for the first time, newly or recently translated retellings of Ramkatha originally published in South Indian languages during the last hundred years. In consultation with respected scholars and writers of Tamil, Kannada, Telugu, and Malayalam, I chose the twenty-two selections in *Ramayana Stories in Modern South India* from more than two hundred suitable texts. The aim was to maintain a balance between languages, genres, historical periods, and range of perspectives. The anthology focuses on shorter literary forms, such as short stories, songs, poems, and plays rather than, for example, novels or epics.[2] Since the book highlights modes by which Rama's story has been adapted, two essays are included; one analyzes how a dramatic script meant primarily for reading was transformed into a theatrical production and the other analyzes how a play was modified for film.

The anthology presents readers with texts, contexts, and insights into broad narrative patterns within the Ramayana tradition. By including framing remarks, selection headnotes, and annotations, the volume provides knowledge about the social, political, and literary contexts of texts. By grouping the selections according to whether they deal with Sita (part 1), marginalized characters (part 2), or demons (part 3), the book reveals three aspects of Ramkatha that have drawn extensive, deeply thoughtful, and innovative treatment from modern South Indian authors.

Folklore scholar A. K. Ramanujan once called the Ramayana tradition "a second language."[3] The rest of this introduction could be considered an intensive "immersion" course in Ramkatha language. Its goal is to equip even novice readers of Ramkatha with the knowledge to appreciate the subtleties of the selections in this volume. "Foundations" gives a synopsis of the plot, followed by a survey of categories into which tellings of Ramkatha have been classified. "Modern Retellings in the South" assesses why modern printed tellings have been largely overlooked by scholars and surveys Ramkatha's role in the cultural life of South India. "Shared Features" investigates how social critique and new forms of literary expression have shaped modern recastings of Ramkatha. "Transformations" articulates the logic of the volume's three-part structure and explains how modern retellings of Ramkatha show the flaws in popular generalizations about today's India.

Foundations

Almost all Hindu adults in India, and a significant number of Indians of other religious affiliations, are familiar with Rama's story, which most learned as children. While those who already know the basic narrative may want to move on to the section (p. 8) titled "Classifying Ramayanas," those encountering Ramkatha for the first time will find a summary of the basic plot helpful. In the overview below, incidents are summarized in as neutral a manner as possible. This synopsis does not follow any single telling of Ramkatha exactly. Instead, it is a heuristic synthesis, designed to show readers where each of the selections in this anthology belongs in the Ramkatha plot line. Each selection recasts or reinterprets one or several incidents found in the synopsis. The plot line that follows is intended to provide a conventional template of events within which one can locate selections in the remainder of this volume and appreciate their originality.[4]

Plot Line for Reference

Rama's Birth and Childhood

Ravana, the ruler of the *rakshasa* (demon) kingdom of Lanka, practiced such long and rigorous *tapas* (asceticism) that the gods had to offer him a boon (a promise to be fulfilled). When Ravana asks that he not be killed by a deity or a demon, they agree, so the king believes himself invincible. Due to his arrogance, he does not request protection from humans or animals, creatures whom he considers too weak to threaten his life. Subsequently, Ravana causes Earth to suffer under his tyrannical rule and the gods beseech the Supreme God, Lord Vishnu, for succor. Graciously agreeing to become an *avatara*, he descends from heaven to take birth in human form in order to destroy rakshasas and restore *dharma*, the code of proper conduct that sustains order in the world.

Meanwhile in Ayodhya, the capital of the kingdom of Kosala, King Dasharatha lacks an heir, so his court ministers urge him to perform a *yajna* (sacrificial rite) for the begetting of sons. From the sacrificial fire emerges a special food that the king feeds to his wives, after which they conceive. His first wife, Queen Kausalya, gives birth to Rama, avatara of Lord Vishnu.[5] His third and youngest wife, Kaikeyi, bears Bharata. Dasharatha's middle wife, Sumitra, has twins: Lakshmana, who grows especially attached to Rama, and Shatrughna, who becomes particularly fond of Bharata.

As members of a distinguished *Kshatriya* (warrior) lineage that traces its origins back to the Sun God, the princes receive training in statecraft and warfare.[6] One day, Sage Vishvamitra arrives at court. Although born a Kshatriya, Vishvamitra has transformed himself into a *Brahmin* (priest) through tapas of singular intensity; when he is displeased, his anger is similarly intense. He has come to request Rama's aid in destroying rakshasas who are interfering with the performance of yajnas in a nearby forest. Dasharatha is reluctant to dispatch his young son on such a dangerous mission, but fearing that refusal might anger the short-tempered sage, the king finally agrees and sends his younger brother, Lakshmana, along with Rama. In the forest, Vishvamitra bestows divine weapons upon the two brothers and teaches them *mantras* (efficacious Sanskrit syllables) to unleash the supernatural powers of the weapons. The princes then slay Tadaka, a monstrous ogre, and her son, Subahu, thereby restoring peace to the forest.

Vishvamitra and the boys then proceed toward the kingdom of Mithila, where King Janaka rules. Famous for his interest in philosophical debate, he shows warm hospitality to learned sages who honor his court with their visits. On the path to Mithila, dust stirred up by Rama's feet falls upon a stone, which turns into a woman. Vishvamitra explains that in a moment of fury, her husband, Gautama, had cursed Ahalya to become a stone. Since a curse cannot be retracted after it is uttered, the regretful husband had ameliorated its effect by decreeing the curse would end when dust from the feet of Rama touched the stone.[7] Now delivered from the curse, Ahalya praises Rama's goodness.

Long ago, King Janaka had been ritually plowing a field as part of a ceremony when he discovered a tiny infant lying in a furrow. Janaka and his queen named her Sita ("furrow" in Sanskrit) and raised her as their own daughter.[8] In order to ensure that Sita marries a suitably valiant Kshatriya, King Janaka has proclaimed that only the warrior strong enough to string the huge bow of

Lord Shiva will win his daughter as bride.[9] Among all the princes who took up the challenge, none had been successful. Rama enters Janaka's court and astonishes onlookers by lifting the bow easily and bending it to string it. He grips it so firmly that the bow snaps, demonstrating his superior power and winning him Sita as wife. At the wedding, Lakshmana also marries Sita's sister, Urmila.

Conflicts over Dynastic Succession

When King Dasharatha decides to pass on his royal responsibilities to the next generation, he chooses as his successor Rama, adored by the citizens of Ayodhya for his wisdom and compassion. The maid of Queen Kaikeyi, the king's youngest and favorite wife, tells Kaikeyi of Rama's choice and convinces Kaikeyi that, should Rama become king, the fortunes of Kaikeyi and Bharata would suffer. So Kaikeyi demands that the king redeem two promises he made earlier when she saved his life on the battlefield: she asks that Rama be exiled to the forest for fourteen years and that Bharata be crowned in his place. Rama, believing that his father should fulfill his promises, calmly accepts exile to maintain his dynasty's reputation for truthfulness. He sets off at once for the forest, accompanied by his wife, Sita, and Lakshmana, his younger brother.[10] Ayodhya's citizens follow their beloved prince and beseech him not to abandon them, but Rama remains firm in resolve.

Separated from Rama, Dasharatha dies of a broken heart. Shortly afterward, Bharata returns from visiting his uncle to learn that his mother, Kaikeyi, caused Rama's exile. Shocked at what she has done, he seeks out Rama in the forest, tells him about Dasharatha's death, and pleads with him to return and assume the throne. Despite Rama's sadness upon hearing about his father, Rama refuses to break his vow to dwell in the woods for fourteen years. Bharata also refuses to accept the crown, and declares that he will place Rama's sandals on the throne and act only as regent until his brother's return. Although he will serve in the court by day, he will sleep each night in Nandigram, a nearby forest, to share the hardships of his exiled brother's life.

Exile in the Forest

In the forest, Rama, Sita, and Lakshmana meet a tribal chieftain, ferrymen, and ascetic sages as they travel through sites ranging from peaceful to dangerous. Eventually, the threesome decide to settle in beautiful Panchavati, where Lakshmana builds them a small cottage. One day Shurpanakha, Ravana's sister, catches sight of Rama and falls in love with him. When she offers herself to him as wife, he replies that he already has one. Deeming Sita the obstacle to her union with Rama, Shurpanakha decides to devour Sita. As she draws near, Rama orders Lakshmana to cut off Shurpanakha's nose and ears. In pain, she flees to her brother. Railing against Rama, she also tells Ravana of Sita's great beauty.

His sister's words arouse in Ravana desire for revenge against Rama and passion for Sita. Since Sita is fond of animals, Ravana enlists the aid of his uncle who, in the form of a golden deer, entrances Sita. When she pleads with Rama to catch the deer as a pet, he entrusts Lakshmana to look after Sita, and then chases the deer, gradually getting lured far away. Rama eventually becomes suspicious and shoots the deer, but with its dying breath the animal calls out in Rama's voice, asking for help. Alarmed, Sita demands that Lakshmana go to the assistance of Rama right away, but Lakshmana refuses, since his brother ordered him to guard Sita. She angrily accuses Lakshmana of harboring impure designs on her and threatens suicide if Lakshmana does not join Rama at once. Reluctantly, Lakshmana departs.

Immediately after Lakshmana leaves, Ravana takes on the disguise of a holy man and approaches Sita, asking for alms. As soon as he gets close enough, he seizes her and carries her away in his celestial chariot. Jatayu, valiant vulture and friend of Rama's father, attempts to prevent Sita's capture, but Ravana deals him a lethal blow. He survives only long enough to tell Rama and Lakshmana that Ravana has abducted Sita. After performing Jatayu's funeral rites, the two princes begin looking for Sita.

In the Monkey Kingdom

While searching for Sita and gathering allies to fight Ravana, Rama gets embroiled in the politics of Kishkindha, a monkey kingdom. There Rama meets the deposed king, Sugriva, and his diplomat, Hanuman. Hanuman finds himself drawn to Rama and becomes his staunch devotee. Sugriva, like Rama, has suffered the loss of his wife and kingdom so the two make a pact: Rama will help Sugriva win back his wife and throne, both currently under the control of his brother, Vali, and afterward the armies of Sugriva will join in Rama's search to find Sita.

Vali possesses a power that makes it nearly impossible for any opponent to defeat him: when he faces his foe in battle, half of the enemy's strength leaves him and goes to Vali. Therefore, a plan is developed: Sugriva will challenge Vali to a duel, and Rama will conceal himself behind a tree. Vali accepts the challenge and at an opportune moment, Rama shoots Vali in the back. By doing so, he circumvents Sugriva's loss of his power to Vali but transgresses the Kshatriya code that warriors must face each other in a fair battle. When Vali dies from the wounds made by Rama's arrow, Sugriva regains his kingdom and subsequently sends his warriors off in all directions seeking news of Sita's whereabouts. They recover a bundle of jewels that she dropped from Ravana's chariot and eventually learn that Ravana took her to his capital city of Lanka.

Hanuman Visits Sita in Lanka

Hanuman crosses the sea to Lanka and eventually locates Sita, who has refused to enter Ravana's quarters. Instead, she has insisted on dwelling beneath an Ashoka tree in the grove outside the palace, where she remains throughout her imprisonment, living like an ascetic.[11] Hiding in the tree above where Sita sits, Hanuman watches Ravana arrive and alternately attempt to seduce Sita and then threaten her life. After Ravana leaves, Sita feels deeply disheartened that Rama has not yet come to rescue her and considers suicide. At that moment, Hanuman descends from the tree, presents Sita with Rama's signet ring, and assures her of imminent rescue. She sends Hanuman back with one of her ornaments as a memento of her devotion to Rama.

Hanuman then visits the nearby orchard where he voraciously consumes fruit and causes such a disturbance that the king's guards come running. Allowing himself to be captured and taken to Ravana's court, Hanuman urges the king to release Sita. Instead, Ravana orders Hanuman's tail set on fire to teach him a lesson. Easily escaping his captors, Hanuman crosses the city, setting buildings afire and spreading panic. After quenching his burning tail in the sea, he returns to Rama with news of Sita.

The War in Lanka

Rama and his allies meet to prepare for war and Hanuman informs Rama about Ravana's military fortifications. Vibhishana, a brother of Ravana who has repudiated him to join Rama's forces, provides intelligence about Ravana's warriors and their powers. Then, taking counsel with Sugriva and Jambuvan, king and commander of the allied bear army, Rama and Lakshmana plan their attack. Monkeys and bears build a bridge across the waters to Lanka so that the army can cross. Then the battle rages, complete with supernatural weapons and feats of bravery, resulting in heavy losses on both sides. Indrajit, Ravana's son, manages to fell Lakshmana, but Hanuman brings a special herb from a far-off mountain that heals him. Rama ultimately kills Ravana in one-on-one combat, and then crowns Vibhishana king of Lanka.

Next, Rama orders Sita to adorn herself and come to him. When she arrives, he announces that he will not take her back because she has dwelled within the precincts of another man. In response, Sita determines to undergo an *agnipariksha* (fire ordeal) to prove her purity. When she steps into the flames, the fire god Agni lifts her out cool and unharmed. Now that she has proven her innocence, Rama declares her worthy to take her place by his side. Rama and Sita then return to Ayodhya, where Rama is crowned. Under his rule, the kingdom enjoys such prosperity and order that the rule of Rama become synonymous with perfect kingship.[12] Some tellings of the story end here while others go on to recount later events during Rama's reign.

Rama's Later Life and Rule

Rama learns that some of his subjects continue to doubt Sita's purity and insinuate that she has tainted the royal family's reputation. Rama becomes convinced that duty requires him to banish Sita from his kingdom. Earlier,

Sita had expressed a desire to visit some holy sites in the forest, so Rama tells Lakshmana to fulfill her wish and then to forsake her in the forest. Rama assumes that Sita will die, but instead she gives birth to his twin sons, Lava and Kusha, and receives shelter in the nearby ashram (hermitage) of Sage Valmiki. There Sita raises her boys, never revealing to them who their father is. Valmiki composes an epic poem about Rama and teaches Lava and Kusha to recite it.

During Rama's reign, Shambuka begins practicing tapas in the forest. The *dharma-shastras* (treatises that set out the duties of ranked social groups) prescribe and proscribe actions according to one's birth in one of four *varnas* (religiously validated categories of rank). Members of the top three groups are classified as "twice-born": Brahmins (priests, religious preceptors); Kshatriyas (warriors, kings); and *Vaishyas* (merchants, agriculturalists).[13] Members of the fourth and lowest varna, Shudras, are prohibited from practicing asceticism, which is reserved for twice-borns. As king, it is Rama's responsibility to ensure that members of each varna perform only their assigned duties. Therefore, when Rama beheads Shambuka, a Shudra, for his transgression, he wins approval from the gods and his court ministers for restoring dharma.

Subsequently, Brahmin advisors at Rama's court urge him to perform an *ashvamedha* (horse sacrifice) to attain the status of a universal sovereign. The ritual involves letting a white horse wander for a year's time. Wherever the horse roams, that land belongs to Rama (or to a king who pays tribute, thus acknowledging vassal status). In order to assert Rama's claim of sovereignty, he must defeat any king who challenges the horse's passage. Because an ashvamedha requires the participation of the king's wife, and Sita has been banished, the sages tell Rama to remarry, but he refuses. Ultimately, the sages concede that a golden statue of Sita may be used in the ritual and it commences.

Sage Valmiki brings Lava and Kusha to chant his poem about Rama during the ashvamedha rites and Rama realizes they are his sons. He requests that Valmiki bring Sita to the capital as well, but when he returns with her, Rama asks her to undergo another fire ordeal to show the citizens of Ayodhya that she is pure. Rather than endure such an indignity, she returns to her mother, Earth. Bereft by the loss of his wife, eventually Rama ends his earthly life and returns to Vishnu's celestial world.

Valmiki's Roles

Valmiki plays two roles in Ramayana tradition: the first rendition of Ramkatha is attributed to him and he also acts as a pivotal character in his own text. Ramkatha begins its narration by explaining how Valmiki came to be a great sage. He was born into a robber family and, due to his low birth, he was judged unqualified to chant Rama's name directly. Instead, his religious preceptor taught him the mantra "mara mara." When Valmiki uttered the phrase repeatedly, the syllables blended into "(ma)rama rama(ra)," thereby accruing the meritorious karmic fruits of chanting Rama's name.

One day, Valmiki saw a hunter kill a krauncha bird that was mating. When he cursed the hunter, his curse emerged in a perfect metrical form called the *shloka,* in which Valmiki proceeded to write his *Ramayana.* So it is said the shloka originated from Valmiki's *shoka,* "sorrow" about the separation of lovers. By creating the first *kavya* (ornate poetic composition) in Sanskrit literature, Valmiki earned the sobriquet *adi-kavi* (first poet). Loss of the krauncha bird's mate prefigures Ramkatha's narrative arc since its overall story recounts the separation of Rama and Sita and their consequent suffering.[14]

Classifying Ramayanas

The "bare-bones" rendering of Ramkatha's plot above does scant justice to the complex and nuanced ways in which the story has been told over the centuries. Truly, Ramayana is not a story but a tradition of storytelling, within whose capacious limits many different stories are contained. To supplement the plot synopsis above, therefore, a survey of three categories into which Ramkatha texts have been classified is given below: (1) Sanskrit tellings, (2) regional language devotional texts, and (3) folk tellings. Readers already familiar with the history of the Ramayana tradition might want to skip this section and go directly to the discussion of modern tellings in South India.

When referring to a particular recounting of Ramkatha, the term "variant" is avoided because its usage implies that only a single correct version exists, from which every other telling varies. Instead, following the usage of A. K. Ramanujan, in this volume we use the term "telling" to refer to each individual rendition.[15] We do so because each selection is a valid telling of Ramkatha, worthy of attention in its own right.

Sanskrit Tellings

Ancient Hindu tradition lauds Sanskrit as the sacred language most appropriate for praise of deities, so telling Ramkatha in Sanskrit is a particularly auspicious act.[16] Since Brahmins have memorized, preserved, and recited Sanskrit texts and lived, to lesser and greater degrees over time, in most areas of the Indian subcontinent, Sanskrit tellings of Rama's story have circulated *across* India, rather than just in a single region. More than twenty-five Sanskrit renditions of Ramkatha exist in various literary genres.

The first full literary text of Ramkatha in Sanskrit, called simply *Ramayana,* is attributed to Valmiki, the sage in whose ashram Sita took refuge.[17] Within Ramayana tradition, Valmiki's *Ramayana* has earned greater prestige, influence, and authority than all other renditions of the story.[18] Besides being in Sanskrit, it has gained great status because of its antiquity; most scholars date its compilation to ca. 500 BCE–250 CE. The text is venerated by devotees as the primordial story, taken by scholars as the foundational manuscript, and respected by later writers for its literary qualities. These characteristics have won Valmiki's *Ramayana* pre-eminent historical, religious, and aesthetic authority.

On the whole, Valmiki's *Ramayana* tends to affirm the values of the social order of his day, thus helping to uphold institutionalized power. Valmiki emphasizes performing one's assigned duties, including those to spouse, parent, elder brother, lineage, *jati* (sub-caste), varna, master, ruler, and kingdom. The text urges adherence to brahminically defined dharma—even at great social or personal cost. It thus won special favor with rulers and high caste elites, who often supported its recitation, recopying, and illustration. Members of subordinated groups have long heard Valmiki exhort that one must act with proper deference to those higher in the social order.

Valmiki's *Ramayana* is the most authoritative telling of Ramkatha in India. The phrase "authoritative tellings of Ramkatha" refers to texts that share three characteristics. First, they espouse normative ideologies of ranked social hierarchy. Second, they are influential beyond the temporal and geographical context in which they were written, continuing to be respected, studied, and transmitted centuries after their composition. Third, they have gained recognition as privileged texts. Although Valmiki's *Ramayana* is the most famous and influential "authoritative telling," at least two others are generally recognized as authoritative: the Hindi *Ramcharitmanas* of Tulsidas, and Kamban's Tamil *Iramavataram*.[19]

Not all Sanskrit tellings of Ramkatha reiterate the gender and caste ideologies present in Valmiki's *Ramayana*. In Bhavabhuti's eighth-century Sanskrit play *Uttararamacharita* (The Later Deeds of Rama), for example, Rama accuses himself of unjustifiable cruelty to Sita and rues the fact that, because a king is duty-bound to uphold the social order, he had to execute Shambuka, despite his admiration for him. In fact, some modern writers refer to the ethical questions that Bhavabhuti raises about Rama's treatment of Sita and Shambuka as a precedent for their own critique of Rama. *Adbhuta Ramayana,* a much later Sanskrit text, recounts the arrival of Ravana's hundred-headed cousin to revenge his cousin's death. Sita slays this demon because Rama, who has just killed Ravana, is too exhausted to fight.[20] Although these two Sanskrit texts endorse disparate social ideologies, Valmiki's *Ramayana* is, by far, the most influential telling of Ramkatha in Sanskrit.

Regional Devotional Tellings

Ramkatha in both Sanskrit and regional languages are called "fixed" texts because, whether inscribed on palm leaves or printed on paper, they were composed for oral recitation. Thus, that they were written is less significant than that almost all their verses were composed, preserved, and transmitted word for word. (Manuscripts do, however, contain some variations due to the development of different recensions, but the vast majority of the words are fixed.) Both Sanskrit and regional texts possess all or most of the following features: they are usually attributed to particular poets, composed in elevated literary genres, and initially recited in elite (royal, monastic, temple) settings. The major difference between Sanskrit and regional language tellings of Ramkatha is that, in contrast to pan-Indian Sanskrit texts, regional tellings circulate primarily *within* a single geographical area. In addition, tellings of Ramkatha in regional languages tend to incorporate local practices into the story. For example, when the wedding of Rama and Sita is described, the account might include nuptial rituals particular to that region. Writing in a language accessible to those who do not know Sanskrit enables an author to reach an audience broader than just Sanskrit-schooled elites, so texts in regional languages are accessible to people on all rungs of the social hierarchy.

Sometimes for this very reason, Ramkatha tellings in regional languages have met with suspicion and criticism. Brahmins in sixteenth-century Varanasi are said to have been offended when poet Tulsidas composed *Ramcharitmanas* (Ocean of Deeds of Rama) in Hindi, rather than Sanskrit. To test his text, they put it beneath a stack of Sanskrit works in the sanctum of a temple overnight. The next morning, when *Ramcharitmanas* appeared on top of the pile of texts, it was taken as divine approval for writing Ramkatha in languages other than Sanskrit.[21] In North India today, *Ramcharitmanas* is the most widely circulated telling of Ramkatha.

Most tellings of Ramkatha composed in regional languages before the twentieth century are *bhakti*, or "devotional," texts. Through them poets celebrate, exegetes provide commentary on, and audiences hear the salvific deeds of Lord Rama. Bhakti tellings of Ramkatha praise Rama as God on earth, rather than just as excellent king and valiant warrior. The point of such renditions is not primarily to tell the story, since its incidents are already familiar to the vast majority of listeners, but to savor the goodness and compassion of Rama and participate in expressing devotion to him.

The earliest full, extant, devotional telling of Ramkatha in a regional language is Kamban's *Iramavataram* (Rama, the Avatara). Most scholars date this Old Tamil text to the twelfth century. Beloved among Rama devotees, *Iramavataram* has also won literary respect at least partly due to the sophisticated way in which Kamban draws upon classic conventions of poetry about love and war from Tamil's earliest literary corpus (ca. first century BCE), and transforms them into appropriate modes for expressing devotion to Lord Rama. Before the development of modern Malayalam, religious and political elites in what is today Kerala and Tamilnadu used Old Tamil for elevated discourse, so knowledge of *Iramavataram* extended beyond the limits of today's Tamilnadu into Kerala, thus cutting a wide swath across South India.

Tellings of Ramkatha composed in regional languages between the twelfth and nineteenth centuries were responsible for expanding the diversity of the Ramayana tradition tremendously. India boasts more than sixteen major languages, and nearly every major Indian literary tradition includes at least one well-known telling of Ramkatha. The descriptor *bhasha* ("language") is sometimes attached to authors who deliberately choose to write not in a pan-Indian language such as Sanskrit, Persian, or English but in a language spoken primarily in a single geographical area of India. By writing Ramkatha in these languages, authors of pre-twentieth-century regional Ramayanas laid a foundation for the subsequent modern retellings in Tamil, Kannada, Telugu, and Malayalam in this volume.

Folk Tellings

Folk tellings are more fluid than the first two categories of Ramkatha just discussed and often incorporate topical material. Folk tellings usually possess some or most of the following: they are anonymous or attributed to authors about whom almost nothing is known; composed in folk genres and often in local dialects; and often performed for religious occasions by non-professionals (those who earn their living primarily by other occupations). Folk tellings provide more scope for improvisation than do fixed texts, allowing the narrative to be customized according to the predilections of storytellers and preferences of listeners.

In folk texts, perspectives on characters and episodes often differ significantly from those in the first two categories of Ramkatha discussed above. Folk tellings of Ramkatha have been recounted for centuries and continue to be told in rural areas today across the Indian subcontinent. Furthermore, these renditions vary widely from locality to locality—sometimes even from village to village. Women's songs and songs of men low in social rank have been especially generative of diversity within Ramayana tradition. Two features of folk stories prove especially relevant to modern Ramkatha tellings: they sometimes present episodes from non-authoritative perspectives and include characters not found in more widely known renditions.

For example, some women's folksongs provide a fresh perspective on events by focusing on what they know best. While Ramkatha by Valmiki, Tulsidas, and Kamban focus on deeds performed by men, such as priestly rites to attain royal heirs and details of battles, many women's songs barely mention these events, concentrating instead on the actions of women. For example, songs sung by Brahmin Telugu-speaking women focus on Sita, describing her wedding rites, marital relations, and pregnancy. The songs also spotlight women such as Sita's mother-in-law (Kausalya), her sister-in-law (Shanta), and her sister (Urmila).[22] A set of women's folksongs performed by domestic servants in North India present new characters: the midwife who delivered Rama; a deer killed to make a drum for Baby Rama.[23]

Even if a folk telling includes a fixed text, fluid elements can shape the reception of Ramkatha, as a bi-lingual play from Palghat, Kerala, shows. In this shadow-puppet drama, performers recite selected Tamil verses from *Iramavataram* by Kamban but supplement them with improvised stories and commentary in colloquial Malayalam. For example, one performance features a darkly comic interchange between Ravana's son, Indrajit, and his standard-bearer. Indrajit learns that although he has felled many valiant warriors, the standard-bearer must stab them afterward with his staff's tip to ensure that each one actually dies. Thus, mighty Indrajit actually depends upon a nameless underling never even mentioned in *Iramavataram.* The servant who holds his warrior's banner provides a bottom-up perspective on the grand narrative of battle.[24]

Most of the writers whose works have been translated in this anthology grew up hearing one or more kinds of tellings of Ramkatha discussed in this section. Familiarity with them, therefore, enables one to see how the modern tellings of Ramkatha showcased in this volume relate to earlier Sanskrit, regional, and folk tellings. In this way, continuities between earlier tellings and modern tellings of Ramkatha become visible.

Modern Retellings in the South

This anthology proposes yet a fourth class of Ramkatha: modern retellings (in prose or free verse) printed in Indian regional languages in the last hundred years. Their composition was preceded by three major transformations: the growth of educational institutions, the availability of relatively affordable print technology for India's regional scripts, and the increase in a regular readership for printed serials and monographs in regional languages. These historical changes allowed writers of literature in regional languages to tell Rama's story in their own way for their own time. Yet modern printed tellings have been virtually unstudied as a category of Ramkatha because they are perceived by learned devotees or scholars as lacking some essential characteristic: authenticity, rusticity, devotionalism, respect, or modernity. Let us consider each of these claims in turn.

Modern Tellings as a Category

Some view Valmiki's *Ramayana* as the only "authentic" Ramkatha and, therefore, denigrate recent retellings as merely derivative. Yet most scholars now acknowledge that Valmiki's text, although it is deeply influential, need not be the benchmark according to which all other tellings should be judged as "deviating." Those who believe nothing except Valmiki's Sanskrit *Ramayana* is worth reading do not usually find any counter-argument convincing, but it is worth pointing out that even the most ardent Valmiki fans have usually learned another telling in their regional tongue. In fact, since pious devotees consider hearing, reading, and savoring Rama's name and deeds as a meritorious devotional act, reading multiple renditions of the story provides more opportunities to earn merit.

Others insist that a telling of Ramkatha must "well up" from the consciousness of the "volk" (folk or masses) rather than from a single individual writer who may not represent "true" India. Yet those knowledgeable in the multiple narrative heritages of South Asia reject the claim that any single, monolithic, uncontested story can represent "true" India because India is, inarguably, a land of narrative diversity. In addition, recent research has revealed the misleading romantic premises that led earlier folklorists to postulate that a primordial (de-historicized) "national" consciousness was the source of folklore.

Some pious Hindus reject modern tellings of Ramkatha as not traditional enough. Yet such a stance contradicts the tenets of the bhakti movement, where the intensity of inner devotion, rather than practice of external rites, is paramount. Devotees of Rama have told, sung, and enacted his story in multiple ways. Indeed, expressing devotion to the deity in one's own tongue functions as a defining characteristic of bhakti.[25] Just as Ramkatha extends beyond Sanskrit to Tamil, Hindi, and other regional languages, it can extend beyond older texts to more recent ones. Indeed, several writers in this anthology viewed their rewriting of Ramkatha as an act of devotion.

Some ideologues condemn modern tellings of Ramkatha as disrespectful. In the twentieth century, there were certain works that were written deliberately to shock or insult orthodox Hindus; such texts denigrated or belittled the story and its ideals.[26] In contrast, authors in this anthology have steeped themselves in Ramkatha, savoring and pondering its subtleties. In addition, as works of art, their renditions are carefully crafted through sophisticated use of literary elements such as characterization, allusion, imagery, and irony that are absent in solely political tellings of Ramkatha. The texts by the authors in this anthology stand out for their depth and seriousness of reflection. Whether modern authors agree with specific aspects of earlier renditions or not, they show an intimacy with Ramkatha rare in today's India.

Some people feel that "traditional" stories such as Ramkatha do not fit in today's India. Indeed, social reform novels, Marxist-inspired short stories about landless laborers, naturalistic dramas, and then minimalist and post-colonial writings have pushed aside older narratives. Referring to such stories as "mythological" texts, some see such materials as suitable only for pandits or folk performers. Yet many modern writers would disagree, citing as counterevidence that they draw upon, allude to, or rethink classic stories in their work. Although much has changed since the days when poets earned their literary credentials by composing a verse Ramayana, retelling Ramkatha today still demands a gravity of intent that many writers welcome as a literary challenge worthy of their best effort.

South India as a Ramayana Region

The writers who composed the selections translated in this anthology grew up in, or were closely linked by family ties to, the region of South India. Their understanding of Ramkatha is often shaped by the roles that the Ramayana tradition has played in South Indian cultural life. The following overview provides information about the geography and culture of South India and how they shaped the transmission, interpretation, and assessment of Ramkatha. Those familiar with the region may want to move on to the next section of this introduction.

Geography

Tamil, Kannada, Telugu, and Malayalam belong to the Dravidian language family, the world's fourth-largest language family, and share linguistic features that distinguish them from the Indo-Aryan language family that predominates in North India. Each Dravidian language, written in its own distinctive script, possesses a vital and growing literary tradition. Each language also ranks among the forty most widely spoken languages in the world. According to the 1991 census, Tamil speakers in India number more than fifty-three million, Telugu about sixty-six million, Kannada nearly thirty-three million, and Malayalam (including inhabitants of the Lakshadweep/Laccadive Islands off Kerala's west coast) about thirty million.[27] Kerala tops all other Indian states in literacy with an official rate of 91 percent.

Today South India consists of four states (see map 1). The Tamil language predominates in the state of Tamilnadu, Kannada in Karnataka, Telugu in Andhra Pradesh, and Malayalam in Kerala.[28] Geographically, Telugu predominates on the upper east coast and inland, Tamil in the lower east coast and inland, Kannada in the center and upper west coast, and Malayalam along the lower west coast between the sea and the Northern Ghats. In addition, Malayalam speakers have lived on the Lakshadweep Islands off the Kerala coast and Tamil speakers have lived across the straits in today's Sri Lanka, especially in the northern part of the island. This anthology includes a selection written by a Tamil poet from Sri Lanka (#15) because Tamils there and in Tamil-speaking areas in South India share a literary culture and ongoing intellectual exchange that began long before the twentieth century.[29]

A long-standing geographical connection has existed between the Ramayana tradition and the South Indian region. First, the kingdom of Lanka over which Ravana rules has long been linked with South India or Ceylon (today Sri Lanka). Second, from at least the fourteenth century, the Vijayanagar area in today's Karnataka state has been identified as the site of the capital of Kishkindha, the monkey kingdom in Ramkatha. Third, Rama is said to have amassed his army at Rameshvaram, the city at the southeastern edge of today's Tamilnadu, directly across the straits from Sri Lanka. Thus, only Rama's kingdom was located in North India (the Ayodhya and Faizabad region), while Sugriva's kingdom and Ravana's kingdom are believed to have been in South India or Sri Lanka.

The association of Ravana with the South has played a key role in the cultural politics of twentieth-century South India. Ancient Sanskrit texts glorify the role of *Aryas* (a term that originally meant "well-born" or "noble" ones), a group credited with preserving the earliest Vedic strata of Hindu texts. Beginning in the late 1800s, some South Indian social critics identified Aryas as Brahmins and other high castes who colonized the South. In turn, they identified the creatures called rakshasas in Ramkatha with indigenous inhabitants of the South whom they classify as "Dravidians" (after the linguistic term). These critics and social reformers glorify Ravana as a great Dravidian mon-

Map 1. South India.

This map is not intended to present every major city and town in South India or to show every place where one of the authors whose work is translated in this book was born. Instead, the map provides a basic geographical understanding of the shape, extent, and borders of the four regions in South India where Tamil, Kannada, Telugu, and Malayalam are spoken. Readers unfamiliar with India in the twenty-first century are also warned that many cities on the map possess more than one name and spelling. The British formalized cartographic spellings, sometimes in idiosyncratic ways, during colonial rule. Indeed, some have been renamed in the last decade. The preferred name today for Madras is Chennai; for Trivandram/Trivandrum, Thiruvananthapuram; Bangalore, Bengaluru; Calicut, Kozhikode. Spellings on the map were used because they circulated for more than four-fifths of the twentieth century, when the majority of authors in this anthology wrote.

arch and depict as tragic his slaying by Rama, whom they decry as a land-hungry colonizer from the North eager to expand his kingdom by annexing the South.[30]

Despite such recent oppositional readings of Indian history, a number of South Indian sites continue to be centers of devotion to Rama and Hanuman (also known as Maruti). In Tamilnadu, the Thanjavur area has been closely associated with veneration of Rama as perfect king, especially during the Chola dynasty's imperial expansion.[31] In Karnataka state, not only is worship of Hanuman widespread but the city of Mysore also celebrates a Dussera Festival that includes ritual veneration of Rama's weapons. In Andhra Pradesh, Bhadrachalam is a major pilgrimage site for Rama devotees, while Kerala abounds in temples to Rama. Many temples sponsor dance-dramas that depict Ramkatha episodes: men act out Ramayana stories in Kathakali dance-dramas while women perform in Mohini Attam dance-dramas. Ramkatha incidents are also presented in Karnataka's Yakshagana repertoire.[32]

Tellings of Ramkatha in the South

Valmiki's *Ramayana* is well known among South Indian Brahmins who are learned in Sanskrit. Among those who do not know Valmiki's text itself, many people who know Sanskrit have encountered summaries or abridgements of it. Others may have studied short collections of its Sanskrit verses with a guru or in school. Thus, a number of authors whose selections appear in this anthology had at least some knowledge of Valmiki's text. Even those who do not know Sanskrit can encounter Valmiki's *Ramayana* through its translation into their regional language. "Translation" here denotes a rendition that not only preserves the original's plot and rhetoric but also attempts to represent its metrical form, number of lines, and other features of Sanskrit literary style.[33] Such translations usually provide equivalents for each word or phrase. Although relatively rare in the pre-colonial period, in the last hundred years such translations of Valmiki into regional languages have proliferated.

Although the Hindi *Ramcharitmanas* has also been translated into South Indian languages in the past century, it plays a more limited role in South Indian cultural life than Valmiki. Hindi is an Indo-Aryan language, so it provides many challenges to those whose linguistic experience is limited to other Dravidian languages. In addition, because the impetus to learn Hindi came from the central government, a certain resentment of it runs high in the South, especially in Tamilnadu. Finally, animosity toward religious texts that propagate social hierarchy has been strong and recurrent in the South, leading to harsh criticism of *Ramcharitmanas* verses such as this notorious one: "Drum, rustic, Shudra, animal, woman: one has the right to beat all these."[34]

Rather than word-for-word translations, it was adaptations that played the greatest role in South India Ramayana discourse in the pre-colonial period. An "adaptation" retells Ramkatha in light of the context of the literary culture and social world of the target language. Most regional devotional tellings of Ramkatha (discussed in the section above titled "Classifying Ramayanas") are adaptations. Adaptations have exerted great influence on local perceptions of Ramkatha because they allow far more scope for creativity and artfulness than a literal translation.

The earliest major adaptation in South India, Kamban's Tamil *Iramavataram,* follows Valmiki's plot closely and Kamban openly acknowledges his debt to Valmiki. Yet Kamban's poetry, composed of individual couplets each of which functions as a tiny poem in itself, makes the experience of hearing and reading *Iramavataram* quite different from that of Valmiki's text.[35] Not only in genre but in content as well, Kamban adapts the work of his predecessor. In terms of characterization, for example, he depicts Bharata as nearly as self-sacrificing as Rama. In terms of setting, he shifts Ayodhya from a North Indian landscape to the landscape of Tamil country. As a regional adaptation of Valmiki's story, Kamban's *Iramavataram* has long been embraced as an authoritative and quintessentially Tamil telling of Ramkatha.[36]

In South India, Eluttacchan's *Adhyatma Ramayana* is the other pre-eminent adaptation of an older Ramkatha text. An adaptation sometimes announces itself as a retelling of a prestigious earlier Ramkatha rendition: Eluttacchan's sixteenth-century Malayalam Ramkatha takes the same name as the anonymous fourteenth-century Sanskrit text, *Adhyatma Ramayana.* Nonetheless, Eluttacchan's text differs greatly from its namesake in form since Eluttacchan wrote it as a *kilippattu,* a South Indian literary genre in which a parrot recites the text to a poet. Among Malayalam speakers, Eluttacchan's *Adhyatma Ramayana* remains beloved today. Many Hindus in Kerala recite parts of it in domestic daily worship.[37]

If Tamil and Malayalam each have a telling of Ramkatha recognized as pre-eminent, the situation in Telugu differs noticeably. No single Telugu telling of Ramkatha has won the status of *the* classic Telugu rendition.[38] Instead, Telugu authors produced a series of texts between the thirteenth and eighteenth centuries, with none winning unanimous recognition as pre-eminent, although the fourteenth-century *Ranganatha Ramayana* is sometimes proposed for that niche. Telugu literature thus shows how recognition accorded to regional tellings of Ramkatha differs from language to language.

Finally, Kannada literature nurtured two robust strands of Ramkatha that flourished side by side. For several centuries, the prestige gained by composing Jain Ramayanas rivaled that of composing Hindu Ramayanas in the Kannada-speaking region.[39] The Jain lineage of Ramkatha in Kannada begins with Nagachandra's celebrated twelfth-century *Ramachandra Charita Purana* (History of the Deeds of Ramachandra), while the fifteenth-century *Torave Ramayana* of Narahari was the most widely recited and read Hindu Ramkatha in Kannada. The ideological differences between Jain and Hindu beliefs and practices shaped narrative differences between the two texts. For example, most Hindu tellings culminate with Rama slaying Ravana, but most Jain tellings culminate

with Rama taking vows to become a Jain monk. In addition, while Hindu Ramayanas depict the superhuman deeds of divine and demonic characters, Jain
tellings debunk claims of miraculous deeds or give naturalistic explanations for
them. For example, Jain texts say that Ravana does not have ten heads. Instead,
when he was a child, his mother gave him a mirrored necklace whose ten gems
reflected his head.

Kannada's two lineages of Ramkatha exemplify another key feature of South
Indian literary tradition: diversity across religious affiliation. In addition to
Kannada Jain Ramayanas, other non-Hindu Ramkathas circulate elsewhere in
the South as well. For example, Muslims in the Malabar region of Kerala developed their own telling of Ramkatha, a translation of which appears in this anthology (#19). In addition, for generations, Muslim Tamil savants have studied
and commented upon *Iramavataram*.[40] Thus in the South, Ramkatha extends
beyond exclusively Vaishnava (devotees of Lord Vishnu), or even exclusively
Hindu, communities.

Whether authors represented in this anthology regard a single telling of
Ramkatha as authoritative or not, most know at least one major Ramkatha in
their regional language and some know several, ranging from written texts to
local folksongs. Several writers in this volume, such as K. V. Puttappa, explicitly
reject the idea that Valmiki's *Ramayana* should be considered the authoritative
text (#11). Other authors express indifference toward all prior renditions. For
instance, Pudumaippittan precedes his story of Ahalya by announcing defiantly
that he does not care whether readers find his story unfamiliar or unpalatable
(#14), a statement that implies that at least some readers would be familiar with
previous tellings of Ahalya's story.

Since the writers in this anthology retell Ramkatha episodes innovatively,
almost all of this volume's selections differ in some way from the influential
Sanskrit and regional language adaptations. Consequently, the selections in
this anthology—either in intent or results or both—oppose or supplement one
or more earlier Ramkatha tellings. As a region where Ramkatha has been told
openly in multiple ways, South India has nurtured narrative diversity in the
past. As this anthology's selections demonstrate, the South continues to support narrative diversity today, in the first decade of the twenty-first century.

Shared Features

The Tamil, Kannada, Telugu, and Malayalam authors whose work appears in this volume wrote in a multi-linguistic context. Some could have
imitated earlier South Indian poets by composing in Sanskrit, the pan-Indian
language patronized by most monastic, temple, and royal elites. Others could
have chosen English, a second language for many educated South Indian pro-
fessionals in the twentieth century.[41] In contrast, each work translated here was
composed in a South Indian regional language and intended for readers who
became literate in it through home tutoring or study at educational institutions.
The development of new print technology, the advent of standard orthogra-

phies, and the burgeoning of periodical literature (newspapers, magazines) enabled writers to address an audience broader than those restricted earlier by the limits of manuscript circulation or attendance at oral recitations.

The section below examines two factors that shaped how the authors in this anthology retold Ramkatha and how readers responded to their tellings. First, authors openly criticized caste and gender hierarchy. Second, writers developed emerging genres and styles in ways that created opportunities for new forms of expression. These factors encouraged the asking of fresh questions and contributed to the growing tendency to rethink ancient narratives. By doing so resourcefully and creatively, the authors in this anthology have prompted readers to reconsider a story heard many times before.

Caste, Gender, and Hierarchy

A number of selections in this anthology retell Rama's story in ways that contest the gender and caste prescriptions in Valmiki's *Ramayana,* as well as in later texts that reiterate Valmiki's ideological commitments. Many writers in modern South India differ openly with Ramkatha predecessors about the role of caste, a form of hereditary social stratification. Modern ideals of equality, liberty, and individuality shape how today's readers assess actions taken by characters in Ramkatha in relation to caste hierarchy. The stakes for reinterpreting such Ramkatha episodes are high, both for authors and their audiences.

One of the first retellings of Ramkatha to provide an explicit and trenchant critique of gender hierarchy *along with* caste hierarchy was written in Malayalam by Kumaran Asan. He was born into a family of Ezhavas, a "backward" jati (sub-caste) considered among the lowest in Kerala, whose members were, in his day, prohibited from even walking on the road leading to certain temples.[42] Asan became a follower of the pre-eminent Hindu reformer of Kerala, Shri Guru Narayana (1856–1928). Himself an Ezhava, he was known for the belief encapsulated in his formulation: "One Caste, One Religion, and One God for Man." Asan served for many years on his teacher's ashram, where he began his poem "Sita Immersed in Reflection" (#6), which contains an acutely observant evaluation of Rama's treatment of women and Shudras.

One of the earliest documented public controversies about rewriting Ramkatha according to egalitarian principles emerged in response to "Kuvempu" K. V. Puttappa's 1944 play *Shudra Tapasvi* (Shudra Ascetic) (#11). The controversy, played out in print and public debate, throws into relief the issues that surface when Ramkatha is retold by writers consigned by brahminical ranking to the low rungs of caste hierarchy. Puttappa, born into a Shudra family, venerated Rama and respected his compassion for living creatures. In Valmiki's telling, when a Brahmin complains to Rama that the Shudra Shambuka is performing tapas (asceticism), Rama cuts off his head. Puttappa did not believe either that Rama would condemn a person for performing a religiously sanctioned form of self-discipline or that Rama would kill an otherwise admirable human being for doing tapas, so he rewrote the story in way that spared Shambuka's life and confirmed that Rama was compassionate. Puttappa's rendition has Rama put the Brahmin in a position where he personally experiences the dharmic power produced by Shambuka's *tapas*. At the climax of the play, the Brahmin realizes his error; simultaneously Rama shows that asceticism is a religious practice open to all.

Famed Kannada writer "Masti" Venkatesha Iyengar, a prominent Brahmin intellectual who viewed Puttappa as his protégé, found the play offensive.[43] Iyengar scolded Puttappa for trying to "rescue" Rama's reputation at the expense of denigrating a learned Brahmin. Furthermore, he instructed Puttappa to desist from writing mythological stories unless he was willing to respect traditional beliefs. Indeed, Iyengar warned Puttappa to focus on contemporary rather than ancient themes, and to employ the new style called "social realism" if he wanted to advocate new forms of social behavior. Puttappa refused. In fact, he published Iyengar's critique, along with his own rejoinder, in all subsequent editions of his play, turning their debate into a famous episode in Kannada literary history.

Other writers in this anthology who, like Puttappa, sought new relationships with traditional narratives refused, as did Puttappa, to view material found in religious texts (such as epics and puranas) as off-limits to them. Instead, *they* insisted on setting the terms by which they would relate to past texts. In particular, some writers in part 2 identify strongly with marginalized characters subordinated because of caste and/or gender in Ramkatha. Their stories give voice to these characters, to the satisfaction of many readers and the dismay of others—particularly those with strictly authoritative interpretations of the story.

Criticism of caste is one of the most prevalent themes in this anthology. Although many have decried caste hierarchy, its denunciation by writers in this anthology carries a particular sting because it occurs narratively in a retelling of Ramkatha, rather than just in a political debate. Furthermore, writers in this volume have created multiple ways to incorporate questioning of caste restrictions into their literary works. For example, Puttappa did so by reconceptualizing the character of Rama and Shambuka (#11), Asan by exploring the crests and troughs of Sita's inner thoughts (#6), and Kavanasarma by satirizing contemporary life (#18).

Modern tellings also denounce women's oppression in Ramkatha. Critique of women's subordination to men in Ramkatha emerged relatively early in the twentieth century. It appeared in Asan's 1919 poem on Sita (#6) and Gudipati Venkata Chalam's 1924 play about Sita (#5). Later, women published their own responses to the depiction of women in Ramkatha, as can be seen, for example, in Lalitha Lenin's extensive critique of patriarchy (#10). It is noteworthy, however, that Asan and Puttappa, both "low caste" authors keenly aware that patriarchy can encompass other forms of discrimination as well, were among the earliest modern writers in the South to censure openly caste *and* gender subordination in Ramkatha.

The authors in this anthology include Non-Brahmins and Brahmins, as well as women and men. Despite Iyengar's defense of orthodox views of Ramkatha, other prominent Brahmins in South India have subjected the brahminical tradition, upon which caste and/or gender hierarchy rests, to critique and sometimes condemnation.[44] C. Subramania Bharati's animal fable lampoons elaborate brahminical sacrificial rites (#17), while the publications of Chalam, who rebelled violently against his Brahmin upbringing, include some of the most virulent and thorough-going criticisms of patriarchy in the first three-quarters of the twentieth century (#5). Brahmin writer Kavanasarma attacks caste and gender hierarchy as they intersect in the sexual assaults of high caste men on low caste women (#18).

One might surmise that Non-Brahmins would not bother to rewrite Ramkatha since they have a smaller stake in making brahminical texts seem acceptable in today's world, but evidence suggests otherwise: Non-Brahmin writers from the middling ranks of Hindu society also rewrote Ramkatha. For example, Pudumaippittan was a Vellala, a Non-Brahmin jati whose members often received education in Tamil religious texts. Furthermore, because Pudumaippittan read broadly and voraciously in Tamil, he had knowledge of religious beliefs and ritual that enabled him to write cutting satires of brahminical practice. Pudumaippittan was steeped in Kamban's *Iramavataram,* upon which he drew to retell Ramkatha (#14).

In addition to authors born into middling or Shudra families, the anthology also includes the works of those whom higher castes viewed as outside the caste hierarchy altogether. Today, members of such groups usually refer to themselves as *Dalits,* which means people who were "ground down" or "crushed."[45] Basavalingaiah, who was born into a Dalit family, ranks among the most innovative directors in Kannada theater. His talent won him the chance to direct plays at the cutting edge of Kannada theater, but he chose to revive Puttappa's play, *Shudra Tapasvi,* because he realized that it could speak to both Dalits and Non-Dalits about some of their deepest aspirations for equality (#11).

Reinterpretations of Ramkatha by women from various social locations are showcased in this anthology as well. As was true of male authors, a number of the female authors were born into Brahmin families. In the earliest period covered in this volume, very few women wrote stories that found their way into print, at least under their own names.[46] From the 1930s onward, however, family magazines and newspapers began to include sections targeted at female readers, creating new opportunities for women writers. Among them was Kumudini, who grew up in and married into an observant Brahmin family in the temple city of Sri Rangam. She felt so comfortable with, and knowledgeable about, the characters in Ramkatha that she introduced humor into her accounts of their daily dilemmas, treating them like next-door neighbors (#2). Also contained in this volume is a short story by K. B. Sreedevi, who was raised in an orthodox jati of Kerala Brahmins. Her protagonist, Ahalya, condemns Rama's unfair treatment of Sita in a particularly dramatic manner (#13). Even more recent is the poem by Vijaya Dabbe, which asks Sita why she did not voice protest against being silenced and humiliated (#1).

Although the work of female Ramkatha writers was seldom published in South Indian languages during the lifetime of male authors such as Asan and Bharati, women's voices in these earlier decades could be heard elsewhere: in their folksongs. Revealing how some non-elite women perceived Ramkatha, these songs circulated before, during, and after the first few decades of the twentieth century. Since an individual singer cannot be held responsible for the contents of songs that have been passed down for generations, views that women would be unlikely to express in public, such as those that contest authoritative tellings of Ramkatha, are expressed in a number of women's songs. Thus, it is not surprising that some women's songs share with other selections in this volume a tendency to re-assess the lives of characters depicted as virtuous in authoritative Ramkatha.

Some of these women's songs depict women and men of lower, as well as higher, castes in realistic, un-idealized ways, thus suggesting the unreasonable nature of standards of virtue, as exemplified by certain characters as they are portrayed in authoritative tellings of Ramkatha. "Do You Accept My Truth, My Lord?" (#4), for example, reveals how Rama tests Sita throughout their marriage, rather than just after her return from Lanka. The song condemns the ongoing patriarchal treatment with which some married women must live on a regular basis. "Lakshmana's Laugh" (#22) suggests that each character in Ramkatha has shortcomings, all the way from Sita to Nala, the engineer supervising the construction of the bridge to Lanka.[47] Such songs form part of a women's Ramkatha lineage to which later female writers can lay claim.

It is crucial to recognize that, along with the other selections in *Ramayana Stories in Modern South India,* the folksongs are also part of modern print culture. Intriguingly, early Indian nationalism created a market for the publication of folklore, enabling narratives previously transmitted by word of mouth to reach people through print.[48] If the other selections in this anthology were written for print venues (newspapers, magazines, literary journals, books), the folksongs translated in this volume were collected and transcribed specifically for publication. Two Telugu folksongs appeared in a compendium of Telugu Brahmin women's songs (#3, #22), whose compiler declared that the quality of these songs entitles them to the same attention as men's published poetry. Thus, books of folklore took for granted literate readers, distribution networks, and the habit of reading.

Yet the transition from oral rendition to print can sometimes be an explosive one, as is shown by the events following the publication of *Mappila Ramayana* (#19) thirty years ago. The song had circulated among Mappilas, Muslims living in the forested Malabar area of Kerala, but had remained virtually unknown outside that area until 1976, when M. N. Karassery transcribed it as part of his Ph.D. dissertation on Mappila songs and later published it in Malayalam. Some Non-Mappila Muslims in Kerala insisted that Muslims would *not* sing such a song because it dealt with a "Hindu" story. Instead, such a claim shows how notions of "Muslim" and "Hindu" were too narrow to account for the diversity of cultural production circulating in northern Kerala. Outside Kerala, readers had little idea that a Ramkatha episode was sung by Muslims in Malayalam until debates about the song were covered in non-Malayalam newspapers.[49]

Mappila Ramayana's use of northern Malabar dialect and local kinship terms, its context within the larger Mappila song cycle, and its spoof on methods for making women look younger bear witness to the range of topics and possibilities for innovation encompassed within the Ramayana tradition. Along with the Jain Ramayanas of Karnataka, the *Mappila Ramayana* in print also attests to the multiple religious affiliations of those who retell Ramkatha in South India.

Modes of Expression and Literary Genres

Modern authors helped to transform South Indian literary culture through use of new modes of expression to represent and interpret Ramkatha. One hundred years ago, most literary elites viewed poetry, rather than prose, as the appropriate form for elevated literary expression. Furthermore, poets adhered to highly stylized conventions governing the subject matter suitable for particular genres, the depiction of protagonists, and the meters appropriate for such subject matter. Over the past one hundred years, Ramkatha writers have actively experimented with new modes of expression. Several poets whose texts appear in this anthology shifted from meters whose form was highly prescribed to blank verse (*vers libre*) or prose. Some writers modified written expression to bring it closer to spoken language. Others pioneered, broadened, or established new literary genres.

During the period covered in this anthology, several ways emerged to provide more freedom for writers of elevated literary works. For example, in his early plays, K. V. Puttappa created a special form of verse for use in dramas by removing from the *lalitha regale* meter its initial and end rhyme (#11). The new form, *sarala regale,* lacks rhyme and restriction on the number of metrical feet, thereby allowing the semantic freedom of prose while providing the intensity of expression supplied by verse.[50]

Other South Indian writers established prose as a respectable form for elevated literature in South Indian regional languages. For example, hitherto prose in Tamil had been used mainly for writing government reports, translating English newspapers, serializing novels in popular magazines, or composing grammatical exegeses on religious texts by learned commentators. Pudumaippittan, whose short stories helped to transform Tamil prose into a form for high literature, stated in 1934, "Until the present time, Tamil prose has not had any [literary] standing."[51] Pudumaippittan's efforts, along with those of his cohort, revolutionized the status of prose and modeled new ways to enhance sophisticated literary craft in Tamil.

Even the words used in literature were changing during this period. For example, previously Ramkatha characters in Telugu conversed in formal written language. As Narayana Rao explains, "Tradition so far had dictated that all mythological characters speak a dialect removed from modern speech, filled with Sanskritic and archaic forms of Telugu. This strategy elevated the characters above the human level and provided them with an aura of distance and divinity."[52] The situation changed when writers began to depict Ramkatha characters employing everyday speech. For example, Chalam (#5) depicted both gods and demons as talking in ordinary language. As written language broke free of requirements of formal expression, fresh options opened up. For instance, Tamil poet C. Subramania Bharati (#17) was inspired by, and wrote poems drawing on, folk meters.

The transformation of prose facilitated experiments with new stylistic techniques. Unlike court-bound literary precursors beholden to patrons interested primarily in eulogistic verse, twentieth-century writers enjoyed a range of formal options. Techniques such as flashback (#13), stream of consciousness (#16), use of regional dialect (#20), and narrative exposition about characters' states of mind (#6, #14) expanded the repertoire of literary effects that writers could produce. These techniques enhanced the extent to which writers could express new perspectives on an ancient narrative.

In terms of genre as well, writers utilized new options. For example, Kumaran Asan found *maha-kavya,* a form of epic poetry appropriate for depicting epic events in court and on the battlefield, unsuitable for the psychological depth he sought to depict in some of his poetry about Sita. Instead, he created the *khanda-kavya* (*khanda* means "piece" or "part"), which enabled him to focus on one small portion of a story and depict the interior life of chosen characters. This new poetic genre proved especially suitable when Asan delved into Sita's feelings in "Sita Immersed in Reflection" (#6).[53]

Some writers who chose the short story to retell Ramkatha used the genre in notably creative ways, thereby winning for the Ramayana tradition attention from short story fans.[54] A short story must have a clear focus; because most readers are familiar with Ramkatha's basic plot, the genre enables authors to focus on a particular incident from a fresh angle without worrying about recounting the entire story of Rama and Sita. For example, the story of Ahalya (#13, #14, #16) has drawn widespread attention from modern writers who have examined her situation from a variety of perspectives. Indeed, cognoscenti of fiction rank Pudumaippittan's re-consideration of Ahalya's fate among this master writer's most brilliant short stories. Two narrative techniques have yielded fruitful results in short stories: imagining what would have transpired after the incident, as recorded, ended (#13, #14) and imagining how the incident would have occurred if it took place today, rather than in ancient times (#2, #7, #16).

The theatrical genre too was enriched by playwrights who sought to write new forms of drama. The plays translated in this anthology differ notably from existing kinds of theater prevalent in the first decades of the twentieth century. At that time, performances consisted primarily of ritual theater for temple festivals, musical spectacles presented by itinerant theatrical companies, or social dramas enacted by amateur members of dramatic societies. In contrast, the scripts translated in this volume are of two types: those for reading and those that incorporate folk elements.

Rather than intended for enactment, two theatrical scripts were composed primarily to be read. The authors, therefore, focused their literary efforts not on blocking out action but on crafting sophisticated dialogues between characters who held opposing views. Chalam's seldom-performed two-person script, *Sita Enters the Fire,* is too short and unconventional for commercial theater (#5).[55] Instead, Chalam wrote to showcase Sita's logical argument and persuasive evidence that she uses to respond to Rama's allegations about her purity. Puttappa employed dramatic dialogue in *Shudra Tapasvi* to create a spellbinding debate between Rama and a caste-minded Brahmin about the nature of asceticism. In Puttappa's preface, he states that the play works better if one envisions it in the mind's eye rather than on stage (#11). The growth of literacy as well as the linked habit of solitary reading ensured readers for the plays of Chalam and Puttappa, whether performed or not.

As many involved with modern forms of theater moved away from elite texts, some came to view local folk theater as a repository that could be drawn upon in addition to, or instead of, Sanskrit dramatic traditions. For example, when Basavalingaiah re-staged Puttappa's 1944 *Shudra Tapasvi* in 1999, he transformed the play into riveting spectacle by incorporating masks, songs, and dance drawn from folk theater in Karnataka (#12). Folk drama also plays a crucial role in *Portrait Ramayana* (#20), a play that explores Sita and Shurpanakha as two sides of today's woman. A chorus that sings in a Kannada folk performance style provides ongoing commentary about unfolding events, using a zesty rural dialect that locates the story in a specific place. Each production uses folk elements not superficially as add-ons but knowledgeably to enhance narrative intensity and to connect it to local geography.

The specificity of locale so crucial in folk drama also influenced G. Aravindan's film, *Kanchana Sita* (#9). Aravindan shot his footage in a remote area of Andhra Pradesh, using as his cast selected members of a community of Koyas ("tribals") based in that area, whose members believe that their lineage descends from Rama. As with *Portrait Ramayana*'s use of rural Kannada dialect, Aravindan uses the Koyas to locate his telling of Ramkatha in the soil of South India and set it among a group of people for whom Rama looms large in self-conception and oral history.

As this section has demonstrated, tracking the development of modern retellings of Ramkatha simultaneously reveals insights about major changes in South Indian literary culture. Through poetry, prose, short stories, plays, and films, the South Indian writers in this anthology have done more than add their own tellings to the Ramayana tradition. They have also added to the modes of expression through which literature has flourished in modern South India.

Transformations

Authoritative tellings of Ramkatha such those by Valmiki, Tulsidas, and Kamban tend to tell us a great deal about characters with established authority: Kshatriyas such as Rama and his brothers; Brahmins such as Vasishtha and Vishvamitra; royal women such as Kausalya and Kaikeyi. The majority of commentary on the Ramayana tradition both by scholars and devotees has focused on these characters. The selections in this anthology both complement already existing commentary on Ramkatha and also supplement it by subjecting other characters and themes to close scrutiny. Each of the three sections of this anthology explores ways in which one theme or character has been transformed across South Indian languages and literary genres.

Three Nodes of Narrative Diversity

Much orthodox discussion of Sita focuses upon her devotion to Rama and how her purity relates to his reputation as a monarch. In part 1 of this volume, Sita is transformed from an iconic ideal into a complex character. Part 2 documents the transformations that emerge when characters portrayed as "minor" in authoritative tellings of Ramkatha become the focal point of a narrative. Part 3 reveals how authors have transformed the depiction of rakshasas by sculpting them into complex and ambiguous figures.

Sita in Context

The portrayal of Sita in India has been loaded with cultural freight, because she is conventionally identified by the orthodox as the quintessential proper Hindu wife. Especially in the Hindi *Ramcharitmanas* (and other texts that share its gender norms), Sita is presented as the exemplar of a *pativrata*, "a woman with a vow to her Lord (husband)." She could have remained in the palace (as did Urmila, Lakshmana's wife), but instead she insisted on sharing Rama's harsh forest exile. When abducted, Sita could have lived within Ravana's luxurious palace but instead dwelled outside with only an Ashoka tree for shelter. Even when Ravana offered her riches and the status of Chief Queen, she remained unswervingly loyal to Rama. When Rama doubted her purity, she could have left but underwent a fire ordeal instead. Like other women seen as ideals of self-denial, she sacrificed her desires for the sake of her husband and reputation.[56]

Such a character raises the bar of virtue too high for most human beings. For example, Ravana never forced himself on Sita because he had been cursed that were he ever to touch a woman without her consent, his head would split into pieces.[57] When an ordinary woman faces a rapist, no such curse exists to protect her. When Sita walked into the fire to prove her fidelity, the fire god raised her up, unharmed by the flames, and testified personally to her purity. Were an ordinary woman, whatever her state, to enter blazing flames, she would burn to death. Consequently, Sita's example can be an oppressive, even terrifying, burden, as Lalitha Lenin's poem, "In the Shadow of Sita" (#10), suggests. Generally, orthodox Hindus regard Sita as an avatara of Goddess Lakshmi. This divine-human woman might walk into a fire and emerge unscathed, but writers today would be loathe to perpetuate the notion that husbands should submit their wives to ordeals that only a goddess could pass.

To emphasize her humanity, some authors in this anthology imagine how Sita might feel at certain moments in the story. Others imagine Sita participating in day-to-day life, emphasizing her involvement in ordinary tasks. Certain stories portray Sita's involvement in actions unrelated directly to her father, husband, or sons. Others present her in phases of her life ignored by earlier writers. Such narrative strategies portray Sita as someone with agency.

Two writers in part 1 portray Sita as a form of power. On the one hand, Aravindan's film *Kanchana Sita* presents her as *Prakriti* (the female power of the universe), whose spirit guides Rama to act compassionately even after her physical presence on earth is gone (#9). On the other hand, Lenin's "In the Shadow of Sita" presents her as a powerful yet haunting construct that functions to reinforce the subordination of women (#10). When the agenda of such a depiction of Sita is revealed, however, women can recognize and combat the power of patriarchy.

However they represent Sita, the writers in part 1 depict her as a dynamic, rather than a static, character. Readers come to care about her as they watch her thoughtfully respond to, for example, the trials of captivity in Lanka or the burden of single parenthood. Rather than a passive woman slavishly following her husband's dictates, this anthology's authors present Sita as a resourceful person—an inspiration, not a burden. This Sita chooses actions in light of the various contexts in which she finds herself at different moments in her life.

Marginalized Characters

Unlike Sita, who remains central throughout the story, the characters in part 2 have hitherto been understood as minor characters who appeared briefly in Ramkatha to demonstrate Rama's virtue: (1) Shambuka, who contravened the dharma of a Shudra by performing tapas, and (2) Ahalya, who transgressed wifely dharma by committing adultery. In ancient tellings of Ramkatha, both Shambuka and Ahalya are stigmatized and despised by those around them.

The authors in part 2 transform a story centered on Rama into a narrative where a character previously at the periphery moves to the center of the action. In two selections, a story originally told in praise of Rama's vigilance in upholding caste prescriptions changes into a Shambuka-centered story. The other selections in part 2 transform a story that originally demonstrated Rama's compassion for a fallen woman into an Ahalya-centered story. In Valmiki's *Ramayana*, Shambuka and Ahalya come and go from the story within a couple of short chapters. In contrast, each of part 2's selections is a self-standing text centered on either Shambuka or Ahalya.

Even the title of Puttappa's play, *Shudra Tapasvi* (Shudra Ascetic) (#11) signals that the drama focuses upon Shambuka and his rigorous asceticism, rather than Rama's defense of caste restrictions. Shambuka, who speaks only briefly as befits an ascetic, remains a towering presence in the script, a benchmark against which the ignorance of others is measured. Basavalingaiah's re-staging of *Shudra Tapasvi* (#12), half a century after the play's original composition, makes Shambuka even more prominent. Sitting on stage throughout the final scene, absorbed in deep meditation, Shambuka's equanimity is almost palpable. In contrast, the Brahmin's demand for Shambuka's beheading is unmasked as a means to protect brahminical privilege from assault from the lower orders. When the repentant Brahmin prostrates himself before the Shudra ascetic at the play's end, the staging, lighting, and choreography center the audience's attention on the self-discipline and compassion of Shambuka.[58]

Part 2's remaining selections portray an Ahalya whose identity is defined neither by her relations with Indra nor her deliverance at the feet of Rama. Instead, two authors transform Ahalya into a judge of Rama's treatment of Sita, and he is found lacking (#13, #14). Next, a poem presents events from Ahalya's perspective but, uniquely, from her perspective *as* a stone (#15). In a final short story, Ahalya explicitly and frankly recounts what is only suggested in earlier renditions: the tragic consequences when a husband remains indifferent to his wife's sexual desires (#16).

The selections in part 2 dramatize the terrible human cost of caste and gender hierarchy, thereby participating in the public critique of caste and gender oppression circulating in the public sphere during the authors' lifetimes. Furthermore, the stories of Shambuka and Ahalya have taken on their own narrative momentum in South Indian literature.[59] In addition, these stories insist that religious practices such as tapas should be equally open to all and that married women deserve physical affection in wedlock. Finally, modern retellings remove the burden of *adharma* (deviation from dharma) from the shoulders of previously stigmatized figures.

So-called Demons

Literary characters designated demons, enemies, or foreigners have received new scrutiny in recent debates about narrative constructions of alterity, or "otherness." Scholars have delved into analysis of which narrative techniques serve to demonize groups of people and how they accomplish such cultural work. South Indian writers often treat demons differently than do writers in the North.

The modern rakshasas in part 3 transgress expectations for proper behavior in myriad ways. Some display excessive conspicuous consumption, while others attempt to shift into more youthful and attractive shapes. Some articulate desires that others keep repressed, while others express their rejection of "proper" male-female behavior. One defends herself without recourse to the aid of senior males (#17), while another prays for the ability to conceive children without intercourse with a male (#18). Each writer in part 3 employs a compelling logic to represent rakshasas; the range of depictions pushes us to view rakshasas through multiple lenses.

First and foremost, the selections in part 3 reject binary oppositions between heroes and rakshasas found in many older Ramkatha texts. Modern playwright Venkatesha Murthy (#20) aptly articulates this view when he comments that Ramkatha characters are "so difficult to understand because there are no black and white characters." Instead of black and white, authors have probed the actions of rakshasas in an attempt to figure out what makes them "tick." Part 3 features stories that retrieve rakshasas from older texts and re-imagine them with more complexity than in earlier tellings. Some writers do so out of empathy for so-called demons, while others reject the idea that any character could be utterly evil and strive to comprehend what motivates their actions. Intriguingly, these representations of rakshasas are parallel to recent theoretical explorations of the motivations of figures such as subalterns, underdogs, anti-heroes, and peasant leaders who practice everyday resistance in the context of repressive social norms.

Reflections on gender play a major role in part 3's depictions of rakshasas. One fable satirizes the link between violence and romantic love by having Shurpanakha cut off Lakshmana's ears (#17). Only a rakshasa female, not a human one, could get away with attacking a male Kshatriya. A short story shows Rama and Ravana as male chauvinist pigs, but Rama evades chastisement due to his political clout (#18). A poem depicts Ravana empathizing with Sita's feelings of humiliation and resentment toward Rama by rejecting the hierarchical norms that guided Rama's behavior not only toward women but toward rakshasas and monkeys as well (#21).

Portrait Ramayana (#20) scrutinizes the role that cultural construction plays in representing rakshasas. When Sita draws a portrait of Ravana, her husband becomes obsessed with destroying it, because society would perceive such a portrait as undermining his masculinity and his control over Sita's sexuality. Chalam also views rakshasas as cultural constructions, depicting Sita telling Rama, "since you cannot understand that love [of Ravana for Sita], you call it animal lust, a demon's idea of love and reduce it to nothing" (#5). In other words, because Rama does not possess the ability to comprehend the magnitude of Ravana's love for Sita, Rama labels it "demonic" in order to discredit it.[60] Because these five modern tellings in part 3 take for granted the constructed nature of rakshasas, they refuse to demonize an entire category of characters in Ramkatha.

Why Ramkatha?

The Telugu women's song titled "Lakshmana's Laugh" (#22) functions as an epilogue to this anthology. Depicting a moment when a set of Ramkatha characters scrutinize their past and feel ashamed of their misdeeds, the song suggests that when one looks closely at Ramkatha, many things are not what they seem upon first glance. The song takes us deeper and deeper into the complexities of Ramkatha. The power of this complexity to generate new tellings won my attention and motivated me to compile this anthology of translations.

Nonetheless, a question remains: Why have modern writers focused on these complexities instead of creating their own characters and incidents from scratch? One might assume that writers would prefer to do so, rather than re-tell Ramkatha yet again, but, for a variety of reasons, that is not the case. Some writers retell the story in light of their own experiences as a form of devotional practice. For example, Telugu poet Viswanatha Satyanarayana explains:

> In this world, everyone eats the same rice every day,
> but the taste of your life is your own.
> People make love, over and over,
> but only you know how it feels.
> I write about the same Rama everyone else has known,
> but my feelings of love are mine.[61]

Satyanarayana's love for Rama moved him to spend twenty-eight years composing a six-volume poem on Rama's story, one largely in conformity with Valmiki's text. On the other hand, the account of Shambuka by Puttappa, which contradicted the tellings of all known predecessors within the Ramayana tradition, was also motivated by his personal love for Rama (#11).

Other writers retell Ramkatha because it gives them a higher point of entry than a wholly original story; since most readers already know the story, an author need not bother with the mechanics of the plot and can, instead, plunge immediately into creatively reshaping some well-known incident. For example, Asan picked a single day in Sita's life, knowing that his audience would understand exactly why the day between her sons' arrival at Rama's ashvamedha and her return to Mother Earth was charged with enormous emotional weight (#6). In some cases, the author depends upon previous familiarity with Ramkatha in order to suggest that well-known events might produce surprising and unintended consequences. For example, by playing on the reader's knowledge of Ahalya's curse and her deliverance, Sreedevi envisions a previously unimagined aftermath to the curse (#13).

Retelling Ramkatha also offers a writer a potentially wide readership. Ramkatha characters are not ordinary characters—their exploits have kept audiences spellbound for centuries and they have wide "name recognition," so a retelling of the story is more likely to catch a reader's attention initially than an unfamiliar work of fiction. As playwright Venkatesha Murthy noted in reference to *Portrait Ramayana* (#20), "The Ramayana and Mahabharata are not only great epics—they are a language themselves. I want to converse *in* Ramayana. By writing in it, I can easily communicate with people because everyone in India knows it."[62] By writing within the Ramayana tradition, one's work can move beyond the merely local or parochial.

Equally attractive to writers is the power wielded by Ramkatha, a narrative that has been granted moral authority for centuries. Even writers who openly reject the hierarchical ideals set out in authoritative texts such as Valmiki's *Ramayana* have rewritten Ramkatha in order to harness its power for their own ends. Telugu writer Volga has peopled her short story titled "Reunion" with Shurpanakha, Sita, Lava, and Kusha not because she was unable to create fictional characters but because she knew that for more than two millennia epic stories, mythology, and exemplary tales have wielded the power to influence behavior (#8). She realizes how effectively the story has functioned to shore up constructions of gender in the past, and uses it, as she remarks, "to subvert patriarchal agendas from a woman's perspective."[63] Art forms such as literature and dance are currently "trapped in a patriarchal idiom," but Volga harnesses them to combat patriarchy in her story about the inner beauty of the disfigured Shurpanakha, a story that shows that both form and deformity are integral parts of natural processes.

Other writers in this volume retell Ramkatha as a way to de-idealize its characters. Some authors feel that unrealistic exemplars such as Sita and Rama inflict substantial social damage; Lenin describes how the shadow of Sita haunts women and paralyzes them when they cannot live up to her impossibly high standards (#10). Other writers present Ramkatha characters as if they encountered the dilemmas of everyday life, rather than just recounting stories of royalty set in the hoary past. Such writers portray Sita dealing with quotidian activities such as deciding what to wear each day (#2) or learning how to play a musical instrument (#7). They want to relate the entire life of Ramkatha characters, not just the grand exemplary events. Yet other authors consider what would happen to human beings if they underwent an experience recounted in Ramkatha, such as turning into stone and then returning to life again (#14).

Certain authors take up Ramkatha to set the record straight. Malayalam writer Vayalar Ramavarma once wrote, "Let those of us who now study the times gone by / tear the dark curtain of smoke with their sharp pens."[64] Many write to tear down that curtain. Puttappa removes the stigma from the shoulders of Shambuka, while Basavalingaiah identifies brahminical practices that deprive Shudras of respect (#11, #12). Madhavan clears Ahalya of blame and reveals the cruelty of domestic abuse (#16), while Bharati shows Shurpanakha getting the best of Lakshmana, for once (#17). Satchidanandan's Ravana reminds us that thousands of rakshasa and monkey soldiers died in the war, not just famous warriors in the army's upper echelons (#21). Ahalya and Shambuka, rakshasas and monkeys—they now receive the chance to have their say.

Because authors retell Ramkatha for many reasons, readers will also find these narratives compelling for a number of reasons. The selections gathered here allow the reader to listen in on debates in the recent past and present within Indian culture. The book's tri-partite structure encourages readers to consider each selection in light of others in the same part of the volume. For those who regularly read literature in one South Indian language, this volume provides access to the story of Rama and Sita as told in other major South Indian languages, thereby giving insights into a broad regional literary experience. For all readers, the book's multiple perspectives guard against the tendency to essentialize Indian culture by draining it of its complexity.

In the last one hundred years, a conjunction of historical, social, political, technological, and literary developments—together with the narrative inclinations of specific writers—has fostered a lively, intense, and challenging set of contributions to the Ramayana tradition. Across the state borders and linguistic boundaries of South India, Sita's life has been re-conceptualized, marginalized figures have moved to center stage, and so-called demons have been rethought. This anthology provides readers with the chance to taste myriad modern retellings of Ramkatha and shows how the narrative continues to play a role in South Indian life today. The vitality of these tellings suggests that authors will continue to retell Ramkatha long into the future.

Notes

1. Goldman (1984: 14–49) assesses the available evidence and dates the oldest portion of Valmiki's *Ramayana* to the second quarter of the first millennium BCE.

2. Almost all the retellings of Ramkatha in the last hundred years were written in these shorter literary forms, but there are two major exceptions to this pattern. K. V. Puttappa wrote a full-length, four-volume Ramkatha in Kannada (1955), which won a Sahitya Akademi Award (1990). Viswanatha Satyanarayanan wrote a six-volume poem in Telugu hailed by many as the literary masterpiece of its day (1944, rpt. 1992).

3. Ramanujan (1991: 45).

4. This synopsis of Ramkatha is organized chronologically, according to the traditional division of the story into seven *kandas* (major sections or cantos): *bala* (childhood) or *adi* (first, original); *Ayodhya* (name of Kosala's capital city); *aranya* (forest); *kishkindha* (name of the monkey kingdom); *sundara* (literally, "beautiful"; tells of Sita's captivity in Lanka); *yuddha* (war) or *lanka;* and *uttara* (later or final). Some kandas here receive more detailed summary than others because they contain incidents that are central to selections in this volume. Few of the selections deal with battles, so the synopsis of the war kanda is relatively brief, while a number of selections deal with Sita's life after banishment, so the synopsis of the final kanda is fairly extensive.

5. Rama is the avatara (literally, "one who descends," or "a descent") and is a form of Vishnu. Sita is an avatara of Lakshmi, Goddess of Good Fortune and consort of Vishnu. Some tellings identify other avataras as well. For example, Lakshmana is said to be an avatara of Adisesha, the celestial serpent upon whom Lord Vishnu rests while floating in the milk ocean.

6. For this reason, epithets for Rama often refer to him as a member of the *surya vamsha,* "solar dynasty."

7. See W. L. Smith (1986) for an analysis of how curses function in Indian literature.

8. A Kannada folk telling says Ravana gives birth to Sita with a sneeze; "Sita" in Kannada means "sneeze" (Gowda 1973: 150–151). In another set of stories, Mandodari, Ravana's wife, gives birth to Sita under miraculous circumstances (Ramanujan 1991: 38). Dineshchandra Sen collected a Bengali ballad attributed to Chandrabati of Mymensing that relates how Sita was born from an egg (1932: v. 4: 323–352).

9. According to one story, King Janaka once saw Sita lift Shiva's bow to clean the floor beneath it, so Janaka sought a husband who could also lift the bow.

10. Sita has long been linked to fertility and prosperity. When Sita dwells in Ayodhya, the trees and flowers flourish. When she leaves, they wilt and die. See Dimmit (1982).

11. Conventionally, when a text mentions Sita beneath the Ashoka tree, it refers to her during her captivity in Lanka.

12. Thus, the Sanskrit *ramarajya*, "the rule of Rama" (Hindi, *ramraj*), has become synonymous with a perfect society, where wealth, health, and perfect dharmic order exist. See Menon and Schokker (1992) on depictions of Rama's reign in Ramkatha.

13. Male members of the top three varnas undergo a physical birth when they are born and then a second, spiritual birth that initiates them into Sanskrit teachings. Thus, they are "twice-born."

14. In Indian poetry, the separation of the male and the female is considered the most poignant aspect of love, since it produces the most intense longing for one's beloved and, hence, the most intense sentiment. The Indian term "krauncha" is retained through this volume to refer to the crane whose death Valmiki witnessed because the krauncha has come to be a metonym for the separation of lovers and the creation of poetry.

15. Ramanujan (1991: 25).

16. Pollock (2006: 62–63) identifies the key features that contribute to Sanskrit's status: its "paradigmatic analyzability" by grammarians, its association with Vedic liturgy, and its use in scholastic discourse. It functioned as an elevated language rather than one for ordinary daily use.

17. The first two categories of Ramkatha discussed here, Sanskrit and regional tellings of Ramkatha, were written in highly stylized poetry. Yet it would be a mistake to assume that these texts circulated only among social elites. Even though the majority of the population were illiterate, and hence could not read Sanskrit manuscripts, extant records provide evidence that kings established endowments for public recitation. See Pollock (2006: 59).

18. For a discussion of the influence of Valmiki's *Ramayana*, see Goldman (1984: 3). For an analysis of authoritative tellings of Ramkatha, see Richman (2001: 8–12).

19. Some would also argue that Sagar's televised Hindi Ramayana functions as an authoritative Ramkatha for the late twentieth and early twenty-first century.

20. For *Uttararamacharita*, see Shulman (2000), and for *Adbhuta Ramayana*, see Coburn (1995).

21. Lamb (1991: 237).

22. Narayana Rao (2001: 118–130).

23. Nilsson (2000: 157).

24. Blackburn (1991). Similarly, a subaltern view emerges when the general of the bear army, Jambuvan, bitterly observes that the human officers in charge are indifferent to the fate of ordinary soldiers, treating them as equivalent to "cannon fodder."

25. See Zelliot (1976).

26. For example, E. V. Ramasami used sarcasm and parody of Ramkatha to win attention for critique of Hindu belief and ritual. See Richman (1991a).

27. These figures are taken from the official statistics of the 1991 Census of India, as provided on page 5 at www.censusindia.net/results/eci11.pdf. By now, more than a decade later, these figures are significantly higher, even though exact numbers will not be known until the results of the 2001 census are released. All such figures for language speakers are approximations but are useful for comparative purposes in relation to other

Indian languages. For example, only five Indian languages have a higher rate of speakers than Telugu and Tamil: Hindi, Urdu, Bengali, Panjabi, and Marathi.

28. Today's boundaries of the four states date back only to the linguistic reorganization of India's states that occurred after independence. During the colonial period, the British broke the country into three administrative units called "Presidencies" and many "Princely States" under the control of local rajas. Madras Presidency included parts of today's Tamilnadu, Andhra Pradesh, and Karnataka. Travancore, Cochin, and Mysore were separate Princely States. Portions of today's northern Karnataka were part of Bombay Presidency. It is also helpful to keep in mind that modern state boundaries are less linguistically isomorphic than maps would suggest, since many bi-lingual people living in villages near borders shift back and forth between two or more languages in daily life. Finally, in addition to the four major South Indian languages that are the focus of this anthology, minority populations in the South speak a number of other languages, including Tulu, Konkani, and Urdu.

29. Until after Indian independence, many Tamil writers in South India had greater literary bonds to Tamil writers in Ceylon than they did to most North Indian writers. Literary interchange between the two countries continues even today, suggesting how misleading it is to imagine an airtight border between two nation-states. (The number of Tamilians in Sri Lanka has decreased markedly in the past four decades due to civil war, which led many refugees to flee to other countries.)

30. For Ravana as an ancient Dravidian king, for example, see Purnalingam Pillai (1928). A radically different notion of Ravana as ancient king of the Sinhalas was propagated in the 1930s and 1940s by Munidasa Cumaratunga, whose Hela ideology rejected any connection between Sinhala and Indo-Aryan identity. See Dharmadasa (1992: 261–264).

31. Blackburn (1996: 29–30). Thanjavur flourished under the imperial Cholas, whose power, status, and ambition peaked in the twelfth century. See Shulman (1985) for analysis of the iconic representation of Rama produced during this period. Outside the Thanjavur region, however, the vast majority of Tamil Hindus, with the exception of Shrivaishnava Brahmins, venerate Shiva (not Vishnu) as their highest deity.

32. For the repertoire of Kathakali, see Zarilli (2000). For Yakshagana in Karnataka, see Ashton and Christie (1977) and Chaudhuri and Bilimale (2000). The Terukkuttu tradition in Tamilnadu concentrates mostly on stories from the Mahabharata, but a Telugu puppet tradition in Andhra Pradesh deals with Ramayana incidents (see GoldbergBelle 1984).

33. For example, see C. Rajagopalachari's translation of Kamban's *Ayodhya-kanda* (1961) for an example of an effort to replicate not just the meaning but the form of the original.

34. For a discussion of debates on this verse, see Hess (2001: 26, 357–358).

35. Valmiki composed in Sanskrit shlokas, but most of Kamban's text is in *kali viruttam,* which produces quite different sonic effects. See the discussion of the challenges of translating Kamban's Tamil text in Hart and Heifetz (1988: 11–19).

36. Kamban received patronage from the Chola imperial dynasty, viewed by many Tamils today as their golden era, so Kamban's time is recalled with great pride in Tamil literary circles.

37. Freeman (2006: 480–482).

38. See Narayana Rao (2001: 165–172) for a survey of Telugu medieval and modern Ramkatha.

39. See Aithal (1987).

40. Umaru Pulavar (ca. 1665–1773), a Muslim Tamil poet, wrote an epic on the Prophet's life using Tamil literary conventions in ways inspired by Kamban's *Iramavataram*. For *Iramavataram* in the Tamil Islamic community, see Narayanan (2001: 266–273).

41. No South Indian renditions of Ramkatha originally composed in English have been included in this anthology, but a number of innovative ones exist. Among poems, for example, see Srinivas Iyengar's *Sitayana* (1987), written in unrhymed English quatrains. Among recent plays, Poile Sengupta's *Thus Spake Shurpanakha, Thus Said Shakuni*, performed in Bangalore in May 2003, stands out for its intertextuality and its contemporizing of epic characters. Set in an airport, it depicts Shurpanakha's encounter with Shakuni (of the Mahabharata), who carries a bomb in his briefcase to blow up the plane in service of his terrorist agenda.

42. The status of the Ezhava (also called Thiya) community is complex. Although designated "backward," some Ezhavas studied Sanskrit and were known for their knowledge of Ayurvedic medicine. According to Sreenivasan (1981: 18), during Asan's lifetime Ezhavas constituted 45% of the Hindu population of Kerala and 26% of the state's total population.

43. Iyengar first published his review of *Shudra Tapasvi* in the July 1944 issue of *Jivana,* a Kannada literary journal that he edited. See Puttappa (2004: 193–198). In the remainder of this volume, reference is made to Iyengar and Puttappa, which is the proper formal way to refer to them. However, aficionados of Kannada literature refer to the two writers as "Kuvempu" and "Masti," as markers of their respect and affection for them.

44. Brahmin intellectuals might be thought to have a great deal at stake in the project of modifying and updating Ramkatha since they are charged with preserving religious texts. If they demonstrate only selective acceptance of religious texts, they can defend themselves from the common criticism that they practice slavish adherence to texts.

45. In the past, higher castes referred to such groups as "Untouchables." Government documents usually refer to them as "Scheduled Castes," often abbreviated to "SCs" because they appear on lists (schedules) of communities eligible for affirmative action. However, today "Dalit" is the self-chosen nomenclature of most born into such groups.

46. British colonial authorities required that one copy of each printed book be submitted to the Registrar of Books, so we know that a few early printed Ramkatha materials by women were published. One, providing words to a women's Ramkatha folksong sung to a folkdance called *kummi*, was by [Ms.] M. Parvati Ammal (1918), but was printed anonymously to preserve the author's modesty. [Ms.] A. A. Vanamalai (1927) wrote a short play based on Valmiki's account of the bow contest and Rama's wedding to Sita. [Ms.] R. S. Cuppalesksumi Ammal's 1928 work tells the story of Kusha and Lava, Sita's sons. These books do not criticize or openly interrogate authoritative tellings of Ramkatha.

47. In light of the subversion found in some women's Ramkatha songs, it comes as no surprise that Venkatesha Murthy and Jayashree found it appropriate to base *Portrait Ramayana* (#20) on a woman's song and stage it through folk drama.

48. Indeed, Blackburn (2003) has shown that folk materials numbered among some of the first Tamil printed books. For example, Pandit Mahalinga Natesha Sastri (1859–1906) pioneered the compiling and publishing of Tamil folklore, making local folktales available regionally and drawing attention to them through the prestige accorded printed matter. Also, by translating Tamil folktales into English, Sastri made them accessible to English readers both within and outside India.

49. Interview with M. N. Karassery, November 2002, Calicut. Intriguingly, this Islamic folksong was preserved by a Hindu Brahmin.

50. This discussion of Puttappa's transformation of dramatic verse is based on T. S. Venkannaiya's Kannada preface to *Birugali*, summarized in Chandrasekhara (1960: 42).

51. Pudumaippittan (1998: 101).

52. Narayana Rao (2001: 178).

53. Sreenivasan (1981: 53, 67).

54. In oral Ramkatha, the story is seldom recounted from beginning to end in a single sitting. Instead a session focuses on one or a few episodes, as do the short stories in this volume. Short stories in South India today are in high demand, featuring regularly in periodicals, especially literary magazines and weekend or holiday editions of newspapers. In Tamil and Telugu, the short story is today's most accessible literary genre.

55. Mehtha (1963: s.v.).

56. One exception to her self-denial is her request for the golden deer.

57. Once Ravana ravished his daughter-in-law, the celestial Rambha. Her husband (and Ravana's nephew, son of Kubera) cursed Ravana that if he ever touched an unwilling woman again, his head would split into seven pieces.

58. As Puttappa's play reveals, combining devotion to Rama with rejection of caste privilege creates a particularly moving retelling of Ramkatha. The Ramanamis of Chattisgarh believe that Tulsidas would never have composed the verses in *Ramcharitmanas* denigrating Shudras because of Rama's compassion for all living beings, so they have excised verses that belittle Shudras from their copies of the text. One of them said, "The *Ramayan* is so great that we cannot possibly damage it. We can only make it better" (Lamb 1991: 251). Puttappa would have probably agreed.

59. See Richman (2004) for an analysis of three plays about Shambuka (one each in Telugu, Kannada, and Tamil). Each was greeted with public controversy when staged.

60. Although he did not use phrases from today's literary theory such as "cultural construction of the other," Chalam's analysis of rakshasas is presciently in agreement with current literary criticism dealing with constructions of alterity.

61. The translation is by Narayana Rao (2001: 181–182), but I have modified the formatting. Because Satyanarayana's poem is essentially conservative and this volume is dedicated to innovative tellings, no excerpts from his poem feature as selections in this book.

62. Interview with Venkatesha Murthy, January 11, 2006, Bangalore.

63. These quotes appear in the program notes that Volga wrote for "Lakshmana Rekha," a dance-drama performed on March 7–8, 2004, for the Andhra Pradesh International Women's Day Celebrations by the Asmita Collective, Secundarabad.

64. Ramavarma (1988: 585), from the poem "Tadaka, the Dravidian Princess."

Part One   *Sita in Context*

Why haven't we heard Sita's own voice and viewpoint?[1] Vijaya Dabbe's poem (selection #1) begins part 1 by articulating this question and considering the consequences of Sita's silence. While authoritative Ramayanas focus primarily on events in Rama's life and his views of them, the selections in part 1 instead direct attention to Sita's life and her perspective. Indeed, Ambai's "Forest" (#7) portrays Sita telling Sage Valmiki why she feels compelled to write her own story: "You were a poet of the king's court. You created history.... I absorbed into myself all manner of experiences. My language is different."[2] Sita sees Valmiki's *Ramayana* as advancing the royal project to glorify Rama and his dynasty. Sita's rendition, in contrast, reveals her own perspective on the events that she has experienced.

Part 1 presents a sampler of selected South Indian writings that recount Sita's experiences from her point of view, as a diverse group of authors have imagined it. These renditions include four notable narrative strategies: they portray Sita responding to particular contexts, they contemporize aspects of her story, they imagine what ensued during periods of Sita's life neglected by earlier authors, or they take Sita as personifying an abstract entity or principle.

Contextualizing

While authoritative Ramayanas tend to portray Sita as an iconic and unchanging image of the *pativrata* (pure wife utterly devoted to her husband/ lord), part 1's texts depict Sita as determining how to act on a case-by-case basis, according to what best suits each context in which she finds herself. Furthermore, she learns from the situations that she encounters and acquires the ability to be resourceful. Thus, contextualizing Sita's actions turns Sita from an icon into a multi-dimensional character who, as a result of her experiences, develops wisdom, practicality, and compassion over the course of her life.

Rather than emphasizing her divine powers as avatara of Goddess Lakshmi, the stories in part 1 spotlight her human limitations and the resources she uses to cope with those limitations. For example, Kumudini's "Letters from Lady Sita" (#2) imagines how Sita adapts to life in the city and then in the forest. In the palace, she figures out how to cope with multiple expectations for a new daughter-in-law by drawing upon the resources of her natal family, especially her mother. In turn, when she accompanies Rama to the forest, she learns how to cultivate detachment and embrace a life of ascetic simplicity. Her ability to make context-specific choices reveals a Sita of greater complexity and flexibility than the Sita depicted in authoritative Ramayanas.

Part 1's stories also reveal insights about relations between women in the household. For instance, "Sita Locked Out" (#3), a song of Telugu Brahmin women in Andhra, tells how Rama grows impatient waiting for Sita to complete her household chores so she can join him in bed and locks the door to their room in anger. When Sita appeals to her mother-in-law, Kausalya scolds her son and insists that Rama let Sita enter. Realizing that a wife's power rests in her relationships with family members, Sita cleverly resolves a marital deadlock by drawing upon her mother-in-law's empathy.

Sometimes a story provides a prehistory to a complex event in a way that foregrounds Sita's perspective, rather than Rama's. The Kannada women's song "Do You Accept My Truth, My Lord?" (#4), for example, shows that even prior to Sita's fire ordeal, her husband demanded that she perform superhuman deeds to prove her purity. First, Rama insisted that she carry water in a vessel of sand. Then, he told her to grab hold of a snake, put it on her head as a pot rest, and then balance her water vessel on it. By enumerating other impossible demands that Rama made, the song presents the fire ordeal as just the latest in a series of trials that Sita has had to undergo.

By contextualizing Sita's many actions in various settings and during different phases of her life, the stories in part 1 also decenter Sita's agnipariksha. In part 1's stories, it is neither the defining moment in her life nor is she the only woman who has faced such an ordeal. Even the notion of precisely what constitutes Sita's fire is questioned, for example, in Gudipati Venkata Chalam's *Sita Enters the Fire* (#5); the title refers not to the fire ordeal demanded by Rama but to the funeral pyre of Ravana, which Sita enters when Rama refuses to take her back. Metaphorically, the story's title also refers to the fiery debate between Rama and Sita, in which she rejects his claims over her. In Volga's "Reunion" (#8), when Shurpanakha tells Sita how her life was traumatized because of her mutilated face, Sita realizes that Shurpanakha's ordeal "was no less than her own." Rethinking the agnipariksha places it in the context of the many forms of suffering with which women have had to cope.

Contemporizing

A writer depicting Sita in modern times must portray a character recognizable as the Sita in the ancient epic but also a Sita relevant enough to modern readers for them to care about her. Some authors meet the challenge by depicting Sita in a short story, a fictional genre that provides an author with the freedom to transport Sita to the present time.[3] For example, in Kumudini's story mentioned above (#2), Sita sees other women in court wearing fashionable foreign-made saris brought by merchants traveling along the trade routes. Yet she soon discovers the flaws of imported goods, and then embraces the enduring qualities of the saris woven in her birthplace. By portraying Sita's sartorial dilemmas in relation to local vs. trade goods, Kumudini represents Sita as an early votary of *swadeshi* ("own country"–made). Championed by nationalists through the boycott of foreign goods, swadeshi was central to the political discourse of her twentieth-century readers.

Semantic choices can also contemporize a story. For example, in Chalam's *Sita Enters the Fire* (#5) mentioned above, Rama casts aspersions on Sita's purity with language drawn from dharma-shastraic discourse. In contrast, Chalam arms Sita with linguistic ammunition from the discourse of rights (*hakkulu*) found in debates about social reform raging in Chalam's own day. Such language enables Sita to combat Rama's construction of his wife as a baby-making machine.[4] By supplying Sita with new vocabulary to critique sexual objectification of women, Chalam frees her from the linguistic hegemony of dharma-shastra texts.

Neglected Periods

Authors also add fresh dimensions to Sita's life by exploring times not treated in depth or even ignored in earlier Ramayanas, such as the periods before, between, or after familiar incidents. Authoritative texts deal primarily with those parts of Sita's life that aid in glorifying Rama or advance the plot toward Rama's war against Ravana. In contrast, part 1 contains stories that focus on alternate phases of Sita's life, including incidents with little direct relationship to the climactic battle between Rama and Ravana.[5] Authors thus re-conceptualize Sita in fresh situations, creating more subtly contoured views of her than were previously available. Especially compelling to modern writers has been the opportunity to re-envision the period of Sita's life after her children have grown.

In "Sita Immersed in Reflection" (#6), Kumaran Asan considers what it would really have meant for Sita to spend twelve years in an ashram devoted to cultivating detachment from pain and pleasure. With the premise that such a life would have furnished Sita with equanimity of mind, Asan portrays her observing the intense feelings of resentment toward Rama that pass through her thoughts. After refuting his inaccurate insinuations about her purity, she then calmly and compassionately reflects upon Rama's own constraints, trapped into fulfilling the demands of kingship, at the cost of personal happiness. The poem culminates with Sita foreseeing the culmination of her spiritual goals: liberation from the cycle of death and rebirth (*moksha*). Hoping that Rama too will attain this goal, she contemplates imminent return to Mother Earth.

In contrast, Ambai's "Forest" (#7) imagines a different trajectory for Sita after her sons leave for Ayodhya. Texts and folklore from South India portray Ravana as a learned and cultivated musician of the *vina*.[6] Ambai builds upon this motif by having middle-aged Sita encounter Ravana again and accept his offer to teach her the vina. The story shows Sita realizing that, after years of sacrificing for others' needs, it is time to cultivate artistic fulfillment in her own life. While Valmiki presents Sita as returning to Mother Earth after her sons are grown, Ambai depicts Sita embarking on a new phase of life.

In "Reunion" (#8), Volga portrays middle-aged Sita and Shurpanakha meeting again, now that each has radically reshaped her life outside of conventional expectations for marriage.[7] Sita has gained peace of mind while raising her sons in Valmiki's ashram.[8] Shurpanakha has endured the anger and self-hatred caused by her disfigurement, come to terms with her scarred body, and now cultivates a garden whose beauty is unrivaled on earth or in heaven. When Sita suggests that she will return to Mother Earth after her twins leave for Ayodhya, Shurpanakha convinces her instead to retire to Shurpanakha's garden, where she can savor the presence of Mother Earth without leaving the world.

By re-imagining Sita in her later years, Ambai and Volga simultaneously reconceptualize the notion of renunciation as well. Although the forest is traditionally portrayed as a place to practice bodily mortification, Ambai's Sita uses the forest's lack of worldly distractions to devote herself to the vina. In Volga's forest, the many women at Valmiki's ashram cultivate fruit trees, assemble garlands for puja, and care for their children together, while Shurpanakha runs a nursery of rare flowers. These women find alternatives to conventional urban married life by moving to the forest.

Asan, Ambai, and Volga all depart from Valmiki's portrait of Sita as a victimized woman driven to give up her life due to male cruelty.[9] Asan depicts Sita as an intelligent and thoughtful woman who realizes that her work on earth is done and therefore calmly returns, without regret, to the source of life, Mother Earth. Ambai and Volga represent Sita as continuing to live a rich and meaningful life after her sons leave for the city. Sita has long served as a model of the proper wife for many people. If one does choose to view Sita this way, Ambai and Volga present a model of a wife who continues to develop in her post-child-rearing years as an ascetic, artist, or gardener and nature lover.

Representing Principles

Hindu tradition has long encompassed an understanding of the world as composed of two gendered principles: Prakriti, the animating force of the natural world conceived as female, and Purusha, the principle of the world conceived as male. Within this dualistic framework, goddesses are identified as an embodiment of Prakriti. Since Sita is an avatara ("descent" or "incarnation") of Goddess Lakshmi, we should not be surprised that authors sometimes conceive of Sita as a form of Prakriti. This interpretation of Sita circulated widely within Kerala beginning with Eluttacchan's sixteenth-century *Adhyatma Ramayana* and continuing in recent texts such as C. N. Sreekantan Nair's modern play *Kanchana Sita* and G. Aravindan's film of the same name, based upon the play (#9).[10]

Aravindan sought a way to represent a philosophically grounded principle in a cinematic medium without having a human actress play Sita. The visual depiction of Sita that he conceptualized is virtually unique within the Ramayana tradition; he literalized the notion of Sita as the animating force of the natural world. When Rama is about to slay Shambuka, for example, Sita speaks through the rustling of the leaves of the trees, urging him to desist. Later, when Rama draws near the Sarayu River, its rippling waves manifest the presence of Sita. In response, Rama as Purusha rejoins his primordial mate, Prakriti, in perfect unity.

An altogether different kind of abstraction exists in Lalitha Lenin's poem "In the Shadow of Sita" (#10). In it, Lenin reflects upon Sita as a construction that represents the ideology of patriarchy, as internalized by women. Since childhood, many Indian women have been socialized into believing that Sita is the image of the perfect woman, and she has been understood as the standard against which their actions will be measured. Hence, observes Lenin, society tries to isolate women from new ideas as they would from an epidemic, for fear that women would discover that they can move beyond Sita's shadow.

Part 1 begins with Dabbe's interrogation of Sita and it ends with Lenin's consideration of Sita's lingering effects on women's lives today (#10). Lenin examines the appeal, as well as the dangers, of identifying with long-suffering Sita. Lenin's scrutiny of the many hues within Sita's shadow helps readers put into a broader context the multiple elements of Sita's legacy sketched out in the ten selections of part 1.

Notes

1. Sally Sutherland Goldman argues that sections of *sundara-kanda* do reveal Sita's voice, but only in a highly muffled form (2000: 223–238).

2. Ambai (2000), p. 140.

3. The use of "contemporizing" here follows the practice of A. K. Ramanujan in his analysis of how folk performers contemporize classical Sanskrit epics (1986: 63). Pudumaippittan's "God and Kandasami Pillai," a short story in which Shiva drops into modern Madras and is appalled at what he finds, is one of the most famous examples of contemporizing in modern Tamil literature. See Holmstrom (2002: 157–180).

4. *Hakku* is a Telugu transliteration of the Arabic word *haq.* In Telugu, *hakku* appears often in phrases such as *prathamika hakkulu,* "fundamental rights," and *paura hakkulu,* "civil rights," drawn from twentieth-century discourse about democratic government.

5. A major characteristic of non-authoritative tellings, including folk Ramayanas, is their willingness to shift away from the story of Rama and Ravana to explore other characters in greater depth. The sixteenth-century Bengali poet Chandrabati, for example, includes in her Ramayana a long account of the birth and childhood of Sita. See Sen (1997).

6. A vina is a stringed musical instrument with a long bamboo fingerboard and a gourd resonator at each end.

7. In authoritative tellings, the two women are usually portrayed as opposites. See Erndl (1991).

8. I overheard the following comment in a discussion of Sita's banishment among a group of retired female Brahmin schoolteachers in Chennai (January 2004): "Sita always looked for the best. She didn't go to just any ashram. She went to the #1 best ashram in the area, Valmiki's ashram, to ensure that her boys got a tip-top education."

9. The notion of a pure, submissive, and self-sacrificing pativrata looms large in

many discussions of Sita as a role model for Hindu women (e.g., Kakar 1988). In contrast, others view Sita not as submissive or passive but as uncompromising, focused, and dignified in her pursuit of noble goals (e.g., Kishwar 2001: 305–306).

10. See Freeman (2006: 479–481) for Eluttacchan's literary, social, and caste context.

1   Asking Sita

Vijaya Dabbe (b. 1952) is a scholar, activist, and Kannada poet. Among her Ramayana interests is Nagachandra's *Ramachandra Charita Purana* (also known as *Pamparamayana*), a Jain Ramayana in Kannada about which she has written a monograph. She has also played a leading role in Samata, a Mysore-based organization committed to the empowerment of women. The poem below, from Dabbe's award-winning collection of poetry, ponders why Sita never wrote her view of events in the Ramayana when she had the resources and time to do so.

Source: Vijaya Dabbe, *Iti Gitike* [Here Are the Songs] (Mysore: Kuvempu Institute of Indian Studies, 1996), p. 51.

Figure 2. Sita sitting beneath the Ashoka tree in the garden outside Ravana's palace. Images of Sita almost always depict her in the presence of males, usually with Rama, Hanuman, her twin sons, or Ravana. Illustrations of her alone, such as this one, are rare. From C. Ramasvami Sastri's collection of abridged Ramayana stories in Kannada, *Ramayana Kathasangrahavu,* published in 1915.

The Questions Return
BY VIJAYA DABBE

You had the words
Father Janaka taught you,
the songs your nursesmaids gave you.

Palm leaves lay all about.
Sita, why didn't you speak?

The Ashoka tree spread its shade.
There was your own brimming sorrow
and time enough.
What more did you want?
Sita, why didn't you speak?

Later, leisure once more yours,
Lava and Kusha grown,
the ashram full of peace
and your whole life flowing past you:
Sita, why didn't you speak?

To all my questions,
only her silence,
heavy as earth.
I look up and the feelings flow
from her eyes into mine
—but wordless.
And my own questions
    come back to me.

Translated from Kannada by
Shashi Deshpande and
Pratibha Nandakumar

2 Sartorial Dilemmas

Ranganayaki Thatham (1905–1986) wrote regularly for Tamil magazines in the 1930s and 1940s under the pseudonym of "Kumudini."[1] A follower of Gandhi, she shocked neighbors by wearing *khadi* (homespun cloth) even to weddings. Striving to achieve personal simplicity and self-reliance, she experimented with a stove that allowed air in on four sides to reduce consumption of fuel, wrote a pamphlet about draping cloth so that it resembled a traditional Brahmin nine-yard sari but required far less material, created an inexpensive and nutritious recipe for eggless cakes, and invented an ice cream made from local plantains. Her interest in the quotidian manifested itself as well in her series of magazine articles called "Mail from the Inner Palace," in which she tried to imagine what everyday life would have been like for characters such as Draupadi and Sita.

Married into an orthodox family in the pilgrimage town of Sri Rangam, Kumudini knew well the expectations for proper female comportment. Because her mother-in-law disapproved of women reading magazines, she awoke in the early hours of the morning to finish her writing before starting her daily household chores. Her husband secretly passed her work onto her father, who sent it to publishers. Her sense of humor, resourcefulness, and familiarity with characters from religious narratives enabled her to imagine them in engaging and original ways, as can be seen in the story translated below. Composed of four epistles that Sita ostensibly wrote from Ayodhya to her mother after moving to the women's quarters of Dasharatha's palace, these letters, which depict Sita struggling to act in accordance with the behavior and comportment expected of a young daughter-in-law, reveal a great deal about the complex gendered dynamics of power within the joint family.

Sita must balance a bewildering variety of charged relationships in her new marital home. For example, Sita must not identify males of higher status by their proper names, instead using elaborate circumlocutions such as "my respected father-in-law" for King Dasharatha. She even tells her mother about Rama by calling him "your son-in-law." She learns as well that even a royal queen must carefully conceal her responses to a king's decisions. For instance, Sita recounts how Kausalya, the king's senior queen, wins public respect and sympathy by performing elaborate *pujas* (ritual offerings) designed to bring welfare to the family, thereby masking Dasharatha's neglect of her due to infatuation with his youngest wife, Kaikeyi. Similarly, another of Sita's letters re-

---

1. Kumudini took her pen name from the heroine in *Yogayog*, a Bengali novel by Rabindranath Tagore that Kumudini translated into Tamil from a Hindi translation.

veals the intense financial pressure on new brides to ensure that their parents present gifts of sufficient value to members of her marital family: Sita secretly informs her mother exactly what kind of jewelry Rama's parents gave to their son-in-law (Rishyashringa) so Sita's parents can give Rama the same gift, thereby upholding her natal family's status. Special pressures fall on the daughter-in-law whose husband receives the crown, causing Sita intense worry about whether she has the right clothing to wear for the coronation ritual.

While previous letters concern the role of sartorial choices within the marital family, in the final letter, the ethos connected with a life of withdrawal to the forest comes to the fore. As Sita prepares for life in exile, she realizes that all her worries about what to wear have become irrelevant. Ultimately, the story suggests the superiority of a Gandhian life of simplicity over the luxury-filled, but anxiety-ridden, one at the palace.[2]

Source: Kumudini [Ranganayaki Thatham], "Sita Pirattiyin Kataitankal" [Letters from Lady Sita], *Ananta Vikatan* 9:36 (9 September 1934), pp. 65–73; rpt. in *Cillaraic Cankatikal, Limitet* [Triffling Matters, Limited] (Tricchi: Natesan Books, Limited, 1948), pp. 75–78.

Letters from Lady Sita
BY KUMUDINI

Letters written by Sita Devi in Ayodhya to the Chief Queen of Janaka, Ruler of Mithila

One

Profound obeisance to mother from her humble daughter, who reverently writes this:

Good health to all!

The servants and chariots you sent have arrived. Your messengers conveyed your request that we all come to Mithila for the Dipavali Holiday. If you knew everything going on here, you would understand how unlikely it would be that we could accept your invitation.

My respected father-in-law spends all his time with Mandavi's mother-in-law [Bharata's mother] Kaikeyi Devi.[3] My mother-in-law [Rama's mother] is

----

2. Here Kumudini likens the forest exile of Rama and Sita to living in a Gandhian ashram. Gandhi, Kumudini's inspiration, also found himself drawn to the actions of Sita. For example, he cited Sita's refusal to submit to Ravana's desires—despite threats and promises of luxurious gifts—as inspiration for the non-cooperation movement. Similarly, when urging people to spin their own cloth, Gandhi said, "Sita also spun on her own *carkha* [spinning wheel] which might have been bedecked with jewels and probably ornamented with gold, but all the same it was still a *carkha*." Philip Lutgendorf analyzes this and similar passages in discussing Gandhi's allusions to Ramkatha (1991:379–380).

3. Kumudini portrays Sita as entering a joint family, in which Dasharatha's three wives, four sons,

terribly angry. In order to hide her anger, she busies herself performing pujas and feeding Brahmins. So I must wake at the break of day, carry out my ritual ablutions, and help her. I work all day long. I don't get even the slightest bit of rest.

As soon as we returned from the wedding, Bharata's uncle took him for a visit to his house. And we know that Bharata's younger brother Shatrughna is like a tail, following his elder brother everywhere. Even after they return, I don't know whether we could all get permission to come to Mithila. It seems quite doubtful that we could arrive in time for Dipavali.

Your son-in-law [Rama] has resolved that it is best to spend Dipavali right here in Ayodhya. A letter will arrive soon about it from my honored father-in-law.

So, send the cream-colored cloth here. Your son-in-law only likes cream-colored silk, so be sure to send only that kind.[4] For Dipavali here, they have designed a new kind of wristband for our brother-in-law, Rishyashringa. It is excellent. Make one just like it for your elder son-in-law [Rama]. Perhaps I can find an expert in this kind of craft and send him back to you with the servant whom you sent here. No one must know that I have written to you about this matter.

You have written that you are having a vermillion-colored sari woven for me. Here in Ayodhya, everyone wears extremely sophisticated clothing.[5] They say that traders from foreign lands bring yellow cloth.[6] Be sure that the borders are very elegant. My husband's elder sister Shanta was wearing a sari in a sky-blue color.[7] I want one like it. All the saris that you presented to me at the time of my wedding have very wide borders. Now I am ashamed to wear them. Everyone makes fun of me. You should not buy that kind. Give my greetings to my honorable father.

With reverence, Sita

---

and their children live together as a unit. This arrangement differs from a nuclear family, which is usually composed of one or two parents and offspring. In an Indian joint family, it is usually customary for daughters-in-law to work under their mother-in-law's supervision, sharing the chores required to feed the family and keep the house in order.

4. This allusion is targeted to Vaishnava. "Pitambaram" is the ritual term for the cream-colored garment priests use to clothe the icon of Vishnu in the sanctum of a Vaishnava temple. Since Rama is an avatara of Vishnu, wearing clothing of this color is suitable.

5. Cosmopolitan Ayodhya, a major stop on the North Indian international trade route, boasts the latest in ever-changing women's fashions. In contrast, Sita's trousseau contains only saris that weavers produced according to traditional patterns in customary colors in Sita's conservative home region of Mithila (today in northern Bihar and southern Nepal).

6. Kumudini uses the term *yavana*, "foreign," anachronistically for comic effect to refer to the British. Ancient Sanskrit texts use the term to refer to Bactrians, Scythians, Greeks, and other groups who entered India from the West.

7. Shanta, wife of Rishyasringa, is Sita's sister-in-law.

Two

A message for mother:
Good health.
After I finished my last letter to you, I saw my husband's elder sister-in-law, Shanta. She said that the blue shade is not colorfast; it bleeds in the wash.[8] So I have absolutely no desire for that sky-blue color now. Send me a vermillion-colored sari of the traditional type made in our country. Or, if you can find cloth with a guarantee that the blue color will not wash out, then send it. Don't be afraid that I might get bored with a color after I have worn it only once. Just don't send the sky-blue color.
Your servant, Sita

Three

Message for mother:
Good health.
Suddenly an idea has occurred to father-in-law. He says that he wants to have a coronation ceremony for your son-in-law. I absolutely *must* wear a sari with your blessings on the coronation platform. What kind are you going to send? Would the new jasmine color be good? If I am to wear it on the coronation platform, it must look very elegant. Are saris with the spotted deer decoration in the border easy to find quickly? Or do you recommend that I wear the one I mentioned before? Honored father-in-law does not like cuckoo-colored or peacock-colored cloth. Perhaps I should wear the tiger-colored one. I don't know what I should do! Since I have been thinking constantly about these saris for hours, my mind is very confused. I cannot seem to reach a decision. Send help.
Your dear, Sita
P.S. Or, you could combine the Dipavali sari and the coronation sari, and get me a really grand sari.

Four

To Mother.
Don't send me any saris. Everything is over. It seems that we are going to live in the forest. Bharata will be crowned. I'll send you the details of what happened. Now all I need is bark cloth. Nothing else is suitable to wear, if you consider how much it rains in the forest. So you can send an outfit of bark. It would

---

8. Sita calls Shanta's sari *astiramaka,* "not firm" or "impermanent." The term *stiramaka* (when not preceded by the privative "*a*") alludes to the firmness of mind gained by cultivating detachment from possessions. This term foreshadows Sita's later realization that sartorial concerns distract one from more significant matters.

be good if you could send betel and *appalams*.[9] Your son-in-law likes your appalams the best. We are going to Chitrakuta. No one must know this. Hurry!

Sita

P.S. Now I need not ponder the color of saris. I feel great peace of mind. It appears that if every woman spent some time in the forest, it would do a lot of good. The worries in life would be reduced by half.

Translated from Tamil by Paula Richman

---

9. *Appalams* (also called pappadams) are round, deep-fried, crispy lentil flour snacks that resemble large potato chips and are served as treats at family get-togethers or festival days. Often the dough for appalams would be made ahead of time in large batches, rolled out, and then stored until it came time to fry them for a special occasion.

3   A Mother-in-Law's Support

"Sita Locked Out," a Telugu song sung by Brahmin women in Andhra, focuses upon an unusual set of events in the married life of Rama and Sita. This song shares some features with a genre of folksongs that are meant to be performed at the door of the house. Such songs are popular at weddings in the Andhra region, but those "open the door" songs depict the husband locked out by the wife, whereas the roles are reversed in the song translated here. In a series of strategically orchestrated sections, the song depicts how Sita extricates herself from a difficult situation, establishes solidarity with her mother-in-law, and enjoys Rama's intimate attention.

Traditionally, a good daughter-in-law should prioritize service to parents-in-law over love for her husband, but Rama is eager to have his wife with him in bed, and resents time she spends on household chores while he waits. Determined to teach her a lesson, he bolts the door and pretends to be asleep. The song describes Sita rushing to finish her chores so she can join him promptly. While she puts service to her in-laws above her own pleasures, she wants to please her husband too. As soon as she completes her work, Sita bathes, combs her hair, and dresses in finery. The song takes its time describing each ornament in detail, as well as a leisurely five-course dinner and a long look in the life-size mirror. Sita goes to her husband when she is ready.

When she finally arrives at Rama's door bringing flowers, she thoughtfully boosts his ego by noting that he has never bent his head to any rival. Alluding to Rama's heroism is meant to create a mood conducive to the role of lover Sita wants him to play soon. When she finds the door barred, Sita tries various strategies to enter. Pleading that she is no match for his anger, she laments about her aching feet and the soaking rain. By locking Sita out, however, Rama has locked himself in. His pathetic claim that items such as the lamp-stand and sandalpaste keep him company only reveals his desperate loneliness. If Rama thinks he has humiliated Sita by equating her with these inanimate items, he is wrong.

Sita knows that Rama would never disobey his mother, so she fetches Kausalya, who scolds Rama with a mother's power as well as her affection: only she can simultaneously reprimand her son by asking "Have you lost your sense?" and then show affection by calling him "my little boy." Rama opens the door with a smile to show his mother he is not really angry. He sheepishly complains, however, that if she pampers her daughter-in-law, he, as a husband, will lose control of her. In effect, he asks his mother to join in disciplining Sita, rather than siding with her.

As soon as Rama opens the door, Sita adopts a delicate strategy to send her mother-in-law on her way: she observes that Dasharatha (Sita's father-in-law) is alone and Kausalya (his wife) should go to him. These carefully chosen words hint at the active sexual life of her in-laws, and that Dasharatha prefers Kausalya to his other wives—a hint that enhances Kausalya's self-image. These words actually mean: your son wants to be alone with me, so leave me free to attend to him.[1]

Finally, Sita joins Rama in bed but faces away from him. Next, the song lists fragrances from various items, those that Sita brought on a golden platter, along with bukka, a scented powder used to perfume clothes. To signal her anger, Sita just puts the platter down instead of offering it lovingly to Rama. The scents are maddening, as is her closeness, but, too proud to admit he was wrong, Rama turns sullenly toward the other side of the bed, away from her. She knows what to do next, commenting that a woman's anger lasts no longer than butter near fire. This gives her enough excuse to turn and, without losing any time, to engage in lovemaking. Rama's anger disappears like fog in sunlight. He happily turns to her, playing along in the games of love.

The song ends with a *phalashruti,* a formulaic statement that tells the results of performing the song. Since the poem concludes with Rama living a life of power and luxury, its content suggests to listeners that a husband who lives happily with his wife succeeds in his work as well. More explicitly, the phalashruti announces that the singers and listeners, who all happen to be women in this case, will earn a life of riches. Readers, too, will find the song filled with the subtleties of diction and ironies of meaning that enrich a well-written poem. [V. N. R.]

Source: "Sita Gadiya" [Sita Locked Out], in "Krishnasri" [Sripada Gopalakrishnamurti], ed., *Strila Ramayanapu Patalu* [Women's Ramayana Songs] (Hyderabad: Andhra Sarasvata Parishattu, 1955), pp. 105–106.[2]

Sita Locked Out
WOMEN'S FOLKSONG

She is born of Earth, and raised by Janaka.
She serves her in-laws with devotion.

Her loving husband calls her, but she doesn't come.
Flowers in his hair, fragrance on his body, her husband is in a joyous
    mood.
Looking for her, he waits and waits.

---

1. For a discussion of subversion in women's verbal art, see Raheja and Gold (1994).
2. In his preface to the collection from which this song comes, "Krishnasri" acknowledges his debt to Nandiraju Chelapathi Rao's *Srila Patalu* [Women's Songs] (Eluru: Manjuvani Press, 1899) and Mangu Jaganandha Rao's *Nuru Hindu Strila Patalu* [One Hundred Hindu Women's Songs] (ca. 1905). Translator Velcheru Narayana Rao thanks Professor K. Malayavasini and Ms. Bhavaraju Lalitha Devi for their comments on an earlier draft of the translation. For analysis of these songs, see Narayana Rao (1991).

He is impatient about the time she takes.
"Why doesn't she come? What's taking so long?"
The hero of the solar lineage is upset with her.

He closes the door and bolts it.
"You and your chores, Daughter of Earth!
You've grown too proud," he says shaking his head,
and totally deluded, lies down on his bed.[3]

Sita comes rushing.
She quickly presses her mother-in-law Kausalya's feet,
gives betel leaves to her father-in-law.
Fans Kaikeyi and Sumitra too,
and makes the bed for Kausalya.

Then she takes her turmeric bath,
chooses a sari with golden flowers,
combs her hair and ties it into a bun.

She puts on her jewels—
tamarind-leaf of gold in the part of her hair;
a drop of pearls crowning her forehead;
a spread of gems around her bun;
earrings worth a thousand,
a gold chain worth two thousand,
a nose ring worth three thousand,
a choker worth some four thousand,
and a pendent worth ten thousand,
a belt of gold with bells on it,
and bracelets with sapphires inlaid,
and a necklace of precious stones.

She brushes kohl along her lashes
and looks in the life-size mirror.
Pleased with herself, the woman smiles.

She eats her dinner, five different courses,
sweets and all, then washes her hands.
She covers herself with a golden shawl.
Takes water to drink in a jug of gold,
betel leaves, areca nuts, fragrances, sandal paste,
jasmine water, fruits, and snacks on a platter of gold.
She puts jasmine and jaji flowers in her hair
and arrives with joy to meet her husband.

---

3. The word used to indicate that Rama has misunderstood Sita, *bhrama,* has a range of meanings from simple misunderstanding to total delusion. It suggests that Rama is so deluded by his own ego that he cannot bear Sita's tardiness after he has summoned her.

"Lord, My Hero, I've brought you flowers.
You never bend before any rival.
You're the one that humiliated
the other Rama who challenged you.
You are my lord, my Kakutstha."[4]

"Can I bear your anger? You closed the door.
My feet are aching, my hands are tired.
Open the ivory door, My Lord.
It's beginning to rain. I am getting wet.
Open that golden bolt, My Handsome!
It's raining hard, my sari is soaked.
My Emerald Young Man, open the door.
It is the fourth phase of the night, Lord of My Life.
I'll give you my necklace of precious gems.
Let me lie at your feet, to get a little sleep."

Rama says,
"If you lose sleep, what do I care!
The lamp-stand here keeps me company.
If you stand out there, what do I care!
Flowers and fragrant bukka scent keep me company.
If you stand out there, what do I care!
Sandal and musk keep me company.
If you stand out there, what do I care!
The mattress and pillows keep me company."

Upset at Rama's words, Sita quickly runs to her mother-in-law's house.
When she hears it all, Kausalya comes to Rama's door.

"You're the son of King Dasharatha,
married into the house of the great Janaka.
Earth gave her daughter to you.
Have you lost your sense?
What did Sita do?
Tell me, my little boy, if something's wrong."

"Mother, if you pamper your daughter-in-law,
Will she ever care for me?" says the hero of the house
As he opens the door, with a big smile.

"Mother, my father-in-law is waiting. You go to him, he is all alone,"
says Sita to Kausalya, and Kausalya leaves.

---

4. Sita lauds Rama by alluding to his defeat of Parashu-rama (the "other Rama"), a Brahmin who destroyed generations of Kshatriyas. She also praises Rama as a descendant of Kakutstha, an ancestor whose great deeds brought glory to the Raghu dynasty, suggesting Rama has lived up to the reputation of his illustrious lineage.

When Sita goes shyly to her husband, the lamp laughs with joy.

Fragrance of betel leaves all over the bed.
Fragrance of betel nuts all over the bed.
Fragrance of flowers all over the bed.
Fragrance of musk all over the bed.
Fragrance of bukka all over the bed.

Who knows how angry Sita is?
Rama turns to the other side.

"Just how long it takes for butter to melt
when it is near fire,
is how long a woman's anger lasts,"
says Sita and moves swiftly
to make love.[5]
Rama plays all the games of love.

He lives in glory and honor.

Women who sing this song or listen to it,
will live on earth with riches.

Translated from Telugu by Velcheru Narayana Rao

---

5. The use of a well-known analogy about the relationship between butter and fire here is intriguing: Sita reverses the usual comparison of woman to fire and man to a pot of butter, thereby underscoring Rama's sexual vulnerability. Describing Sita's move toward Rama, the song uses the verb *kalisenu* (literally "met"), a Telugu euphemism for sexual union. The term indicates a man making love to a woman, or in plural a man and woman making love together. Since it is never used in singular with a woman as the subject, the word signals that in this situation Sita takes the initiative, a bold usage, considering the conventions of female modesty prevalent among the women who have sung these songs.

4 Sita's Powers

This song, translated from Kannada, comes from a three-part collection of folk stories from Ramkatha where each part focuses on one aspect of Sita's experiences: her birth, her marriage, and the tests of her fidelity to Rama. The editors of the collection inform us that they transcribed the song translated below, focusing on Sita's tests, in 1972 from a performance by Honnajamma, a woman then approximately forty-five years old.

The song belongs to a vast repertoire of women's expressive traditions that construct and imagine the detail of everyday life of women, detail that is often missing from Sanskrit epic narrative. Ringing of experience and wisdom, such folksongs are mostly sung by older women. The village of Ankanahalli, to which Honnajamma belongs, is part of Mysore District in Karnataka state. At the base of the Nilgiri mountains, this region is characterized by hilly tracts. The song's references to paddy and the images of water—indeed the rural ambience—reflect the traditional farming occupation of the Vokkaliga jati to which Honnajamma belongs.[1]

The song shows Sita undergoing a series of trials before the climactic fire test (agnipariksha), with each trial demonstrating her quintessential purity and the powers she derives by virtue of that purity. The analogies Rama makes to unfading jasmine, unsullied silk, untainted vermillion, and unwilting leaves are shown immediately to be realized on Sita's own body. She wears jasmine and silk, is adorned with auspicious vermillion and turmeric, and holds a tender leaf at the moment when she prepares herself for the flames. As the last lines suggest, her purity extends far beyond the usual units of measurement. Still, Rama does not accept Sita's "truth" and the refrain "Do you accept my truth?" becomes ironic, revealing the incongruity of the tests to which Sita is subjected. The further irony is that the late Dasharatha (who says "Accept my word as truth, Son") has to vouch for Sita, who has succeeded in performing all the difficult tasks that Rama sets for her in the first half of this song. Sita's appeal to Dasharatha plays on the well-known theme of Rama's unquestioning devotion to his father, whose word Rama has always accepted as "truth." The song highlights ironies in the male-authored tellings about Rama, making these ironies available to those who hear this song of Sita.

---

1. Almost all the Vokkaligas in Mandya, Mysore, and Hassan districts of Karnataka are Gangadikara Vokkaligas, whose name derives from their ancestral origins, believed to be in the land of the Ganga kings of Mysore. According to the *Mysore Gazetteer,* they worship Shiva, Vishnu, and many village deities (Hayavadana Rao 1927: 243–244). Ankanahalli is part of K. R. Nagar Taluk in Mysore District.

The moral complexity of the song is reflected in its development. It begins with the searing words of Rama to Sita, moves on to provide examples of Sita's extraordinary powers created by her purity, climaxes in the fire test, alludes to gossip about Sita's purity in Lanka, and ends with Sita's return to cool, deep Mother Earth, Sita's natal home and ultimate refuge. [L. P.]

Source: Rame Gowda, P. K. Rajasekara, and S. Basavaiah, eds. *Janapada Ramayana* [Folk Ramayanas] (Mysore: n.p., 1973), vol. 1, pp. 16–17.

Do You Accept My Truth, My Lord?
WOMEN'S FOLKSONG

Go to the river bank and make a ball of sand.
Make a vessel of sand and fetch water in it, Sita.
Then will I accept your truth.

Making a vessel of sand, taking water in it,
she placed it in front of Rama—did Sita.
Do you accept my truth, My Lord?

Using a serpent's coil for a pot-rest on your head, Sita,
if you fetch me water in a sheaf of paddy,
then will I accept your truth.
Going to the anthill, standing there,
reaching into the snake hole—what did she say?
You who reside in this anthill, O Serpent, Sovereign of the Earth,
won't you at least bite me to death?

Bringing out the hissing one, coiling it around her arm,
slipping it off to make a pot-rest, she places it on her head.

With the serpent coiled into a pot-rest, Sita,
carrying water in a sheaf of paddy, Sita,
placing it near Rama—what did she say?
Do you accept my truth, My Great Lord?

As jasmine in the hair does not fade,
as draped silk does not get soiled,
as vermillion does not get discolored by turmeric,
as the hand does not get weighed down by a tender leaf,
like that, you must stand in the fire
that I will make in front of the palace.

She has combed her hair, she has decorated it with jasmine.
She has donned a silk sari—has Sita.
She has adorned herself with turmeric and vermillion—has Sita.
She holds a tender leaf in her hand.

A fire has been made in front of the palace.
She has gone around the fire three times.
Going around the fire three times, she says—what does she say?
Dasharatha, father-in-law, you who have passed on,
won't you at least come to my rescue?

He came, did king Dasharatha, and said—what did he say?
I am your father, Ramachandra.
Don't bring ill-repute to Mother Sita.

Just because of somebody's idle talk, don't make Sita a laughingstock.
Accept my word as truth, Son, and
make your devoted and pure wife Sita happy.

The water-fed furrow in which Sita was born
is the netherworld of Sitala.[2]
Sita, who sank into a furrow twelve man-lengths,[3]
that Sita's virtue is true virtue.

Translated from Kannada by Leela Prasad

---

2. Sitala, the Goddess who causes and cures smallpox, is said to live in the cool earth, to which Sita ultimately returns. She is also known as Shitala in other parts of India.
3. This unit, an *alu*, measures from a man's toe to the tip of his finger when his arm is raised straight above his head.

5 Talking Back

Gudipati Venkata Chalam (1894–1979), popularly known simply as "Chalam," was a prolific and skilled writer of Telugu fiction. His social and literary contributions stemmed from his relentless advocacy of women's social and personal freedoms (especially sexual freedom) and his talent for portraying women's lives in their own voices as he imagined them. A master of spoken Telugu, he made dialogue, especially intimate speech, a major component in his novels and short stories as well as his plays.

Sita Agnipravesam (Sita Enters the Fire) is representative of Chalam's iconoclasm. It was originally published in a collection of five short plays, all of which recast puranic and epic tales by provocatively reversing stories of pativratas. Rarely produced, his plays were primarily read as literature. They imagined possibilities of women's liberation through heroines who were confident, powerful, independent, witty, and sensitive, heroines for whom love and desire were inseparable. In this play, Chalam takes the paramount figure of the pativrata ideal, Sita, and rewrites her reunion with Rama after the battle in Lanka. Challenging Rama's status as the ideal man, Chalam uncovers Rama's patriarchal egoism and depicts Ravana, his arch-enemy, as a worthy rival. Chalam adeptly creates a psychologically convincing Sita with a complex subjectivity.[1] Chalam transforms the famous scene in which Sita's fidelity to Rama is tested by her entrance into fire into another kind of test altogether. [S.E.P.]

Source: Gudipati Venkata Chalam, *Savitri: Pauranika Natikalu* [Savitri: Plays from the Puranas] (n.p.: Panduranga Press, 1924; rpt. Vijayawada: Aruna Publishing House, 1993), pp. 50–58.

Sita Enters the Fire
BY GUDIPATI VENKATA CHALAM

In the ages to come, there will be neither sons like Rama, nor wives like Sita.[2]

SITA: Rama, my good fortune, at long last! How wonderful it is to see you again!
RAMA: Wait . . .
SITA: (Unable to stop)

---

1. Chalam's work proved so compelling that "quite a few Telugu feminist writers today trace their direct line of descent from him," note Alladi Uma and M. Sridhar (2001:13).
2. The epigram at the beginning of the play is Chalam's.

Oh, Rama! After all that you've sacrificed for my sake, you must be dying to feel my love. You must have been so worried about me and everything I've suffered through. My hero, you destroyed this brutal demon with your amazing strength, with your bare hands!

I've been praying constantly for this moment, this blessed moment, when I would turn and see you again.

I knew I would see you again. Oh, those endless nights when I chanted your sweet name like a mantra—they are burned into my memory forever. With great compassion, you heard my prayer. It was my hope that kept me alive. Now that your love has saved me, I will never fear anything again, in life or death.

This separation was a true test of our love. It has strengthened the bond that unites us. Our love is now stronger than ever, eternal, unwavering. This great war has proven how completely my heart belongs to you, how steadfast my heart has remained. In the face of all temptations and terrors, no matter how long we were separated, I knew your deep love for me would never disappear. Not even death frightens me now, because it cannot change my heart. I know now that your love for me is everlasting.

Come, come, hold me in your arms. Ignore all these people around us. Think of them as our friends. They are my army now, my servants. Let me soothe your aching chest. It must hurt from warding off Ravana's arrows.

RAMA: Sita, stop! You really need to listen to me. You were born a woman. You were abducted by my enemy. After living inside his palace for so many years . . .

SITA: No, in the forest—[3]

RAMA: Whatever you say, wherever it may have been. You were touched by another. You are impure. I am the moon rising over the sea of Bharat, the precious gem of the solar dynasty.[4] You are no longer fit to be the queen of this great empire.

SITA: (Not mincing words)

What do you mean, I was "touched by another?"

RAMA: Ravana loved you.

SITA: Is it my fault that he loved me?

RAMA: He stole you away.

SITA: Is that my fault?

RAMA: You lived with him in his palace gardens.

SITA: No, in the grove. Is that my fault, too?

RAMA: It is your bad luck.

---

3. Rama accuses Sita of living luxuriously in Ravana's palace. Sita corrects him, noting that she lived austerely in a grove outside the palace like a renouncer in the forest.
4. Conventionally Rama is identified as part of the Raghuvamsa (lineage of the Raghu clan), but Chalam uses Bharatavamsha instead, perhaps to indicate a general realm or country, thus suggesting modern overtones of nationhood.

SITA: You made a vow when we married that you would share both good and bad with me. You said you would bear my burdens and protect me. It was your responsibility to keep a rival king from carrying me off. Does our marital knot unravel if another man claims he loves me and abducts me? People say the bond between a husband and a wife is forever! Am I food just to be eaten? Do you think you can throw me away with disgust if you suspect that someone has polluted me with his saliva?[5]

I am the beloved daughter of Janaka. I am not womb-born, I am born of the very Earth. How dare you treat me like a dirty dish! Do I deserve all of this abuse just because I became your wife? The queen of a great king, who holds the whole Earth in his hands?

(Rama remains silent)

SITA: If the great Shri Rama did not want his wife back, why did he bother to fight this war?

RAMA: Because of my righteous anger. A warrior's dharma is to punish the wrongdoings of his enemies.

SITA: You fought this war for the sake of your dharma? May I assume that you are also going to seek another wife for the sake of your precious dharma?

Don't I have dharma? Even if you throw me away like a worn-out shoe, don't I still have a right to bear great warriors, to bear an heir to the realm of Bharat? My dharma as a wife, my dharma as a mother, my dharma as a queen—what happened to those?

Fine, you got married to fulfill your dharma to have a family. You dragged me around the forest to fulfill the dharma of your oath to your father. To have loved me was the dharma of a husband; to fight this war was the dharma of a warrior. And what particular dharma do you think requires you to abandon me now?

RAMA: The dharma of a king.

SITA: Think about what you are feeling now. Can you honestly say that your suffering for me, your love, your pain, your anger are all just following what is prescribed in the shastras? Are you a machine run by the shastras?

RAMA: I am not a weeping peasant, I am a king! I have responsibilities that go beyond those of a husband. Nothing should taint the glory of Shri Rama.

SITA: Doesn't leaving your wife damage your integrity? Do you think your subjects would approve of that?

RAMA: I would never give them any reason to disapprove of me.

SITA: Shri Rama, is what your subjects say really so important to you? When your father ordered you into exile in the forest, did you care that the people

---

5. This refers to pervasive Hindu ritual and social mores that regulate purity and pollution in eating and sexual practices; both are strictly guarded arenas of commingling. For example, sharing food and saliva implies the sharing of sexual intimacy, which is only permitted between a husband and wife under pativrata ideology.

of your realm, without exception, begged you not to go? You told them then that obeying the will of one's father is always the highest good. Now you want to reject your wife before the people have even made their will known. A father's word is absolute—but you can easily break all the promises you have made to me, all the dharmas of love and marriage, only because I am a woman.

What do you care if my heart breaks? Do you care if my life is wasted—a life I have devoted to you? I have suffered for you. I have shared dreams with you for all these years. If leaving me meant your life would be ruined, like mine would be, would it be so easy for you to leave me?

Of course, you want to be renowned as a perfect king, dazzling future generations with your deeds. But just remember, you will also be a role model for all the men who treat their wives like dirt and throw them out— that's why you invented this fantasy in your mind about me. That's why you are throwing me in the dust. You are just hungry for fame, Rama!

And this is a country that claims to worship women! Right? So this is the respect a devoted wife, a pativrata, gets in this world! When people think of a model for low standards, they will think of you.

If you kick me and throw me out, should I behave like a dog, following after you, falling at your feet and crying? Shall I confess to wrongs I did not commit, and be expected to atone for all of them, accepting shame with a bowed head for anything and everything? Then will people praise me as a pativrata for all time to come?

But if I stand up to you, defend my own honor, reject your cruelty and look after my own life, I'll be suspect. I'll be called a whore.

If you really love me, then listen to me. You're not king yet. The coronation has not taken place. You have no real responsibility to the people at this moment.

RAMA: The coronation will take place soon.

SITA: Of course, once you are made king, you will have an obligation to respect public opinion. But why can't you give up the kingdom now for my sake—for the sake of my love—for the sake of my life?

RAMA: My dharma is to be king. And it is my right.

SITA: *You* have dharmas and rights, but what about me? Apparently, you have the right to claim me or reject me. Why don't you give up your rights for me?

RAMA: What! For a woman? Won't I be blamed for losing my kingdom because I was tangled up in lust?

SITA: Is sacrificing your kingdom for the sake of your beloved wife the same as being tangled up in lust? By falling in love with you, I denied myself the opportunity to be Ravana's queen. Was it my dharma to fall in love with you? Or was it my stupidity, my karma?

You are selfish, Rama. You care only about your kingdom and your fame. You want your fortune to flourish forever, but you want me to die alone. When I'm treated as impure and helpless, am I supposed to just sigh? Did you gather all these people here to humiliate me? If you care so much about serving your people, why bother with a wife at all?

RAMA: To continue my family line, and to keep it pure. But you are unfit to continue my sacred lineage.

SITA: So all I am is a machine to produce children for you? You think that since this machine is broken, you can simply get another?

So, in the end, only you have dharma? A woman is not even a living being to you. She has no breath, no heart, no dharma. What if I accept that it is only you that have dharma? You are dharma-bound to your father, mother, brothers, the people of your domain, animals, and stones—everybody except your wife![6] Does the dharma you had to your wife disappear with a single word?

But enough of that, what does your heart say?

RAMA: How my heart feels does not matter.

SITA: Let me tell you something. Ravana loved me. Even your sharp arrows could not kill his love for me. But your love was destroyed by childish suspicion the moment you thought that another man might have loved me. His love did not waver for an instant, in spite of the protests of his people, his brothers, his wives, his sages, even the gods—in spite of losing his kingdom, his riches, his beloved sons, and his brothers, he still loved me. Even when his ten heads were cut off and rolling across the battlefield, he still loved me. Since you cannot understand that love, you call it animal lust, a demon's idea of love, and reduce it to nothing!

Did I love him in return? That's what you really fear, don't you? If I had loved him, I would have covered his body with mine to shield him against your arrows. Did he molest me? No, he was too noble a person for that. If he had forced himself on me, shouldn't you be soothing my heart and the pain my delicate body would have suffered at the hands of this so-called demon? Is this all the compassion you can show me? No, you are a dharma-bound machine and you want me to be reduced to a machine to bear your children.

I refuse to be renounced by you. I reject you as a husband, you heartless machine, you base wretch who breaks his vows. Ravana loved me, even when he knew I would never love him in return. He did not view me as a child-bearing machine. He wanted my love, that's all he wanted. When I refused him and treated him like dirt, never even looking at him, it was enough for him to be near me. He felt that his life was useless without me. He gave up everything. I ended up here, like this, because I was stubborn and did not love such a hero.

I regret that I did not return his love. I shall pay a price for it now. I shall purify my body, which was soiled when I uttered your foul name, by the same fiery flames that consumed his blood-stained limbs. Rama, you have

---

6. "Stone" refers to Ahalya (see part 2, #13–16).

rejected me because you feared that my body was defiled by his touch, even though you knew my heart remained pure.

(She jumps into the funeral pyre of Ravana.)

This demon wanted my heart, even though he knew my body belonged to you. Some day, intelligent people will be able to see whose love was more noble. How long will a woman be merely something for man's use? When will the world open its eyes?

Translated from Telugu by Sailaza Easwari Pal

6   The Pensive Queen

"Sita Immersed in Reflection" by Kumaran Asan (1873–1924) consists almost entirely of Sita's extended soliloquy, interspersed with a few descriptive verses that signal shifts in her train of thought. The poem, first published in 1919, presents Sita's inner feelings at a pivotal moment between two of the epic's most dramatic events: Rama's ashvamedha (horse sacrifice) and Sita's return to Mother Earth. "Sita Immersed in Reflection" begins after Valmiki has taken Sita's twin sons to Ayodhya to recite Valmiki's poem for Rama. There the king will learn that his wife, whom he thought had perished in the jungle long ago, has survived and raised his sons. The departure of the sage and twins leaves Sita to herself—a rare experience for a woman cared for by father then husband, supervised by mother then three mothers-in-law, kept under surveillance by rakshasa guards, and then serving as single parent to her growing twins. In the poem, from nightfall to sunrise the next day, Sita considers her life with Rama. Concluding that her role in the earthly drama has ended, she decides to return to Mother Earth.

"Sita Immersed in Reflection" depicts Sita moving through a set of moods and reasoned reflections that are mirrored by changes in the natural world, as she and her surroundings pass from darkness into light. Within this overall pattern that provides the poem with its momentum, Asan presents Sita's multiple, complex, shifting, ambivalent, and conflicted thoughts about a marriage that provided loving companionship but also intense suffering. Some have criticized Asan for portraying Rama in a negative light, while others have praised him for considering the relations between Sita and Rama from many angles.[1]

Much of the poem's originality consists of Asan's imagining how living in Valmiki's ashram would affect Sita.[2] There, she slowly reconstructs her life by cutting herself off from everything connected with Rama. For example, she never reveals to her sons that Rama is their father—they know only that they are Janaki's sons.[3] Over the years, Sita has imbibed the ascetic ethos of the hermitage and cultivates feelings of compassion for others, a sentiment in short supply

---

1. Sreenivasan (1981: 110) and George (1972: 54) discuss some of the ways in which Asan's poem has been criticized for its depiction of Rama.

2. Kumaran Asan knew ashram life well. As a disciple of Shree Narayana Guru, the pre-eminent reformer of Hinduism in Kerala, Asan lived in the guru's ashram from 1891 to 1892 and from 1900 to 1920. For a useful chronology of Asan's life, see Sreenivasan (1981: vii–ix).

3. "Janaki," another name for Sita, emphasizes her royal status as daughter of the great king and philosopher Janaka. Asan also calls her "Sita Devi" or "Devi," to stress her ultimate status as a goddess who descended to earth only briefly.

at the court of Ayodhya, where jealousy, slander, and striving for power seem to harden people's hearts. In the ashram, Sita overcomes her grief and, eventually, by cultivating equanimity of mind, frees herself from resentment toward Rama for disgracing her. The poem culminates with a monist-inspired vision of Sita's body merging with Mother Earth and her *atman* (eternal self) soaring to the highest spiritual realm, released from the cycle of death and rebirth.

In the translation below, the four major sections of "Sita Immersed in Reflection" have been indicated with a heading at the start of each section.[4] The first section explains how Sita came to be alone and to recall events from her earlier life. The second portion considers the virtues of the women dwelling in the ashram, highlighting the wisdom, asceticism, and piety practiced there in contrast with women in court. In the third section, Sita articulates an acutely insightful indictment of how Rama treated her by comparing his love for her during their forest exile to his rigidity, self-absorption, and subterfuge after their return to the kingdom of Kosala. Eschewing euphemisms or delicacy, she accuses Rama of being in thrall to public opinion, failing in his duty to protect her, and caring so much for his position that he does not consider renouncing the throne to remain with Sita.

Asan's most masterful transition is the carefully modulated one between the third section and the final one. At the height of Sita's condemnation of Rama, she suddenly sees her husband from a different perspective: imprisoned by his own position as ruler, like a caged bird longing for freedom from the burden of governing. This insight releases her from her bitterness toward Rama and enables her to view him as a person mired in the contradictions of existence in an imperfect world. Her realization prompts another: that her time on earth is drawing to a close. The poem ends with her anticipation that she and Rama will meet after they both quit their earthly existence. In the final verse, she goes to Rama's court and, there, leaves the world.

Asan was familiar with the Ramayana tradition and in fact published his retelling of Valmiki's *Ramayana* in Malayalam as a story for children before he completed "Sita Immersed in Reflection."[5] Asan's telling of the story of Rama and Sita, however, focuses upon the section of the story that most scholars consider a later addition to Valmiki's text. Furthermore, Asan's poem portrays Sita's return to Mother Earth not as a desperate or tragic act, but as the result of a decision reached after probing and judicious reflection. Sita's soliloquy provides an elegant and deeply intelligent assessment of her life, viewed in retrospect.

Source: Kumaran Asan, "Chintavishtayaya Sita," in *Kumaranasante Sampurna Padyakritikal* [Complete Poetic Works of Kumaran Asan] (Kottayam: Sahitya Pravarthaka Cooperative Society [1981]; rpt. ed. 1986), pp. 521–563.

---

4. In the Malayalam original, verses that describe Sita, rather than quoting Sita's words, indicate the shift between sections.
5. Called *Bala Ramayanam,* it was published in 1916.

Sita Immersed in Reflection
BY KUMARAN ASAN

Twilight

On an evening, long after her sons
had left for Ayodhya with Sage Valmiki,
Sita, lost in her thoughts, wandered
into the twilit yard of the forlorn hermitage.

A sirius tree in bloom hung for her
a fair canopy of interlaced boughs;
the sapphire grass appeared
a silken carpet where she reigned.

The pensive queen did not heed
the sun dropping on the horizon
or the earth brimming with moonlight;
nor seemed aware that she was alone.

The Tamasa River looked ecstatic
in the breeze wakening its water lilies;
the swaying forest turned silver
beneath the shimmering moon.

The dark-haired one wore
the fireflies falling on her tresses
as though they were wild jasmines
wafted to her through the air.

Her rich mane of raven hair,
now glistening in the dark,
seemed a piece of twinkling night sky
seen through the woods.

Swathed in a single drape,
petal-soft, Sita Devi sat there;
the lovely one rested on her thighs
her slender bough-shaped arms.

Fixed in an empty gaze, not once
did her partly-closed eyes flicker
even as her coarse untended curls
grazed her eyelids in the wind.

Languidly, she raised her body
that bent slightly inwards,

and a sigh escaped her at times,
like a wayward draft of wind.

The turbulent sea of thought
that raged within Devi's mind
brought shifting waves of moods
to the pure shores of her radiant cheeks.

Finding no way to calm
her fond heart in tumult
the valiant lady contemplated
thus in great anguish:

"Nothing is certain;
our fortunes are fleeting;
we plod along our feverish ways, yet
the world reveals its mysteries to none.

At times like a bead of mercury,
or in the vein of a popping grain of rice,
my mind shifts incessantly,
one time mightily, another time lightly!

I recall those happy days
that once embellished the fair earth,
and their fading, too,
like the treacherous smiles of evil Fate.

The scorching summer passes every year,
the cool rains arrive soon on earth.
Winter trees sprout tender shoots
and burst into bloom before long.

Misery that befall earth's creatures
spends itself quickly, but,
due to our proud nature,
woe remains ever with us.

My left shoulder still quivers, but like
a lowly worm.[6] What is now a tryst with love?
I shall no longer follow desire
like a child chasing shadows.

---

6. In Indian love poetry, the quivering of the left shoulder usually indicates that the lover and be-loved will soon have a tryst. Conventionally, this is a good omen, but here Sita comments on how inappropriate a meeting between her and Rama would be now, so the omen is not romantic but instead is as lowly as the action of a quivering worm.

Today, listening to the poignant song of Sage Valmiki,
Rama, the reigning Sovereign of Manu's dynasty,
besieged by compassion, must have
recognized the sons born to him.[7]

The tender stirrings that once sprung
from marital love have not utterly ceased,
yet, as faint now as dying echoes,
they do not sway my thought anymore.

Even a moment's separation
still seems so severe that it singes my heart,
but love has fallen into a deep slumber
like a viper that dares not raise its head.

Severed of the feelings
kindling sensuous pleasure,
my mind is now in a wretched state,
a sad nest deserted by doves.

The golden moon in my heart that once
neither rose nor set, but always shone
with its resplendent rays, is now seen
only in my memory's mirror.

Austerity being a habit now,
grief has been spent; my days
are calmer from spiritual learning.
Disgrace alone is not yet cured by wisdom.

Compassion for the ones I bore within
stopped me that day from taking my life.[8]
The artless games of my lively sons
soon filled me with wonder and joy.

The winning rays of their smiles
removed the darkness in my heart.
Children are indeed a balm
for the pain that is human life.

Night is illumined by bright stars,
islands relieve the vast ocean.
There will always be an instance
that abates even the greatest ill.

---

7. Asan subtly insinuates that Rama has been overly rigid by calling attention to his ancestor, Manu, the lawgiver.
8. Sita refers obliquely to the day when she was banished from Ayodhya.

So it is seen that Fate does not hold
lasting spite for the creatures on earth.
While she wields the scourge in one hand,
with the other she caresses her prey.

It is inevitable that the paths trodden
by living beings remain uneven
reflecting joy and pain alike
as though they were light and shade.

A condition may appear
painful at times, joyful at times.
Swayed by none, the wise endure
their shifting fortunes with equanimity.

I shall no longer desire the devious pleasure
that leads only to a tryst with misery.
If the mind willingly courts sorrow
fate might discard its malice.

Endurance can slowly turn
sheer darkness into light.
Even a bitter taste, with habit,
can feel sweet on the tongue.

Life in the world may go on forever
with good and evil inseparably fused
like the ever-changing moon
that endures her waxing and waning.

An atman might eventually cross
the vast ocean of illusion
after the long roaring ride
on the fickle waves of joy and sorrow.

Or, perhaps, the divine hand
drives us along the pathway of grief
to hasten our arrival at
the great citadel of joy.

Even the advent of good fortune,
the mind takes as a guise of evil,
and quivers like a timid bird, fluttering
in the kind hands that try to fondle it.

As Lakshmana revealed the king's decree
that I be forsaken in the jungle,
darkness at once fell upon my world
and, as if struck by lightning, I collapsed.

Then I most desired death, yet the life
that grew inside me checked my fatal thoughts,
though I was shaken by the heavy blow which fell
on my old calluses of separation.

I yearned for madness, too, in which
my anguish would have declined.
But sanity seldom left me, and
I lingered in intense despair.

Yet, good fortune insured that no sickness
befell my mind to double my torment.
Death is surely preferable
to living a senseless life.

I no longer want the monkey of madness
to enter the virtuous garden of my wits.
Nor do I wish to mumble away
like the bamboos split in the wild wind.

There is no better companion
than fortitude that vows to favor a person,
and no greater preceptor than grief
which instills such wisdom.

It was sheer chance that I did not
nurture the sinful thought of death: thus
the perpetuation of the line was ensured,
and I gained this equanimity of mind.

I cannot bear any recollection;
darkness fills my heart's environs,
hosts of distressing thoughts
rise like clouds of moths.

At times the shadow of apathy lifts
and the stream of memory lights up
like a creeper that bursts into bloom
on the arrival of spring.

I remember Lakshmana: powerless to leave,
his brows quivering in grief like worms,
bowed head propped in his hands
and tears streaming down his face.[9]

---

9. Lakshmana felt duty-bound to obey Rama, his elder brother, but agonized about abandoning pregnant Sita in the jungle, weeping as he left her alone.

Seeing him in such agony, that brave heart
of untold strength, keen discernment
and supreme devotion to his brother,
my own despair was diminished.

You lived with us, pure one,
heedless if it were jungle or home.
Brother, how hard it is to forbid your dear face
from appearing in my mind's eye!

Terror of foes, your loving devotion
alone had made our days merry.
We basked safely in the magnificent beauty
of great woods and mountains.

In the forest, unable to bear my indictment,
you once fled from me. Later the charge
chanced on me, and it fell on you to desert me.
Fate seems vengeful in its ways.[10]

My brother, by the grace of your heart,
forgive my thoughtless and cruel words.
Is there any wicked path into which
an unruly mind may not wander!

You shielded him from danger
and thus saved the regal line when,
distraught by my absence, Raghunatha
wandered alone in the wild forests.[11]

It was when I heard the fretful story
of your combat with the tireless Indrajit,
that I tremulously fathomed the depth
of my heart's devotion to you.[12]

You must have embraced my boys in compassion
when Sage Valmiki presented them at the court.
Your pure mind, ever free of jealousy, today
must have swum in the river of joy.

---

10. Sita delicately refers to the moment during their forest exile when she forced Lakshmana to join Rama in his attempt to catch the golden deer. Sita had charged that if he did not leave to aid Rama, it would show that he had impure designs on her. Shocked by the allegation, Lakshmana quickly left. Now it is Sita who has been impugned with accusations of impurity and wonders if the negative effects of her earlier charge against Lakshmana have returned to her.

11. Asan refers to Rama as Raghava, "He of the Raghu lineage," and Raghunatha, "Lord of the Raghus," to emphasize the extent to which Rama's identity is based on his royal lineage.

12. Indrajit, son of Ravana, wounded Lakshmana in battle but Hanuman crossed the earth to bring back a special herb that saved his life.

Dismiss all thoughts of me, dear one.
Live long as the King's sole companion,
safe in the company of the kinsfolk
whom Virtue's hands have blessed!

I remember the cold faint
that deprived me of discernment
and obscured my senses, yet acted
like a balm on my wounded heart.

Though I looked the very scion of death
in that state which made onlookers shudder,
to one deeply aggrieved
such oblivion lent abundant comfort.

With no ill will to my beloved
nor any fear or shame, I simply sank
into the murky depths of forgetfulness,
my reason submerged.

My soft body, then full-bellied, so tender
that it hurt even on a bed of flowers,
lay on the hard ground full of thorns
and teeming with insects.

I remember the learned seer
coming up to me like the early autumn
that arrives, bringing relief to the earth
lashed by turbulent rains.

'Come to my nearby hermitage, my child,
and consider it your own home.'
Speaking these guileless words, Sage Valmiki,
my father's friend, cooled my heart.

Night

The great sage revealed to me
that earthly life is a mirage
of the mind, and seeking
everlasting peace alone is the way.

Was this a soothing lake
near a forest on fire? Or,
the calm shore of the raging sea?
Serene is this retreat of the sages.

Pious women with faces untainted
by the smoke of fury

glowed as eternal lamps
in this calm hermitage.

I recall the warmth of the love
they tenderly bore in their hearts
for all creation: trees, birds, beasts,
humans and gods alike.

And the profound piety
with which they paid homage
to the sun, moon, fire, forests,
the Vedas and the mountains.

They are like the very Vedas of the world,
these ascetics, mothers of saints,
revealing what is good and what evil
through the rituals of their ashram life.

Reciting the epics and sacred lore
they irrigate the terrain of life
and offer everyone flowers that blossom
on the creepers of their souls.

Chaste deities of pure love,
they who find utmost joy in the service
of their ascetic husbands, victory be to those,
who do not fall under the illusion of desire.

Even if the smrti be forgotten
or the Vedas submerged in the sea of Time
the land would be blessed where
these chaste women lead their pure lives.[13]

The fellowship of these jewels of womankind
that shine in their compassion
would soften even the austere sages
who grow hard with self-denial.

Perhaps their compassion made the great bard,
to whose sharp mind the three worlds
are no more than a leaf of grass, take pity
on the krauncha bird that was slain before him.

It so chanced that I was to be grateful
to the cruel Fate that drove me

---

13. *Smrti* is a treatise on correct action written by a learned teacher. Hindu texts are often divided into two types: *shruti* refers to religious texts of divine origin (such as the Vedas) while smrti refers to religious texts composed by humans.

to these women, just as a patient
would feel obliged to a skillful surgeon.

On the other hand, city women
act as fuel to the flames
of love's insatiable desire, and burn
themselves away into charcoal and ash.

Nurturing scorn, jealousy, avarice
and indulgence in their hearts,
generations of women
have ruined their lives.

Blinded by their own flaws, they cannot
understand the virtuous way of life.
Discontented, they perish from illness
inflicted by the host of their sins.

Like a jewel is covered with mud,
the soul of the vicious loses its luster.
Like a worm in the mind's cave,
it falls into a dark pit of filth and putrefies.

As the carnal serpent exhales
noxious fumes in heat
through the mouth of that cave,
it blights everyone nearby.

Gorgeous clothes, fabulous jewels
and expensive ornaments
are the beautiful flowering vines
covering treacherous forest wells.

Smiles that overawe the moonlight
and words sweeter than honey
are the minions of the demon of deceit
reigning in the hearts of men.

Without flags, chariots or forts,
battlements or men-at-arms,
the flaming tongues of evil men
burn away a whole forest of their enemies.

Even the directives of a king
issued after days of deliberation
are maligned and turned upside down
in an instant by slanderers.

Listening to malicious words, monarchs
may set out to perform imprudent acts,

forgetting time-proven love
and throwing aside all mercy.

Some would pledge the crown to a son
then send him in exile to an ascetic's life.
Their sons, in their turn, would impudently
abandon a pregnant queen in the jungle.[14]

Alas! The wind of that memory
suddenly intensifies the fire in my heart,
and scorches my already-shattered life,
thus utterly devastating it.

If illustrious rulers themselves
thus turn away from the righteous path,
Dharma will come to ruin, and soon
the world will turn uninhabitable.

That day, in Lanka, Raghava had privately
revealed he was discontent with me.
Again, did he have to muddy his feet
to wash them clean in public?[15]

Heavens, it is a cruel rope
one gets for loving intensely!
Men display their prowess by offering
their women as bloody sacrifices.

The pyre of jealousy that consumes
even those deeply in love and
bonded in conjugal felicity
may be the lot of mankind.

Most Pure Wedlock,
the loveliest flower of virtue
that was once the joy of earth, now
how you have fallen into the dust!

Though the practice of morality
should refine one's nature, one's flaws
can instantly defile all rites
and make even Dharma seem invalid.

---

14. Sita suggests that recklessness runs in the family: King Dasharatha announced Rama's coronation but subsequently let Kaikeyi send Rama into exile. Rama banished his queen after fighting a
war to win her back from Ravana.
15. Asan suggests that when Rama first saw Sita in Lanka he privately denigrated her, but then
forced her to undergo a public ordeal to prove her purity.

Was it my fault that, in the wilderness,
we had to spend long years in exile?
Was it my misstep that made
the demon king lust after my body?

True, a king is obliged to esteem
the verdict of his subjects, but when
the public is divided in opinion,
shouldn't the king assess its clashing views?

Before the conceited masses fed by the lies
of the wicked, whose thick tongues would deny
even what they have seen with their very eyes,
I am sole witness to my own purity.

Did this king care for his people's wishes
when Bharata's mother mercilessly
snatched away the sovereignty
which was so near at hand?

That was to uphold Truth
and this to safeguard Dharma![16]
Even the misdeeds of shrewd men
may be praised by the populace.

Earlier, the subjects hailed me
as their beloved queen. How could they
dishonor me so suddenly
when I conceived the king's heir in my womb?

Perhaps some jealous people
who only pretended love for me
because they believed I was barren
might have spewed this base slander.

Is it possible that the mind
that suspected Bharata to be a cheat
when he came to the forest
can be pure with no touch of spite?[17]

---

16. Members of the Raghu lineage won fame for always adhering to truth (*satya*), so they pride themselves on carrying out vows that they make.

17. Bharata returned to Ayodhya from a visit to his uncle and discovered that his mother had caused Rama to be exiled, so he set out to find his brother, tell him of King Dasharatha's death, and insist that Rama become king. When Lakshmana caught sight of Bharata's huge entourage approaching the forest of Chitrakuta, he thought that Bharata might be coming to slay Rama so Bharata could secure his claim to the throne. Rama scolded Lakshmana for harboring such suspicions about Bharata and welcomed Bharata with great affection.

Wasn't I a devotee who offered herself
to her husband, her Lord?
He should have told me; I treated his word
as my law even if it harmed me."

Recollecting banishment, overcome
by emotion, tears fell from Sita's closed eyes
like dew dropping from between two leaves
parted by the gentle wind.

Still Dark

Still, the dove-eyed one
sustained her stream of thought; can
the strong current of water be blocked
by the wall of waves the wind draws up?

"Mountains, caves and wild forests,
lions and leopards, deadly serpents,
the perilous sea, the habitations
of demons, and all such threats—

I had suffered all the horror
of hell in this human world, and
nothing could scare me anymore. Then
why did the king hide the truth from me?[18]

Could Janaki have even thought
against her husband's wishes?
Would the currents of the Ganges
defy the great ocean?

Fearing dishonor, and keen on nothing
but removing the stain on his own name,
the king, with his selfish act, confirmed
the disgrace that had fallen upon me.

Due to pity, a dharmic man might give
the benefit of doubt even to an evildoer.
How will this king expiate the sin
of banishing his blameless queen?

---

18. Sita endured wild animals and rakshasa attacks, as well as abduction by Ravana and the threats of her rakshasa guards in Lanka. Nothing could be worse than what she had already suffered, so if Rama had simply asked her to leave the kingdom, she would have complied. He hurt her when he deliberately misled her into believing that she was visiting holy sites, rather than being banished.

Full of love and trust, I had revealed
to him my craving during pregnancy.
And—I cannot bear this—
he used that to ensnare me.[19]

When, on his father's orders, he went
in exile to the forest, I followed him.
In return, my beloved made me the victim
of his decree to cast me off in the wild.

Heartfelt love sees oneself in the other.
He forgot that and also marred
his own reputation for gratefulness
when he treated his desperate queen thus.

Even the ant takes great pains
to care for its young ones.
Yet the noblest of men, my beloved,
cast away his unborn child in the forest.

His father had performed many sacrificial rites
to beget him, yet that very son listened to
the lies of the malicious and ruined the joy
his own child could have brought him.

Not without a shudder can I recall
his cruel slaying of the Shudra saint.
It seems the king was swayed by the laws
against women and the Shudras.[20]

His inborn kindness, dharma
and other noble qualities must have
fast forsaken the king, even before
his wife separated from him.

How often had the eyes of my lord
filled with tears while watching
my pet doe, weary with pregnancy,
coming to our forest shelter!

Perhaps, kindness sprouts in the forest
as beautifully as tender leaves,
while the duties of the crown
might harden one like an iron shield.

---

19. It is customary to offer to fulfill a request made by a pregnant woman. Rama used Sita's request to visit holy sites as a pretext for removing her from his realm.
20. This line refers to Rama's beheading of Shambuka and, strikingly, links Rama's treatment of Shambuka with his treatment of Sita.

His love for me was consummate
during our sojourn in the forest.
Even such ardor may fade away
when worldly power and wealth swell.

I remember how after the daily rites
I, at once his love and dear devotee,
spent my time with my beloved
on the alluring banks of the Godavari River.

No other pair on earth could have envisioned
the game of love we played in our hiding:
oblivious of our separate selves,
we were like a single being with two bodies.

Swimming about culling lotuses,
diving into the cool depths, and
chasing me on the riverbed, then
my lord had frolicked like a child.

Why speak more? Like the animals
of the forest not lacking in feral grace,
or akin to wingless wild birds,
we found our joy in the woods.

Innate and pure Love, you are
the most luminous gem from the heart's mine;
you are the cherished jewel
the spirit joyously wears on its breast.

Love, you are the thrust of man's quest,
you are the virtues of woman.
Ah, you can even turn the arid desert
into an captivating garden of flowers!

The rising flame of your lamp
leads the righteous to heaven.
Your justice invariably leads
the unrighteous to hell.

Even Death will not harm you,
Love, may you reign forever!
In one's memory where the dead abide,
tears are offered daily to pay you homage.

Love, it is not honest anger
that is your foe, but conceit
that blocks the way to communion
and ruins your abode in man's heart.

The rat of arrogance in one's heart may
slowly gnaw away one's forbearance,
sense of equality and fairness,
and esteem for the other's virtues.

Anyone could turn supercilious
on account of affluence,
power, fame, sovereignty
and triumphs one after another.

When the storm of conceit
has blown out the lamp of love, lo,
sycophancy may delude one's mind
and lead it to perilous situations.

Otherwise, would the king abandon
in the wild forest, his devout wife
in her pregnant state, and continue
to rule the country ever so impassively?

Does not the king have brothers
valiant enough to rule the land?
Isn't the forest sufficiently vast
for him to live there with his spouse?

Hasn't the king himself experienced
the pure ways of forest life?
Does not the king know for certain
the lofty manner of spiritual reflections?

Perhaps he does not, since even a rogue
would resent anyone slandering his wife;
yet the noble king took as Vedic truth
the aspersions cast on me.

He was the paragon of chivalry who had,
for my sake, acted out his fury even on a crow,[21]
and reduced the forest of demons to a desert.
How could he have so changed?

Perhaps, the king, who deemed
his repute as his greatest asset,

---

21. According to a story told in several regions of India, one day during the forest exile, Rama was asleep on Sita's lap. A crow began pecking at her but Sita refused to move because she did not want to disturb Rama. When Rama awoke and saw the blood caused by the crow, he shot an arrow and instructed it to follow the crow, no matter how fast it flew. Finally, the arrow caught up with the crow and killed it. The story shows how angry Rama became when any harm came to his beloved wife.

was deeply hurt by the spiteful rumors
his spies had brought him.

The sudden blaze of moral valor
on hearing his people's judgment
must have swayed his action
in a manner that heeded no hazard.

The king must have acted thus
owing to his duty to his people;
the wise would rather sever a limb
than let the poison spread.

Terrific indeed is the passion
that a man of strength restrains.
Whirlpools within deep waters
are more frightful than waves.

A noble man will instantly do
what he takes to be his duty;
Honest Rama could not have rested
until he fulfilled his promise.

At Dandaka, he took on the task
of annihilating the demon clan;
and at Rishyamuka he pledged
that he would take Bali's life.[22]

The jewel of the Solar Dynasty
has performed many such reckless acts;
certain lapses add luster to a great man
like mysterious caves to a mountain.

His father killed a sage's son
mistaking him for an elephant.[23]
And King Dasharatha died of regret, lamenting
his rash act of granting his wife's wish.

Viewed without bias, these actions
were imprudent. Yet, a similar streak

---

22. When Lakshmana mutilated Shurpanakha at Dandaka Forest, her brother Khara and his army general Dushana attacked, but Rama defeated the two rakshasas and all their soldiers. When Rama met Sugriva on Rishyamuka Mountain and learned that his brother, Vali (also called Valin or Bali), had usurped his throne and taken his wife, Rama immediately pledged to kill the brother, without finding out the full history of the conflict between the two monkeys.

23. One day as a young man, Dasharatha was hunting in the forest. Hearing the gurgle of water being drunk from a stream, he shot his arrow at what he assumed was an animal. Instead, he had killed the only son of two blind parents, who cursed him to lose his own son at a young age.

in his son may be defensible, considering
how traits are passed down to offspring.

The virtuous nature of his grandsire Aja
who died of grief and suffering
at the death of his beloved wife
might also be reflected in his character.

It is beyond doubt that the king
is still constant in his love for me;
even if separation afflicts Raghava,
he will not desire another woman.

During our first separation,
my passionate lord went mad.
And by returning victorious, he
proved his deep love for me.

Then how much more distressed
would he be now by this breach?
Would that penitent soul bear the shame
that my proud self suffers now?

Ha! A gold statue of Sita will adorn his side
as his partner in the great hall of sacrifice.
Complex are the ways of the virtuous
when one considers them deeply.

The course of justice is terribly painful.
Sadly, even kings are not free in this world.
My husband banished me, but now
has chanced to worship my statue."

Her cheeks shone in a sudden glow
and the petite one felt a thrill all over,
like the golden riverbed
sprouting tender paddy shoots.

Light

Struck by profound sympathy,
the sylvan stream of Sita's musings
gently stopped for a moment,
and then resumed its flow.

"Alas! I do perceive how,
under the guise of splendor, you,
my remorseful lord, are living as a captive
in the prison of Justice.

Oppressed by convention, even
the free will of a sovereign may perish,
a bird caged for long may forget
the innate power of its wings.

Envisioning the woodland haunts
of your mate and tiny fledglings,
and desperately stretching your neck,
you might be frantic in your cage.

Deluded by various calls, and
imagining familiar forms,
you might be flapping your wings
and extending your bill in anguish.

In your bed you might be alone,
tossing in inexorable anguish,
murmuring in pity, and even
suffering nightmares.

One may cease to love one's mate
or part ways with her by ill fate, but
rarely does one's devotion to duty
entail a sacrifice so tremendous.

One may forfeit the crown and beg
or surrender one's life for another, but
hard is the resolve to live on
only to rule a land as the people wish.

Even the ascetics greatly esteem
his supreme strength of will;
he surpasses all other great kings
in performing the duties of a ruler.

For the righteous, life on earth
is not for self-indulgence.
The inimitable Rama was renowned
for battling great dangers.

If one becomes utterly desperate
in the pursuit of sensual pleasures,
and lives in fear of death,
I would not regard that as living.

Though superhuman in his powers,
Raghava has more restraint than an ascetic.
That radiant beacon of ideals
earns my esteem in every way.

Every condition has its own justice
owing to its time and space, yet
for all devout men, O King,
you are an unrivaled paradigm.

Lord, kindly forgive me, your wife,
who lives with my pride,
for the flaws I saw in you
when my mind was agitated.

Though I am blameless, my past
could prove to be unworthy.
I have indeed caused my lord
great sufferings, one after another.

Many women have, on account of me,
lamented the loss of their husbands.
How many children were made destitute,
and had mourned the death of their fathers?[24]

The core of justice is hard to grasp;
it may change directions like the wind.
Still the relentless effect of karma
will hit the target like an arrow.

Sharp arrows, quit your toil,
you cannot hurt my callused mind.
Cosmic wheel, roll on, and
abandon the despondent Sita here.

Continuing to live does no good
to one who has fulfilled his duty;
an actor who has finished his part
should promptly leave the stage.

The rice plant withers in the field
after yielding its crop of grain,
the shells of oysters lie bare
in the profound depths of the ocean.

The horizon of my mind is clearing up,
my perception turns brighter day by day.
The river that joyously joins the ocean
reflects the light of self-revelation.

---

24. Because Ravana abducted Sita, many humans, monkeys, bears, and rakshasas lost their lives in battle.

Let me now take my leave of you
O, Emperor of the domain of day,
Lord of the firmament fully clad
in golden rays of consummate glory.

I bow to you, O Moon, clothed in white,
aged, with white hair like the threads
of the lotus stalk, smiling brightly,
and washed in the fair sheen of ash.

Greetings to you, most winsome stars
that project your rays against
the dense darkness and pierce it.
Spread your light to the far distance.

Salutations to you, dear Sandhya,
who at every dawn and dusk
weaves a gorgeous carpet
for the gateways of heaven.[25]

Charming woods and tremulous flowers
swarmed by bees, I who found
unbound joy in your presence
now bid farewell to you.

Perhaps I need not part from
the delightful world about me;
when my body unites with the earth,
my spirit may merge with this beauty.

Mother Earth, I can see you
going into your splendid chamber
carrying me in your pure arms
with maternal care and affection.

I will lie in that arbor, listening to
the mountain stream's song of peace.
The trees and shrubs nearby
will shower their blossoms on me.

Up above, birds will fly about
and sing in their sweet voices,
deer will gambol on the meadow
that rolls out like a gleaming cloud.

---

25. Sandhya means twilight.

The store of fresh gems
and the minerals of the mountainside
will always enthrall me, nay,
all this will become part of me.

Mother Earth, thus shall I delight in
a deep sleep on the bed of your lap.
No! I shall offer my respects to you,
Mother, and then rise and soar up.

Like a star that pays its homage to the Earth
when it is reflected in the river below,
I am a light in the heavens
even as I merge at your holy feet.

I salute you, beloved Raghava, and
now rise, leaving the bough of your arm.
I will fly off into the vast sky
undaunted, all by myself.

The mass forming the cosmic spheres
is absent here. In this pure dwelling
of peace, beyond day and night,
is only the radiant Primal Principle.[26]

Chastened by suffering, relieved of
all burden, and happy, Grandson of Aja,
you too will reach this abode, which
only a resolute one can discover."[27]

Then Sita was startled: a tremor passed
through her petal-soft body. Greatly agitated,
she thus spoke aloud in a jumble
of words and thoughts:

"Why would I endure this? Does the king intend
that I should appear before him, prove
my innocence and live as his consort again?
Does he take me for a puppet?

Seer Valmiki, pardon me,
do not think I am arrogant.

---

26. *Adi dhamam.*
27. Asan refers here to Rama's ancestor Aja, who loved his wife so much that he died of grief when his wife passed away. Sita suggests that her love for Rama is of similar magnitude and that their inner selves will reunite in the celestial world. Also Rama, as an avatara of Vishnu, and Sita, as an avatara of Lakshmi, will join each other in heaven after each completes life on earth.

Neither my mind nor spirit will yield;
only the body, wont to submission, might come."

She struggled with the scorching thoughts
that were fast spreading over her mind,
like a girl whose clothes were on fire
and body burning in flames.

A nun ran to her saying, "The beaming stars
that rose at dusk have set in the western ocean,
and those heralding the day have started rising.
Sita, what is the matter?"

She dashed cold water on Sita's face,
helped her into the hermitage, and laid her down.
It was near daybreak when Sage Valmiki
returned from Kosala with Rama's message.

Her head bent and eyes fixed
on the lotus feet of the sage who said:
"Don't grieve my child, come with me,"
she reached the Royal Court,
went up to Rama in silence,
and in one glance saw her lord
amidst the nobles, looking remorseful;
and then, she left this world.[28]

Translated from Malayalam by Rizio Yohannan Raj

---

28. These last eight lines function as a kind of epilogue to the poem.

7   Choosing Music

C. S. Lakshmi (b. 1944) has been writing fiction under the pen name Ambai since the age of sixteen. In addition to being a prominent short story writer in modern Tamil, she is also a historian, critic, and archivist. "Forest," one of her more ambitious stories, contains many layers, moving between two protagonists and their life-stories: Chenthiru living in today's world, a modern Sita; and the other, the Sita of the epic world, rewriting her story. There are clever parallels between the two: both marry men of their choice; both are rejected after years of faithful companionship. "Forest" begins with both women, now middle-aged, rethinking their lives through time spent in the forest, which becomes a place of quest and self-discovery.

All Ambai's work has a firmly feminist base. She is passionately interested in women's lives and experiences, the spaces they claim, the resources with which they negotiate that space and manage their lives, their support systems, and their sustaining dreams. But most of her stories also concern the quest for self-realization and liberation; the *rudra-vina* music in "Forest" is a trope for that self-realization. Just before the final episode of Sita's story, excerpted here, Chenthiru, in her final appearance, meets a music guru, who plays his rudra-vina to her and explains the importance of "getting the pitch right," being in tune with oneself wherever one is, and therefore in tune with the universe. Ambai's story then culminates with the section translated below, in which Sita too meets a *tapasvi* (ascetic) in the forest who offers to teach her to play the rudra-vina. The tapasvi is Ravana. [L. H.]

Source: Ambai, "Adavi" [Forest], in *Kaattil Oru Maan* [In the Forest a Deer] (Nagercoil: Kalachuvadu, 2000), excerpt pp. 166–168 (entire story pp. 138–168).

Forest (excerpt)
BY AMBAI

Nobody was willing to accept Sita's decision. They said it was not proper to refuse to go, when the king of Ayodhya himself came to take her back. What was her goal, after all? What was she seeking? Then there were Hanuman's long appeals. The denunciations of the rest of them.[1] She could not recover from her

---

1. Rama has just met his grown sons at the ashvamedha ritual in Ayodhya. Rama wants Sita to rejoin him. "Having gone somewhere beneath the earth" alludes to Sita's return to Mother Earth but that journey is interpreted figuratively here.

sense of having gone somewhere beneath the earth, somewhere so deep that nobody could reach her.

She rose to her feet and looked around the cottage. This time it would be a total renunciation. A lone journey which left behind all those who were known to her, those who spoke lovingly, who dispensed advice. A journey that would be long, that went very deep.

The more she walked, the more the forest seemed to extend. She crossed the river, went past a waterfall, and walked on; saw the deer drinking at a small stream, was shocked by deer-eating tigers, delighted in the sight of baby elephants running alongside the herd, encountered nights through which owls' eyes glowed, observed the shimmering of green leaves as the sun's rays fell upon them, was surprised by the leaping of monkeys from branch to branch, their young clinging to their bellies. She walked on. Eagerly. Wearily. She rested.

And yet again she walked on.

Their meeting took place early one morning. A time when not even the sound of birds was to be heard. The sun was hidden, secretive in the skies. Far away, she saw a small hut. The dim light of a lamp flickered through it. The sound of a musical instrument came to her, tearing the darkness. As she came nearer and nearer, she recognized it as vina music. A tune that she had surely heard at some time. As she came nearer, the music held her bound in its melody. The door of the hut was open. She looked inside. Someone who looked like a tapasvi, living a life of austerities, was playing the vina. When she asked whether she was disturbing his practice, he said no. He had been waiting for her, he said. "Don't you know me? I am Ravana."

Startled, she stepped back.

"I thought you died in the war . . ."

"This life is full of magic, is it not? When Rama demolished everyone in my palace, there was one bodyguard left. He pleaded with Rama to spare his life. And he then prayed that a friend of his should be brought back to life. Rama brought his friend back to life and told them both to flee before Lakshmana appeared. When they said they no longer had the strength to run, he gave them wings. They changed respectively into a kite and a parrot and flew away. This is a story that people tell. Could I not be that parrot that has been flying about in these forests? A parrot waiting for that moment when he would meet Sita once more. A tired old parrot."

"Even now, this infatuation? I have seen so many tragedies. My life has been like a game of dice in which I am a pawn. I am tired. I am weary. I am more than forty years old."

"It is then a woman needs a friend. To support her when she is distressed by her changing body. To serve her. To encourage her. To stand at a distance and give her hope."

Sita sat down on the floor.

Ravana went on, "I have never refused to give my friendship to anyone. Before the battle began, Rama wanted to make a puja. There were only two people in the world who could have conducted the puja for him. One was Vali. The other, myself. Rama had killed Vali with his own hands. So only I was left. He sent an invitation to me. I went to him. I did the puja as he desired. I blessed him and invoked his victory."

Sita addressed him by name for the first time. "Ravana, words make me tired. Language leaves me crippled. I am enchained by my body."

Ravana smiled. "The body is a prison. The body is a means of freedom," he said. "Look," he said, showing her his rudra-vina. "A musical instrument that was created by imagining what wonderful music would come forth, if Parvati's breasts, as she lay on her back, were turned into gourds, and their nipples attached by strings. It is an extension of Devi's body. You lifted Shiva's bow with one hand.[2] You should be able to conquer this instrument easily. Will you try?"

"Will you teach me?"

"I am the one who did battle for you, and lost. Would I deny you music? I will be your guru and give you lessons every day. Let the music break out of the vina and flow everywhere in the forest. Don't think of it as an ordinary musical instrument. Think of it as your life, and play on it. Here."

He lifted the rudra-vina from his lap and stretched it out towards her.

"Let it be there on the ground," said Sita.

"Why?"

"It is my life, isn't it? A life that many hands have tossed about, like a ball. Now let me take hold of it; take it into my own hands." So saying, Sita lifted the rudra-vina and laid it on her lap.

Translated from Tamil by Lakshmi Holmstrom

---

2. As a young girl, Sita was cleaning the floor and picked up Shiva's huge bow to wash beneath it.

8   Forest of Possibilities

"Volga" Popuri Lalitha Kumari (b. 1950) has combined feminist activism with writing, film work, college teaching, and publishing. A versatile author, she writes novels, essays, plays, short stories, literary criticism, and translations from English to Telugu. In addition to a number of novels, many of which explore the meaning of freedom in women's lives, she has also published a study of trends in feminist cinema, edited an anthology of feminist Telugu poetry, co-edited a report on the women's anti-liquor struggle in Andhra Pradesh, and composed a play about six characters from the writings of Gudipati Venkata Chalam (see selection #5).

"Reunion" envisions a feminist-inspired forest alternative to urban society. Although authoritative tellings of Ramkatha portray Sita and Shurpanakha as opposites, Volga imagines them meeting late in life and realizing how much they have in common.[1] Volga depicts the forest as a space where an individual can come to terms with the past through self-reflection free from worldly distractions. In "Reunion," Sita learns to calm the waves of her mind in Valmiki's ashram. Shurpanakha too reinterprets her life, rejecting the binary opposition between beauty and ugliness when she realizes that both form and deformity contribute to nature's bounty.

"Reunion" plays a role in Volga's larger project to fight patriarchy through art, especially classical dance and well-known religious narratives.[2] Because the stories in authoritative texts promote gendered stereotypes that uphold patriarchy, rewriting such narratives provides crucial opportunities to subvert their sexism. By writing short stories that artfully and convincingly portray Sita and Shurpanakha as three-dimensional characters, rather than polar opposites, she encourages readers to move beyond the stock images of pativrata and demoness.

Source: Volga, "Samagamam" [Reunion], *Sunday Magazine* of *Andhra Jyothi*, 4 May 2003, pp. 20–23.

---

1. For an analysis of the ways in which various authoritative Ramayana texts have portrayed Sita and Shurpanakha as opposites, see Erndl (1991).
2. Volga wrote lyrics for two feminist dance-dramas about characters in Ramayana and Mahabharata. "War and Peace: A Dance Ballet" depicts Sita, Shurpanakha, and Draupadi narrating their experience of war. "Lakshmana Rekha" deals with constraints on women, focusing on Gandhari and Urmila. It was produced by Asmita Resource Center for Women for the Andhra Pradesh International Women's Day celebrations in 2004.

Reunion

BY VOLGA

With the evening glow on one side and creeping darkness on the other, the jungle at dusk resembles a huge fire belching smoke. As birds flock to their nests, the cacophony of their songs generates a pleasant clamor. Herds of deer are shaking off their daytime lethargy to get ready for a saunter under the moonlight. The sage's hermitage and its serene surroundings within the jungle seem like the flawless creation of a skilled painter.

Evening rituals have begun at the hermitage. Holy fires burn and the melodious sounds of religious chants fill the air. Women of the hermitage are resting after watering flower and fruit trees. Some assemble garlands for the evening worship. Children are returning from their forest rambles to the eager laps of waiting mothers. Some mothers hurry their children to prepare for the evening rituals. There, in a small cottage, a mother waits for her children who have not yet returned from the forest. Her eyes reveal how her very life revolves around the safety and well-being of those children. Those eyes, normally eager, affectionate, and kind, are now filled with anxiety.

This is Sita, waiting for her two sons.

They would usually have returned from the forest by this time. They would bring many wild flowers from the thicket and beg their mother to use them in her worship. Sita would refuse to use nameless flowers for the sacred ritual, so the children would name them creatively. She would make fun of them, making them pout. Then, she would pacify them by offering the flowers to the gods to restore their cheer. In the evening, the whole jungle would listen intently as the boys sang in their mellifluous voices.

Lava and Kusha haven't returned yet. Sita doesn't worry that they are in any danger. For the boys, the jungle is a well-trod path. They were born here. They are children of the forest. But, why so late? Not knowing why causes fear and doubt. Sita has been anxious ever since the children visited Ayodhya. An unknown apprehension. It's the same now—not apprehension of the jungle, but of the city.

Darkness settles in. Sita's eyes are searchlights in that darkness.

Into the dim light arrive the two boys. Sita breathes a sigh of relief and asks about the undue delay. "Mom, look here," says Lava, as he empties flowers from his shoulder cloth into a plate. A delicious fragrance instantly fills the cottage.

Flowers. Red, white, yellow flowers never seen before; smiling all over that plate. It's a fragrance she has never experienced before. Lava and Kusha, proud of their floral conquest, gaze at their mother.

"They are so beautiful! Where are these from?" inquires Sita, gently touching the flowers with her fingertips.

"Mom, today we've discovered a new garden in the forest. We've never seen one like it before. The Nandana garden that Grandpa Valmiki describes can't hold a candle to this one," says Kusha.[3]

Lava confirms his elder brother's assessment with his equally appreciative eyes.

"Whose garden is it, Kusha?" asks Sita.

"Mom, the garden is beautiful but its owner is so ugly! She arrived while we were collecting flowers. We were afraid. Brother somehow recovered his composure and said, 'We are the children of the hermitage. We're collecting flowers for worship.' We hurried back. Oh my! What a disfigured face! Utterly ugly," said Lava, with disgust in his expression.

"No, Honey. One should never judge people by their appearance. She may be ugly, but, didn't she grow that beautiful garden?" suggested Sita.

"Her body is fine, Mom. But, she doesn't have any nose or ears. There are large gouges as if someone cut them off," Kusha said, making a face.

Sita was as startled as if someone had whipped her. "No nose and ears?"

"Well, maybe they were there at one time. But someone cut them off. Didn't it look like that to you too?" said Lava, seeking support from his brother.

Sita was certain now.

Shurpanakha! Definitely Shurpanakha!

It has been eighteen years since she appeared, desiring Rama. How beautiful she was! She was disfigured viciously by Rama and Lakshmana. Is the same Shurpanakha living in this forest now? How time has passed!

Rama humiliated Shurpanakha and Ravana avenged the humiliation by abducting me, she thought.

Are women there only for men to settle their scores?

If they hadn't known that Shurpanakha was the sister of Ravana, they would not have ill-treated her. Rama really intended to provoke Ravana into war. Shurpanakha provided the cause for a battle with Ravana.

These events were all about political battles.

Poor Shurpanakha, she came to him in the agony of love. Who will love her now, disfigured, without nose and ears?

Has she led a loveless life all these years?

Has she nurtured that garden with all her love?

Is that garden a manifestation of her desire for beauty?

Are these flowers the result of her tenderheartedness?

Poor Shurpanakha!

The tears in Sita's eyes surprised Lava and Kusha.

"What's this, Mom? Why have you gotten so sad just from hearing about the deformity of someone you don't know?"

Sita wiped her tears and smiled.

"Will you take me to that garden tomorrow?"

Lava and Kusha looked at each other in disbelief.

---

3. The Nandana-vana referred to here is a delightful forest in the celestial realm where deities go to picnic and enjoy themselves.

"Really, I will come with you. Will you take me there? Do you remember the way?"

Sita's words skyrocketed the brothers' enthusiasm.

They felt ecstatic at the thought of their mother joining them for a stroll in the forest. They had always wanted to show her all their favorite haunts in the forest. But Sita never obliged. Whenever she went to the forest, it was only with other women from the hermitage. The children couldn't contain their excitement at the thought of holding their mother's hand, leading her through the treacherous paths, reassuring her when she was afraid, and showing her all the wonders of the forest.

They couldn't wait for the night to pass.

Sita spent the night with a heavy heart. No matter how much she tried, however, memories of the distant past wouldn't go away.

Those were happy days in the forest with Rama.

The arrival of Shurpanakha—how gracefully she walked! Pure white jasmines in her hair, yellow oleander garlands around her neck, lilac bluebells around her arms; she was practically a walking floral vine. She gazed at my jewelry with wonder, as if she were asking me, "Why are you carrying around those weights lacking fragrance or grace?" She looked at me, but said nothing. She went straight to Rama. Listening to their conversation, I continued with my chores. Soon, there was bloodshed at the cottage.

Heart-wrenching wails of a female . . .

How much she cursed them for their brutality.

Doesn't look like that curse ever left me.

No man loves her.

The one that loves me distanced me.

Are both tales the same in the end?

What will Shurpanakha say when she sees me?

She may still be so full of anger that she won't speak to me. We'll see. I have to meet Shurpanakha.

———

The next morning, after completing all the morning chores, Lava and Kusha started their journey to the forest with their mother.

"Mom, I will show you my Raja today," said Lava.

Lava had captured a wild elephant of the forest and tamed it. The brothers ride that elephant.

"Mom, will you ride Raja, please?" intoned Lava.

"No, Honey. I prefer to walk," said Sita, remembering royal ceremonial processions in the past on the backs of elephants.

The boys thought that Sita was afraid of elephant rides.

"How can Mom ride the elephant? Besides, she might be afraid." Kusha admonished Lava.

The boys continued their journey through the forest, introducing all the animals to their mother.

As she listened to her sons, she didn't even get tired while she walked.

"Mom, this is the garden."

Sita stood dumbfounded as she gazed at the garden. It was like a smile of nature itself! This garden was much more beautiful than even the Ashoka Grove.[4]

"What an accomplishment, Shurpanakha!" mused Sita.

"Come on, Mom. Let's go in."

"I'll go alone. Why don't you two wander around the forest until evening and come back here? We'll return to the hermitage together." She sent the children away.

She entered and called softly, "Shurpanakha!"

Shurpanakha turned around. She didn't recognize Sita.

"Who are you madam? Lost your way? How do you know my name?"

"I didn't lose my way, Shurpanakha. In fact, I came looking for you. I'm Sita."

It was Shurpanakha's turn to be dumbfounded. Sita . . . ? This is Sita? How she's changed!

All she remembered was the Sita laden with heavy jewelry. Of course, she hadn't looked at her for long.

Is this the same Sita, the queen of the all-sustaining Emperor Shri Ramachandra who killed Ravana and established the Aryan empire in the entire South?

Shurpanakha couldn't believe it.

Why these cotton clothes? Why these garlands in place of jewelry? Why the sunburn on her golden skin? This is Sita? Shri Rama's wife Sita?

"Sita? You mean . . . Shri Ramachandra's . . ."

"I'm Sita. Janaka's daughter, Janaki. Daughter of the Earth," said Sita with pride, interrupting Shurpanakha.[5]

"Then . . . Shri Rama . . . ?" asked a confused Shurpanakha.

"Shri Rama abandoned me. I'm living in Valmiki's hermitage now."

Shurpanakha couldn't utter a word. Shri Rama abandoned Sita? No one knows the strength of the love between Rama and Sita better than she. The price she paid for it was not small.

Couldn't women in love with Shri Rama escape this agony?

Shurpanakha saw no signs of agony in Sita, only a profound peace. "How she has matured," mused Shurpanakha.

"My children saw your garden yesterday. They saw you too. It's they who brought me here today. Your garden is so pleasant and beautiful," said Sita, with a smile.

"Those kids are your sons? How adorable they are!"

A flash of pride in Sita's face didn't escape Shurpanakha.

---

4. Shurpanakha's garden surpasses Ravana's Ashoka Grove, where Sita dwelled during her imprisonment in Lanka.
5. Sita pointedly corrects Shurpanakha, identifying herself in relation to her father, King Janaka, and her mother, Mother Earth, instead of in relation to her husband.

"The plants, vines, and trees in this garden are all my children too," said Shurpanakha.

"Yes. That's why they are such heartthrobs," agreed Sita.

Shurpanakha's pride was evident in her eyes.

"Tell me Shurpanakha, how is your life?"

"It is as beautiful and pleasant as this garden."

"I am really happy for you, Shurpanakha. I was worried about what would happen to you after that gruesome incident. I know your love for beauty. Could you live with your disfigured face? Every time I've thought of you, I've always wondered if, unable to bear the disfigurement, you had committed suicide."

The love and kindness in Sita's eyes melted Shurpanakha's heart. Tingling sensations swept through their bodies at the thought of a friendship developing between two inner selves.

"You are brave and courageous," said Sita.

"You see me now, Sita, but don't assume that it was easy. The struggles in my life have toughened me, and I've discovered happiness in understanding the true meaning of beauty.

"Life was unbearable in the early days of my mutilation. Looking at me, men, the handsome men I was infatuated with, used to hate me.

"'Why should I continue to live?' I thought. Those were the hellish days for me. My mind was raging with pain and anger. How much I cursed Shri Rama, his brother, and you. My thoughts were venomous against you three. There was not even an iota of love in my heart. Sheer hatred settled in. I, who worshiped beauty, started hating everything that was beautiful. My quest for beauty was transformed into jealousy towards everyone beautiful.

"I became a walking volcano. A raging sea of sorrow."

Painful memories of Shurpanakha grew heavy in their hearts.

"How did you emerge from all that pain, Shurpanakha?"

"It was very difficult. It was quite difficult to discover the real meaning of beauty. I was proud of my infinite beauty. You don't know how ecstatic I used to feel looking at my nose. I felt funny about the long noses of you Aryans. Of course, there is a certain beauty in them too. My nose was neither too long nor short. I was always proud that my nose was just the way God intended a nose to be at the time of creation. I used to decorate my nose with yellow and white grass-flowers as jewelry. They used to twinkle like two stars on my nostrils. I was rapturous when my lovers gently kissed my nose.

"No one but I can understand what it meant to lose that nose. I endured all that. I carried the weight of all the strange thoughts that the disfigurement and the resulting ugliness brought me. At times, I wanted to disfigure everything and everyone.

"I had to fight a great battle within myself to emerge from that anger, to love beauty again, and to find the essence of form and deformity.

"The infinite beauty of nature helped me through that battle.

"I labored hard to realize the oneness of form and deformity in nature. I observed all forms of life. I observed the uniformity in their stillness and their movement. I discovered the secrets of colors. I had no teacher to guide me. I taught myself. I've observed every nook and corner of nature. That observation transformed my very eyes. To those eyes everything appeared beautiful. I had developed hatred towards everything including myself, but now I started loving everything including myself.

"When other birds attacked a small bird, for whatever reason, and plucked its feathers to hurt her, I became very emotional. It was no ordinary effort on my part to realize those emotions as manifestations of love and appreciation of beauty.

"I gradually learned to love these hands. I've learned to labor, create, and serve with these hands. It took more than ten years for this transformation. After those ten fruitful years of incessant focus and perseverance, I started raising this garden." She laid out the true beauty of her life's voyage in front of Sita.

"How beautiful you are Shurpanakha! No man may be able to recognize your beauty, but . . . ," Sita choked.

The realization that Shurpanakha's trial was no less than her own by fire brought tears to Sita's eyes.

Shurpanakha laughed heartily.

"Don't men also have eyes and a heart? I am not talking about men who only know hatred and mutilation."

Although Sita asked, "You mean . . . ," she knew what Shurpanakha meant.

"You're right, Sita. I found the companionship of a man. There is a fortunate man who for a short while enjoys the beauty that flows from my hands into nature and gives himself up for me." She turned around and called out, "Sudhira [Well-built]!"

A well-built man, appropriate to his name, came there.

"Sudhira, this is Sita."

Sudhira bowed respectfully.

"I called you just to introduce you to Sita."

With that, Sudhira turned back and left. With that simple act, Sita gleaned a unique relationship between them that she had never seen before between any other woman and man.[6]

"So, you have attained fulfillment in your life."

"I've realized that the meaning of fulfillment is not just in the companionship of a man. I found true companionship only after learning that."

Sita was listening to Shurpanakha attentively. There was depth and wisdom in her words. She felt like listening to her again and again.

"How about you, Sita?"

"My life finds its fulfillment in raising my sons."

"Is that the ideal for your life?"

---

6. Sita has only seen relationships between a man and a woman based on the institution of marriage, in which a wife is subordinate to her husband throughout her life. Instead Shurpanakha and Sudhira are partners, as long as they enjoy each other's companionship.

"Yes. I am Rama's wife. I could not fulfill my duties as the queen. At least, I have to provide heirs to Rama's kingdom, don't I?"

"How entwined with that kingdom your life is, even though you rarely lived in it."

"Can you escape from it once you become the wife of the king?" laughed Sita.

"For some reason I was afraid of the kingdom from the very beginning. No matter how my brother tried to convince me, I couldn't stay in Lanka. Nowhere else will you find the happiness that comes with wandering in the forest."

"I too like the forest life. Though Rama abandoned me, this forest life lessened my anguish."

Much time had passed in their conversation without them realizing it.

"My children don't know that they are Shri Rama's sons. I haven't told them. They'll know when the time comes."

"Once they know, do you think they will stay in the forest for even a moment?" asked Shurpanakha, looking sadly at Sita.

"They also like living in the forest," replied Sita, weakly.

"Maybe. But, how much does the kingdom care for the forest anyway? Perhaps it is inevitable for these two children who grew up in the forest to migrate for the sake of developing the cities and to protect the civilized folks."

Sita too is aware of that inevitability.

"What will you do then? Will you stay alone in Valmiki's hermitage?"

"No, Shurpanakha. I'll take refuge with my Mother Earth."

"Sita, where is it that you don't have your mother? However, I think her form is more beautiful here than anywhere else." Shurpanakha looked around the garden with pride.

Sita smiled, acknowledging Shurpanakha's intention. She was very moved by Shurpanakha's kind invitation. Sisterly sentiments filled her thoughts.

"I'll certainly come Shurpanakha. When my children leave me for the city, I'll once again become the daughter of this earth. I'll find a new meaning in my life as I rest under these cool shady trees."

The conversation stopped with the arrival of the children.

Shurpanakha served them delicious fruits. The children promptly devoured them.

"Who is that lady, Mom?" the children queried, on their way back.

"She is a close friend, very dear to me."

"How come you never told us about her?"

"When the time comes, you'll know everything. But you should never forget the way to this garden in the forest. No matter where you go or whatever you do, don't forget this way. Promise?"

"We'll never forget, Mom," replied Lava and Kusha, in unison.

Translated from Telugu by Krishna Rao Maddipati

9   Union with Nature

In his film *Kanchana Sita,* Kerala filmmaker G. Aravindan (1935–1991) portrays Sita not in human form but as a representation of the philosophical concept of Prakriti, the animating force of the natural world conceived as female.
In the film, Sita speaks only through movement in nature, such as when leaves
rustle or the surface of the river ripples. Although *Kanchana Sita* touches upon
several episodes from the final section of Ramkatha, Aravindan's attention to
the absence and presence of Sita animates his film.

Aravindan was a painter, cartoonist, musician, and film director who worked
most of his adult life as a Kerala Rubber Board administrator. Aravindan's
second full-length film, *Kanchana Sita,* contains features that developed into
his distinctive cinematic style.[1] He created a visual look of stark purity by film-
ing large vistas in remote Andhra. The film reveals the inner life of characters
such as Rama and Lava, rather than focusing on plot. Aravindan's interest in
marginalized people led him to cast Adivasas in most of the film's roles. Finally,
his incorporation of music to signal the presence of Sita is masterful.[2]

As Zacharias's essay on Aravindan's *Kanchana Sita* demonstrates, even particular *retellings* of Ramkatha generate their own subsequent retellings. In his
original 1960 play, *Kanchana Sita,* C. N. Sreekantan Nair had rewritten the final
section of Valmiki's *Ramayana* as a critique of brahminical privilege and political repression. Using Nair's play only as a starting point, Aravindan transformed the script according to his interpretation of Indian philosophy and his
minimalist aesthetic. He replaced Nair's crisply articulated exchanges of dialogue with a cinematic meditation on Rama's separation from, and eventual
union with, Sita, thus carrying the concept of Sita as Prakriti to its visual limit.

Prakriti and Sovereignty in Aravindan's *Kanchana Sita*
FILM ANALYSIS BY USHA ZACHARIAS

Aravindan's unique contribution to world cinema and to the Ramayana tradition emerged out of the creative energy that colored the artistic milieu of
Kerala in the 1970s and 1980s. His work related to, and was inspired by, a generation of iconoclastic artists, filmmakers, writers, painters, and sculptors who

---

1. He created the cartoon serial "Small Man and Big World" for a major Malayalam newspaper for
eighteen years. In the early 1970s, his cartoons emphasized large blank spaces with tiny people at
the bottom of the frame, similar to the look of his later films.
2. For surveys of Aravindan's oeuvre, see Madhavan Kutty (1981), Rajadhyaksha and Willemen
(1994: 45), and Robinson (1979: 92).

were deeply disillusioned with post-independence "modernization" and leftist democratic politics. The solitary colors of this generation's rebellion, its self-destructive impulse, and its masculine profile are etched into Aravindan's film as well.

A written commentary that throws light on Aravindan's interpretation of the play precedes his film proper. This opening scroll reads, "This film is an interpretation of the *uttara-kanda* of the Ramayana. Our mythologies and the epics are constantly re-created in retellings. The epic is the basis for this visual interpretation as well. This film deviates from established norms in how it visualizes the protagonists and portrays the course of events in the epic." The scroll explains that the film will try to reflect what it calls the epic's *adi-sankalpam*, "original conception," of the theme and protagonists. It states that "the inner essence of this film" is that woman is *Prakriti*. Ultimately *Purusha*, here conceived of as the (masculine) self, dissolves into Prakriti.

Interpreted in this context, Rama's journey (*ayana*) follows a compelling narrative path: the dissolution of the self, Purusha, into the female animating power of the universe, Prakriti.[3] Eluttacchan's *Adhyatma Ramayana*, the classic Malayalam telling of Rama's story, views Rama as Purusha and Sita as Prakriti, an interpretation familiar to audiences in Kerala.[4] However, in contrast to almost all other tellings of the *uttara-kanda* (final section), and in what probably constitutes Aravindan's single most significant creative intervention in the film, Sita herself is physically absent. The title of C.N. Sreekantan Nair's play, *Kanchana Sita,* refers to the golden image of Sita that substituted for her presence by Rama's side in rituals that required a queen. In Aravindan's film, Prakriti takes Sita's place.

In an interview, Aravindan stated that "C. N. [Sreekantan Nair] had made clear the prakriti-purusha notion in Ramayana" but, as director, Aravindan did not think that Sita should be represented in the physical form of a woman. Instead, Aravindan takes the extraordinary cinematic step of representing Sita as Prakriti. Aravindan sought to visualize Sita's emotions—pain, sadness, joy, and equanimity—through the moods of Prakriti, and, therefore, describing dialogue as "redundant," he used it minimally in the film.[5] Aravindan interpreted the uttara-kanda's ending, when Rama enters Sarayu River, as Rama's own self-immolation at the end of a journey which has left him truly solitary.[6]

In this essay, I investigate how the relationship of power and sovereignty is

---

3. Prakriti and Purusha, as philosophical concepts, have their genealogy in the Samkhya-Yoga school of Indian philosophy. In Samkhya thought, Prakriti is the generative source of the universe. Through its threefold *gunas* or characteristics of the physical universe, Prakriti binds Purusha, the self (in the minimal sense of awareness or sentience), which itself is not distinct from Prakriti. In this school of thought, detachment and meditation (yoga) are the paths to knowledge, ignorance is the main cause of suffering, and discriminating knowledge removes the bondage of rebirth (Hiriyanna 1993: 267–297).

4. Eluttacchan (1994: 26).

5. Aravindan (1992: 26).

6. Ibid., p. 27.

thematically unraveled in Aravindan's *Kanchana Sita*.[7] Aravindan's film distinctively differs from both the uttara-kanda of Valmiki's *Ramayana* and Sreekantan Nair's play. If the uttara-kanda's critique of sovereign power is buried in the karmic webs of Rama's life, Sreekantan Nair's play carries a sharply materialistic edge in its critique of Kshatriya-Brahminical power. In contrast to both, Aravindan's thematic content is much more directly focused on Rama's inner conflict between the desire for enlightenment (*moksha*) and the desire for sovereign power (*artha*). Aravindan highlights this conflict through his choice of location and actors, as well as his thematic elaboration of the killing of Shambuka and, most of all, the presence of Prakriti.

The film assumes the viewer's textual familiarity with prominent narratives in the uttara-kanda, the final section of the epic text.[8] The uttara-kanda records the waning half of Rama's sovereign power and divine aura. Earlier sections of Ramkatha have affirmed sovereign power and glorified Rama as warrior-king, but the uttara-kanda provides a powerful counterpoint to Rama's authority by focusing upon figures outside Ayodhya: Shambuka, Sita, and Valmiki. Following the advice of Brahmin sages, Rama conducts the horse sacrifice to consolidate the sovereignty of his power.

In uttara-kanda's most dramatic sequence, Valmiki brings the twins to the horse sacrifice, where their singing of Rama's story forces him to recognize them as his sons. The horse sacrifice will ensure the king's complete sovereignty over the kingdom and any rival ruler who challenged the king to a battle by capturing the horse. Yet Rama demands a second trial by fire from Sita, who refuses to prove her purity again. In the final scene, Rama departs from the world by entering the Sarayu River. All this functions as the implicit narrative background for Aravindan's film.

Aravindan, however, selectively focuses on particular events that unfold around the horse sacrifice, creating critical changes in how Sreekantan Nair's play depicts Sita. As Rama proceeds, under the dictates of Brahmin sages, to ensure absolute power through the sacrifice, he enters into a series of dharmic confrontations. Critical among them are his interrogation of and beheading of Shambuka; the conflict between Rama, Bharata, and Urmila over whether the horse sacrifice should be performed; the unexpected challenge from Sita's twins, Lava and Kusha, who capture the sacrificial horse that has been let loose

---

7. Aravindan's film casts the question of power into a philosophical context sharply distinct from, and epistemologically prior to, the theorizing of disciplinary mechanisms of the state, social institutions, and subjects analyzed in Anglo-American scholarship. Following Michel Foucault's monumental work, in the last two decades members of the Anglo-American academy (especially in cultural studies) have analyzed the mechanisms of power in depth. Yet few of these discussions examine how the idea of power is itself conceptualized in non-western philosophies, mythologies, and texts. Foucault's decentering of power into micro-political networks and his theory of how power works through both totalizing and individualizing impulses have opened up rich veins of study.

8. This section is often lacking in popular North Indian versions of the epic, such as *Ramcharitmanas* by Tulsidas, at least partly due to its critique of Rama as sovereign.

at the beginning of the horse sacrifice; Valmiki bringing the twins to chant Rama's story at the sacrifice; the necessity for Rama to recognize and accept his sons there; and his decision to enter the Sarayu River. What began as a kingly exercise to assert absolute power over an external territory turns into a battle of the self, in which Rama seems to abandon each unfolding chance for enlightened action.

Throughout the film, Rama is caught in a dharmic predicament. The external world, which Brahmin ritualism takes as the place for the proper exercise of Kshatriya royal power, comes into conflict with his own inner self which, detached from kingly power, appears to hear and feel Sita's presence everywhere. In the film (as in the play), Urmila, Lakshmana's wife and Sita's sister, asks why Rama abandoned Sita and why he submits to the dictates of Brahmins. The emotional intensity of these dialogue-dominated conflicts in Sreekantan Nair's play is muted, however, through Aravindan's reticent, subdued cinematic rendering of long, silent takes of Rama and Lakshmana wandering through the dense forests and the ochre river banks, as if on a spiritual quest.

Aravindan's Journey

The cinematic rendering of *Kanchana Sita* seems to have been shaped by the outcome of Aravindan's own serendipitous quest for location and actors. The story of the making of the film detailed below reveals his emphasis on the search for the thematically apt visual landscapes, actors, and mise-en-scene. Aravindan's quest for the realization of these elements is nearly as crucial as the aesthetics of the completed film. Sreekantan Nair's play followed the style of epic presentation that is familiar to Indian audiences used to viewing mythological films and dance-dramas.[9] The scenes in such renderings would alternate between the visually distinct spatial environments of outdoor forest settings and ornate palace interiors, complete with royal trappings.

In contrast, Aravindan abandoned such alternation in setting by moving Rama's story into the landscape of Adivasis (tribal people), imagining Ayodhya in the forest.[10] Its palaces are forest caves, its streets are tracks in the wilderness, and its Sarayu River is the Godavari River winding through rural Andhra Pradesh. Aravindan identified locations 100 miles away from Rajamundhry in Andhra, along the expanse of the Godavari River and its ribbed red earth banks. Such a spatial visualization of Rama's story had not been attempted before: the epic retold as if it occurred in the Adivasi world.[11]

Relocating the narrative into this spatial and temporal context makes it en-

---

9. Sreekantan Nair (2000) and a recent English translation (Sreekantan Nair and Joseph 2005). "Modern" and "realistic" here refer to Sreekantan Nair's following of western practices of realistic representation, as opposed to a highly stylized Indian aesthetic (e.g., Kathakali).

10. The term *Adivasi* (primordial or original inhabitant) is used currently to refer to communities who live now in India's mountains and forests, often continuing their traditional ways of living, which are closely dependent on and integrated with nature.

11. Portrayals such as Aravindan's may no longer be politically possible. Followers of the Bharatiya Janata Party and Hindu majoritarian politics judge such representations as transgressive.

tirely possible to imagine that the events of the film could be happening now, or thousands of years ago. From the choice of this setting, it would seem that Aravindan's vision of the original conception of the epic reflected the experiential conditions in which Rama's story could unfold as a journey of the self. Stripping the epic narrative of any historical details in the setting that would date the scene allows the viewer and the director to focus on the pure dharmic questions that Rama faces at each turn.

Filmmaker Padmakumar, who worked closely with Aravindan in several of his films, described in an interview how *Kanchana Sita* was shot in less than three weeks during November and December 1976.[12] Padmakumar recounted how Aravindan noticed the Koyas, who believed themselves to be descendants of Rama, in the streets of Hyderabad, and then sought actors among them. Koyas are traditionally nomadic healers who wander the forests and mountains to search for medicinal herbs, and then sell these cures in cities and towns. Koyas who were practicing as healers at the time in Hyderabad play the central roles of Rama, Lakshmana, Bharata, Lava, and Kusha in the film.

Aravindan's idea, said Padmakumar, was not to use conventional actors, but to find people who had reached the state of awareness that the role required. So Shambuka was played by a wayside tapasvi, while a destitute woman acted in the role of his wife. Communication with the actors was carried out with the help of Manohar Dutt, painter and lecturer at the College of Fine Arts, Hyderabad. Dutt also accompanied Aravindan and his associate, journalist and filmmaker "Chinta" Ravi, on a preliminary trip to Andhra Pradesh to finalize the locations.

The shooting took place at the time when Congress Party Prime Minister Indira Gandhi had declared a national emergency to suppress the mass democratic uprising against her government. Police were combing the entire area around Rajamundhry in their hunt for the members of the Maoist People's War Group. As a result, recalled Padmakumar, members of the production team were picked up and questioned by the police several times because they looked different from the average person. At a time when the politics of absolute power was playing out in history, Aravindan's film relocated the question of sovereign authority to a narrative in which it played a major role as part of the conflict between the desire for power and the desire for enlightenment.

Shambuka's Significance

The incident in which Rama kills Shambuka plays a heightened role in Aravindan's film at least partially because the Brahminical dictates that sustain sovereign power come into direct conflict with the desire for spiritual knowledge. Aravindan stated that he used the Shambuka episode "to highlight Rama's troubled conscience and evoke within him and the film the memory

---

12. Interview with Padmakumar, August 4, 2001, Thiruvananthapuram. I owe many of my observations here to Padmakumar's deep understanding of Aravindan's work.

and presence of Sita."[13] In Sreekantan Nair's play, Rama seeks out the Shudra tapasvi, finds Shambuka performing penances hanging upside down, and takes Shambuka's life.[14] In contrast, Aravindan broke Rama's single, fatal encounter with Shambuka into two scenes.

In the first scene, set at the very beginning of the film, Rama finds Shambuka practicing penances forbidden to Shudras, but Shambuka's wife pleads with Rama not to kill her husband. At this moment, soft music begins to play, Rama looks up as if he discerns another presence, and a gentle wind blows through the tall trees. As if overcome by emotion, Rama spares Shambuka. "A king ought not to dream," Rama tells Lakshmana later, yet we know that he has allowed himself to be guided by Sita, who appears as the force of compassion. The second brief scene shows a Shambuka who has already been cut down by Rama's arrow, his body having fallen into the lap of his grieving wife. The scene precedes an image of the white horse's head, now severed for the horse sacrifice. Both killings reassert the primacy of the desire for sovereign power, and the necessity for such power to assert itself through extremes of violence. The nature of power, it would seem, is not to safeguard itself, nor to counter another, but to extend constantly beyond its own realm.

Scholar V. Rajakrishnan noted that Aravindan had not fully considered the implications of locating Rama's story in an Adivasi community.[15] Shambuka's killing, Valmiki's confrontation with Rama at the horse sacrifice, and Sita's withdrawal into the earth all contribute powerful examples of social critique in the uttara-kanda, but all three incidents are muted in the non-dramatic, subdued narrative style that Aravindan used. So too is Sreekantan Nair's reading of the Rama-Ravana war as an Aryan-Dravidian conflict (an interpretation that could be implied by the casting of the Koyas) in which Rama safeguarded interests of the Aryans.[16] Rajakrishnan pointed out that the rigid economy of expression and the subdued acting styles, which appear to render all dialogue artificial, reduce the element of human drama so prominent in Sreekantan Nair's play.

Unlike Sreekantan Nair's play, in which he was committed to developing character conflict, Aravindan consistently and deliberately edits out passionate emotional expressions and outbursts in the play (such as Rama's encounters with Urmila, Bharata, and Kausalya) in favor of a non-dramatic, non-dialogic style of expression that diminishes greatly the centrality of feeling. Indeed, the contrast with Sreekantan Nair's play that Rajakrishnan has noted is one that the filmmaker has painstakingly sought to create through his use of specific cinematic techniques. The Shambuka episode illustrates Aravindan's disinterest in dramatic conflict as a mode either for social critique or for philosophical elaboration. Indeed, the narrative logic for Shambuka's death and an interpretation

---

13. Aravindan (1992: 27).
14. See part 2 of this volume for detailed analysis of the Shambuka story.
15. Interview with V. Rajakrishnan, August 28, 2001, Thiruvananthapuram.
16. See, for example, Richman (1991a: 175–201).

of it that use it to advocate a progressive politics of caste are absent from the film. This detachment flows from Aravindan's philosophical position as a filmmaker, and therefore is inseparable from his aesthetics.

In using Shambuka's penance to evoke Sita, Aravindan bypasses the element of caste subordination in the story, which has made it a common example in Kerala of caste hierarchy in Rama's story (which Sreekantan Nair drew upon). Interpreting this episode, scriptwriter P. S. Manu pointed out that Shambuka's upside down body metaphorically challenged the system which ranked Brahminical castes as the highest in the social hierarchy.[17] The inverted body stood Rama's world of security, built on Brahminical manipulation and Kshatriya might, on its head, challenging the very foundations of its sovereignty. Shambuka's upside down body is also a temporal symbol, one that heralds the imminent demise of the foundation of sovereign power that Rama represents.

In Aravindan's film, it is not caste hierarchy that is the issue, but again, Rama's conflict between the desire for power and the desire for enlightened action. Caste hierarchy, it would seem, is a result of these fundamental drives. The question of power is located not in the external structures of oppression, such as the Kshatriya-Brahmin hierarchy, but within the self. The Brahmin sages who advocate the killing of Shambuka are directly countered by the absent presence of Sita as Prakriti. The Shambuka incident in Aravindan's film is not a social critique. It is, rather, about the instinctual drives for power and their encounter with compassion.

Sita's Absent Presence

Through his aesthetic choices, Aravindan erases the motivating power of human emotion and action that impel ordinary plot structure, not to yield to the supremacy of fate but to ameliorate the centrality of human agency as the cause and measure of events. Indeed, Sita as Prakriti—and Rama's almost inevitable journey into becoming a part of her—is the heart of Aravindan's narrative. Thematically, the detachment from social issues is consistent with the film's focus on the union of Purusha and Prakriti. Sita's physical absence liberates her presence from the limitations of a specific spatio-temporal location or physical form such as a body, a scene, a place, or a voice.

Instead she now permeates the narrative through her immediate and all-pervasive presence as Prakriti, the cosmic life-force. Aravindan clearly indicates through visuals that Prakriti is not nature in the passive sense in which the word is often employed; instead Prakriti actively gives life to nature. Thus she appears as the sunlight that marks an ever-changing path through the thick forest trees, she is audible and visible as the wind that rustles the leaves, and she moves in the river as ripples in the water. She is the animating principle of

---

17. The reference is to the Rg Vedic verse describing the Purusha, the cosmic body. Brahmins (priests) emanate from his head, Kshatriyas (warriors) from his arms, Vaishyas (the productive varna) from his thighs, and Shudras (servants) from his feet.

nature that energizes all visible life-forms, including the creativity of the poet
Valmiki who begins to compose the uttara-kanda in her inspiring presence.

Poet and scholar Ayyappa Paniker views Sita's absence as typical of Aravindan's style in which there is a conscious, meticulous effort "not to communicate
in order to communicate."[18] Such a style is especially difficult in the visual medium of film. "Sita is not a woman, or an individual, but an eternal concept in
the film," Paniker said. Paniker described Aravindan's expressive style using his
own concept of *antarsannivesa,* or the poetics of interiorization.[19] In this form
of expression, relish (*rasa*), mood (*bhava*) and purpose (*artha*) are withheld,
denied overt expression, or negated, in order to draw the reader into deeper and
less obvious levels of communication. "In the work as a whole there inheres,
like a living inner spring, another work, an inside work," writes Paniker.[20]

To Rama, Sita in the form of Prakriti also appears as a guide to dharma, indicating the path of action that he must adopt. Signs from Prakriti, presented
through the music and images of nature's movement, stop Rama from killing
Shambuka at first sight and from fighting with Bharata. Likewise, the turbu-
lence in nature appears to warn Rama against the performance of the horse sacrifice. For Aravindan, however, Prakriti appears to be primarily a maternal force
that heightens Rama's awareness of his own destructive actions. The mood of
the music that accompanies the presence of Prakriti, which Aravindan repeats
throughout the film whenever Rama experiences the presence of Sita, is nostal-
gic, compassionate, and tender.[21] Only in the final scenes does Prakriti begin to
consume Rama's universe, as the fire that burns down the sacrificial hall and as
the waters of the Sarayu that await Rama's final journey.

For Aravindan, Prakriti also seems to bear no resemblance to woman in
her temporal, sensual, and worldly form. The radical role given to Urmila in
Sreekantan Nair's play, and her fiery speeches to Rama which expose his own suspicion and betrayal of Sita, are edited down to the bare minimum and shorn of
their resonance with the modern idiom of women's rights. The argumentative
voice of Urmila, the "real" woman of the film, remains significant but periph-
eral, her physical presence shadowed in the interiors of the caves which serve as
the palaces of Ayodhya. In the refined sensibility of the film that foregrounds
the masculine tapasvi's journey to Prakriti, the Sita of the uttara-kanda, cast
out of the kingdom, the "woman crying aloud in despair" outside Valmiki's
hermitage, is not heard.[22] To Aravindan, Prakriti's silence is more eloquent than
the speeches of her womanly manifestations. The horse sacrifice is not so much
an external ritual as a preparatory rite for Rama's final liberation from the self
caught in the bonds of phenomenal existence.

The physical absence of Sita also led Aravindan to transform the final scenes
of Sreekantan Nair's play, where Sita appears at the sacrificial site and descends

---

18. Interview with Ayyappa Paniker, August 29, 2001, Thiruvananthapuram.
19. Interview with Paniker.
20. Paniker (2003: 1–8).
21. Aravindan (1992: 27).
22. *Valmiki Ramayana* 7: 49 (1992: 2072).

into the opening earth rather than undergo a second ordeal of sexual purity at Rama's behest. In Valmiki's *Ramayana,* and in Sreekantan Nair's *Kanchana Sita,* a golden image of Sita substitutes for her presence at the horse sacrifice. The golden image which Aravindan uses for the horse sacrifice is a traditional South Indian bronze sculpture of the goddess seated in a benedictory posture. To Rama, meditating directly in front of the sacrificial fire, the image appears enveloped in flames, as Sita must have appeared when she entered the fire after the great battle of Lanka to prove her purity. Sita, enveloped in flames, appears to be fire itself, since she is unscathed by the flames. Clothed in fire, yet transcending the flames, she is at once Rama's awareness and the life-force within him which fire symbolizes.

As the last scenes of the film unfold, it appears to the viewer that the agni-pariksha (fire ordeal) is ultimately for Rama to attain final awareness, not for Sita. As Kanchana Sita, the golden image of Sita enshrined in flames, she is the fiery means of his enlightenment, and the goal of his enlightenment as well, since there is nothing that transcends her presence. In the final scene, Rama walks into the waters of the Sarayu. He carries the sacrificial flame with him into the waters of dissolution, into Prakriti that waits to absorb all the elements of life back into herself. Collapsing the final sections of the epic into a few minutes, Aravindan merges Rama's recognition of his sons and Sita with his desire for final liberation. The conflict between the desire for enlightenment and the desire for power now vanishes as the significance of the horse sacrifice changes from attaining absolute power over the kingdom to attaining moksha or enlightenment from the kingdom. The search for absolute sovereign power ends in the failure of the material conquest it sought, even as enlightenment is revealed as the ultimate goal of human life.

10 Struggling with an Ideal

Lalitha Lenin (b. 1946) served as Reader in, and then Head of, the Department of Library and Information Science at the University of Kerala in Tiruvananthapuram until her retirement in 2006. Among her many publications are articles in the field of Library and Information Science, short stories, children's books, television scripts, and several collections of poetry.

"In the Shadow of Sita," first published in 1997, considers Sita's ambiguous legacy for today's women. Sita may be clad in pure white, but she is haunted by darkness and restrictions. Sita's life took shape through the deeds of others: abandoned in a field, found in a furrow being plowed, married to a man who broke Shiva's bow, exiled due to Kaikeyi's ambitions, and subjected to danger during the exile. If one clings to the image of Sita, one gains certain kinds of security and evades troubling questions, but the price is collusion in self-imprisonment. Yet breaking free of Sita's mold can seem terrifying. The poem reveals how deeply a single character has influenced generations of women. Precisely for this reason, many modern writers have striven to re-imagine Sita's life in a way that does not exact such a high price from women.

Source: Lalitha Lenin, *Namukku Prarthikkam* [Let Us Pray] (Thiruvananthapuram: D.C. Books, 2000), pp. 39–41.

In the Shadow of Sita
BY LALITHA LENIN

I am still
in the shadow of Sita.
Heartbeat, bat of an eyelid,
voice lilting—everything
is caught in the dark nights
of wingless white-clad Sita.

It cuddles me
like a cow that licks her calf
to draw it closer to her udder.
Feeds me with the sparkle of the dawn
and the prayer of the dusk
to keep me away from epidemics.

Measures up the pitch
and boundary lines

of my laughter and tears.
Blesses me profusely to fill
ruled notebooks and written words
with fine contours.

Leads me down the steps
of images of ploughs,
dreams about Three-eyed Shiva's bow,
and the conceit of the king's favorite queen,
and walks me blindfolded
among the wild woodland fears.

Teaches me how,
sitting under the Ashoka tree,
and chanting the mantras
of the anguish of separation,
I should cast the mold
of the chaste woman.

Trains me in self-oblivion
by being servile to custom,
and without sowing the seed
in the fret of the loose terrain.
Tames me on the trident of restraint
into paying the fine without fail.

I am still
in the shadow of Sita.

When it stifles me
like an old dress that no longer fits,
they tell me, it is the sea of death
beyond the shadow.
Others say, it is the desert.
I am unnerved, it is danger either way.

They tell me,
shadow is shade, too.
Some others hold
that it is fulfillment itself.
I just know, it sticks like glue, and
petrifies my heart into a piece of marble.

How could Sita
shroud the entire universe
with this tiny shadow?
Who said this shadow
does not have colors?

In its dark cavities,
there is the merger
of purity and apathy,
the blaze of sacrifices,
calls of prohibition, and
past sins buried in black holes
while great stars burn themselves out.

How I wish
I could take a step,
just one step,
beyond this shadow
in search of truth!

Translated from Malayalam by Rizio Yohannan Raj

Part Two   *Stigmatized Characters*

Modern South Indian writers have paid particular attention to Rama's relationship with two characters, each of whom was stigmatized for departing from religiously validated gender and caste norms: Shambuka and Ahalya. On the one hand, Valmiki's *Ramayana* depicts Rama slaying Shambuka, a Shudra tapasvi (ascetic), because he violated the prohibitions against Shudras practicing asceticism. On the other hand, even though Ahalya was stigmatized by her husband as an adulteress, Rama released her from her husband's curse.

The selections in part 2 do not condemn Rama for his generosity toward Ahalya, but they do point out that he does not extend the same compassion to Sita, who suffered a fire ordeal and later banishment in the jungle despite her scrupulous fidelity to her husband (#13–16). Nor does the modern retelling of Shambuka in part 2 condemn Rama for executing Shambuka; instead it rejects the idea that Rama *would* kill him (#11, #12). Although Shambuka and Ahalya are usually considered "minor" figures within the Ramayana tradition's large cast of characters, the kind of attention that each has received from modern South Indian writers suggests that neither character's significance is minor.

Shambuka

The earliest and most prestigious account of Shambuka's story appears in the last book (uttara-kanda) of the *Ramayana* attributed to Valmiki.[1] Most scholars view this book as a later interpolation, but whether it dates from Valmiki's time or somewhat later, it soon became part of the ongoing Ramayana tradition.[2] It relates how a Brahmin arrives at Rama's court carrying the body of his dead son, a virtuous child who had never deviated from dharma. The father declares that an undeserved death never occurs in a kingdom where a just ruler ensures that each citizen performs *varnashrama-dharma* (duty enjoined according to one's social rank and stage of life). When Rama consults his ministers about the state of the kingdom, they pinpoint a single deviation from dharma: the Shudra Shambuka has been performing tapas.

Since tapas is a form of ascetic self-discipline reserved by the orthodox exclusively for "twice-borns," members of the upper three varnas, Rama's ministers urge him to slay Shambuka. Rama mounts his celestial chariot, speeds to the forest where *Rishi* (Sage) Shambuka dwells, and interrogates him. Upon confirming that he is indeed a Shudra by birth, Rama draws his gleaming stainless sword and cuts off his head. "Well done!" shout the gods in praise. The Brahmin's son returns to life and fragrant flowers rain down from the sky, a sign of celestial approbation.

Although the execution of Shambuka can be seen as proof of Rama's vigilant defense of dharmic order, criticism of Rama's slaying of Shambuka dates back at least to the eighth century, when playwright Bhavabhuti composed *Uttararamacharita* (Later Story of Rama). In his Sanskrit play, Bhavabhuti expressed profound unease with Rama's willingness to execute a person whose only alleged misdeed was performing tapas.[3] By the twentieth century, Bhavabhuti's veiled criticism gave way to explicit attacks on Rama's killing of Shambuka. Some critics claimed that Rama realized that Shambuka's tapas was valid but succumbed to pressure from his Brahmin advisors to slay the ascetic because otherwise they would refuse to legitimate his claim to kingly office. Other critics attacked all religious practice as superstition, seeing Valmiki's depiction of Rama killing Shambuka as a warning to low caste people of the lethal consequences that would ensue should they attempt to transgress the boundaries of the social hierarchy.[4]

Rejecting both of these interpretations of Shambuka's slaying, K. V. Puttappa composed an incisive re-interpretation of Shambuka's story in a Kannada play titled *Shudra Tapasvi* (Shudra Ascetic) (#11). An ardent devotee of Rama, Puttappa had studied both Sanskrit and Kannada literature deeply, so he knew Valmiki's *Ramayana* well. Yet Puttappa plainly rejected the assumption that Valmiki had a monopoly on the truth about Rama's story. Puttappa explains this stance at the start of a long lyric poem that presents his distinctive telling of Rama's story:

> It is not correct to say that Valmiki is the only Ramayana poet.
> There are thousands of Ramayana poets.
> There is a Ramayana poet in every village.[5]

Thus, instead of feeling obligated to follow Valmiki's rendition, Puttappa retold Shambuka's story in a way that is, to our knowledge, virtually unprecedented within the entire Ramayana tradition: his play bears witness to both Rama's compassion and the validity of Shambuka's tapas. Today Puttappa is lauded as a Kannada pioneer in the literature of Dalits (people "ground down" or "oppressed"); he earned that stature at least partially on account of *Shudra Tapasvi*.[6]

The play focuses on three characters: (1) Rama; (2) Shambuka, who seeks to attain *moksha* (religious salvation); and (3) the Brahmin, who admonishes Rama for allowing a Shudra to usurp the privilege of performing tapas. Puttappa, who was born into a Shudra family and was also a votary of *ahimsa* (non-violence), believed that Rama loved all creatures, irrespective of their social rank. In *Shudra Tapasvi*, therefore, when Rama determines to end deviation from dharma, rather than slaying Shambuka, he destroys misperceptions of tapas in the mind of the Brahmin.

Furthermore, while most earlier accounts of Shambuka's slaying (e.g., Valmiki, Bhavabhuti) are Rama-centered tellings placed in the midst of a much longer narrative of Rama's glorious deeds, Puttappa centers his entire play on Shambuka. The play's title, dialogue, and even the stage directions in the script focus directly upon Shambuka or the broader issue of Shudras performing tapas. When theatrical director Basavalingaiah revived Puttappa's play half a century after its composition, he staged the play in a way that intensified the production's focus on Shambuka (#12). And, although Shambuka speaks only briefly, as befits a tapasvi, he remains a towering presence on stage, as he sits utterly still amidst the anthill, functioning as a witness to the Brahmin's arrogant and prideful interchanges with Rama.

Ahalya

While Puttappa questions the validity of caste-based restrictions, three short stories and the poem in part 2 question the validity of gender-based restrictions. Valmiki's *Ramayana* and Kamban's *Iramavataram*, both authoritative texts in South India, narrate the same basic plot of Ahalya's story as follows.[7] Every day Ahalya's husband, Gautama, leaves their forest cottage to practice austerities in the forest. One day, while Gautama is performing his daily ablutions at the river, Indra, king of the Vedic gods, takes on Gautama's form and seduces Ahalya. After enjoying sexual relations with her, Indra leaves the cottage but then encounters Gautama returning home. All Gautama's accumulated tapas turns into rage, from the depths of which he curses Indra and his wife.

Despite agreement about the general plot, the two authoritative tellings of Ahalya's story differ in specific ways. First, Valmiki's Ahalya eagerly welcomes the embraces of Indra, while Kamban's Ahalya believes that Indra is Gautama (since he took on Gautama's form) and finds out only later that he is not. Kamban's version therefore portrays Ahalya not as an adulteress but as a wife longing for affection from her husband, whose celibacy and intense tapas precluded marital intimacy. Second, in Valmiki's text, Gautama curses Ahalya to become a ghostly presence in the ashram, consuming nothing but air and lying amidst the ashes, invisible to all creatures. In contrast, Kamban depicts Gautama as cursing Ahalya to turn to stone, an object incapable of the ability to feel pleasure. Both Valmiki and Kamban *do*, however, present Ahalya's story primarily as Rama-centered, taking her deliverance from the curse as proof of Rama's compassion.

In stark contrast, four selections in part 2 present the narrative as Ahalya-centered, exploring how she experiences events. In addition, the stories by K. B. Sreedevi and Pudumaippittan extend their narratives beyond where earlier renditions end. In continuing the narrative, these two writers imagine how Ahalya would have reacted to Rama's subsequent treatment of Sita. Why would Rama free Ahalya but punish his own wife—especially if he believed that the rumors of her adultery with Ravana were false? Rather than glorifying Rama as do Valmiki and Kamban, both these stories testify to Rama's double standard in relation to Ahalya and Sita. Pudumaippittan's "Deliverance from the Curse" (#14) shows Ahalya turning into a stone again after she hears of Sita's trial by fire in Lanka, while Sreedevi's "Woman of Stone" (#13) depicts Ahalya lithifying after learning that Rama has banished Sita.[8]

"Deliverance from the Curse" goes even a step further, examining how Ahalya's release affects Gautama and his relationship with her. Pudumaippittan portrays Ahalya as stricken with what physicians today call "post-trauma repetition syndrome," in which a victim compulsively relives again and again a fearful incident in the mind's eye. Indra's seduction and Gautama's anger scar Ahalya so deeply that she cannot break free of their memory even after the curse ends. Because Gautama blames himself for giving in to anger and cursing Ahalya, he becomes imprisoned in self-recrimination. Pudumaippittan explores the psychological nature of marriage after adultery, showing that the couple could not just pick up the threads of their lives as if past events had no consequences in the present.

A poem by S. Sivasekaram (#15) represents Ahalya in a singular way by delving into the multiple meanings of stone. When Ahalya married an ascetic absorbed in self-denial, she endured an existence devoid of companionship, as if married to a stone. The poem suggests that only when she united with Indra did Ahalya finally taste life. If, after deliverance from the curse, she must return to the same stony marriage, might she be better off remaining a stone? If she did, at least she could maintain her dignity.[9]

The final selection in part 2, by N. S. Madhavan (#16), contemporizes Ahalya's story by setting it in the modern city of Cochin, Kerala. While Sreedevi, Pudumaippittan, and Sivasekaram portray Ahalya as a stone, Madhavan follows Valmiki's earlier rendition, where Ahalya is instead cursed to become a ghostly presence. Madhavan depicts her as unconscious after her husband beats her when he learns of her adultery with a film star. Rama's skill as a neurologist temporarily restores Ahalya. Madhavan's story explores the pressures that physical beauty creates for today's women and the consequences of domestic violence.

The four accounts of Ahalya in part 2 represent only a fraction of the many ways Ahalya's story has been retold in modern South India.[10] Is it right for a beautiful young woman to be paired off with an older husband who leaves her alone day after day due to his own self-absorption? Was Ahalya naïve, deluded, tricked, wanton, tragic, passive, traumatized? All four of the selections about Ahalya imply that a wife deserves a spouse with whom she can share her life. Assumptions about companionate marriage have invested the story of Ahalya with particular poignance in the modern period. The ambiguity of Ahalya's experience as a wife and the extremity of her curse have haunted a number of twentieth-century writers, as part 2's selections demonstrate.

Caste and Gender

How is Shambuka connected to Ahalya? A scene in *Shudra Tapasvi* provides one answer. In Puttappa's play, Rama first catches sight of Shambuka meditating intensely amidst a huge anthill. The sight of the anthill immediately calls Valmiki to Rama's mind because, according to popular legend, Valmiki's name comes from "*valmika*," anthill. He then recalls that Valmiki is, according

Figure 3. Ahalya simultaneously woman and stone. When Ahalya is depicted, usually she is shown at the forest hermitage when Gautama has just returned and found Indra slinking away. This unique drawing depicts Ahalya as both woman and stone. Artist: Bapu.

to legend, of low birth.[11] Rama realizes that at the very moment when the Brahmin seeks to punish Shudra Shambuka for practicing tapas, Shudra Valmiki is sheltering Rama's wife in his ashram.

Puttappa suggests that both Sita's banishment and Shambuka's execution derive from erroneous judgments premised on constructions of purity and pollution, rather than the actual quality of one's actions. Among the varieties of pollution enumerated in dharma-shastras, a twice-born male can be sullied by contact with a Shudra or an impure (adulterous) wife.[12] Rama now apprehends that although Valmiki, Shambuka, and Sita performed many virtuous acts, public opinion assessed them only according to a harsh dichotomy based on purity vs. impurity, thus perpetuating injustices based on caste and gender hierarchy. Here Puttappa suggests that actions must be judged according to moral standards rather than those of "purity," if caste and gender rankings are to lose their power to dehumanize and humiliate human beings. The two forms of hierarchy are entwined.

Each selection in part 2 retells a story about Shambuka or Ahalya in a way that removes the stigma of adharma from their shoulders. Since such stories present the narrative in light of current political issues, these selections both reflect and contribute to vigorous protest against caste and gender hierarchy in South India. Indeed, the view that tapas should be open to all and that refuge should be given to wronged women dates back at least to the time when legends about low caste Valmiki giving refuge to banished Sita began to circulate.[13] Protests against caste hierarchy have grown stronger over the last century and continue to the present day. Thus, Puttappa's Shambuka-centered play and the four Ahalya-centered selections in part 2 demonstrate that, for modern writers and readers, Ahalya and Shambuka are not minor characters. Instead, their experiences of caste and gender inequality are deeply implicated in modern South Indian life. Indeed, the experience of stigmatized characters evokes deep empathy, and even identification, from many of today's readers.

Notes

1. For Valmiki's Sanskrit rendition of Shambuka's slaying, see Bhatta (1958: 7: 413–425, sargas 73–76). For an English translation, see N. Raghunathan (1982:569–574). Since Kamban's *Iramavataram* ends with Rama's coronation, it does not contain Shambuka's story.

2. For a discussion about interpolations in Valmiki's *Ramayana,* see Goldman (1984: 14–29) and Richman (1991b: 8–9).

3. For the Sanskrit rendition, see Kane (1971). Lal provides an English "transcreation," not a literal translation (1957).

4. Between 1920 and 1960, many other authors retold the story of Shambuka in ways that criticized Rama's actions and prompted public controversy. For example, Tripuraneni Ramasvami Chaudari (1887–1943) wrote a Telugu play, *Shambuka Vadha* [The Slaying of Shambuka] (1966: 1–79), which argued that all have a right to practice tapas, no matter what their status at birth. Pursuing a somewhat different line of critique, Thiruvarur K. Thangaraju's Tamil play *Ramayana Natakam* (1954) depicts Shambuka articulating a set of arguments based upon science to convince Rama that one's status should derive from meritorious action, rather than birth. See Richman (2004: 129–133).

5. Puttappa (1955: xii).

6. For Shambuka and Ekalavya in recent Dalit literature, see Sivasagar's poem "Ongoing History," (2000) and Omvedt (1995: 96–103).

7. For Valmiki's story of Ahalya in Sanskrit, see Bhatta 1: 268 (sarga 47). An English translation appears in R. Goldman (1984: 215–218). For Kamban's telling, see Kopalakirushnamacariyar 1: 388–389 (*akalikaippatalam*). For an English translation of Kamban's telling, see Hande (1996: 39–41).

8. Strikingly, neither writer knew of the other's story, yet each portrays Ahalya returning to stone when she learns of Rama's harsh treatment of Sita.

9. See note 29 in the introductory essay to this anthology for a discussion of the relationship between Sri Lanka and South India.

10. For an overview of Ahalya's story in pre-colonial tellings of Ramkatha, see Shastri (1988). For Ahalya in Sanskrit drama, see Sahdev (1982: 17–19). In modern South India, Ahalya's story has drawn the attention of an impressive number of writers. In

Tamil alone, the story's retellings are legion, as Kailasapathy (1970) has shown. In Gundappa's Kannada *Rama Parikshanam,* characters accuse Rama of deviating from dharma or compassion and he defends his actions. Ahalya's testimony is the most poignant among the characters depicted in the text (Aithal: 10). Also famous is "Putina" P. T. Narasimhachar's "Ahalye" (1941).

11. For analysis of this legend about Valmiki, see Narayana Rao (2001: 162–164).

12. On purity and pollution in India, see Dumont (1980).

13. See Leslie (2003).

11 Transforming a Brahmin

Kuppalli Venkata Puttappa, known as "Kuvempu" (1904–1994), composed innovative works in each of Kannada's major literary genres, earning particular acclaim for rewriting epic narratives in fresh ways.[1] After growing up in the Malnad district (Western Ghats) of Karnataka, Puttappa attended Mysore University for multiple degrees and rose through the ranks of academia to serve as vice-chancellor of the university. By the mid-1940s, when *Shudra Tapasvi* was published and then performed, Puttappa was among the most successful, prominent, and respected "Shudras" of his day and the first to rise so high in the university system of Karnataka, enjoying an extraordinarily successful career as a writer and public intellectual. In 1955, his four-volume retelling of Ramkatha won the Sahitya Akademi Award for literature. As devotee of Lord Rama, Ramkatha was close to Puttappa's heart. His commitment to ahimsa (non-violence) and reasoned reflection is evident in the radical ways that he has transformed Shambuka's story.[2]

The excerpt from *Shudra Tapasvi* (scenes 2 and 3 from a three-scene play) shows particular rhetorical skill in the use of epithets to highlight the power of knowledge and demonstrate the drawbacks of assuming that dharma-shastras contain all truth. For the sake of variety, Indian poets often use epithets, words, or phrases expressing some quality possessed by the person being addressed, in place of a character's name. Puttappa's epithets function more profoundly, disclosing that the Brahmin's thinking depends on prejudice, superstition, and self-contradiction. At this point in the play, Puttappa's stage directions instruct Rama to speak "ironically but seriously." This section of the play turns into a verbal duel.

Each man uses a carefully chosen epithet to warn that the other must act according to precedents that function as standard for approved behavior. Rama begins the battle by asking the Brahmin whether tapas is a holy practice. The Brahmin first addresses him with the epithet "King of the Raghu Lineage,"

---

1. In addition to rewriting Shambuka's story, Puttappa also rethought the sacrifice of Ekalavya's thumb in *Beralge Koral* [A Head for a Thumb], from the Mahabharata. See Chandrasekhara (1960: 35–37). Puttappa ["Kuvempu"] is one of the early giants of Kannada literature. It is said that "for Kannadigas," Kuvempu is "like Tagore is for Bengalis." Nonetheless, outside of Karnataka, few people seem aware of how radical his telling of Ramkatha has been. For example, in his lyric poem *Sri Ramayana Darshanam* that recounts the whole Ramayana story, he portrays both Rama and Sita going through the fire ordeal in order to purify themselves and Sita promising that Ravana will receive her affection in one of his future births (1955).
2. Puttappa's innovative championing of non-violence is even more radical. He omits Hanuman's burning of Lanka because it would be wrong for Hanuman to cause the death of so many innocent people (1955).

thereby warning Rama to maintain his lineage's unsullied prestige, and then affirms that tapas is unequalled in virtue. Rama calls the Brahmin "Eminent among the Enlightened Ones," indicating his respect for eminence in spiritual wisdom, the only kind of knowledge that can cut off rebirth, and hence lead to enlightenment. The epithet suggests that a person schooled in the highest knowledge cultivates detachment from worldly affairs, and hence would not seek Shambuka's death, since ultimate truth transcends life and death.

The duel soon ratchets up to a higher level of intensity. Addressing the Brahmin as "One Who Knows Wisdom" to imply that one must abandon ignorance, Rama inquires whether it is a sin to kill a person who performs tapas. The Brahmin concedes that such a deed would be a sin but, in a surprising turn, addresses Rama as "Killer of Vali." The Brahmin thus insinuates, through his choice of this unexpected epithet, that to rid Rama's kingdom of Shambuka, Rama must again stoop as low as he did when he murdered Vali.[3]

Rama, now valiantly curbing his anger, demands to know whether it would be a sin to kill Shambuka. Addressing Rama as "Disciple of Vasishtha" to remind him that his guru Vasishtha taught strict adherence to caste hierarchy, the Brahmin responds that one must look not to logic (*tarka*) but to dharma-shastras for the answer to Rama's question. He adds, definitively, that although milk is sacred, that doesn't mean you can drink dog's milk, and he compares a Shudra's tapas to dog's milk. With tongue in cheek, Rama praises the Brahmin as "Great Teacher" and compliments him on his erudition, thereby implying that he is clever but lacks wisdom. Only after this verbal battle does the Brahmin announce that he wants Rama to shoot Shambuka with the deadly missile called "Brahma's arrow," which Rama used to kill Ravana. The Brahmin insinuates thereby that Shambuka's practice of tapas falls in the same category as Ravana's tyrannical acts that oppressed all the inhabitants of the earth.

When Rama grants the Brahmin's request by launching Brahma's arrow, it first venerates Shambuka, then heads straight toward the Brahmin. Rama urges him to "open the eye of intellect," but the Brahmin clings to the idea that even logic is adharmic if it contravenes shruti, a term for teachings revealed in the earliest Hindu texts. As if texts themselves were answering the Brahmin, a voice from the heavens then declares, in Sanskrit verse, that recourse to scripture is insufficient for determining what constitutes dharma. As enlightenment finally dawns upon the Brahmin, he takes refuge with Shambuka and the weapon spares his life.

This outcome proves the potency of Shambuka's asceticism, since it was the accumulated power of his tapas that saved the Brahmin's life. The missile accomplished its aim, since it destroyed the Brahmin's bigotry. In addition, Puttappa's ending also adheres to the convention that classical Indian plays should end auspiciously: the drama concludes with Shambuka blessing both the Brah-

---

3. At the time of Vali's death, when Rama was questioned about shooting Vali in such a cowardly way, Rama justified his action in largely strategic terms: he resorted to an adharmic act because there was no other way to rid the monkey kingdom of Vali.

min and his son, who has come back to life. By the play's end, Rama has shown himself to be dharmic, non-violent, compassionate, and—not least—a teacher who has destroyed the Brahmin's ignorance.

Source: Kuppalli Venkata Puttappa, *Kuvempu Samagra Nataka Samputa* [Complete Plays of Kuvempu], ed. K. C. Shivareddy (Hampi, Shimoga: Kannada University, 2004), pp. 199–225.

———————

Shudra Tapasvi (excerpt)
BY "KUVEMPU" KUPPALLI VENKATA PUTTAPPA

Scene 2

RAMA: (Enters with a royal gait)
Where is the mourner
whose heartrending wails
shatter the peace of Ayodhya
on this bright spring night?
(Sighs)
When I heard him grieving,
my own wretchedness about Sita
surged back.
Where is he? Where's he gone?
(Looks around)
That weeping came from this garden.
(With an ironic smile)
Lamentation has become
the leitmotif of my life.
Grief and tears are the price one pays
for being an avatara.
(Notices Brahmin)
Someone is coming this way.
(Looks)
A Brahmin—bent with age and sorrow.
He might be the one who was grieving.
(Takes a couple of steps towards him)

BRAHMIN: (Rushes forward)
Protector of the wretched on this earth!
Refuge of the tormented,
Lord of all the worlds,
Help me, help me!

RAMA: Please, get up.
You are a Brahmin, aged, and my elder.
You are like a guru to me.

BRAHMIN: My distress has made me rave. Forgive me.
Despair paralyzes one's mind.
Desperation strips one of one's dignity.

RAMA: Who are you? What is your sorrow?
BRAHMIN: That you should ask is enough.
> You!
> You brought forth from your navel
> Brahma, who created all Brahmins.
> Time is a mere child compared to you.
> How can one talk of age
> when you are older than the Creator of the World?

> It is natural to prostrate oneself
> before you.
> Even ordinary decorum dictates
> that one should prostrate oneself before a king.
> And, you are a great sage
> who has succeeded in tapas through love.
> Tapas is always great.
> How could one belittle tapas?

RAMA: Generosity is the mark of the great.
> Tell me, please, what ails you?

BRAHMIN: My five-year old child
> has been snatched away.

RAMA: What villain did that?

BRAHMIN: Yama, the Lord of Death.

RAMA: Oh, I see.

BRAHMIN: If you come with me,
> I will show you the spot.
> And there, the body of my only child.
> (Weeps)
> You are a treasure of kindness.
> Faced with catastrophe,
> everyone calls your name
> and receives your aid.

> Ocean of Compassion,
> nothing is too difficult for you.
> We have seen your adamantine strength:
> Faced with slander,
> you did not hesitate to discard your wife
> the beautiful Sita
> and send her off to the jungle
> although she was pregnant
> and had already proved her innocence
> by entering the fire.

RAMA: (His face becomes clenched and he sighs)
> Enough, sir, of that saga.

Are you using my anguish
to contain yours?
Setting the town ablaze
does not extinguish the forest fire.
BRAHMIN: Forgive me, King!
Please bring my son back to life.
RAMA: I am puzzled by your tale.
Yama, the Lord of Dharma,
would not act so rashly
in my kingdom.

I am sure there's been
some transgression of dharma somewhere.
If he has been guilty
of taking away the life of a young child,
he shall pay for it.
But I doubt if that's the case.
Perhaps you have unknowingly
erred somewhere?
BRAHMIN: My parents were impeccable in their conduct.
Also, my guru trained me in piety.
I am a born Brahmin, King.
RAMA: My kingdom is blessed
to have a personage like you.
Do you then suspect anyone else
of misconduct that may have
cost your son his life?
Tell me if you do.
I shall destroy him.
When the root cause is eliminated
the effect mends itself.
(With authority)
No adharmic person shall live in my kingdom.
(Rama's virtuous rage frightens the Brahmin. He stands blinking. Rama
reassures him.)
RAMA: Don't be afraid. Speak your mind.
BRAHMIN: Forgive me, Great Being,
but my tongue hesitates.
RAMA: To speak the truth?
BRAHMIN: No, to hold up your own name
to your face.
RAMA: (A little startled, speaks to himself)
I seem to be the source
of all offenses—

the Washerman that day
and now this Brahmin.[4]
(Aloud)
Revered Brahmin, truth is worshiped.[5]
It is not right to be afraid of it.
Certainly, I have never shied away from it.
Truth is beneficial to all—
the young and the old,
those who speak it and those who hear it.

So tell me, where I have erred?
You are a guru not only by birth
but by practice.
So please tell me right away.
BRAHMIN: Protector of Good People, I'll tell you.
This morning my son and I went
to pick flowers for our daily puja.
We entered the woods
that shall remain nameless.
RAMA: Do they have a name?
Where are they?
BRAHMIN: Saying the name would pollute a person.
It lies in the direction of death.
RAMA: How can a name be so vile?
Tell me.
BRAHMIN: That wild jungle is known
as the ashram of Shambuka.
RAMA: (Thoughtful)
Ah, I see light.
And then?
BRAHMIN: Then? What then, Great Lord?
We saw him doing tapas.
Shambuka! A Shudra!
A heretic in the garb of an ascetic!
(Rama frowns. The Brahmin to himself.)
Whatever that Shudra deserves
Is going to happen.
The mere mention of that adharma
inflames the face of Ravana's Slayer.
RAMA: (Assumes a soft manner)
Did you do obeisance to him?

---

4. According to a story that tells of events that occur after Rama's cornation, a washerman has taunted his unfaithful wife by saying that, unlike King Rama, the washerman will not accept back an impure wife.
5. Alludes to the Sanskrit adage *satya sarvo pujam*, "truth is worshipped everywhere."

BRAHMIN: (Covers his ears)
>Shiva! Shiva! Shiva!
>We did nothing so foul.
>It is true that my innocent child
>was about to do obeisance,
>but I reprimanded him.
>"No," I said, "no deference to a Shudra!"
>Never!

RAMA: (Ironically)
>After all, you are the Vedas incarnate.

BRAHMIN: I should deserve to go to hell
>if I didn't correct
>at least such adharma
>while living in your kingdom.

RAMA: True enough. Now you have done the deed
>that could win you heaven.
>So you think your child
>has gone to heaven from that good deed?

BRAHMIN: No, no, Ramachandra,
>your young subject
>has fallen victim
>to the adharma
>of a Shudra doing tapas.
>To the transgression
>of varnashrama dharma.

>Had my child lived
>who knows what heights
>he may have scaled,
>what shastras studied,
>what epics composed,
>what secret powers mastered
>through tapas?
>That ward of yours
>has been the victim of
>a Shudra's tapas.[6]

RAMA: (In anger, but also with kindness, says to himself)
>How shall I teach a lesson
>to this bigoted pedant
>drunk with the pride of varna?
>Shambuka is a great yogi.
>Dharma, angered by this man's affront to the rishi,

---

6. In the first scene of the play, the audience learns that the Brahmin's son died of a snake bite. The Brahmin believes the bite is bad karma that occurred because Shambuka was performing tapas.

has brought sudden death to his child
even in my kingdom.
But blind to his own faults
he vituperates Shambuka openly
and me by implication.
(After thinking, he continues)
Venerable Twice-born,
show me the woods of Shambuka.
Let's go there.
Let's obliterate the evil.
In Rama's kingdom
adharma is death.
Justice shall triumph over death.
When Dharma succeeds
Death is defeated.

BRAHMIN: (To himself)
If censuring him can be so productive
what couldn't praise achieve?
(To Rama)
Let's go, Destroyer of Demons.
I am indeed blessed.

RAMA: Come.
(Looks at the sky)
Let's fly to the hermitage of Shambuka
in my celestial chariot.
(Celestial chariot arrives and takes them into the sky)

Scene 3

(The wilder regions of Shambuka's ashram, bathed in moonlight, immersed in silence. Stretched out next to a flower bush growing out of an anthill lies the body of the Brahmin child. The shadow of Death hovers over the dead body.[7]

Not too far in the distance, one can see the indistinct figure of the Great Rishi Shambuka, lost in meditation. Thick foliage covers him. His wild whiskers and knotted hair have grown entwined in vines. An anthill has climbed up the lower half of his body. A glow envelopes the entire scene. So completely has the figure of the rishi merged with the surrounding nature that it can be made out only when inspected closely.

Suddenly the wilderness becomes animated. Wind blows. The vegetation begins to toss about. Death reverently bows her head towards the direction from which Shri Rama emerges, accompanied by the Brahmin. Rama's face glows with heightened emotion. He speaks to himself.)

---

7. Although Death in Sanskrit texts is usually a male, Yama, Puttappa has portrayed Death as a female figure in this play.

RAMA: Such peace informs this beauty.
　It's palpably a rishi's abode.
　Truly, nothing can equal tapas in its glory.
　(He is so moved, he seems lost in meditation.)
BRAHMIN: (To himself)
　This king is most unusual.
　How intensely this palace-dweller
　Adores wilderness!
　How deeply he adores it.
　Having sent Sita to the forest
　the forest has become Sita for him.
RAMA: (To the Brahmin)
　Please, show me the spot.
BRAHMIN: Come, Lord, I'll show you.
　(Leads)
　There. There, Lord of Kosala—
　lying there is the jewel of my family.
　(Rushes forward)
　Save him. Please, save my darling.
　(Collapses by the body)
RAMA: (Fighting back tears, to himself)
　This father's grief
　would agitate a stoic's heart.
　It brings back in a rush
　my own father who died heartbroken
　separated from me.
　Isn't it strange?
　Death distresses even those
　who've known immortality.
　It's only backstage
　that the truth of the drama strikes home.
　(Comes to the Brahmin)
　Don't cry like a child.
　You are an enlightened man.
　When adharma is set right
　your son will escape death.
BRAHMIN: (Ecstatic with happiness)
　'Your son will escape death.'
　Your words can't fail to come true.
　My son will escape death!
　So, King, dispatch that adharma right away.
RAMA: (Beaming to Death, who is still standing by reverently)
　What brings you here to this forest of tapas?
　(Smiling)
　Are you fasting?

DEATH: (Smiles)
    I am doing tapas.
RAMA: (Joking)
    With what inauspicious objective?
DEATH: I am performing tapas
    for your victory over adharma.
RAMA: Many thanks to you.
DEATH: I am blessed.
BRAHMIN: (Looking at Rama in dismay, he says to himself)
    Who is the Dark One talking to?[8]
RAMA: Eminent one among the Twice-born,
    show me the place where the Shudra
    without authority to do tapas
    is practicing tapas.
BRAHMIN: (Points)
    There. Next to that anthill.
RAMA: (To himself)
    What a tongue this Brahmin has.
    Every word of his rips open an old wound.
    That reference to the anthill
    touches me to the quick
    by recalling the great poet
    who is sheltering Sita today.
    That poet too is a Shudra
    like Shambuka.
    Born a hunter, he too achieved
    greatness through tapas.
    Truly, nothing can equal tapas in its glory.
    (He looks in the direction pointed out by the Brahmin and, on
    the pretext of preparing his bow, he does obeisance to Rishi
    Shambuka.)
BRAHMIN: (Startled, to himself)
    What's this? Is he doing obeisance
    to the heretic doing tapas
    or is he adjusting his bow?
    I can't make any sense
    of this king's eccentricities.
    (He stands in awe)
RAMA: (Turning to the Brahmin)
    Eminent One among Gods on Earth,
    would you kindly dispel
    a small concern of this Kshatriya?

---

8. Krishna and Rama, Vishnu's avataras, are portrayed as having dark skin. Puttappa thus takes the opportunity to remind his reader that Rama has dark skin, as do many "Shudras."

BRAHMIN: (Modestly)
    I'll draw upon what little
    my feeble intellect knows.
RAMA: (Ironically, but serious)
    I shall be grateful for illumination.
BRAHMIN: Great King, I'll do my best.
RAMA: Isn't tapas an action to be venerated?
BRAHMIN: King of the Raghu Lineage,
    is there anything equal to tapas?
RAMA: Eminent One among the Enlightened Ones,
    the person who performs tapas—
    is he not worthy of reverence?
BRAHMIN: One of Good Conduct,
    he is, certainly.
RAMA: One Who Knows Wisdom,
    isn't it a sin to kill such a person?
BRAHMIN: Killer of Vali,
    undoubtedly.
RAMA: (Frowning slowly)
    Brahmin,
    in that case,
    isn't it a sin to kill this rishi?
BRAHMIN: Disciple of Vasishtha,
    you should know that
    Revealed Wisdom, not logic,
    has ultimate authority.

    And the shastras declare that
    a Shudra has no right to perform tapas.
    In the Krita Age
    only the Brahmin had the right.
    In the Treta, it was
    extended to the Kshatriyas.
    In the Dwapara, to the Vaishyas
    and in the Kali Age
    even Shudras will aspire to it.[9]
    That is why Dharma,
    which stood firmly on four feet in Krita,
    was reduced to three in Treta,

---

9. According to Hindu teachings about the nature of time, each eon has four ages (*yugas*). At the eon's start in the Krita Age, Brahmins perform the highest deeds and Dharma stands strong and firm on all four legs. As time passes during the Treta and Dwapara ages, Dharma stands, respectively, on three and then two legs, with Kshatriyas and then Vaishyas performing the highest deeds. In the degenerate Kali yuga, when Dharma can barely stand, even Shudras try to perform deeds reserved for Brahmins.

hobbled on two in Dwapara,
and in Kali Age tottering on one,
will collapse and be destroyed
at the end of time.

Protector of Varnashrama Dharma,
milk is worthy of worship and nourishes life.
But that doesn't mean you can drink dog's milk.
A Shudra's tapas is like dog's milk.

RAMA: (Hiding his anger behind irony)
Great Teacher, your erudition
has proven its worth.
Now, do you want me to shoot
my arrow at him?

BRAHMIN: Wielder of the Bow,
indeed I do.
This Shudra ascetic
deserves to be punished.

RAMA: Even though he is a Shudra,
his tapas gives him power.
A common arrow won't bring about his death.

BRAHMIN: Subduer of Enemies,
why don't you launch
the Brahmastra, that divine weapon
with which you chopped off
the ten heads of Mighty Ravana?
This man is in no way inferior
to that one in sinful deeds.

RAMA: Twice-born One,
that is a terrible weapon.
Once it bursts forth, it will not relent
until it has destroyed its enemy.

BRAHMIN: Then, it will be the perfect instrument
for this scoundrel.
Bearer of the Kodanda Bow, go ahead.[10]

(Shri Rama reaches for his quiver. The earth trembles. The sky thunders. The Brahmin hides behind Rama in sheer terror. Death, lost, shouts out.)

DEATH: Master of Destiny, wait. Wait.

RAMA: Why are you afraid?

DEATH: Are you merely play-acting
or is this in earnest?
What course am I to follow?

---

10. Name of Vishnu's bow.

RAMA: (Frowns)
Death,
no one is exempt from doing one's duty.
Let this great weapon be your guide.

DEATH: As you order!

(Head bowed, Death prepares to follow in the wake of the arrow. Rama commands her, "Seek out the sinner and destroy him!" and launches the arrow. Storm, thunder, and lightning ensue. Dust obscures the earth. The forest screams out in terror. Death pursues the Brahmastra, which approaches Rishi Shambuka, becomes docile, and finally prostrates itself in front of him. Death does the same. With a smile, Rama addresses the Brahmin who stares, stunned.)

RAMA: Guru, what is this?

BRAHMIN: Son of Dasharatha,
it is the dark influence
of this Shudra's tapas.
It has rendered your Brahmastra fruitless.

RAMA: Can a Brahmastra ever be fruitless?
It will soon bear fruit.

BRAHMIN: (Surprised)
How will that be?

RAMA: After prostrating itself before the Great Rishi,
it will head back this way.

BRAHMIN: This way? Why?

RAMA: To exterminate its enemy.

BRAHMIN: Who is that?

RAMA: The one who did adharma.

BRAHMIN: You mean the Shudra?

RAMA: No, I mean the Eminent Brahmin!

BRAHMIN: The Eminent Brahmin?

RAMA: The one who has insulted
those who deserve worship.
The one whose brain
is addled by the shastras.
The one who is irreverent
towards his betters.

BRAHMIN: (Slowly realizing Rama's meaning)
What?

RAMA: (Without looking at him)
You, Best of the Twice-born.

BRAHMIN: Protector of Orphans!
Refuge of Deprived Ones!
Save me!

RAMA: (Without looking at him)
It's not me you have insulted.

BRAHMIN: Master of Forgiveness,
    show me the way.
RAMA: (Without looking at him)
    The weapon will be the guide.
BRAHMIN: I'll do as you command.
RAMA: It is not enough that
    you follow my command.
    You must open the eye of intellect.
    Then the father will live
    and so will the child.
BRAHMIN: Best among Kshatriyas,
    I am afraid because
    it is against the shastras.
RAMA: A good act prompted by a good mind—
    does it need the support of the shastras?
    And yet, for your sake,
    I'll quote a proof text.
    Listen, One who Studies Shruti!
A VOICE IN THE SKY: [in Sanskrit]
    Recourse to scriptures alone
    will not help decide duty.
    A thoughtless act
    can only do harm to dharma.
BRAHMIN: (Stares silently at Rama and then suddenly)
    Omniscient One, you have taught a lesson
    to one who has been hidebound by tradition,
    warped by shastras
    blinded by jati.[11]

    What does the jati of firewood matter?
    Will it not burn?
    Will the fire differentiate?
    Will a conflagration hesitate
    whatever it may be?

    A tapasvi is to be venerated,
    whoever it may be.

    Showing respect brings merit
    Showing contempt brings sin.
RAMA: Now that you've come to understand,
    whatever you do, it will bring merit.

---

11. Jati refers to the specific community into which one is born. For example, "Brahmin" is the name of a varna, but the group of Madhva Brahmins from Mysore is a jati.

Best of Brahmins,
just as sugarcane,
however much you twist it,
will only pour out sweetness
and the ocean when churned
will only yield nectar,
Shambuka will only repay torment
with benevolence.

(The Brahmin walks toward Shambuka in a daze and prostrates himself in front of him. The woods exult. The heavens shower flowers. Divine drums resound. The shadow of Death disappears. The Brahmin boy sits up and rubs his eyes as though he has just woken from sleep.)

BOY: (Calls his father)

Father! Father!
Did I doze off
while picking flowers?
Where's father?
(Picks up his basket and advances. Sees Rama)
Who is this magnificent figure
shining like a God?

RAMA: Don't be afraid, child.

There. There's your father.
(Points to him)

(The boy runs to his father, calling out to him, and embraces him. The Brahmin, tearful with joy, leads his son to Rama.)

BRAHMIN: Child, do obeisance to Shri Ramachandra,

Lord of Sita, King of Kings,
who has protected us both.

(The boy does so. Shri Rama picks him up, caresses him, and points to Rishi Shambuka.)

RAMA: Do obeisance to that great ascetic.

Young Twice-born, by this rishi's grace
you have truly become a twice-born.
Even from a distance,
the fruits of tapas are realized.

(The boy bows to him.)
In my arms, let your hands
convey my homage to him.
May all prosper!
May the kingdom be free of misfortune!
May order triumph!

(The Brahmin too does obeisance along with his son. The thick bushes covering Rishi Shambuka shake. Two arms appear from them and freeze in a gesture of benediction. Vina music fills the heavens. A shower of flowers transforms itself into the final curtain.)

Translated from Kannada
by Girish Karnad and
K. Marulasiddappa

12 Shambuka's Story Anew

C. Basavalingaiah (b. 1977) became involved with drama through Samudaya, a street theater movement begun in 1975 during the Indian Emergency to combine messages of social activism with excitement about new theatrical forms.[1] It organized performance festivals (*jatras*) to foster socio-political awareness among laborers in rural areas. Basavalingaiah entered Samudaya as a student and became a pivotal member of the group. Later, he attended the National School of Drama in Delhi, graduating with a specialization in direction.

During his years as director of Rangayana, a dramatic academy in Mysore, he began theatrical work designed to inculcate an early taste for theater in children, a project that led to the Chinnara Mela, a festival in which twenty-five hundred children participated. In addition to *Shudra Tapasvi*, which has been staged multiple times and won national acclaim, Basavalingaiah has directed many other plays.[2] In addition, he has been involved in direction, stage design, and drama criticism. More recently, he has become active in film as well.

Sources: Productions of *Shudra Tapasvi*, Rangayana, Mysore; discussion with cast and director Prasanna, November 15–17, 2002. Interview with Basavalingaiah, January 4, 2005, Bangalore.

Basavalingaiah Re-presents *Shudra Tapasvi*

Performance Essay by Paula Richman

Valmiki had told Shambuka's story as an affirmation of caste hierarchy and brahminical privilege, but "Kuvempu" K.V. Puttappa radically transformed the narrative in his 1944 play *Shudra Tapasvi* [*The Shudra Ascetic*] by removing the stigma of adharma from Shambuka's shoulders and showing the respect with which Rama viewed Shambuka. In 1999, the play was revived more than half a century after its initial performance by C. Basavalingaiah. He went one step further in rethinking the relationship between the Shudra tapasvi and the Kshatriya king. The director presented Puttappa's story about the power

---

1. This summary of Samudaya is based on Ramesh (2000: 16) and interviews with Basavalingaiah and Prasanna. Samudaya's earliest play was Prasanna's *Huttava Dadidare*, with music by B. V. Karanth, which examined kingship from the perspective of the proletariat. Two early Samudaya plays dealt with the killing of rural Dalit agricultural laborers.
2. Basavalingaiah also directed another major play by Puttappa: *Shmashana Kurukshetra* (Kurushetra, the Cremation Ground), based on an incident from Mahabharata. The play takes place at midnight after eighteen days of battle, when the Dwapara yuga gives way to the Kali yuga.

of tapas performed by a Shudra, using performance styles drawn largely from Shudra folk drama. By doing so, Basavanlingaiah's production actualized Puttappa's principle of respecting cultural acts of "low caste" people.

Most stage directors, following the lead of Puttappa himself, viewed *Shudra Tapasvi* as too static for staging. As the first person to articulate concerns about his play's stageability, Puttappa himself comments on its shortcomings in the play's preface, stating, "the play is useless from the point of view of the theater."[3] Several features account for the assessment. First, the play's main goal is to depict the transformation of a character's mind—not promising material for an action-oriented medium such as the stage. Second, *Shudra Tapasvi* contains a number of lengthy speeches and is written for a small cast of all-male characters. Third, the play lacks comic interludes and grand battle scenes to vary the play's texture. Fourth, *Shudra Tapasvi* does not contain the songs, dances, and complexity of plot that those attending Kannada plays in the 1940s would have expected—whether in ritual dramas at festivals, spectacles mounted by professional companies, or newly emerging social dramas enacted by dramatic groups at colleges.[4] Finally, the play is quite a bit shorter than most performances of its day.

The play's elevated linguistic register also limits its appeal to audiences. Written in a grandiloquent style that features Sanskritized vocabulary, complex word play, and phrases chosen for their musicality and rhythm, the script assumes the listener's familiarity with high literary style.[5] The consensus among most was that Puttappa's script worked better for readers than directors. That Puttappa saw the play's ideal audience as a well-read literary connoisseur with the ability to conjure up its incidents and characters in the mind's eye is indicated by his comment in his preface: "It [*Shudra Tapasvi*] therefore has to be imaginatively visualized on the screen of one's mind."[6]

Theater director Basavalingaiah conceptualized an original and compelling way to stage *Shudra Tapasvi*. His production earned acclaim locally in Karnataka and later at a pan-Indian level, when it was staged at the National School of Drama in Delhi as part of its Indian theater festival in 2001.[7] Basavalingaiah lengthened the duration of the play, involved a substantially larger cast than the original, and incorporated aspects of Kannada folk theater into the performance. Basavalingaiah, who was born into a Dalit family, views theater a means of education and social change that can reach illiterate groups and audiences in both urban and rural areas. His restaging of *Shudra Tapasvi* reflects his longstanding commitment to making modern theater accessible to various audi-

---

3. Puttappa (2004: 191–192). An excerpt from the preface was also included in the program notes for Basavalingaiah's production of *Shudra Tapasvi*.
4. For a survey of the types of theater prevalent at the time, see H. K. Ranganath (1982: 80–163).
5. Indeed, it was for this reason that G. S. Sivarudrappa (2002) decided to translate two of Puttappa's plays into a less exclusive idiom that would be more accessible to general readers.
6. Puttappa (2004: 192).
7. National School of Drama (2002).

ences. His production also reveals a power and topicality to the play that was not fully realized when *Shudra Tapasvi* was first performed in the mid-1940s.

Basavalingaiah's pivotal innovation called for providing Shambuka's story three times within the play: (1) as narrative recounted by members of the chorus, (2) through the lyrics of songs and movement of dance, and (3) by enacting Puttappa's scripted dialogue. In essence, Basavalingaiah did the equivalent of helping an audience appreciate *The Tempest* more fully by (1) relating its story in today's English, (2) then presenting sections of the original script sung to popular musical tunes, and (3) enacting Shakespeare's lines.[8] The prose and musical renditions, which tell the story and reflect upon it, provide a framework within which those unused to the semantics of elevated poetry can first encounter the story. At the same time, those who are schooled in the poetic conventions relevant to Puttappa's language can also enjoy the songs and dances, which transform an otherwise fairly static play into a lively and memorable piece of theater. Multiple tellings, thus, make the play accessible to members of the audience possessing varying degrees of familiarity with Kannada literary language.

Although Basavalingaiah added songs and dance to *Shudra Tapasvi*, he respected Puttappa too much to threaten the play's textual integrity by adding lines written by others to it. Instead, he incorporated into Puttappa's 1944 play only what he himself had written in his preface and stage directions, making them the basis for added songs and choral sections.[9] In the preface, Puttappa had summarized the story of Shambuka attributed to Valmiki, noted how Bhavabhuti revised the story in *Uttararamacharita,* and explained why he felt compelled to tell the story in a way that differed from both of them. Basavalingaiah took this prose from the preface and inserted it right at the beginning of *Shudra Tapasvi*. He also drew prose from the stage directions that Puttappa placed at the beginning and end of scenes or before certain speeches, which explain which sound effects should be produced or provide guidance about emotions to be conveyed by the actor at a particular point in the play.[10] Consequently, more of Puttappa's words appeared in Basavalingaiah's production than in the 1944 production that Puttappa supervised.

Incorporating parts of Puttappa's preface at the beginning of Basavalingaiah's production also invested the play with a notable self-reflexivity about Ramayana tradition. Self-reflexivity occurs when one, while in the midst of hearing one version of the story, reflects upon other ways in which Rama's story has been told or upon the process of telling the story itself. For example,

8. The comparison to a play by Shakespeare is not an arbitrary choice, since Puttappa wrote a Kannada play based on *The Tempest.* Puttappa sets the incidents in the play on a river island in the Western Ghats of Malnad district, the area of his birth and childhood.
9. Also added were affirmative responses and exclamations of agreement, surprise, emphasis, and encouragement such as "*howda*" (yes) spoken by members of the chorus in response to words uttered in the play.
10. An example of such stage direction is, "His [Rama's] face is melancholy. He looks around as though he is searching for something. He walks gently, seriously, like hope, like grace itself."

one telling of Ramkatha portrays Sita asking Rama, who refuses to let her accompany him to the forest, "Have you ever heard of a Ramayana in which Sita doesn't accompany Rama to the forest?"[11] The question foregrounds the multiple ways the story has been told, doing so in relation to the dilemma being explored by the characters at that moment. In a similar way, Basavalingaiah directs the audience's attention to the multiple tellings of Rama's story when he begins *Shudra Tapasvi* with Puttappa's thoughts on renditions by Valmiki and Bhavabhuti.[12]

By putting words from Puttappa's preface in the mouths of a nearly all-female chorus, Basavalingaiah casts his play in light of Rama's soliloquy where Puttappa links Shambuka, Sita, and Valmiki (see the remarks that introduce part 2). The passage suggests that the dichotomy between pure and impure has subordinated Sita as well as Shambuka. Viewing high caste males as the pinnacle of caste hierarchy simultaneously subjugates low caste males and women of all castes. By creating a primarily female chorus, Basavalingaiah incorporates gender issues quite visibly into the fabric of a play whose scripted characters are all male.[13] As several actors in the chorus noted, "Basavalingaiah told us often that the most oppressed people in our society are women, especially untouchable women. So it is appropriate that they should be part of the storytelling in this play."[14]

Basavalingaiah incorporated a choral style that intensifies the process of exploring relations between caste and asceticism, a theme central to *Shudra Tapasvi*. The costumes, song patterns, and gestures he chose are those of the Jogatis of Karnataka, a group of staunch devotees of Yarlamma.[15] Jogatis are Shudra women who have renounced marriage or hijras (men who dress as women) who have renounced masculinity.[16] The renunciation of sexuality that these performers undertake makes it well-suited to a play whose central character is an ascetic. Basavalingaiah's choice of Jogati style reiterates the major theme of the play since Jogatis are Shudras, as were Shambuka and Puttappa.

---

11. Nath (1913: 39). Ramanujan (1991: 33) calls attention to the self-reflexivity of this passage.

12. For analysis of Bhavabhuti's presentation of the story, see Shulman (2001: 54, 60).

13. Usually, a repertory company's director seeks scripts that make resourceful use of the troupe's talent. Adding a chorus allowed Basavalingaiah to include more actors than if the production contained only the characters in Puttappa's script. Also, since the script contained only male roles, the actresses in the company would otherwise have been excluded from the play.

14. I thank Prasanna, Director of Rangayana in Mysore, for inviting me to a rehearsal, making it possible for me to see two performances of *Shudra Tapasvi*, and arranging a group discussion with actors Ramu S., Jagdeesh Manevarte, Mahadev, Ramnath S., Manjunath Belekere, Hulugappa Kattimani, Prashanth Hiremath, Santosh Kusunoor, Geetha M. S., Prameela Bengre, Shashikala B. N., Nandini K. R., Saroja Hegde, Vinayak Bhat, Noor Ahmed Shaikh, and Krishnakumar, as well as designer Dwarakanath, costume designer Raghunandan, manager Gangadhar Swamy, music director Srinivas Bhat, and musician Anju Singh.

15. Yarlamma's husband, the ascetic Jamadagni, ordered their son to behead her. After the boy did so and was granted a boon, he asked for his mother's return to life. By mistake, the head that was put back on her body was that of a Dalit woman. Now worshipped as a goddess, she is known in Sanskrit tales as Renuka and Yarlamma, Yellamma, or Yerlamma locally. For an English translation of a Sanskrit version of the story, see van Buitenen (1973: 445–446).

16. For information about the Jogatis, see *Encyclopedia of South India* (1991, 1: 586).

Equally crucial, Shambuka and the Jogatis both perform tapas, the religious practice at the core of the play.

Basavalingaiah also weaves into *Shudra Tapasvi* theatrical devices from two other Kannada folk traditions. He uses the oversize masks of Somana Kunita drama in his costumes for the characters playing Death and her minions. The huge, terrifying masks make visible the lethal risk that Shambuka has taken, since a Shudra who performs tapas should be beheaded, according to dharma-shastras. Basavalingaiah also draws upon Yakshagana, dance-drama that de-picts warriors engaged in battle with potent weapons.[17] Basavalingaiah uses the intricate footwork and stylized whirling of Yakshagana to choreograph Rama's movements, particularly as he prepares to launch his Brahmastra. In each case, Basavalingaiah uses folk elements judiciously to enhance the representation of what Puttappa had depicted in his script.

Analysis of a device drawn from Yakshagana shows that Basavalingaiah's choices serve not as distracting add-ons or slick gimmicks but as ways to reveal heretofore hidden aspects of characterization. Basavalingaiah borrows from Yakshagana a specific prop: a large piece of cloth that prevents an actor from being seen by the audience while on stage behind it. In *Shudra Tapasvi,* the cloth works to separate from each other (in time and space) the two actors who play the Brahmin, so that only one of them can be seen by the audience at any given time. To bring the second person playing the Brahmin onto the stage, two men enter the stage at either side of a person-size piece of cloth, concealing an actor who walks behind it. When they reach the point where the hidden actor should appear, the men turn slightly parallel to the audience and begin to walk in a circle. Consequently, the actor who has been playing the Brahmin until now soon disappears behind the cloth and a new Brahmin becomes visible, seeming to emerge from behind the other side of the cloth.

What is the payoff of this staging device? The first Brahmin, who requested that Rama kill Shambuka in revenge for his son's death, looks frail and an-guished, his hair shaven and his body shrunken from fasting and mourning. Lest sympathy for the father blind one to the Brahmin's pride, bigotry, and vindictive obsession with killing Shambuka, a second Brahmin replaces him on stage. The Brahmin whom the cloth discloses is tall, broad, and muscular with knee-length dark hair unbound and whirling about him like a vengeful demon. As this Brahmin gleefully waits for Brahma's arrow to end Shambuka's life, the whole apparatus of caste hierarchy is revealed—its brutality, power, and menace. The second Brahmin, concealed except in this one section of the play, reveals how brahminical ideology and practice insure that Shudras who refuse to stay in their place die at the hand of the king. By using the revolving cloth to present the brahminical power behind individual Brahmins, the play reveals what supports each Brahmin: a regime of social discipline designed to main-tain subordination and murder those who resist brahminical hegemony.

---

17. The most popular Yakshagana performances feature epic battles, especially from the Maha-bharata. See *Seagull Theatre Quarterly* (2000: 25/26) and Ashton and Christie (1977).

Puttappa called his play "useless from the point of view of the theater," and in 1944 Kannada theater may have lacked the dramatic resources to do full justice to *Shudra Tapasvi*. Kannada theater has developed significantly during the last fifty years, however, and has the means to stage *Shudra Tapasvi* in a way that enacts the nuances of Puttappa's script. Rather than "dumbing down" a play that many found inaccessible, Basavalingaiah enriches it with the cultural capital of Kannada folk tradition. He draws upon regional non-brahminical dramatic traditions not like a tourist seeking local color but like Puttappa's heir enhancing the visibility of those people marginalized by brahminical exclusivity.

The subtlety and craftsmanship of Puttappa's play was, and still is, savored by literary connoisseurs and students of Kannada literature. Basavalingaiah's recent restaging of *Shudra Tapasvi* makes it accessible to a larger group, while showing that it is not only as an excellent literary composition but an effective script for performing. His staging demonstrates how *Shudra Tapasvi* can be produced in a way true to Puttappa's deepest convictions. Multiple performance styles, suggests Basavalingaiah, can express Puttappa's central teachings of respect for Shudra forms of religious expression and Puttappa's belief in the compassion of Rama.

13 Ahalya Later

K. B. Sreedevi (b. 1940) was born into an orthodox Nambudri family, steeped in Vedic learning, in northern Kerala.[1] After secondary school, she continued her study of music and Sanskrit and began her career as a writer. She has written four novels, one of which was made into a film. Among the many short stories she has published, she has shown particular interest in female characters from the Ramayana narrative.[2] The story translated below, "Woman of Stone," takes place after Ahalya has been released from Gautama's curse and is traveling through the forest to attend a ritual at Valmiki's ashram. The short story also includes some flashbacks to earlier moments in Ahalya's life.

"Woman of Stone" reflects upon the relations among tapas, freedom, and blame. As a wife, Ahalya lived without affection because her husband had committed himself to a life of harsh penance. Although Ahalya was turned to stone after her union with Indra, Sreedevi suggests that her stony state enabled her to perform penance for her misdeed. For that reason, she earned deliverance from her curse when the dust from Rama's feet touched her. At various points in Sreedevi's story, Ahalya considers who is to blame for her curse, comparing Rama's gentle compassion to the anger of her husband, Gautama, and considering whether tapas makes one more compassionate or more stone-hearted. Just after Ahalya decides that it would be better if all men could be like Rama, she learns he has banished Sita. The news prompts her to realize that even Rama cannot transcend the anger of a jealous husband. When she then turns back into stone, she ensures that neither Gautama nor Rama will disappoint her ever again.

Source: K. B. Sreedevi, "Shilpe-rupini" [Woman of Stone], in *Grihalakshmi*, 1990.

Woman of Stone
BY K. B. SREEDEVI

How long it was since she had come this way.... She had last come a long time ago, as a child, with her father. When one journeys through the skies, one

---

1. "Nambudri" is the name of a jati of Brahmins in Kerala whose members are known for their adherence to the elaborate prohibitions believed to ensure their purity. According to their origin story, they were invited to Kerala by Parashurama himself, as part of his efforts to perform penance for killing Kshatriyas. These Brahmins adhered to some of the strictest ritual practices of any Brahmins in India. Information about the lives of Nambudri women in the twentieth century appears in the introduction to a collection of Lalithambika Antherjanam's stories and memoirs (1988) written by its translator, Gita Krishnankutty. Antherjanam was active in the Indian nationalist movement as well as the Kerala movement to gain increased rights for women.
2. For example, Sreedevi's "The Disrupted Coronation" (2001) concerns Manthara, Kausalya, Bharata, and Rama.

does not fully understand the beauty of the earth. Still, she remembered how, guessing what she wanted from the expression on her face, her father had reined in Brahma's swan to slow down the celestial chariot whenever they reached the banks of a sacred river or a hermitage. She would breathe in the pure fragrance of the ghee, the rice, and the nine sacred grains cooking in the sacrificial fires of the sages performing their rituals. When had all that taken place? Thousands of years ago? She had changed so much since then, hadn't she? Hadn't her whole life changed?

Or had it?

Time had changed, not Ahalya.

She walked forward. The flowering forest. Under the huge trees with roots that snaked down, the ground was like a carpet of flowers. The sun's rays, filtering through the branches, scattered more blossoms over the carpet of flowers. They made her happy.

Her husband had not objected to her wish to attend the final auspicious rituals that Great Rishi Valmiki would perform at the close of his tapas. All he had said was, "Convey my respects to that devotee of Rama, that greatest of sages."

In the old days, she had not been allowed to walk alone through this forest. Nor would she have dared to do so. But today, her husband harbored no doubts about her. Nor did she lack courage. When she went to ask leave of him, he placed both his hands on her bowed head and blessed her: "Peace be with you." Had this change taken place in him because the times had changed?

Shri Ramachandra had freed the forest of demons and freed human beings from fear. Shri Ramachandra himself had taught her not to fear anything except adharma. She had been astonished at the way in which he had vanquished Khara, Dushana, Trishira and an army of soldiers in just three and three-quarter hours.[3] He had told her: "Once you acquire spiritual strength, a quarter-minute is all you need to kill 14,000 evil demons. Spiritual strength surpasses physical strength."

She had never tired of hearing those words, limpid as the peal of temple bells, over and over again. The moment she saw him, she had realized the rewards of her tapas. His gentleness had enraptured her. "Ahalya, I see your heart. Awaken from the sleep which traps you in illusion."

Why couldn't sages speak like this? Because they had mastered curses with the power to destroy? Ahalya shuddered. She, mocking the virtuous?

She corrected herself at once. Had she forgotten the great Valmiki? Even his curse was just an explosion of anger springing from an incomparable compassion for life.[4]

Ahalya waited for a minute or two. She told herself it was the expression of

---

3. A reference to Rama's battle with Khara and his troops after Rama ordered Lakshmana to mutilate Shurpanakha.
4. Ahalya wonders whether the curses of all ascetics are driven by malice but remembers that Valmiki's curse emerged from compassion for a krauncha bird whose mate was slain.

a far-sighted vision rather than a curse. The great sage must have already understood the sacrificial fire that was Sita. He had realized that, to preserve the
human race, he had to prevent that fire from being extinguished, from being
evaluated before the whole world. That was why he . . .

Ahalya looked at her arms. The hair on them stood on end!

What was astonishing about that? Which woman would not be thrilled at
the memory of Sita?

Ahalya walked on. The murmurs, the bird calls in the forest delighted her
ears. She felt the past opening many doors in her mind and peering out.

How often, how endlessly she had felt these sensations: noting the change
of the seasons, seeing so many things, hearing so many! Experiencing all the
heights and depths with naked, unshielded eyes.

She tried to think each time—who had more compassion? The husband who
had enabled her to have all this? Or . . .[5]

One scene stood out with particular clarity in her mind: she had been stay-
ing in Gautama's hermitage, vulnerable to all the cruelty and tenderness of
nature. One day, while she stood with her head bowed after venerating the dusk
according to the prescribed ritual, she overheard a conversation nearby. Both
voices were women's. She knew they were from Mithila from their dialect and
their way of speaking. They had come to pluck the special lavanyakam flower
which grew only in the vicinity of Gautama's hermitage.

"Why does the young mistress [Sita] like this flower so much?" asked the
younger of the two women. The elder one answered: "Don't you know? She
knows that offering this flower in worship will earn her husband's love. Ahalya
Devi herself brought it from the abode of the gods, planted it here, and nurtured it."

"The young mistress is always absorbed in worship and meditation."

"And why wouldn't she be? Didn't you know those two krauncha birds are
here? They say Shri Ramachandra, King Dasharatha's son, will marry Sita."

"Ah, how fortunate. Indeed, it will bring good fortune to all of Mithila!"
Putting down her basket of flowers, she joined her palms and raised them to
her forehead.

"Ever since, the young mistress's mind has been immersed in thoughts of
Shri Ramachandra. She spends her days here waiting for him."

"Our baskets are full of flowers. Let's go back. I feel so sad when I stand here,
even now."

"Why? Why feel sad in such a beautiful place?"

"This hermitage feels completely empty without Ahalya Devi."

For a while neither of them spoke. Then she heard the younger woman's voice: "How did Ahalya Devi, so full of virtue, become the subject of a
scandal?"

"Che! What did you say?" The older voice was full of anger. "Ahalya Devi was

---

5. By marrying her, Gautama gave Ahalya the status of an auspicious wife. By delivering her from
the curse, Rama gave her back her life as a woman.

not born womb-born and she was very large-hearted.[6] Who knows whose fault it was? Come, let's go. Remember, the flowers we gathered are sacred and to be used for offering worship. Evil thoughts and words must not taint them."

They left.

She found the conversation of these servant women entertaining. Her mind envisioned Sita Devi, who used the flowers that Ahalya had grown and cared for as worship offerings and who spent her time longing for union with her husband. After that, she meditated on even Shri Ramachandra through Sita. And when that moment that she had prayed for so long finally arrived. . . .

When she had transcended love and hate and was almost emptied of all emotion, Rama had arrived before her, filled with radiance, looking more handsome than anyone in the world, to break through her inertness and awaken her.

She prayed for only one thing then: Sita Devi, may your waiting soon be fulfilled!

Ramachandra appeared to Sita after he had restored Ahalya to the way of action. She thought again, who had more compassion? Her detached husband, the observer of harsh tapas, who threw her cruelly onto the breast of the vast world, saying to her: "You know nothing about this world of illusion. Go and learn what it is, Ahalya!"

Or . . .

Ah, she had left the forest behind. Ahalya turned and looked all around. Had she reached the banks of the Tamasa River so quickly? How auspicious the river looked! As pure and beautiful as the minds of good people. She decided to stay there awhile and look at it. Then she heard the terrible sound. Of someone weeping. She saw a bark-clad woman who looked like an resident of Valmiki's hermitage, went up to her, and called gently, "My good woman!"

The woman wiped her tears and looked at her.

Ahalya asked with disbelief, "How can you be sad, in the precincts of this hermitage?"

"How can I tell you? The destruction of the world is at hand, that is certain."[7] She sobbed even harder.

"What happened?" Ahalya went closer to her to comfort her.

After a minute or two, the ascetic said, her voice trembling, "Shri Rama, the ruler of Ayodhya, has abandoned his wife Sita, full with child."

"What!" Ahalya's mouth fell open. "Is it true, what I hear?" Her voice was shrill with helplessness.

"Yes, my sister. Just a while ago the sage Valmiki, who had come to the Tamasa River to perform his afternoon rituals, came upon Sita Devi seated alone on the banks of the river, like an incarnation of sorrow. The great man offered the wife of Shri Rama shelter. I've come to look for the fruits she . . .

---

6. Brahma created Ahalya himself in heaven, endowing her with beauty unsurpassed by any other woman and then giving her to Gautama as a wife.
7. The woman from the ashram takes Sita's banishment as a harbinger of the imminent destruction of the universe.

Before she could complete the sentence, Ahalya's lament tore through the air.
"The fire has abandoned its own flame?
Prakriti has been disowned by Purusha?[8]
This terrible experience . . . his insult . . . his act of contempt . . ."
The ascetic who stood next to Ahalya realized that her voice was growing fainter and fainter. Watching her, she cried out anxiously, filled with consternation:
"My sister, my noble lady . . ."
There was no response.
She moved towards Ahalya. She laid her hand lovingly on that form. But she stepped back at once in fear.
"What? This is a stone statue!"
The words echoed along the banks of the Tamasa River like a great lament. People bathing in the river heard the sound and came running. They stared at that immobile and tender figure from head to foot. A beauty at which a man could gaze with a thousand eyes and yet feel he had not seen enough.
Then they saw that on its head were footprints with a thunderbolt and a fish on them.
They bent down quickly to look—the imprints of Shri Rama's hands on those infinitely beautiful feet.[9]
They raised their heads.
A face filled with the radiance of long tapas.
They all looked at one another and said in one breath: "But this is Gautama's wife."
The woman from Valmiki's hermitage who had become the companion of Rama's wife, Sita, said in a stern voice:
"Yes. Ahalya has turned into stone."

Translated from Malayalam by Gita Krishnankutty

---

8. According to Samkhya philosophy, the universe is made up of Prakriti, the animating materiality conceived of as female, and Purusha, the fundamental principle conceived of as male. Some have interpreted the story of Sita and Rama as recounting the union of Prakriti and Purusha. For a more extensive description of Purusha and Prakriti, see #9.

9. This passage suggests that Ahalya prostrated herself at Indra's feet, when he disguised himself as Gautama, to show respect for her husband. The thunderbolt and the fish signify Indra's role as the deity of rain. The monsoon brings abundant fish in rivers, as well as abundant harvests. The imprint of Rama's hands came when, as a young boy, he bowed at Ahalya's feet after freeing her from the curse (see #14). A similar use of the poetic contrast of hands and feet also appears in *Iramavataram,* where Kamban praises Rama's destruction of Tadaka as showing the power of Rama's hands and his deliverance of Ahalya as showing the power of his feet. Young Rama performs both actions when he accompanies Sage Vishvamitra to the forest. See Ramanujan's translation (1991: 31) of this passage in Kamban.

14 Consequences of a Misdeed

"Pudumaippittan" C. Virudhachalam (1906–1948) employed many genres during the fourteen years of his writing career. Within the genre of the short story, he engaged with a range of themes and forms as he observed the social changes and shifting political affiliations of the times. His early stories tend to be short and stark, biting in their satire, and he invented a staccato style for them, single sentences spread across a page, as he said, "like a frog leaping." Later, he developed a more discursive style. "Deliverance from the Curse" uses both styles. Many of his finest stories are in the realistic mode, but Pudumaippittan also explored fantasy, dream, and myth as modes of fictionalizing. In "Deliverance from the Curse," he explores alienation and loneliness within the mythic story of Ahalya and Gautama.

The story begins with Ahalya's release from Gautama's curse, after the dust raised by young Rama's feet settles on her. Rama absolves Ahalya of adultery, saying that any action must be judged by its intention or lack of it; Ahalya cannot be held responsible for Indra's deceit to which she did not give assent. The rest of the story takes off from this point, commenting on the main events of the entire Ramayana story from the perspective of Ahalya through an exploration of what dharma means.

Pudumaippittan introduces the element of psychological depth into the story, developing subtle symbolism to explore it. Unable to find any peace, Ahalya and Gautama undertake a pilgrimage that parallels the years of exile and wandering of Rama and Sita. But the landscape merely reflects their inner *palai* (aridity, wasteland) wherever they go.[1] When, eventually, Sita tells Ahalya the story of the fire ordeal, Ahalya's hope of the possibility of an alternate, more daring, definition of dharma is finally lost. The symbolism of stone is deployed with acuteness and force. At the beginning of the story, it is a punishment for passion; at the end, a voluntary withdrawal in protest against betrayal. Turning to stone once more, Pudumaippittan implies, is Ahalya's real deliverance from the curse of long ago. [L. H.]

Source: Pudumaippittan, "Sabavimosanam" [Deliverance from the Curse]. *Kalaimakal*, 1943; rpt. *Pudumaippithan Kathaikal*, ed. A. R. Venkatachalapathy (Nagercoil: Kalachuvadu Pathippagam, 2000), pp. 527–540.

---

1. In classical Tamil poetry, *palai* is the landscape denoting the wasteland or arid desert, which signals the theme of lovers' separation. Here separation is metaphoric: Ahalya and Gautama have experienced so much suffering and grief that their inner state is reflected in the bleak outer landscape.

Deliverance from the Curse
BY "PUDUMAIPPITTAN" C. VIRUDHACHALAM

(For those familiar with Ramayana, this story might be incomprehensible—unpalatable, too. I am not concerned about that.)

Along the path, a stone statue. A form so beautiful that it inspired a leaping desire in the most weary onlooker. It was as if a sculptor of rare ability had appeared on this earth for this single work alone, and had put all his dreams into stone. But from the eyes of the figure, a sadness—an inexpressible sadness—springs, overcoming the desires and lust of her onlookers and plunging them into sadness, too. For this is no sculptor's dream. This is the result of a curse. This indeed is Ahalya.

She lies in the forest path, a tragedy in stone, on Nature's lap; and Nature, like a renunciant, looks upon her tragedy with impartial eyes. The sun beats down. Dew descends. The rain falls in abundance. Dust and chaff, sparrows and small owls sit on her; they fly away. She lies there unconscious, a tapasvi lost in her penance; a stone.

Some distance away there is an anthill. Lost in meditation, empty of thoughts, forgetting his sorrow, Gautama performs his austerities. Nature, impartial, protects him too.

Still further off, in the same way as the cage of the couple's family life collapsed without a cross-beam, so too the roof that gave them shelter has fallen down for lack of support; has become dust, has scattered with the wind. The walls have disintegrated. All that is left now is the raised ground. It looks like the scar of the sorrow which filled their hearts.

In the distance, the rustle and ripple of the Ganga. Mother Ganga. Is she aware of the infinite tragedy of these two?

And so, aeons have passed by.

One day. . . .

The early morning sun was harsh enough. Yet the greenness and shade from the creepers, together with the kindly breeze, brought a certain comfort to the heart—like a religion which attempts to hide the sorrows of this world, and to inspire belief and courage.

Vishvamitra comes striding along, majestic, like a lion, reliving in his mind the sheer joy of having completed the duty he had taken up. Maricha and Subahu are not to be seen anywhere. That ancient malevolence, Tadaka, had been crushed. Vishvamitra enjoys the satisfaction of having been the means of bringing tranquility to all those engaged in dharmic concerns; meditation and sacrificial offerings.[2]

He turns round frequently, looking behind him. Such a tenderness in that

2. Rama and Lakshmana have just killed Tadaka, freeing the sages to practice their rituals without interference. Vishvamitra is now bringing the young boys to Mithila, where Rama will break Shiva's bow and win Sita as a wife.

look! Two young boys come along, playing, chasing each other. They are none other than Rama and Lakshmana, young avataras. They have already begun the destruction of the rakshasas, but do not yet understand its import; they run along, chasing each other.

Their game of chase raises a cloud of dust. Lakshmana comes running ahead; Rama is chasing him. The dust cloud settles over the statue. Vishvamitra, himself full of joy, turns round to see what the boys' hilarity is about. He stands still and gazes.

The dust cloud falls and spreads on the statue.

Within the statue, the heart that stopped and turned to stone, heaven knows when, begins to throb once again. The blood that clotted and dried in its many tracks begins to flow. A life-warmth pervades the stone and it becomes living, rounded flesh. Awareness returns to it.

Ahalya shuts her eyes and opens them. Her consciousness awakens. Deliverance! Deliverance from the curse!

Oh God! This fleshly body, once tainted, has been purified.

And the divine being who gave her, once again, a new life? Could it be that child?

She falls at his feet, folds her hands and makes obeisance. Rama looks towards the rishi in surprise.

Vishvamitra understands at once. She must be Ahalya. That artless girl who was deceived by God Indra in his magical disguise. Because of her excessive love for her husband, she allowed herself to be deceived by that magic disguise; allowed her body to become used. Gautama's wife. All this, Vishvamitra tells Rama. You see that anthill there; there is Gautama, lost in meditation, forgetful of himself, like the butterfly in silent penance in its cocoon. Look, he too stands up now.

His eyes, coming out of deep meditation, swirl around, like knives just sharpened on a whetstone. The life-force knits and courses through his body as if he has been fed on an elixir. He comes forward in haste, yet with some hesitancy, as if he cannot quite free himself from the woman's disgrace.

Once again, this snare of sorrow? His mind had not considered what sort of life there could be, after a deliverance from the curse. For the present, it still encircles his life, like a gigantic wall. She too is lost in perplexity.

Rama's entire education had trained him to look with the eyes of dharma. With the clear light of knowledge. He had not yet been sharpened against the whetstone of experience. Yet he had been taught by Vasishtha, who could look steadily upon each separate braided thread in life's tangles without breaking it. There was no smallness about him. He had the courage as well as the wisdom to strike upon a new path.

What kind of world is this that it ties itself into these troubling knots? Should someone be punished for something that happened without the assent of her conscious will and reasoning mind? "Amma," says Rama, falling at her feet.[3]

---

3. The Tamil term *amma* (mother) is used as a term of respect when a young person greets an elder woman.

Both rishis (the one who thought boldness essential to knowledge, and the other who saw that love alone is the basis of dharma) understood the youth's perspective and his reasoned conclusions; and they rejoiced.[4] What an easy truth, full of love yet so daring.

Vishvamitra says, quietly, "It is only right that you accept her; she did not err in her heart."

In the cooling air, the different harmony in his voice is apparent.

Neither Gautama, nor his wife, nor that scarred foundation without pillars, their former hut, had moved. Yet sentient life began to manifest itself in that once-dead place.

The forces that had come there to change the entire course of their lives, as if with a whiplash, had now disappeared. Should they not try to reach Mithila at least by nightfall? Married life beckoned now, with both hands.

Gautama could not speak to her, as he could once, from an unblemished heart. It was as if his burning accusation of her as a harlot, that day, so long ago, had succeeded only in scorching his own tongue. What could he say? What should he say?

"What would you like?" asked Gautama. In the swirl of emotions, commonsense and wit had deserted him and he could only push out these meaningless words.

"I am hungry," said Ahalya, like a child.

Gautama went to a nearby field and gathered all kinds of fruit. The desire and love which had played over everything he did in the very first days of their married life was apparent once again, in the movement and stillness of his hands.

"After all, our marriage only came to flower after we found pity and sympathy for each other; after an early disappointment. I only gained her hand after circling the divine Kamadhenu."[5] So said Gautama's heart, changing direction, accusing himself.

Ahalya ate her fill.

Between them flowed absolute compassion. Yet each was in anguish; trapped in a different prison.

Ahalya's only concern was whether she was right for Gautama.

Gautama's only concern was whether he was right for Ahalya.

The flowers that bloomed along the forest path watched them and laughed.

---

4. The rishis mentioned here perceive dharma in different ways. (1) Vishvamitra, a Kshatriya, originally ruled a kingdom. Later, he undertook particularly rigorous tapas for a thousand years, managing to transform himself into a Brahmin sage, thus moving across the nearly impossible-to-cross boundary between the two highest varnas. His experience thus involved boldness leading to some flexibility in a seemingly rigid dharmic system. (2) Sage Vasishtha, the family priest of the solar dynasty, abided by the letter of dharma, seeing each decision in light of it. Vishvamitra and Vasishtha fought when Vishvamitra insisted on taking Vasishtha's cow, Kamadhenu, by force. (3) Later in Pudumaippittan's story, a third theory of dharma is articulated: Sage Gautama, Ahalya's husband, had become convinced that intention, rather than action, determines what is dharmic.
5. Kamadhenu, Vasishtha's cow, fulfills desires, producing whatever a person wants.

2

Deferring to Ahalya's only wish, Gautama built a hut some distance away from the outer walls of Ayodhya, by the shores of the Sarayu, where the stench of humankind would not reach them. And there he studied the meaning of dharma. Now he had absolute faith in Ahalya. He would not have doubted her, even if she were to lie on Indra's lap. He believed her to be infinitely pure. And he was now in such a position that without her daily help all his philosophic enquiries would have been just dust and chaff.

Ahalya nourished him with her immeasurable love. At the thought of him, her mind and body felt overcome with the tenderness of a newly wedded bride. All the same, the stone that had entered her heart had not quite shifted away. She wanted to conduct herself always in such a way that no one would have reason to doubt her; not even to look at her in a particular way. Because of this, she forgot how to be natural; her behavior had changed in character. Those around her appeared to her as Indras. Fear entered her heart and froze it. The easy chatter and play of her former days deserted her, totally. Before she uttered anything, she repeated it like a lesson, a thousand times in her mind, examined each word, from all perspectives, to make sure it was the right one. She agonized over even casual words that Gautama spoke, wondering whether they contained some other meaning.

The very business of living became a hellish torment.

The other day, Maricha, the great rishi, had visited them. Some while ago Dadichi had come to their home. Matanga had looked in, on his way to Varanasi, enquiring after Gautama's health.[6] Although they were all full of concern and goodwill, Ahalya shrank from them. Her mind closed in on itself. She could scarcely bring herself to give them all the hospitalities due to guests. She was too shy to allow her clear eyes to meet even an ordinary gaze from other people. In the end, she hid herself in the hut.

Nowadays, Gautama's thoughts turned towards a different kind of enquiry. Now he held that all the fences and strictures of dharma applied only to those who acted in full consciousness of what they were doing. If a violation of the moral law happened without one's awareness and assent, then even though the entire seed of man is crushed because of it, yet it could not be judged a sin. The full intention of the mind, and the deed we do with such intention, is what marks us. Living in a broken-down hut, and starting once more from a position which was only the collection of other peoples' ideas, Gautama turned his thoughts in a new and different direction. In his mind, Ahalya walked about, sinless. It was he who had been unfit to accuse her; the anger which had invoked his fiery curse had tainted him alone.

---

6. Maricha, Dadichi, and Matanga are well-known forest sages. Especially noteworthy is Matanga, who encouraged the tribal woman, Shabari, to practice asceticism and devotion to Rama in his ashram. For an analysis of the complex relationship among Shabari, Matanga, and the other ascetics on the ashram, see Lutgendorf (2000).

From time to time, Rama and Sita would come in their direction, by chariot, on a pleasure trip. That young avatara in Gautama's imagination had grown into the ideal youth. His laughter and play were like ever-burning lamps, and sufficient commentary to the dharma-shastras. That rare affinity between those two young people! It reminded Gautama of his own life of long ago.

Sita was the dove who came to ease the burden upon Ahalya's heart. Sita's very words and smiles seemed to wash away Ahalya's stains. It was only when she visited that Ahalya's lips would part in a smile. Her eyes would betray a dawning light of happiness.

Growing up under the surveillance of Vasishtha, were not the young couple destined to be the ideals of rulership? They came to the rishi and his wife who lived in seclusion on the banks of the Sarayu, each in a separate world. They revived a former liveliness within them.

Ahalya had no wish to go out and engage with the world about her. Sita's nearness alone eased her heart's burden and gave her a little courage.

She agreed to come to Ayodhya for the grand occasion of the coronation. But how fierce the emotional whirlpool in the palace turned out to be! In one breath, Dasharatha's life was taken, Rama driven into the forest, Bharata distressed, in tears, forced to go and live in Nandigram.

Some great force, impossible to measure in human terms, made it all happen, like dice rolling in a headlong frenzy which bring the game to an end once and for all.

With what scrupulousness Vasishtha had watched over his wards, wishing to establish an ideal governance, the triumph of humankind's dharma! All his calculations had become mere dust and chaff, dwindled to the glimmering light standing alone in Nandigram.

It has to be said that the little hut by the Sarayu collapsed once again for lack of support, Gautama's philosophic investigations were scattered by the whirlwind. Belief dried up in his mind, leaving it waste and void.

And Ahalya? Her sorrow cannot be measured nor told in words. She could not understand it; she was totally crushed. Rama went away to the forest. His younger brother followed him; Sita too. Ahalya's heart was as heavy and dark as it once had been when she was a stone statue. Being alive, though, the consciousness of its weight was unendurable.

At earliest dawn, Gautama finished his prayers and austerities, came ashore, entered his hut.

Ahalya was waiting with the pot of water to wash his feet. Her lips moved.

"I cannot bear to be here any more. Why don't we return to Mithila?"

"Alright, let's go. It's a long time too since we saw Sadananda." And he made ready to leave.

They began to walk towards Mithila. A heaviness had entered each of them and inhabited their hearts.

Gautama stopped. He reached out and took Ahalya's hand as she came up towards him; he walked on. "Don't be afraid," he said.

They walked on towards Mithila.

3

Dawn broke. They walked along the banks of the Ganga.

Someone stood in the water, reciting the Gayatri in a bell-like voice.

The couple waited on the shore, some distance away, until the prayer was said.

"Sadananda!" called Gautama.

"Father ... Mother." Sadananda poured out his happiness, and fell at their feet in greeting.

Ahalya embraced him in her heart. How much like a stranger her child Sadananda had become, moustached and bearded like a rishi!

The radiance of his son's face brought ease to Gautama's heart.

Sadananda invited both of them to his hut. He made every arrangement for their comfort and then prepared to set off for Janaka's court and forum of discussion.

Gautama readied himself to go with his son. Of course the son wanted his father to accompany him. Yet, he thought for a moment, with special filial compassion, of the long journey that the older man had just undertaken. But then again, Gautama's body had withstood the rigorous austerities of aeons; how could a short walk tire him out? Sadananda followed Gautama. He was eager to learn about his father's new philosophic enquiries.

As he walked along the streets of Mithila, it seemed to Gautama that a certain weariness of spirit and of sorrow, growing out of Ayodhya, had pervaded this city, too. It was as if a suppressed sigh had mingled with the very wind.

People went to and fro; they went about their business; everything was done as if in selfless service; there was no involvement; no intense participation.

There was no enthusiasm in the elephant's stride as it carried the sacred waters for the ritual bath of the deity; nor the play of grace on the features of the accompanying priest.

They entered the debating forum. An army of disputants filled the chamber, like an ocean. How could any real discussion even enter such a marketplace, Gautama wondered. In the end, he found he had been mistaken.

Janaka's eyes fell on them immediately.

He came hurrying up towards them, offered the sage veneration, greeted him with all due observances, and invited him to sit next to him.

Janaka's face was touched with sadness. Yet there was no hesitancy in his speech; it was clear his mind had not lost its tranquility.

Gautama hesitated, wondering what he should say.

Stroking his beard, Janaka spoke. "When he established the state, Vasishtha did not build in a sluice-gate for emotion."

Janaka's words touched a nerve center.

"Isn't it from that whirlpool of emotion, that truth is born?" asked Gautama.

"Sorrow too is born, if we have not learnt to use our emotions. When we wish to establish a state, we must take account of this, or there can be no state," Janaka said.

Gautama voiced a doubt: "What of yours, though?"

"I don't reign; I try to understand rulership," said Janaka.

Both were silent awhile.

"What is your enquiry into dharma about?" Janaka asked, courteously.

"I have not even started on it yet; I can only try and understand from now on; so many puzzles and mysteries ensnare my senses." Gautama arose as he said this.

From the next day, he stopped attending Janaka's forum. His mind was full of enigmas, standing as high as the Himalayas. He needed solitude. Yet he didn't seek it. Ahalya should not be hurt, after all.

The very next day, Janaka asked, "Where is the great sage?"

"He spends his entire time beneath the Ashoka tree in front of our hut," replied Sadananda.

"In austerities?"

"No, just in thought."

"The storm has not abated," said Janaka softly, to himself.

———————

Ahalya took immense pleasure in bathing in the river. Here, certain of peace and quiet along the river Ganga, she would set off at earliest dawn with her water-pot.

For a couple of days, alone in the river, she could allow her thoughts to branch out as they wished; unburdening herself, she could play in the river, bathe, and return at last with a full water-pot.

It did not last.

She was walking home after her bath, her eyes cast down, letting her thoughts drift.

She could hear the sound of toe-rings coming towards her. Rishis' wives whom she did not know; they too were on their way to bathe. But as soon as they saw her, they started as if they had seen an outcaste, and then turned and fled, shunning her.

From a distance she heard their voices, "That was Ahalya." Those words burnt into her more painfully than the fiery curse which came flaming out of Gautama's belly.

In an instant she felt as if her inner self was on fire, like a cremation ground. She was distraught. "Oh God," she sobbed, "Even though I am absolved of the curse, am I not to be absolved of the sin?"

She served Gautama and Sadananda their food that day, like a mechanical doll. Her mind was beating out a refrain, "My son has become a stranger; strangers have become enemies; why stay here any longer?"

Like one returning to reality from time to time, Gautama placed a mouthful of food in his mouth, and then became lost in thought.

The heavy atmosphere wrought by his parents' bewilderment made Sadananda, too, gasp for breath.

In order to lighten the air, he said, "The sage Atri was here, to visit Janaka. He has been to visit Agastya. He's traveling towards Meru, now. Rama and Sita paid their respects to Agastya, it seems. Apparently Agastya told them, 'It's a good place, Panchavati. Stay there awhile.' It looks as if they have done just that."

Ahalya asked softly, "What if we too should make a pilgrimage?"

"Shall we start now?" asked Gautama, standing up and washing his hand.

"What? Immediately?" asked Sadananda.

"It doesn't matter when," answered Gautama, collecting his staff and water vessel, and setting off towards the front door.

Ahalya followed him.

Sadananda's heart was heavy.

4

The day was dying, the light had dimmed. Two people were walking along the shores of the river Sarayu, towards Ayodhya.

Fourteen years had gone by, vanished, mingled now into the flood of time. There was no eminent sage they had not met, no sacred place of pilgrimage they had not visited. Yet they had not gained peace of mind.

They stood on snowy mountain crests, and looked with adoration upon Kailasa rearing in front of them, beyond the reach of those who do not possess courageous feet; like Shankara's imagined temple, beyond the reach of timid minds.[7]

They crossed a desert which was identical to their inner drought, their burden of sorrow, their lack of belief.

They circumambulated volcanoes, which, like their own minds spouted flames and threw up the dregs of smoke, ashes, and dust.

They reached seashores where the waves tossed endlessly like their hearts; they returned.

They crossed hills and valleys, like the crests and troughs of their own lives.

A single hope had dragged them onwards: "In a few days more, Rama will return. After this at least we may see a renewal of life."

They arrived at the place where fourteen years ago they had left the cottage they once built, desolated.

That very night Gautama repaired it, so that it was a fit dwelling once more. When the work was done, the rising sun was smiling.

They bathed in the Sarayu and returned.

Ahalya busied herself in serving her husband. Both of them longed for and looked forward to the day of Rama's and Sita's return. All the same, how can we cross the rules of established time, except through the imagination?

One day, Ahalya set off early in the morning to bathe in the river.

Before her, someone else, a widow, had finished her bath, and was returning. Although she could not tell who it was, the other woman had recognized her.

---

7. Shankara is a name for Shiva, several of whose famous temples are located in the high Himalaya mountains, to which only the most persevering pilgrims would journey.

She came running forward and fell at Ahalya's feet, her entire body prostrate on the ground.

Kaikeyi Devi, without her retinue of attendants and maid servants; alone, a renunciant?

Ahalya set down her water-pot and lifted her up with both hands. She could not understand Kaikeyi's gesture.

"Bharata is so engrossed in dharma that he has forgotten to give me a place in his heart," said Kaikeyi.[8]

No anger throbbed in her voice, no leaping arrogance. The Kaikeyi she had imagined and the Kaikeyi in front of her were different people. All Ahalya saw was a yearning heart, like a vine without a supporting frame.

They walked on towards the Sarayu, their arms still about each other.

"And who was the cause of Bharata's steadfastness in dharma?" asked Ahalya. A gentle smile of compassion touched the edge of her lips, and then disappeared.

"If a fire started by a small child razes the city, should we kill the child?" asked Kaikeyi.

Ahalya thought it was certainly necessary to raise a fence between the child and the fire. "But what was burnt was indeed burnt and lost, wasn't it?" she asked.

"Then is it enough just to heap up the ashes and sit by them without cleansing the entire city?" asked Kaikeyi again.

"The person who will remove the ashes will arrive in a couple of days, though," Ahalya reminded her.

"Yes," said Kaikeyi. There was a profound contentment in her voice. It was not Bharata who looked forward the most to Rama's return, but Kaikeyi.

The next day when she met Ahalya, she looked as desolate as if her whole inner self had collapsed.

"Our messengers have been sent out in all directions. There is no sign whatever of Rama. How can we hope that they will be here within the next sixteen hours? Bharata has declared he will perform the *prayogavesham* ritual and give up his life.[9] He is already arranging for the sacred fire to be lit," Kaikeyi told her.

She implied that Bharata wished to extinguish his life at the fire, as an atonement for the love of government that had been forced upon him.

After a pause, Kaikeyi went on, "I too will enter the fire, but alone and in secret." Her inner resolve shone.

After fourteen years, once again the very same whirlpool of emotion. Had the results of that curse that fell upon Ayodhya still not ended?

Ahalya's thoughts flew about, without connection. She even wondered whether that curse had not come from the shadow of her own feet.

---

8. When Bharata returned from his uncle's home and learned how Kaikeyi had coerced Dasharatha into exiling Rama, he was appalled and henceforth treated his mother coldly.
9. *Prayogavesham* is a form of ritual in which the adherent fasts unto death. Bharata has vowed to undergo this ritual unless Rama returns from exile.

"Can you not ask Vasishtha to stop him?" she asked.

"Bharata will be bound only by dharma and not by Vasishtha," said Kaikeyi.

Ahalya was outraged. "A dharma that is not bound by human beings is the enemy of the human race."

A foolish hope that Bharata might, perhaps, submit to her husband's advice, struck her. She was terrified that the wheel of tragedy would begin to turn once more in Ayodhya.

Gautama agreed. But his words were profitless.

But, after all, Agni did not wish to accept Bharata's sacrifice, nor to consume him.

Hanuman arrived; the fire was extinguished. In all directions, sorrow turned into a boundless ecstasy of joy. Dharma whirled its head and danced.

And Vasishtha hid a smile behind his moustache, in the hope that after fourteen long years, his dream would come true.

Thinking that he had no place in that carnival of happiness, Gautama went home.

Ahalya exulted inwardly, certain that Rama and Sita would come to visit her. And they did come after the revelries had quieted down; on their own, without their retinue.

Experience had dug its channels in the brow of the Rama who stepped down from the chariot. And through experience, Sita's radiance had come into full flower. The harmony of their laughter conveyed the bliss of moksha.[10]

Gautama invited Rama to walk with him, and they left the house together.

With that special compassion which flows towards a child who has lain and grown in one's womb, Ahalya took Sita inside. They sat down, smiling at each other.

Sita told her everything without a tinge of sorrow: Ravana's abduction, her suffering and her release. Where was the place for sorrow, now that she had joined Rama once again?

Then she spoke of entering the fire. Ahalya was shaken to the core.

"Did he ask you to do it? Why did you do it?"

"He asked me, I did it," said Sita quietly.

"How could he ask you?" shouted Ahalya, Kannagi's frenzy leaping through her mind.[11]

One law for Ahalya, quite another for Rama?

---

10. Release from worldly bonds that imprison one in the endless cycle of death and rebirth, the ultimate goal of Hindu yogic spiritual discipline.

11. Pudumaippittan links three women mistreated by their husbands: Ahalya, Sita, and Kannagi. Heroine of the fifth-century Tamil epic *Cilappatikaram*, Kannagi had been a faithful wife, devoted to her spouse even when he left her for a courtesan and returned penniless. Kannagi gave him her gold anklet to raise some money. When he went to the city to sell it, the king of Madurai wrongly executed him for the theft of a gold anklet stolen by another. The news of his death filled Kannagi with rage, transforming her into an avenging goddess. Cursing the king, she burned his city to the ground in punishment. By comparing Ahalya's mind to that of Kannagi, Pudumaippittan suggests the depth of Ahalya's anger toward Rama and indicates the injustice of Sita's fire ordeal, since she was abducted against her will and remained as devoted a wife as Kannagi.

Was it a betrayal after all? A judgment, which was equal to the curse that had poured out from Gautama?

For a long time they were both silent.

"Didn't it have to be proved to the world?" Sita said, laughing softly.

"If one knows it oneself, isn't that enough? Is it possible to prove the truth to the world?" demanded Ahalya. She was dry of words.

Again she said, "And will it become the truth if you just demonstrate it, even if it doesn't touch the heart? Anyway, we must let it pass; what is this world?"

They heard voices outside. The men had returned.

Sita came out, ready to return to the palace. Ahalya was not with her.

It burnt Rama's heart. The dust spreading over his feet burnt him.

The chariot rolled forward; the sound of the wheels faded away.

Gautama stood stock-still, lost in thought. The uncertain, impermanent constellation of Trishanku, in the southern sky, fell upon his eyes.[12]

In the cave of his mind, a new thought flashed like lightning and disappeared. What if they were to have a child in order to ease their heavy hearts and revive their old attachment? Surely its tender fingers would set down her heart's burden at last?

He went inside.

Ahalya was barely conscious. In her mind Indra was re-enacting the same scene, the scene she strove to forget.

Gautama embraced her. She thought it was Indra re-entering his role, disguised as Gautama. Her heart hardened into stone. Stillness at last.

Entangled in Gautama's arms lay a stone statue.

Ahalya was stone once more.

Her heart's burden ceased.

———————

In quest of Kailasa, a solitary human form hurried across the wastes of snow. Those heels had hardened through a profound indifference to all things.

It was Gautama. He had renounced the world.

Translated from Tamil by Lakshmi Holmstrom

---

12. King Trishanku wanted to go to heaven. When at his request Vishvamitra sent him to the celestial realm, Indra refused to let him enter, so Trishanku remained hanging, stuck between heaven and earth as a constellation, a symbol of one who is neither here nor there.

15 The Nature of Stone

Sivasekaram, professor and head of the Department of Engineering at the University of Peradeniya in Sri Lanka, was born in 1942. He has been composing poetry in Tamil since the 1970s; he also writes critical articles on literature and politics as well as translating poetry into Tamil from English.

In Sivasekaram's poem, none of the four characters participating in the drama is named: the wife; the stony-hearted husband who curses her; and the two gods—one who is the reason for the curse, and the other the means by which the curse is (casually, almost insultingly) revoked. The poem presents Ahalya as the victim of all three males. Rather than the usual questions of Ahalya's chastity and morality, which are irrelevant to the poem, Sivasekaram takes up her right to a life of feeling, passion, and agency. The tragedy of his Ahalya is that she is condemned to be a stone, whether she is alive or not. Sivasekaram organizes the poem brilliantly and tightly around the image of stones and a complex set of meanings associated with and generated by this image.[1] He also sets it in the palai, a landscape of wilderness, filled with stones and inhabited by ascetics who have left the city behind to practice tapas. [L. H.]

Source: S. Sivasekaram, "Ahalikai," in *Natikkari Muunkil* (Madras: National Arts and Literary Association, 1995).[2]

Ahalya
BY S. SIVASEKARAM

Stones.
Above the earth, beneath the earth,
hillocks and mountains,
rocks and fragments,
upright, fallen,
stones.

Her husband, the sage, was a stone.
The god was a liar, but
no stone he,
only a male deity, who lived
to survive the curse.

---

1. The poem is constructed around a system of alliteration and play on similar sounding words such as *kal* (stone), *kaal* (foot), and *kaalam* (time).
2. For the challenges of translating Sivasekaram's poem, see Kanaganayakam (1992).

And she who had lived like a stone
coming alive for that instant alone
truly became a stone.

On a day much later,
an avatara who crossed the seas to rescue a lover,
only to thrust her
into burning flames—
who feared the town's gossip
and exiled her—

a god, yet unworthy of touching a stone—
stumbled upon her.

Had she not changed again
stone becoming woman
to live like a stone with a stone,

Had she remained truly a stone
she might have stood forever,
a mountain peak, undestroyed by time.

Translated from Tamil by Lakshmi Holmstrom

16 Domestic Abuse and
the Neurologist

N. S. Madhavan (b. 1948) grew up in Cochin, where this short story is set. Soon after his first short fiction was published in 1970, he joined the Indian Administrative Service (IAS) and has served since then in the Bihar cadre. Going on to publish many short stories, he became closely identified with the Malayalam modernist movement. Madhavan is known for subtle connections of crisscrossing dialogues and images that reflect the sensibility of change. After a decade of silence in the 1980s, he began publishing extensively again in the 1990s. In addition to stories, he has also written a novel, two plays, and many articles for Malayalam journals.

Madhavan's short story, "Ahalya," plunges beneath the surface of the epic narrative, imagining what would be the equivalant in today's world to Ahalya turning into a ghost because her husband had no interest in developing marital intimacy. This Ahalya lives in our era, as can be seen from the contemporary quality of the dialogue (full of references to film actresses and television newscasters) and setting (complete with pollution from the Cochin Refineries). The story's characters take IAS exams to get jobs in government service, go abroad for higher education, or work in the Persian Gulf. Yet, the story remains unmistakably a tale of Ahalya's neglect by Gautama, in this case an engineer indifferent to his wife's emotions, feelings, or physical desires.

The story's humor builds cleverly through narrative detail. For example, one meaning of "Ahalya" is "un-ploughed." Ahalya's email address is unploughed@yahoo.co.in. The concept of being "unploughed" takes on symbolic undertones as her story unfolds and we discover that only during her single tryst with a film star, long after her marriage, does she discover that the touch of a man can give her pleasure: her field has remained unploughed, and hence unfulfilled. Furthermore, according to tradition, the Creator God Brahma used celestial resources in heaven to make Ahalya the most lovely woman ever created. In Madhavan's story, Ahalya's friends tease her that Brahma created her by combining parts of the body from stunning film actresses such as Smita Patil and Madhuri Dixit. Madhavan also spoofs Ahalya's legendary unsurpassed beauty by imagining that potential spouses find her so lovely that they are afraid to marry her; instead, an oblivious man marries her without even seeming to notice her loveliness.

The story explores many ways in which Ahalya lacks control over her life. As she grows up, she develops no ambitions of her own. Her husband treats her solely as an object for his pleasure, but when she attempts to make her body a means of revolt, she is beaten into a comatose state. Her beauty has become a form of oppression rather than a means of fulfillment. Her coma, which echoes the ghostly state of Valmiki's Ahalya before the lifting of the curse, occurs after domestic abuse, medicalization, and other experiences of today's society.

Source: N. S. Madhavan, "Ahalya," *Bhashaposhini,* April 2006, pp. 5–12.

Ahalya
BY N. S. MADHAVAN

Infinity was never so endless in childhood. It was the place where the parallel rail tracks faded away into the mist flitting in the sunlight, when one looked southward from Ernakulam Junction Railway Station. And the future was a train which could appear there any moment.

I gave different names to that train—IIT Engineer, Poet, Doctor, Journalist, Indian Administrative Service Officer.[1] By that time everyone had begun playing the game of What-You-Wanna-Be. Rivalry had already entered the game. When Sebastian said he wanted to be a mountaineer, Ashraf was keen to become a Formula One driver. Priya wished to be the wife of someone with a Pronnoy-Roy beard.[2] Sitara longed to be the first woman jockey of India. For quite a while, she used to wear horse-print T-shirts. Sprinting a distance and jumping in an imaginary bowling act, I would declare: "Fast Bowler." Mira wanted the Nobel Prize for Peace. For that, disregarding our jeers, she would greet the handicapped beggars with the gestures of Mother Theresa. But, much to our chagrin, Mira's elder sister Ahalya never participated in our game.

Before long, I too stopped playing the game. My not-so-old father had died before my eyes, unwinding slowly like a toy mouse. Since then, besides studying, eating, playing cricket, staring into the mirror, reading, and discovering my body, I had begun to worry about my future. Eternity for me was no longer a train that could be seen at a distance, but a vast continent without maps. On certain days I set out looking for it like a fifteenth-century navigator. But the seagulls heralding the view of the land never appeared in the lens of my telescope. Very often, trapped in the fishnet of latitudes and longitudes, I went mad.

Sebastian was the first among us to leave the ranks. The train that arrived for him did not go to Darjeeling, where Tenzing's mountaineering school was located. Before Sebastian left for Mangalore to do his degree in pharmacy, all of us got together at Ahalya's house. On that evening, Ahalya looked at all of us

----

1. IIT stands for Indian Institute of Technology. The Indian Administrative Service (IAS) is a cadre of well-educated civil servants posted in top positions all over India. In order to be admitted into this selective group, one must receive a high score on the pan-Indian IAS exam.

2. Pronnoy Roy was a senior television journalist, known for his salt and pepper beard, who conducted a news program, "The World This Week." Many teenage girls had a crush on him.

and said: "I want to be." Then she fell silent. All, except me, pounced on her in a pack: "What do you wanna be, Ahalya?"

Ahalya did not utter a word. But her silence did not seem to us a ruse to draw our attention. We guessed that her future was something that she intensely desired. Again the others asked in a loud chorus: "Tell us, what do you wanna be?" Ahalya sat with her face pressed on her palm and still did not say anything.

"Speak up," Priya touched her shoulder encouragingly.

"Go ahead, Chechi, we won't laugh or pull your leg.[3] Come out with it, say that you wanna be the President of India," Ahalya's kid sister Mira egged her on.

"Is it something that you are ashamed to tell us, Ahalya?" Sebastian asked. Ahalya raised her head and looked fiercely at Sebastian.

"Nurse? Kindergarten Teacher?" Ashraf queried, "or the eye-candy wife of a millionaire? Open up, and tell us whatever you wanna be, Ahalya."

"Whatever you wanna be, someone else must have already become *that* long before you. One just cannot be original when it comes to the future," Sitara was sure.

It was my silence that finally forced Ahalya to reveal it. She looked at me and said: "Raghavan, I wanna be a ghost."

"Ghost!" Priya exclaimed.

"You say that to sound original," Sitara alleged.

"What is wrong with you, Chechi? My God, you scare me." Mira's face went pale.

Finding no words to respond, we boys kept quiet. Standing close to Mira, Ahalya confided in us: "I have never felt anything when you guys played What-You-Wanna-Be. Suddenly, one day I thought: why shouldn't I be a ghost? A spirit. No one would see me. I would see everyone. I don't need to eat anything. Mira, why do we wanna be someone when we are big? To eat, to cover ourselves. Once you are a ghost, you do not need any of these. So I want to be a ghost." We looked keenly at Ahalya to see if she was joking. Her face said she thought it better to turn into a ghost right away. That shocked us slightly.

Nobody said anything for some time. As usual, humor was brought in to break the quiet. Ashraf said, "It would be our loss not to be able to see Ahalya. How the Almighty must have toiled to create Ahalya. First, Srividya's hair was chosen. Then Rekha's nose . . ."

"Smita Patil's eyes," I suggested.

"Meena Kumari's eyelashes," Sebastian proposed.

"The smile of Madhuri Dixit, Simi Garewal's neck . . ." with closed eyes Ashraf whispered.

"Dimple Kapadia's legs from *Bobby* times," Sebastian added.

---

3. "Chechi," a term used to address one's elder sister, locates the events of the story in the mid-Kerala area. In southern Kerala, the term would be the Tamil term "akka," reflecting the strong Tamil linguistic influence of neighboring Tamilnadu, while the term in northern Kerala would be "oppol."

"Hey guys, stop," Priya warned, "don't climb too far up the leg."[4]

"So, how can Ahalya just fade away? Ahalya, whom the Creator had pains-takingly assembled, selecting each part with care? Can we see her as a ghost?" Ashraf asked widening his eyes. We all laughed. But Ahalya was not fazed.

Whenever we talked about Ahalya among ourselves after that, we went back to this story, and laughed. Sometimes the names changed. Smita Patil gave way to Aishwarya Rai.

After Ahalya went into a coma, on every February 2nd—Ahalya's birthday according to the Christian calendar—we repeated the story in front of the cake decorated with candles showing Ahalya's age. The thought that Ahalya was still there, within the unresponsive body which lay in that room, gave us the courage to laugh. One of us would finally say, "For her next birthday, Ahalya will blow out the candles." Today is her fourth comatose birthday, and the joke has worn thin. For the past few months we have stopped telling the story of Ahalya's crea-tion. Our hope has been ending inexorably, like a pier.

Mira, who ran a beauty parlor, and stayed unmarried, reminded us of her sister's birthday every year. Ashraf, who worked in Dubai, attended the func-tion only once when he came on leave. In the year she gave birth, Sitara did not come. Sebastian, employed in government service, managed to visit Ahalya's home each time from a different part of Kerala. Priya, who married a lawyer in Ernakulam, also never missed it. Her husband did not have a Pronnoy-Roy beard. He did not even have a moustache.

After my degree in medicine, I had gone to Edinburgh for advanced studies in neurology, and continued to work there. I met a Scottish girl named Iris and lived in with her for a few months. Then we got married. We were only two while we lived together. But before long, routine entered into our marriage as a third person. It was hard to cope. In two years, after the divorce, I came back to Ernakulam.

My elderly mother cried when she saw me sitting on the veranda and read-ing only the obit page in Malayalam daily newspapers. To bring her neurologist son back to life, from the next-door neighbor she borrowed the back issues of *Reader's Digest* that carried articles on the brain, and gave them to me. I lived on measuring the passing months with haircuts until my mother showed me the ad for the post of the Head of the Department of Neurology in a huge hospital in Ernakulam. I landed the job.

I saw my work as a shield against leisure. I worked late nights in the hospital. One such night, the duty nurse came and said I had a phone call.

"Dr. Raghavan?" said a female voice.

---

4. Most of the actresses mentioned in this section starred in films released in the 1970s. Dixit's films appeared in the 1980s–1990s, while Rai (mentioned later) became popular later, so the reference indicates how much time has passed. Patil, Kumari, and Garewal starred in Malayalam films. The comment "legs from *Bobby* times" refers to the actress Dimple Kapadia in her 1970s film *Bobby,* where she made her first sensational appearance in a bikini.

"Ahalya!" It was the first time I spoke to one of my old friends since I had returned.

"It's Mira." She had the same throaty Sushmita Sen voice as Ahalya. Mira wept for a while. Her cell phone transmitted the din of vehicles more loudly than her cry.

"Yes, Mira."

"I'm bringing Chechi to you in an ambulance."

"What happened to Ahalya?"

"Hit on the head. She has lost consciousness."

"I'll meet you out front."

The last time I had seen Ahalya was a week before I left for Britain. I went to their house to say goodbye to Ahalya and Mira. Mira was not there. When Ahalya came and sat near me on the couch, I suddenly felt a strong desire for her, as I had never before felt toward Ahalya. As I drew in the scent of her breath, I heard my heart pounding.

"What do you plan to do, Ahalya?" I asked.

"Become a ghost as soon as possible."

"You haven't forgotten it?"

"I had, Raghavan. But I have started thinking about it again these days."

"Show me that palm, I will predict Ahalya's future."

"When did Raghavan learn to read palms?" Ahalya asked.

"Yeah, I learned it."

I started examining Ahalya's hand. On her palm, besides the prominent lines, there were Chinese ideograms of thin crisscrossing lines. I just held her hand, unable to read it.

"Raghavan, you don't know how to read palms, do you?"

"No."

"Then?"

"For the touch."

Ahalya shook her hand free and got up. I also rose. The next moment, lust and the shame of being rejected overtook me, and I drew Ahalya close to me and rubbed my cheek against hers. Ahalya stood still. My lips moved to Ahalya's lips, and my hand to her breast.

"No," Ahalya said without a movement. Quietly. It startled me. As I walked to the door, Ahalya called after me: "Raghavan, just a minute."

She went inside and brought out a gift pack.

"A farewell gift to you from Mira and me. A tie. To go with Raghavan's new camel-colored jacket."

I never wore that polka-dotted silver gray tie. As I was preparing to go to Britain, Mother had given me a picture of my father as a youth. I forgot to pack that photograph and the tie Ahalya had given to me. That helped me banish two things from my memory: my father's selfish, untimely death and Ahalya's "no."

Till my relationship with Iris soured, I had email contact with everyone except Ahalya. I composed many letters to Ahalya's email address, unploughed@yahoo.co.in, but never clicked the "Send" button. I saved my electronic monologues for a while. After Iris and I parted ways, I deleted them all in a fit of frenzy to start everything anew. A "no" suddenly echoed in my head. At that moment, the ambulance arrived.

"How did this happen?" I asked Mira while pushing the trolley to the emergency ward.

"Someone hit her on the head with a whiskey bottle."

I arranged to prepare the operation theater, inform the doctors and nurses, and call the barber to shave Ahalya's head. I went to the cafeteria after sending Ahalya for scanning. I told Mira who came along with me, "Brain surgery takes a lot of time. I thought I should have a bite before that. Where is Ahalya's husband?"

"Gautaman's cell phone is switched off. I can't reach him."

"Who hit Ahalya?"

"No idea." Mira started weeping.

"When did this happen?"

"I don't know. In the evening, the milkman rang the bell and no one answered him. After he had placed the milk packets near the door and turned to leave, he felt something sticky on his feet. He looked back and found his red footprints on the steps. He ran back to Chechi's flat. Blood was coming out through the gap beneath the door." She fell silent for a moment.

"In the milkman's words, 'blood trickled out of the flat like a train of red ants.'" Mira wiped her face, and continued: "The people next door called me up. There was a locksmith down the road and it was not difficult for him to open the door. My sister was lying in the living room, bleeding. A broken bottle of Red Label lay near her. Some whiskey was left in it. My sister's skirt was drenched. The mixed stench of blood, alcohol, and urine.

"We took her to a nursing home nearby. They removed the broken pieces of glass from her head and dressed the wounds. The doctor out there told us to rush her immediately to Dr. Raghavan."

I listened to Mira with admiration as she repeated the story she had told me to Sitara and her husband Mukesh. And to many relatives and friends whom I did not know, without adding or omitting a detail. But when she narrated the incident to Priya and her husband Ravi, a criminal lawyer, she added one thing: "The security guards saw Gautaman get in the car and leave at three o' clock."

The scan results showed that Ahalya did not need surgery. She opened her eyes on the third day. The same day Gautaman was arrested in a hotel in Thalassery. I did not permit the police to question Ahalya. But I could not stop the young woman police officer from asking her: "Was it Mr. Gautaman who did this?" Ahalya nodded.

Even after opening her eyes, Ahalya had occasional blackouts. Sometimes she cried due to severe headaches. After two weeks, she stopped relapsing into unconsciousness. Still I kept her in the hospital under observation. On the day she was discharged, I said: "Be careful. We can't afford any complications to develop."

"Won't Raghavan visit me?" Ahalya asked.

"No."

"The ailing me?"

"I don't make house calls."

Ahalya smiled.

The first time I dropped by Ahalya's, she opened the door and said: "I knew Raghavan would come."

"I just dropped in to say we could do one more scan."

"Was it difficult to find this place?"

"No, Mira had told me that all the taxi drivers would know the apartment where movie star Devraj lives."

We sat on the veranda of Ahalya's ninth floor apartment and watched the city lights fade in the darkening sky. At a distance, the flames of burning gases rose from the chimneys of Cochin Refineries and painted those dark stretches of the sky red.

"What was the name of Raghavan's ex-wife?"

"Iris."

"Kids?"

"No."

"Raghavan, do you miss Iris . . . Britain?" Ahalya asked.

I kept quiet.

"Did you avoid me all this time because I didn't allow you to kiss me that day you did that palm reading gambit?"

"I haven't met Gautaman," I said. This time Ahalya kept silent.

The next scan results showed a small blot on Ahalya's brain. Ahalya was admitted in the hospital. I decided that she did not need surgery, and put her on medicine. At times Ahalya was disoriented. She spent almost a month in the hospital. The day before leaving the hospital, Ahalya told me: "I need to ask you something, Raghavan."

I sat down before her in a chair. Ahalya asked: "You did not take the tie we gifted you and your father's photograph to Edinburgh, did you?"

"Who told you?"

"I met your mother at a wedding."

"Mother didn't tell me she met Ahalya."

"She must have forgotten," Ahalya closed her eyes and said.

"Yeah, must have forgotten," I said.

I visited Ahalya one Sunday evening after calling her. I noticed that the little disorientation left in her eyes on the day of her discharge from the hospital had disappeared. We pulled up cane chairs to the balcony and sat.

"Did you notice my sports shoes?" I asked.

"Yes, I did, as soon as you came in. They do not go with Raghavan's clothing. So old," Ahalya said.

"They're my father's. He used to go jogging everyday. Mother found them among his old things. She asked me if they would fit me. I told her to give them away to some beggar. Her face fell. So I just checked them. Size eleven. I suddenly knew who left me these big feet."

We didn't say anything for a while. I rose and walked up to the balustrade. I held the railing and looked at Ernakulam where wind shifted from the land to the Arabian Sea. Ahalya asked softly from behind: "Raghavan, you have come to tell me about your father's sports shoes, haven't you?"

"Yeah."

"I did not have to guess too hard," Ahalya laughed.

"How did you know?"

"It's clear that you have your father on your mind. Size eleven sports shoes, salt-and-pepper moustache . . . Raghavan's body reveals all that is on his mind."

"Isn't everyone like me?"

"Maybe. But I am not. I don't have a mind," Ahalya said.

I felt Ahalya was soliloquizing. I asked: "Don't have a mind?"

"No. I'm my body. It was my desire for a mind that made me yearn to become a ghost. My body is my mind too. My thoughts are brought to me by its portholes . . ."

"The portholes of the body?"

"Yeah. Its pores. I've often felt that all the cavities in the body share a single emotion: urge. Nose's urge is to breathe. The urge of Mouth is to eat. Then there is the urgent call to pee. And the other compelling urgency. The ache of urging breasts that brim with milk. My ears had an urge to listen to Malayalam film songs. I could not bear, for long, the urge of the crack between my legs. I knew the world through Nine Orifices."[5]

Without turning to Ahalya, I stood looking at the ruby tail-lights of the vehicles rushing along one half of the long road below, and the diamond head-lights of those coming in the opposite direction.

"Raghavan, come and sit here," Ahalya said. "I'll tell you why Gautaman hit me, something Gautaman held back from the court."

"Did you know Gautaman before?" I asked.

"No, it was an arranged marriage. He was an engineer in Cochin Port. He looked clean. I felt he would take good care of me. A big attraction was that I did not have to go away from mother and Mira to another city."

"Sitara wrote that Gautaman looked handsome. And, very serious, too."

"Serious! My wedding was strange," Ahalya exclaimed, "In the wedding pavilion, Gautaman sat cross-legged as all grooms do. But he looked straight ahead, and kept his fists on his knees. Like the yoga teachers on TV. I almost burst out laughing. He refused to look at me even when he was tying the knot. The guests and I started feeling awkward. No one except the nadaswaram players made any sound.[6] Only the video-cameramen moved."

"At the wedding feast, I teased Gautaman: 'Are you afraid to show your profile?' Gautaman continued eating carefully and did not answer me."

---

5. The phrase "Nine Orifices" comes from ascetic discourse that provides instruction in detaching oneself from sense desires through meditation. Ahalya uses the phrase here ironically, as she enumerates her desires not for detachment but to describe how she sought to fulfill the desires.

6. Nadaswaram, a long flute, is played at South Indian weddings to celebrate auspicious rites.

Ahalya walked up to the railing. She said, looking at Ernakulam: "I was twenty-six when I got married. You were the only one who had even touched me until then."

"Why were you so late to marry?"

"I was not good at schoolwork. I saw marriage itself as a career. There were many proposals. Nothing worked out. Hadn't the Creator put all the parts together like a watchmaker to assemble me! Maybe they thought it would be difficult to keep a wife as beautiful as me. Gautaman simply lacked thoughts. So that wedding took place."

"Go to bed, Ahalya," I suggested, "don't exert your brain."

"I am not tired," she maintained while walking into the flat.

Ahalya came back with a famous Scotch whiskey and soda. Pouring the whiskey into the glass she said: "There are still whiskey bottles here that have not yet been smashed against heads."

I laughed aloud for the first time in months. I remembered what Ahalya asked Ashraf, Sebastian, and me when we began evading her after she became of age: "Guys, why are you so shy?"

"I punished Gautaman for ruining my wedding," Ahalya said. "My outfit on our first night. I chose an old greenish yellow—the color of baby poop—cotton sari that night. I wore the black-framed glasses that I had never used outside my room. Rubber slippers on my feet. I wanted Gautaman to feel disgust towards me. That was what I had planned for Gautaman.

"Gautaman sat on the chair in front of me. He gestured to my feet. I got up and removed my slippers. Then he gestured at my face with his index finger. I did not quite follow what Gautaman meant. His finger was insistent. I started getting scared. A pleasurable fear deep inside the belly that comes from jitters and wetness, and the urge to piss. Then it struck me that he was asking me to take off my glasses. First step to undress me. My fear vanished. Some more whiskey?"

"No," I said.

"The ten fingers of Gautaman's open palms asked me to rise. I got up. Gautaman's first finger pointed to my baby poop yellow sari. I took it off. No, I didn't feel insulted. Nor frightened. Instead, a primal curiosity. I removed my clothes one by one, obeying Gautaman's finger. Finally, Gautaman pointed to the bed. I went and lay down there."

Ever since I returned from Edinburgh, I have not been inquisitive about anything. But Gautaman aroused curiosity in me again. It was like betraying Ahalya, but I could not help asking: "How was Gautaman otherwise?"

"Being with Gautaman was easy. I could sense what was going on in his mind. He had a kind of face made of glass. Revealing all his thoughts. Gautaman confronted the world with habits. That made my life easy. 'Is it rice gruel or chappati for tonight?' I would ask after kneading the dough ready for chappati. Gautaman would think for sometime with closed eyes and then say: 'chappati.' Gautaman was tightfisted only when it came to one thing. Touch."

"Touch?"

"Gautaman took me to bed whenever he decided. If I warmed up to him sometimes, that would turn him off. After the act, Gautaman was always in a hurry to get into his jeans. But I longed to lie close to Gautaman and sumptuously feel asleep during that time when every part of the body except the eyes becomes as light as a feather."[7]

Suddenly I thought of Iris. After we had sex, she would sit up and light a cigarette. When I continued to be quiet, Ahalya probed me: "Iris?"

"Yeah."

"Sorry."

Ahalya went inside and got a glass full of ice cubes. She poured a small whiskey into it and spoke in between sips: "Raghavan, we have learnt not to look at woman as an object of sex. But I wanted to be just that, and I started looking at Gautaman as a sexual object." Ahalya smiled momentarily.

"A strange object that doesn't yield to my control. I started forgetting my physical needs. Gautaman could sense that, and he would signal me towards the bedroom with his eyes. With my whole body protesting, I would go and lie down on the bed. Sometimes in the afternoon, Gautaman would call up and say he was coming home. Once he called when I was in Anita's place. She is the sister of our apartment building's claim-to-fame movie star, Devraj. She took care of his flat. Anita was giggling when I ran out explaining that Gautaman would reach home soon."

"Was it the day when Gautaman hit you with the bottle?" I asked.

"No," Ahalya continued, "On that afternoon I got a call: 'Ahalya, it's me, Gautaman.' I could tell that someone was impersonating Gautaman. The voice I heard was very familiar. The voice said: 'I will be there at two.' When I heard the knock at two, I said: 'It's not closed.' The familiar voice said: 'I am not Gautaman.' I replied: 'I know that.' When Devraj entered the room, the scent of cologne filled the house. Not counting TV and movies, I had met Devraj only once before in the elevator of our apartment."

"Devraj said: 'From the moment I saw you in the elevator . . .' We walked into the bedroom. Devraj read my body the way a blind man would read a poem in Braille script, touching it line by line. Finally as we were slipping into a calm silence, I jumped up and said: 'Devraj, you better leave. Gautaman may come home.'

"And yes, as soon as Devraj left, Gautaman came in, his face lit up in a smile. Gautaman said: 'While I was getting off the elevator, there went our superstar Devraj! Drenched in cologne.' Gautaman abruptly stopped talking. He stood there for some time trying to catch the scent in the air. Then he started sniffing around, rushing into the bedroom to smell the bedspread, holding me tight and sniffing at my cheeks, lips, shoulders. . . . None of this affected me. Indulging in my languid enchantment, I sat in the living room. A naughty smile might have

---

7. The narrator is not referring to actual sleep here, instead describing a feeling of fulfillment, such as when you want to sleep and imagine yourself feeling sleepy after a hearty meal.

lined my lips. Suddenly, Gautaman came running in with a bottle and hit me on the head."

For the second time that day, Iris touched my memory. It was not a delightful feeling to think of myself as a distanced third person in her conversations in Edinburgh. Perhaps because Ahalya reminded me of Iris, I did not visit her for some time. One night, Mira called me up at the hospital: "Raghavan, Chechi is throwing up."

"Mira, give her a lime to smell. Vomiting is not a good sign. I'll be there soon." When I got out of the hospital, I did not feel like calling a cab. I sat in the front seat of the ambulance.

I saw Ahalya. She had blacked out. I got her inside the ambulance and put her on oxygen. Later, the sound of Ahalya's breath echoed in the hospital corridors. I admitted her to the Intensive Care Unit. She was put on a ventilator. We scanned her head from various angles.

Mira came back to the hospital after a daylong sleep that followed two wakeful nights. She asked me: "Is surgery needed?"

"I don't think so."

"Luck."

"Luck?"

"I was thinking of Chechi's hair," Mira said. I kept quiet.

"I know I'm sounding silly," Mira started sobbing.

"Mira. . . ."

"Will the medicines be effective?"

"Too early to say."

"Raghavan is trying to hide something from me," Mira said pointedly.

"Nothing is certain as of now. I have sent the results to my old professor in Edinburgh. Let's see what he says."

Over the next two weeks, there were lots of accidents in Ernakulam. I had at least two surgeries to perform every day. That was a convenient excuse to avoid Mira. I telephoned Mira on the day that the letter from my professor in Edinburgh reached me: "Mira, shall I come to your place for dinner tonight? Call them all over, your mother, father's brother, and your cousin Mohan."

"Is it that bad?"

"Yeah."

"Tell me now," Mira said.

"No, I want to speak to my professor on the phone."

That night we sat around the dinner table before empty plates. Mira, her mother, and some male relatives were present. Priya and Ravi had come. Sitara and her husband Mukesh were there too. Sebastian came from Alappuzha. I looked at everyone and said: "If her mother and Mira agree, I can take Ahalya off the ventilator. Then she can breathe on her own. But to make that possible, I'll need to perform minor surgery to make an opening in the windpipe. After that, Ahalya can be brought home. Medicine cannot help beyond this."

"Won't my sister recover at all?" Mira was flustered.

"I shall arrange for a masseur who does head massage for comatose patients. And a good home nurse," I said.

"Ayurveda?" Priya and Ravi questioned together.[8]

"I can't say."

All of us got up when Ahalya's grandmother came into the room. Grandmother walked up to me and asked: "Is this all your medical science is about, Raghavan?"

Nobody spoke for some time. Then Mira raised her head and asked: "Food?"

"Through a tube," I answered.

"How long will my child remain like this?" Ahalya's mother started crying. "Why don't you remove all those tubes. Let her go in peace."

Sebastian opened a packet of cigarettes. I asked for one. I lit a cigarette for the first time after many years.

"What is the use of keeping her like this?" Ahalya's mother asked.

"Mother, what are you saying? She is our Ahalya," Sitara said.

"Raghavan, will she ever get well? Or after lying like this for sometime. . . ." Mira hesitated.

Everyone looked at me. I sat with a bowed head.

"What can Raghavan say?" Sebastian wondered aloud.

"I would be more than happy if my family pulled the plug on me if I were laid up like this," Priya said.

I stood up and pointed my two fingers that held the cigarette at each one's face. The way Iris does when she gets angry. I declared: "Nobody should play God." As my voice rose, it now broke like Iris's. "I believe in miracles." I walked out of the house.

As I drove back home, I saw an open telephone booth. After my return from Edinburgh, I called up Iris for the first time. The phone rang for some time and then my voice came on the answering machine: "We are presently not at home. We shall call you back when we return. Please leave your name, message, and telephone number after the beep. . . ."

Mira invited us over on Ahalya's birthday, the first since she was bedridden. Ahalya looked a little shrunken as she lay in her new clothes. Sebastian and I stood silently. Mira escaped into the kitchen. Sitara and Mukesh sat talking to each other. Priya and Ravi played with their child.

That was when Ashraf came in. His driver came behind him carrying a big cake. Ashraf played the CD of Yesudas songs on a music system he had brought from Dubai as a gift to Ahalya.[9] Ashraf and his driver hung festoons in the room. Mukesh and I began to blow up the balloons. Mira cut the cake for

---

8. Ayurveda, an indigenous system of healing that originated in Kerala, cures joint and muscle ailments. Even when it cannot cure illness, it often ameliorates the patient's pain.

9. Yesudas is one of India's most famous playback singers. In addition to recording Malayalam songs, he has sung in other Indian languages as well.

Ahalya. Ashraf sang aloud: "Happy Birthday to you, Ahalya . . ." The rest of us joined in: "Dear Ahalya . . ."

After that we often gathered at Ahalya's. I never forgot to take tapes or CDs of Malayalam songs as gifts for Ahalya. Sebastian came there on most Saturdays. Priya's husband Ravi sometimes played the flute for Ahalya and us. Mira got the girls from her beauty parlor to file Ahalya's nails. Sitara laid her newborn girl on Ahalya's chest and said: "Sweetie, you are lying on Beautiful Aunty."

Mira called me last night to tell me that today was Ahalya's birthday. Then she asked me: "Raghavan, can you come by ten in the morning tomorrow? Jayanti, her home nurse, said she would be a little late."

"Tomorrow is Sunday, isn't it? Yes, I'll be there."

"Chechi's face looks so dull. I want to give her a facial. Could you bring one-hundred grams of Fuller's Earth and one-hundred grams of sandal powder? I forgot to bring them from the beauty parlor."

I reached Mira's home at ten this morning. Mira mixed Fuller's Earth and sandal powder in two egg whites and the juice of two lemons. She put a little turmeric powder into it, and added half a bottle of rosewater to make a paste. The mixture was applied to Ahalya's face. Mira made me a cup of coffee while waiting for Ahalya's face to dry. Then she wiped Ahalya's face clean and said: "I have to go and bring Grandmother. Raghavan can leave as soon as Jayanti comes."

I sat in the living room watching cricket. In the break between wickets, I switched off the TV. Then I noticed that the music had stopped in Ahalya's room. I went into her room and put on a Yesudas tape. When I returned to watch TV, I vaguely felt something was different about Ahalya. I went back and checked on her. Everything looked as before. I came back, but still felt restless and went in again to check. Now I saw the two small lumps of Ahalya's erect nipples breaking the usual evenness of the sheet that covered her. I could see that her breasts were firm. The sheet had seized the quickening of her breath too.

I ran to my car, took out the torch from the glove compartment, and rushed back. I reached Ahalya, and shone the torch into each of her eyes. Her roving eyes took me by surprise. In that moment of wonder, I felt exhilarated and alone.

Then, did I feel Ahalya's fingers on my head? Like wisps of smoke wafting through my hair. A sudden blaze of fire. Ahalya's hand gripped my hair and drew my lips nearer to hers. I forced my head away, and whispered into her ear: "No."

And, like snow melting, I saw the lumps on the sheet disappear. I walked back.

Translated from Malayalam by Rizio Yohannan Raj

Part Three   *So-called Demons*

Thinking about Ramkatha as depicting interactions between different categories of creatures (such as deities, humans, and rakshasas) reveals how each category provides specific imaginative resources for authors. The writers in part 3 reject binary oppositions between rakshasas and humans that drive older tellings of Ramkatha. Their rakshasas do not conform to clichéd images of villainous demons who perform utterly wicked deeds. Instead, modern South Indian authors view rakshasas as neither completely evil nor the same as other creatures. Part 3's authors move beyond polarized representations, creating instead characters who raise questions about, make visible in dramatic ways, or flaunt resistance to conventional behavior.

Among features linked with rakshasas, scale is a long-standing element. In Tamil a task of huge proportions is called *rakshasa velai*, "rakshasa's work," because only one with prodigious energy, strength, and stamina could complete it. Someone described as "having ten heads" (as does Ravana) is a brainy person. The noun "rakshasa" derives from the Sanskrit verb root *raksh*, "to protect," and Ravana views himself as a protector of epic dimensions. As creatures "writ large," rakshasas provide writers ample scope for critique, humor, and psychological exploration.

Modern writers also portray rakshasas as transgressing conventions for social interaction. Part 3's authors have retrieved rakshasas from the realm of terror and remixed them into stories where they contravene society's norms by taking some forms of behavior to an extreme. These rakshasas act upon desires that they have neither denied nor repressed. When writers in part 3 name characters "Shurpanakha" or "Ravana," they play on readers' expectations of how rakshasas will act. When these characters behave in excessive ways, however, readers often find themselves contemplating aspects of modern life. From self-absorption to expressing their sexual passions openly, these rakshasas reveal, through their excess, human desires that others suppress. Each of part 3's writers employs a different logic to represent rakshasas, but none of these writers accepts the polarized view of rakshasas found in both Valmikian and Dravidian representations.[1]

Valmikian Representations

In Valmiki's *Ramayana,* rakshasas transgress several norms for proper conduct. Sanskritist Sheldon Pollock describes them as "creatures polluted by violence, blood, and carnivorous filth, who kill and eat those they kill." Not

Figure 4. Rama with his bow (right) glaring at Ravana within the frame of the portrait (left). Ravana's encounter with Rama in Spandana's staging of H. S. Venkatesha Murthy's play, *Chitrapata Ramayana* [Portrait Ramayana]. Image reprinted with the kind permission of Spandana.

only is their violence condemned as polluting rather than celebrated as heroic, they also deviate from sexual prescriptions: "[I]n their libidinized forms, they enact the deepest sexual urges—total abandonment to pleasure, as well as absolute autonomy and power in gratifying lust. Since they are broadly humanized in so many features, their deviance in others becomes not only a scandal but also a risk."[2] That is, the portrayal of rakshasas reveals behaviors that are feared but also secretly desirable.

Ramkatha has often been called a "textbook" of dharma because it provides examples of dharma and adharma (its opposite, non-dharma). For instance, authoritative tellings of Ramkatha depict Rama as a model of the way a son should treat his father. Similarly, Sita is viewed as paradigmatically devoted to Rama while Lakshmana is an ideal younger brother because he puts his elder brother's welfare above his own desires. If dharmic acts fall at one end of the spectrum, authoritative Ramkatha present the adharmic deeds of rakshasas at the opposite end. For example, Valmiki and Tulsidas depict Ravana as lacking self-discipline and thus bringing about his own destruction, while Shurpanakha earns disfigurement because she lacks proper modesty. Thus, as they reap positive or negative consequences of action, rakshasas exemplify the consequences of adharmic behavior.

According to Pollock, Valmiki depicts Rama as representing the divinized socio-political order of Ayodhya, and Ravana, Rama's opposite, as the enemy who threatens Ayodhya's socio-political order.[3] Demonized and othered, Ravana must, therefore, be slain by Rama. Building on Valmiki's portrayal of Ravana as an evil king fit only for destruction, Tulsidas adds a bhakti (devotional) element by depicting compassionate Lord Rama as slaying Ravana so that he can attain moksha and be released from his rakshasa form.

Pollock argues that Valmiki demonizes rakshasas by portraying them as deviant in behavior, with Ravana as a prime example. Ravana threatens the earth's well-being with his tyrannical rule, violates dharmic norms of gender by abducting the wife of a virtuous king, and transgresses sumptuary prescriptions by eating raw flesh. Shurpanakha too conforms to Pollock's description of deviance, especially in male-female relations, when she approaches Rama alone and offers herself to him in wedlock, instead of abiding by the matrimonial arrangements made by senior males in her family. Attributing such deeds to rakshasas "others" them in alienating ways.

Dravidianist Representations

In contrast, South Indian texts often exhibit a great deal of sympathy toward rakshasas. As early as the twelfth century, Kamban's Tamil *Iramavataram* portrayed Ravana not as utterly evil but as a tragic figure, and Nagachandra's twelfth-century, Kannada, Jain *Ramachandra Charita Purana* made Ravana less monstrous by giving him only one head. A number of twentieth-century Tamil texts express compassion for, and sometimes identification with, Ravana.[4] Sympathy for rakshasas received great momentum from Dravidian "cultural nationalism" that began in the early twentieth century, reached a high point in the 1940s and 1950s, and continues in lesser form today in South India. Linguists had labeled "Dravidian" the language family to which the four main languages of South India belong.[5] Identifying linguistic family with cultural identity, Dravidianists laud Ravana as a great Dravidian monarch and patron of the arts. They see Shurpanakha as disfigured by Aryans to humiliate and express contempt for rakshasas.

Dravidianist interpretations identify the rakshasas, monkeys, and bears depicted in Ramkatha with various communities of indigenous inhabitants located in different parts of South India. According to Dravidianists, Rama led an army of Aryans to the Dravidian kingdom in the South, where they decimated the rakshasa community and made so-called monkeys and bears into vassals.[6] In the historical imagination of many Tamil speakers, and some Telugu, Kannada, and Malayalam ones as well, rakshasas are the once glorious, and then cruelly subjugated, indigenous peoples of South India.[7]

According to this southern-centric ideology (which reverses the earlier

northern-centric ideology), authoritative tellings of Ramkatha recount a thinly
fictionalized account of how Northerners conquered Southerners in order to
aggrandize their kingdom's territory. Local collaborators, such as traitorous
Vibhishana who abandoned his brother Ravana to join Rama, revealed Lanka's
military secrets, helping Rama to conquer the otherwise invincible city. After
conquest, Aryans sent Brahmin priests south to inculcate belief in caste so that
the subject population would be deceived into believing that they were inferior, thus destroying their self-respect.[8] Although selections in part 3 assume
readers' familiarity with both Valmikian and Dravidianist constructions of rakshasas, none of the authors accepts in entirety either of these opposing representations.

Rakshasas and Gender

Part 3's selections portray rakshasas in multiple and heterogeneous
ways, but share two characteristics: All five do *not* portray rakshasas as performing supernatural deeds or wielding miraculous weapons and *do* depict
rakshasas as impelled by desires that are excessive, rather than moderate or disciplined. Most of part 3's selections also cast rakshasas in ways that call attention to social constructions of gender.[9]

For example, C. Subramania Bharati (#17) does so by reversing the roles of
Shupanakha and Lakshmana. While authoritative tellings portray Lakshmana
slashing off Shurpanakha's nose (and ears) in response to her bold offer of marriage, "The Horns of the Horse" depicts Shurpanakha cutting off Lakshmana's
ears (and toes), after which Rama's awe at her martial prowess impels him to
offer himself in marriage. When Rama proved his prowess with Shiva's bow, he
won Sita as bride; here Shurpanakha proves her prowess with a fruit knife so
Rama seeks her as his bride. The reversal highlights the peculiarity of falling in
love with a person because he or she performs a violent act, making visible the
premises of the "macho" ethic. Long before feminists began attacking constructions of gender linked with violence, Bharati satirized them in this story.

Kavanasarma's "Shurpanakha's Sorrow" (#18) questions whether humans
actually are more virtuous than rakshasas or simply less likely to get caught
at misdeeds. In the story, businessman Ravana does not act in moderate, re-
strained, or disciplined ways, but neither does Rama. When Ravana fails to get
Rama convicted in court for accounting malpractice because Rama's uncle, an
influential politician, bribes the judge, Ravana decides to exact vigilante justice instead. He takes revenge by abducting Sita, after which Rama disfigures
Shurpanakha. Each man is propelled by greed and by the fear that if he does not
prove his prowess by roughing up a woman, others will doubt his masculinity.
For Kavanasarma, the demonic is that which impels men to perpetrate sexual
assault.

In *Mappila Ramayana* (#19), representation of Shurpanakha and Ravana
functions to spoof the courtship process. Shurpanakha, a fifty-six-year-old
widow who desires youth, beauty, and a new husband, tries to talk Rama into

wedlock by promising him the protection of her brother, Ravana. Rama, a Kshatriya and prince, could hardly find this offer anything but insulting to his male prowess. Equally misguided is Ravana's proposal of marriage. He offers Sita, who willingly shared with her spouse the deprivations of forest exile, the accouterments of conspicuous consumption: fireworks as matrimonial announcements, a four-elephant wedding procession, and heaps of jewelry. In this song, a rakshasa is one deluded enough to think he or she would be seen as an irresistible marriage partner and to promise inappropriate blandishments.

In contrast, Venkatesha Murthy's *Portrait Ramayana* (#20) suggests that Ravana and Sita both experience strong desires, but only he acts upon them. Sita's feelings are compared to a pot of boiling milk that might spill over if tipped—even a tiny bit—so they must be ruthlessly and fully repressed. Ravana, in contrast, openly covets her and insists that, since he emerged from Sita's imagination, she shares the same intense desire. The play explores conflicts between expressing and suppressing feelings of love, ending ambiguously with Sita postponing physical affection for Ravana until her next birth.

Satchidanandan's "Come Unto Me, Janaki" (#21) suggests that Ravana's power as a rakshasa lies in his ability to sustain his love for Sita by persevering against any and all obstacles. Only a rakshasa has the strength and will to counteract the acidity of Rama's venomous "love" for Sita and to convince her to return from Mother Earth to experience love anew. Only Ravana's intense rakshasa desire can dissolve the hardened chastity that Sita cultivated at great cost as Queen of Ayodhya during exile, imprisonment, and banishment. Ravana's love even transcends death.

Humor and Rakshasas

Modern writers often find themselves drawn to representing rakshasas through the lens of humor. The extreme nature of rakshasa behavior makes them especially appropriate for comic treatment. For example, it is only a short step from a ten-headed demon to Kavanasarma's riff on Ravana as a playback singer who can produce ten different film actors' voices. Few would make heroic characters the butt of such treatment, but poking fun at rakshasas is safer. They have long been larger than life and thus available for caricature.[10]

In several selections, rakshasas receive almost cartoon-like treatment. Slapstick emerges in *Mappila Ramayana* when Shurpanakha dyes her hair with coal, hammers in her buck teeth, cleans years of snot from her nostrils, and sticks mangoes in her blouse to look sexy. This caricature of female concern with outward appearance mocks human vanity, especially of a widow seeking a husband.[11] Bharati too pokes fun at rakshasas by depicting Ravana, a rakshasa, and Vali, a monkey, attending the same math class in school. This incongruity of a human activity performed by non-humans produces amusement, just as does a *New Yorker* cartoon of various animals all dressed up in three-piece suits exchanging chitchat at a cocktail party.

Bharati also highlights intriguing contradictions about Ravana in Ramkatha.

Although King Ravana talks and acts a great deal like a Kshatriya, he is actually a Brahmin and takes great interest in the details of Vedic sacrifice. In describing the grand Vedic rites that Ravana patronizes, Bharati highlights the animal sacrifice prescribed in the ancient brahminical scriptures so sacred to South Indian Brahmins, who pride themselves on their strict vegetarianism. Furthermore, by presenting Ravana as a king who rules so perfectly that the entire natural world runs its course with such regularity that the annual rains fall at mathematically elegant intervals, Bharati uses a rakshasa to exemplify dharmic kingship. When Bharati reverses previous representations of rakshasas, a satirical edge to his humor emerges.

Shurpanakha as Rakshasa and Woman

Modern South Indian retellings of Ramkatha portray Shurpanakha as a more complex character than in authoritative Ramayanas, where she drops out of the narrative after instigating Ravana to abduct Sita, as if she were a mere plot device. In older Ramkatha texts, notes Erndl, even though male characters are divided into good and bad (e.g., Rama vs. Ravana), "the split between women is far more pronounced and is always expressed in terms of sexuality," and "when a woman such as Śurpanakha performs a wrong deed, it is typically ascribed to her female nature, whereas Ravana's evil deeds, for example, are never said to spring from his male nature."[12] In contrast, modern authors do not treat Shurpanakha as a mere plot device; they delve into her motivations and rethink her agency. They also balance representing Shurpanakha as rakshasa and as female in differing proportions, producing a diversity of depictions.

"Shurpanakha's Sorrow" suggests that sexual assault as a result of male rivalry is not an isolated event and, to the contrary, is an experience to which many females have been subjected. Kavanasarma presents Shurpanakha's mutilation as having little to do with being a rakshasa and everything to do with being female. Even Mandodari, Ravana's pativrata, agrees with Shurpanakha's analysis that men express cowardice when they act out hostility by assaulting their opponent's woman. Nor is Shurpanakha's rakshasa status the operative aspect in "The Horns of the Horse": her ability to repel Lakshmana by wielding a fruit knife, rather than turning to her brother, derives not from supernatural rakshasa (demonic) power but from her refusal to let men take advantage of her.

Even *Portrait Ramayana*'s representation of Shurpanakha builds upon her spunk, ingenuity, and ability to adopt disguise—qualities not limited to rakshasas. She cleverly concocts a plan to get past the palace guards by posing as a fortune-teller. Then she claims to be Sita's childhood playmate so she can inveigle Sita into drawing Ravana's picture. Furthermore, Shurpanakha uses the same method to enliven the portrait of Ravana as do the human artisans who make icons of deities: enlivening the image by painting in the eyes. Venkatesha Murthy, thus, presents Shurpanakha as an artist, as he does Sita.[13]

Although Kavanasarma presents Shurpanakha primarily as victim, her comments at the story's end suggest an awareness of the wrongs perpetrated by sexism, an awareness that provides the initial step toward combating those wrongs. Her ability to preclude disfigurement in "The Horns of the Horse" and take revenge for mutilation in *Portrait Ramayana* equips her with an agency she seldom receives in authoritative tellings of Ramkatha. Shurpanakha and Ravana are represented in part 3 in ways that display creative rethinking of the category of rakshasas among modern South Indian writers. Each way that rakshasas are reconceived has consequences for how self and other are understood, represented, critiqued, or strategically invoked.

Notes

1. The phrase "Valmikian tradition" is used here to refer to Valmiki's *Ramayana* and subsequent tellings that share his representation of rakshasas as wholly "other" and deviant. "Valmikian" is descriptive, not judgmental, in contrast with "Valmiki and his epigones," used by Pollock (1993: 263), which denotes Valmiki and his heirs, but can imply that the heirs are unworthy or inferior successors. The term "Dravidianist" refers to interpretations of Ramkatha that view Ravana as a glorious monarch who represents the greatness of Dravidian culture before the coming of the Aryan invaders from the North.

2. Pollock (1991: 83–84).

3. Because Valmiki portrays Rama as a divine avatara serving as a king and because Rama comes to symbolize the institution of kingship in many subsequent Indian literary texts, Pollock (1993) sees Rama as a representation of a divinized political order. Not all scholars agree with Pollock's thesis here. See, for example, Chattopadhyaya (1998).

4. In the 1950s, some Ravana fans even named their children "Ravanan."

5. Trautmann (1997).

6. This view of the past was invoked by the former chief minister of Tamilnadu, Karunanidhi, when he declared, famously, "Anyone who insults Ravana insults me."

7. For two overviews of this period that emphasize different facets, see Geetha and Rajadurai (1998) and Irschick (1969).

8. For a discussion of the many books that espoused this view and the main characteristics of the discourse, see Richman (1991a, especially nn. 36, 48–49).

9. For a discussion of specifically how Valmiki's constructions of rakshasas focus upon sexual and gustatory deviance, see R. Goldman (2000).

10. For example, children often find Ravana more intriguing than Rama. Ravana's ten heads have prompted their questions such as whether any of the heads ever get into arguments with each other and whether all the heads get a cold when one head contracts a cold.

11. T. H. Kunhirambi Nambiar heard *Mappila Ramayana* from Piranthan Hassankutty in 1928 and found its humor so striking that its words lodged themselves in his memory. He sang the song over the decades, amusing audiences of varied backgrounds. M. N. Karassery, who heard Nambiar sing it while conducting research on Mapilla songs in northern Malabar for a Ph.D. from Calicut University in the 1960s, savored the song's satire and published the version that he recorded from Nambiar so readers could too.

12. Erndl (1991: 83) compares depictions of Shurpanakha in Valmiki's *Ramayana*, Kamban's *Iramavataram*, *Adhyatma Ramayana*, Tulsidas's *Ramcharitmanas*, and a Hindi twentieth-century commentary on Tulsidas, *Radheshyam Ramayana*.

13. Several selections in the volume suggest that Shurpanakha and Sita have more in common than has been generally realized. For example, Volga's "Reunion" (#8) portrays the two middle-aged women comparing notes on Rama's treatment of them. In Venkatesha Murthy's play as well, both characters prompt self-reflection about the nature of artistic creation.

17 Gender Reversal

C. Subramania Bharati (1882–1921) worked in a number of capacities over the course of his life, including as court poet for a zamindar, high school teacher, journalist, cartoonist, and translator. Widely viewed as the greatest Tamil poet of the twentieth century, he received the title by which he is commonly known, "Bharati" (a Tamil name for Goddess Sarasvati), from an assembly of poets in recognition of his literary talent. His articles and cartoons criticizing colonial rule made him vulnerable when the British government cracked down on "seditious" writings, so he fled to the nearby French territory of Pondicheri, where he remained for a decade and wrote many of the works that later won him literary fame. After returning to British India in 1918, he passed away at age thirty-nine in 1921.

In addition to poetry, Bharati also wrote "The Horns of the Horse," and some other stories in the same vein, for an unfinished collection he called "Nava-tantra."[1] He envisioned it as an updated version of *Pancha-tantra,* an ancient collection of Sanskrit animal fables allegedly composed to impart practical wisdom about rule to princes. "The Horns of the Horse" contains the nested structure of many animal fables, beginning with a question about how a particular animal gained one of his features, but Bharati's tale answers a different question: why does a horse *not* have a particular feature, namely, horns? The humorous animal fable also tells Ramkatha from Bharati's wry perspective.

The narrator's unreliability is suggested by his name, Pandit Crooked Face, as well as by King Reevana's susceptibility to flattery, generous gifts of gold to fawning storytellers, and excessive interest in the deeds of his ancestor, Ravana. The tale also mocks glorification of Ravana as perfect ruler of ancient Dravidian civilization, a view of the past propagated by Tamil ideologues during (and after) Bharati's day.[2]

"The Horns of the Horse" also makes fun of narrative conceits of various kinds. Bharati mocks epics by depicting kings whose political networks develop from attending the same math class in school, Vedic rites that require absurdly large numbers of sacrificial offerings, and crucial journeys delayed for years due to a paucity of auspicious times. Male-female relations are also skewed. Rather than Lakshmana disfiguring Shurpanakha with his gleaming

---

1. Many Indians know of Bharati's nationalist poetry composed in Tamil, Sanskrit, and English, but "The Horns of the Horse" is little known either inside or outside of Tamilnadu.
2. P. Sundaram Pillai (1855–1897) had identified rakshasas as Dravidians. See summaries of his ideas in Ponemballem Pillai (1909) and V. P. Subrahmania Mudaliyar (1908).

sword, Shurpanakha slashes Lakshmana's ears and toes with an ordinary fruit knife. While disfiguring her face is the most common punishment for a woman's misdeed relating to men, cutting off Lakshmana's toes has no such precedent.[3] Even the story's framing device rests on the hyperbole that the guffaw of Ravana echoes so loudly throughout the universe that the heavenly horses fall and break off their horns.

Bharati recounts the deeds of Sita, Rama, Shurpanakha, and Ravana in ways that differ radically from those by Kamban, Eluttacchan, Valmiki, or Tulsidas. Bharati puts Shurpanakha at the center of his satirical animal fable, instead of making her auxiliary to Ravana. Bharati also breaks down opposition between "good" and "bad" women by having Sita seek help from Shurpanakha. Yet the story ends on a familiar note, with Rama marrying Sita in a proper ceremony in Mithila, thus limiting the extent of the transgression in "The Horns of the Horse."

Source: C. Subramania Bharati, "Kutirai Kompu," in *Kataikkottu* [Collected Stories] (Madras: Parati Piracuralayam, 1938); reprinted in *Paratiyar Kataikal* [Stories of Bharati] (Madras: Poompukar Press, 1977), pp. 285–292.

The Horns of the Horse
BY C. SUBRAMANIA BHARATI

In Andappura City in the land of Sind lived a king named Reevana Nayakkar. He prided himself on his descent from the lineage of Ravana, who ruled as the King of Lanka several aeons ago. His court was renowned for its many pandits who had thoroughly mastered all the shastras. One day the king demanded of his court, "Why doesn't a horse have horns?" All of the pandits were taken aback. Only Pandit Crooked Face, who had come from Karnataka to receive gifts from the king, offered to answer the question. When the king gave his assent, Pandit Crooked Face began this story:

"Emperor Reevana, listen! In ancient times, all horses had horns. In the time of Lord Ravana, your ancestor who ruled in Lanka, Brahma Deva put an end to the practice of having horns on horses, at the king's command."

When Reevana Nayakkar heard [of his ancestor's power], he was thrilled. "What's that? Tell me the whole story." Pandit Crooked Face continued as follows.

During the time of Ravana's dharmic rule in Lanka, rains fell three times a month. In those days, every year uniformly contained thirteen months and each month had thirty-three days. So annually thirty-three rains fell at the rate of 1

---

3. Erndl (1991: 82) notes that disfigurement of women was the most common punishment for women's crimes of a sexual nature, ranging from adultery to attempting to poison one's husband.

per 11 days.[4] The Brahmins were so skilled that they could recite backwards—without missing even a single syllable—the four Vedas, the six shastras, the sixty-four kinds of learned arts, 1,008 puranas, and the 10,080 subpuranas.[5] Every day in every Brahmin house—without fail—24,000 goats were sacrificed and a variety of yajnas were performed. (The storyteller has only told us about the arithmetic of goats. He could have told us the totals of other animals as well.)

In the same way, members of the other varnas performed their duties properly as well. Everyone was virtuous and charitable, enjoying all the pleasures of this world and then attaining the shade of Ultimate Shiva's holy feet in the next world.

At that time in the city of Ayodhya, King Dasharatha's son Rama did not want his elder brother crowned. Since he desired the crown himself, he revolted against his father. Dasharatha, enraged, threw Rama and Lakshmana out of the country. From there they fled to the city of Mithila and took refuge with King Janaka. While Janaka was sheltering them, Rama saw and fell in love with the beauty of Sita, daughter of the above-mentioned King Janaka. He abducted her and entered the Dandaka Forest.

There Rama and Lakshmana tortured the sages in all sorts of ways, ruining their sacrifices. Shurpanakha Devi, who ruled there, came to hear of this. Because she was Ravana's sister and because she was from the Brahmin lineage, she couldn't tolerate the trouble Rama gave the rishis. So she ordered her army to catch Rama and his brother Lakshmana, tie them up, and bring them to her. The soldiers caught the brothers just as she had ordered, bound them with a rope, and brought them into her presence.

Commanding that the two be untied, she threatened them with harsh words: "Because you are princes and also because of your youth, I will forgive your past depredations. However, if you ever perform such actions again, you will be severely punished."

After giving this advice, she welcomed them to stay for a few days in the palace and enjoy her hospitality. One day when Sita was speaking to Shurpanakha privately, Sita told her that Rama had abducted her and she wished to return to her father in Mithila. Out of empathy Shurpanakha sent Sita to Lanka, and asked Ravana to have her brought to Mithila. As soon as Sita reached Ravana's palace, the ministers sought an auspicious day to send her to Mithila. There wasn't an auspicious day during the entire year. It was the same thing the following year. So Ravana ordered Sita to stay at his palace for two years.

Back in the Dandaka Forest, Rama asked Shurpanakha, "Where is Sita?"

---

4. This section mocks language about ideal kingship. If a king rules righteously, it is said that people will perform proper dharma and rains will fall moderately in season. Bharati lampoons this notion with spurious mathematical formulations.

5. The Vedas contain hymns; the shastras tell how to carry out one's duties; the sixty-four arts include music, poetry, dance, and other elevated accomplishments; puranas and subpuranas contain stories of the gods.

Shurpanakha told him that Sita had been sent to Mithila. Angrily, Lakshmana began to rebuke Shurpanakha, asking, "How could you do such a thing?"

Immediately Shurpanakha grabbed the knife tucked at her waist, which she used to cut down fruits and eat them. Then she slashed off Lakshmana's two ears and toes.

Infatuated by her heroic act, Rama said, "Oh my! Since you sent Sita to Mithila, why don't you marry me now?"

As soon as Shurpanakha heard this, she felt embarrassed, blushed, and said, "It's true that you are a handsome boy. I could marry you. But my elder brother would get angry, so don't stay here any longer. If you do, it will give rise to scandal."

Rama asked, "When did you send Sita to Mithila? With whom did you send her? How far would she have gotten by now?"

Shurpanakha replied, "Henceforth, abandon all thoughts of Sita. I have sent her to my elder brother in Lanka. Maybe he'll send her to Mithila, maybe not. He can do whatever he wants. He's the king of the three worlds. Forget Sita."

When he heard that, Rama set out, planning to rescue Sita from Ravana, and arrived in Kishkindha. At that time a king named Sugriva was ruling Kishkindha. He had been preceded by his elder brother, Vali. Ravana and Vali were great friends; they had studied arithmetic in the same school. Even though Ravana exacted tribute throughout the three worlds, he had exempted Vali from paying any tribute for Kishkindha. While Vali was sleeping, his younger brother Sugriva cut his throat with a spade and then forced his brother's wife, Tara, to marry him. Through the cunning of his minister Hanuman, Sugriva took possession of the kingdom. When Ravana heard this, he became furious and immediately wrote the following letter to Sugriva:

"Ravana, King of Lanka, writes to Sugriva of Kishkindha: You killed our friend. You killed your elder brother. You stole the kingdom. As soon as you read this letter, you should send Tara to a nunnery in Lanka. You should give the kingdom to Angada, the son of Vali. You should become a sannyasi. Renounce the kingdom and go away. If you refuse to obey my commands about these matters, I will lead my army to attack you."

As soon as Sugriva read these orders, he got frightened, looked for Hanuman, and asked him, "What are we going to do?"

Hanuman gave this advice: "You must pacify him by sending him Tara, whom you took from Vali, as well as seventeen and a half women under seventeen years of age as slaves. And for the expenses incurred for the sacrifices performed by the acclaimed Vedic rishis whom Ravana venerates and worships, send forty crores, eighty lakhs, 34,240 goats and cattle. Also send enough of the juice called "Soma-essence" to fill 400 crores of leather bags, each of which holds 4,000 measures of liquid.[6] Inform Ravana that Angada will receive the

---

6. A lakh is 100,000 and a crore is 10,000,000 (ten million). Soma is a hallucinogenic drink brewed as part of the Vedic sacrifice as an offering to the gods.

title of crown prince and that every year he must pay 4,000 crores of gold as tribute. If you do all this, we can survive," said Hanuman.

Exactly as Hanuman had directed, Sugriva collected and sent in the custody of messengers the slave girls, goods and cattle, juice, and the total tribute for the first year, along with a message.

The messengers delivered the goats, cattle, and juice to Ravana's palace. They gave the slave girls and money to the sages, and the palmleaf letter to Ravana. Because some messengers drank some juice from the leather bags on the way, they failed to carry out their work properly. Ravana and his friends immediately killed and ate all the goats and cattle, and then drank the juice. Only afterwards did Ravana open and read the letter.

He demanded of the messengers, "Why didn't the money and slave women who were in your custody arrive?" They responded that they had delivered the money and slave women to the monastery of the sages. Since the sages had taken all the money as payment for the sacrificial ritual, they said it would be contrary to the scriptures to return it.[7] And most of the slave girls had run off.

Ravana gave the command to kill all the messengers immediately and ordered the Commander-in-Chief of his army to leave at that very minute and make war on Sugriva.

His Commander-in-Chief said, "Fine!" and collected his troops.

Spies conveyed all this information to Kishkindha. Immediately Sugriva mobilized his army, as Hanuman had advised. After Ravana's army got ready, they waited for an auspicious sign before setting off.

Meanwhile, since Hanuman's jati was that of an agile monkey, he quickly set out with his monkey army for Lanka. Rama and Lakshmana both joined his army. It included forty-nine crores, ninety-four lakhs, 37,356 foot soldiers, twice the number of cavalry, four times that in chariots and 70 times that in the elephant corps.

Even before they came to Lanka, a section of Ravana's army attacked them and finished them off. Only Rama and Lakshmana kept some sections of the army and secretly entered Lanka.

This news reached the ears of Ravana. Immediately, he began to roar with laughter. "Hahaha! Has the human army entered our city? What amusement! Hahaha!" The sound of his laughter was so loud that it deafened Adisesha and made the solar disk fall to the ground.[8]

Afterwards, Ravana destroyed Rama's army and had Rama and his younger brother brought to him. But out of compassion for the royal princes, he didn't kill them. Instead, he handed them over to some servants and sent them to Janaka for custody.

---

7. It would be inauspicious for money or other forms of wealth bestowed on Brahmins as payment to be taken back.

8. Adisesha is the serpent upon which Lord Vishnu rests, floating in the milk ocean in the celestial world. The Sun is believed to ride in a horse-pulled chariot across the sky from east to west each day.

Afterwards, Sita too reached Mithila. Janaka also had compassion, so he gave Sita to Rama in marriage. Then Rama and Lakshmana went to Ayodhya and submitted themselves to Bharata.

––––––

"*This* is the real Ramayana story," concluded Pandit Crooked Face in the court of Reevana Nayakar.

Reevana then said, "Venerated Pandit, I asked why horses don't have horns, but you haven't answered that question yet, have you?"

Crooked Face Pandit said, "Didn't I say that when Reevana heard the news that Rama had come to invade Lanka and cried 'Hahaha,' the sun couldn't bear the noise and fell down? At that time, the horns of the sun's seven horses broke. The sun came and fell at the feet of Ravana, beseeching him tearfully:

'My horses possess the boon of immortality. Other horses don't have the swiftness that they possess, but their horns have broken. From now on everyone in the world will laugh at me. What shall I do?'

Feeling compassion for the Sun, Ravana ordered Brahma, the Creator God: 'From now on, you must create horses without horns. That way, there will be no reason to laugh at the Sun's horses.'

"Since that day, Brahma has created horses without horns."

When he heard what Pandit Crooked Face said, Reevana Nayakkam was delighted and gave the pandit a gift of a lakh of gold for each letter [in each word] of the story.

Translated from Tamil by Paula Richman

18   Male Rivalry and Women

Among those included in this volume, Telugu writer Kandula Varaha Narasimha Sarma (b. 1939) has utilized the strategy of contemporizing Ramkatha in a particularly masterful way. A retired professor of civil engineering who writes in Telugu under the nom de plume of "Kavanasarma," he seeks to provide logical explanations and tell "a hard-core truth" in his writing.[1] He has won particular praise for his clever satire. His story of Shurpanakha's mutilation updates the plot, combining astute observation of social hypocrisy with humorous digs at today's politicians, lawyers, and businessmen. The story's incidents could come right out of today's headlines.

Yet, the character's names signal that Ramkatha is the subtext of the story. Kavanasarma's prominent protagonist is "Ravanarao." "Rao" is a widely found caste suffix among Telugu Brahmins, a usage that reminds readers that King Ravana was not a Kshatriya but a Brahmin. Rama is called "Ramaraju," a colloquial way to say "King Rama," while Lakshmana is "Latchumaiah," which has a decidedly local ring to it. Rama's wife is named Sita and Ravana's sister earned the nickname "Shurpanakha" in college. Ravanarao disguises himself as an ascetic called Dasakanthaswami, "Swami with Ten Necks" (addressed by the honorific "Swamiji"). The sobriquet takes "not being what one seems" to a new level, since the reference to ten throats means that the holy man can sing, as do playback singers, with ten different actors' voices.[2]

Kavanasarma has cleverly engineered the plot so that familiar events get a new twist. For example, the conflict between Ravanarao and Ramaraju occurs not in war but in the world of business, where today's real battles are fought in the global marketplace. And rather than defeating enemies by knifing them in the back, one gets one's uncle to bribe judges. Kavanasarma also calls the dwelling to which Ramaraju retreats a *parnasala*, a forest cottage, a title used today for a suburban or country mansion where politicians retire to enjoy the wealth accrued in office.

At the heart of the story is Shurpanakha, who has suffered because cowardly men perpetrate violence upon each others' women, rather than settle their scores man to man. The two competitors abuse women to take revenge on each other and prove their masculinity. The story indicates that such behavior and its motivations are widespread, citing them in recent atrocities perpetrated

---

1. Quoted in an interview with Sarma in the *Hindu*, February 3, 2003.
2. In some Indian films, the stars do not actually sing. Instead, that task is performed by "playback singers," who record the music while actors mouth the words. A talented playback singer can imitate the singing styles of many actors.

by high caste men, with the collusion of the police, against low caste women. Thus, Shurpanakha's sorrow is the sorrow of women who experience sexual violence. Kavanasarma suggests continuities between Shurpanakha's mutilation and events occurring today.

Source: "Surpanakha Sokam" was first published in *Andhra Sachitra Vara Patrika*, 11 May 1984. This version has been translated from Kandula Varaha Narasimha Sarma, *Kavanasarma Kathalu* (Visakhapatnam: RK Publications, 1995).

Shurpanakha's Sorrow
BY "KAVANASARMA" KANDULA VARAHA NARASIMHA SARMA

Ramaraju was fuming. He was fretting, spitting fire, letting off steam. He decided that he had to take revenge for the insult he had suffered.

He felt humiliated because Ravanarao had deceived him and carried Sita away. He was not worried because his wife was suffering at the hands of his enemy but because he felt that people might laugh at him for being so effeminate and doing nothing while his enemy had a good time with his wife. Ravanarao should pay. Only then would Ramaraju have peace of mind. Only then would his manliness have any value.

Ramaraju was so worked up that he took Latchumaiah and went looking around the neighborhood. When he went a little southward he saw a flower garden.

"This is Ravanarao's sister's garden, Elder Brother," said Latchumaiah.

"I know," said Ramaraju imperiously, "So what do you want me to do?"

"Did I say anything, Elder Brother? I only reminded you."

"Do *you* have to remind me that this Shurpanakha is that Ravana Asura's sister?" Ramaraju said, irritatedly.[3]

When Ramaraju was in college, the other students had named Ravanarao's sister "Shurpanakha" because she was of a jealous and mean nature and because she was Ravanarao's sister. She had once nurtured a lot of affection for Ramaraju but Ravanarao had found her a good match. Later her husband left her and took up with another woman and she started looking after this garden where she lived happily selling flowers and fruits. She used to come to their parnasala and speak to Sita. But of late she had stopped that.

"That girl is a bit jealous because you take good care of me," Sita had once laughingly told Ramaraju. Though she had dismissed the whole thing with a smile, she hadn't stopped meeting Shurpanakha. Nor had she turned her away.

Sita would look out anxiously for Ramaraju if he went out anywhere. That

---

3. By calling Ravana "*Asura*" (demon), Kavanasarma says, in effect, "that demon of a Ravana," an inside joke since authoritative tellings of Ramkatha portray Ravana as a demon. The English equivalent in a Christian context would be "that devil of a Satan."

day when he and Latchumaiah came home, Sita was not waiting at the doorstep looking out for him. Ramaraju remembered that day vividly.

"Sita," he called out. There was no reply.

"Sita!" he shouted. Sita didn't answer, "What is it?"

"Sita!" he screamed as if the roof would come down. Still Sita did not come running.

Sita never went to the town, not even to see a film. Thinking she might have left a note, he searched all over the house but found nothing.

Then Ramaraju remembered that he had asked Sita to serve Dasakanthaswami. He walked towards a hut in the corner of the garden. No sign of movement there. He went in and looked around. The prayer things had not been disturbed. There was a smell in the room, the kind of odor found in hospitals. He thought perhaps someone had been injured.

He came out and called, "Latchumaiah!"

Latchumaiah walked towards him.

"Coming, Elder Brother."

"Where's Amma, you rascal?"[4]

"I don't know. I was with you, wasn't I?"

"Why did you come with me without my asking you to come, you wretched rascal?"

"You didn't ask me but Amma told me, 'Go and see. Our car seems to have broken down at some distance. You may have to push it. Or do something else. Go and check. This is a forest. If our car isn't there, come running back. If it's our car, take this bag, tell him to go to town and get me the groceries I want.' When I reached there, weren't you under the car? I pushed the car and it started with a whirr. Thinking I may have to push it again on the way, I quickly got into the car."

"Where's Swamiji?"

"I don't know!"

All was quiet for a while.

"Perhaps Swamiji has taken Amma along with him to the Shiva temple," said Latchumaiah after some time.

"It's good you didn't say he eloped with her, you wretched fellow," Ramaraju snapped.

But the seed of suspicion was sown in his mind. In a little while it grew into a huge banyan tree. Wondering, what that odor was that he smelt in the hut, he went in again. He inhaled and realized that it was chloroform.

"So you're a fake swami, you scoundrel! You threw a blanket over my eyes, didn't you? You deceitful scoundrel! You've kidnapped my wife, haven't you, you bastard!" Ramaraju hissed.

He searched for Sita and the swami. He found a *jutka* driver who was on the verge of death. He said, "Saar, the car sped past me like a rocket. Amma was

---

4. "Amma" literally means "mother" but can be used to refer to any respectable woman.

bundled in at the back. I tried to avoid the car, fell into the pit and was seriously injured."[5]

Ramaraju understood what had happened. He knew now that this was Ravanarao's handiwork.

———————

Ravanarao and Ramaraju were bitter business rivals. Ravanarao's people had lived in that town all along while Ramaraju's father had come from another district and settled there. Ramaraju wanted to enter Ravanarao's family business, which had been with him for generations, and establish his authority. And Ravanarao was infuriated by this.

Ravanarao placed his most trusted people in Ramaraju's service, got copies of documents of his business transactions and gave them to the income tax authorities. Ramaraju entrusted his entire business to his half-brother and stayed away from it. That brother's uncle wielded a lot of influence. He was trying to throw money around and get the cases dropped.

Two years ago, Ramaraju had bought a garden at some distance from the town thinking it might come in useful. He had given up his business for a while and was trying to wash away the sins of his past and earn a good name. So he built a house with all amenities in that garden, called it a parnasala and lived there with Sita. He took Latchumaiah along to keep him company.

Trying to prove that he had no desire for money, he started wearing clothes made of jute. He kept good company so that people would call him an honorable person. Thinking, who better than swamijis—agents of Gods—to give him a clean bill of sale, he turned to them!

It was around this time that he learnt of Dasakanthaswami. He was told that when the swami prayed to Lord Siva, his voice had the power of ten voices, and that he could sing in the voices of Ghantasala, Balasubramaniam, Raja, Madhavapeddi, Pithapuram, M. S. Ramarao, P. B. Srinivas, Raghuramiah, Suribabu and Rajeswararao. He requested that the swamiji come to his parnasala, stay for a week and accept alms from him. The swami agreed.

What Ramaraju did not know was that the swami was none other than Ravanarao in disguise.

Ravanarao's wife was aware of his intentions. "You should fight amongst yourselves and decide who is the stronger of the two. But it is not right on your part to kidnap Sita. Would you be able to tolerate it if Ramaraju kidnapped me?" she asked, trying to make him see reason.

"Shut up! I am not a fool like him. I have not built a hut away from the city and am not living with you there. There are ten people, along with five hounds, guarding you! It's not possible for Ramaraju even to look at you from up close," Ravanarao said, proudly twirling his moustache.

———————

5. A *jutka* is a wagon pulled by a horse, a form of transport used in some rural areas even after cars became available. The jutka driver functions as the modern equivalent of Jatayu. "Saar" is a local pronunciation of "Sir."

Dasakanthaswami had a hut built close to the parnasala in Ramaraju's garden and lived there. He kidnapped Sita at the first opportunity, drugging her
with chloroform and carrying her off. Though he had a house as large as Lanka,
he hid Sita elsewhere, so that even if Ramaraju came with a search warrant, he
would have to go back empty handed. "What can this Ramaraju do? He doesn't
have any proof against me," he boasted.

Ravanarao had forgotten about Shurpanakha.

But that day Ramaraju remembered Shurpanakha was Ravanarao's sister.

The next day, Ramaraju went as if to visit her and invited her over.

"Why don't you come and see our garden? It seems you have stopped coming
over because Sita is no longer around." Shurpanakha immediately understood
that he was really saying Sita is not here and I'm alone. When she was in the first
year of the Intermediate class, she had cast her vote for Ramaraju who was in
the final year of his B.A., and had helped him win the election as President of
the Union. In those days she used to love him deeply. Knowing that they didn't
belong to the same caste, however, she had had no illusions of marrying him.
She remembered those times.

She dressed up in her best clothes and went to Ramaraju's garden the next
day. Eager to be kissed by Ramaraju, she went straight to him.

He smiled maliciously and said, "Latchumaiah! Get that knife you had sharpened this morning and cut off this bitch's nose and ears."

"What kind of love play is this?" Shurpanakha asked, thinking it was all a
joke.

"I'm coming, Elder Brother," said Latchumaiah, drawing a knife.

Ramaraju bolted the doors so that Shurpanakha could not escape. An atroc-
ity was committed on Shurpanakha in that very garden in broad daylight.

"May you be ruined! May your wife be a widow! What did I do to you, you
cunning bastard! May you drop dead!" cursed Shurpanakha.

"Your brother has brought me disgrace by carrying my wife away. I've taught
your brother a lesson by cutting off your nose and ears. Go! Go and tell your
brother! Go and tell your woes to your brother. Tell him that this is just the beginning, not the end. That the worst is yet to come," said Ramaraju and then
ordered Latchumaiah, "Go, push her out into the street." His follower obeyed
the order.

Shurpanakha went to Ravanarao's house. He shouted angrily with his ten
voices, called the doctors, had her wounds dressed, took a certificate and filed
a police case. The police imprisoned Ramaraju. Ramaraju's brother bribed the
authorities, got someone to put in a word and had him released. The brother
also engaged a lawyer for defending the case in court.

The lawyer argued, "This girl has a history of biting ears and having her ears
bitten ever since childhood.[6] It is because of this habit, that she has had her ears
bitten off after she left Ramaraju's place. As the people who bit her ears had long

---

6. "Biting ears" has two meanings in Telugu: (1) literal: biting or having one's ears bitten, and (2)
figurative: gossiping about others and listening to gossip, often used as a pun.

teeth, her ears got torn. What's there in the certificate presented by Ravanarao in the court? That her ears were torn. It doesn't say that Ramaraju had them cut. There's no evidence. As for the nose, this girl has had an English education. She was in the habit of poking her nose into things. Because she poked her nose in the wrong place, it was cut. There is no proof that my client had anything to do with it. Blood on Latchumaiah's knife is only circumstantial evidence. Many hens are killed in the house of the Rajus. It hasn't been proven that the blood on the knife and Shurpanakha's blood type were one and the same."

The court dismissed the case because there were no eyewitnesses.

Outside the court, Shurpanakha, with her deformed face, said, "Why should we become victims of the rivalry between men, the male scoundrels? If my brother kidnaps Ramaraju's wife, Ramaraju should go straight to my brother and cut off his nose and ears, shouldn't he? Because he lacked the courage to do that, he targeted me. Look, how manly my brother is! Because he couldn't compete in business with Ramaraju, he kidnapped his wife. So much for his valor.

"This is a country of courageous men! When *Harijans* revolt, unable to face them, these heroic men invade their homes when they are not around, and the brave policemen, who go ostensibly to protect the weak, violate their women.[7] When the police come and arrest the rogues, the rest of the rogues come, and instead of doing anything either to the men who had tipped off the police or to the police themselves, they rape the women of the town. Whoever wants to settle an account with the other, targets only the women. We become the scapegoats of their vengeance.

"Why don't you settle your own accounts, you rascals? May you all be ruined! Oh God, can you not help us conceive without men? And even when we have children, can you not make sure that we don't give birth to male worms? Or are you yourself male?"

Shurpanakha was inconsolable.

"That's how it is, our life as women," sympathized her sister-in-law, Ravanarao's wife.

Translated from Telugu by Alladi Uma and M. Sridhar

---

7. Harijan, "children of God," is the term M. Gandhi used, instead of the pejorative "Untouchable."

19 Marriage Offers

The selections that follow are taken from an oral version of Ramkatha that was sung and possibly composed by an itinerant performer of the Muslim community of Kerala who wandered the northern part of that region (Malabar) some seventy years ago. The indigenous Muslims of Kerala are commonly known as Mappilas in Malayalam, and this version of Ramkatha was sung by one Hassankutty in the meter and style of their folksong genre known as Mappila Ballad (*Mappila Pattu*), hence the title by which this work was widely known, *Mappila Ramayana*. The performer of this piece was eccentric to the point of earning himself the nickname Piranthan ("crazy") Hassankutty, but his audience was so appreciative that one among them, a fifteen-year-old Hindu boy, committed a fragment of the work to memory. The seven hundred lines memorized by that boy, who later became the venerated folklorist T. H. Kunhiraman Nambiar, are all we have left today of *Mappila Ramayana*. The lines that follow in translation represent about one-fifth of the total lines recalled by Nambiar and were collected from him by a noted scholar of Malayalam, M. N. Karassery, in the 1960s.[1]

While this composition was clearly intended as humorous entertainment, the humor was informed by a sharp wit and underlaid with the fundamental irony of casting the Hindu religious epic and its characters in the social context and language forms of Kerala's Mappila culture. The work's apparent popularity, however, indicates that this handling of what today could be inflammatory themes was received neither as disrespectful of Hindu religious sentiment nor of Muslim social and linguistic practice. The piece's overall tenor of broad humor and gentle irony points rather to a time and place when relations between the different faiths were far different from the murderous communal tensions that surfaced only recently in Hassankutty's own heartland.[2]

The very first line sets the pattern for the piece, where the bearded Hindu sage, Valmiki, is referred to by an Arabic-derived word for Muslim holymen. The juxtaposition continues, in the third line, where Karkadakam (July–August) signifies the month of famine when Kerala Hindus sing their traditional Malayalam and Sanskrit *Ramayanas* as an act of ritual devotion, but where the mode of its singing by stopping the ears, in the next line, mimics the Muslim call to prayer. Indeed throughout the work its "Hindu" characters appear as

---

1. Except for the section I have titled "Prelude," which was passed on to me in hand-written form, the lines translated here appeared in Karassery (1989).
2. I refer to the murder of nine fishermen in the coastal village of Marar, near Calicut, in May 2003, and the subsequent flight of scores of Muslim families from the area to refugee camps, fearing Hindu communalist reprisals.

culturally Mappila, as with Rama's use of Mappila kinship terms to refer to his own relations, or his arguing of Muslim law (*Shari'at*) in refusing the advances of Shurpanakha.

In addition to the meter, the text has a number of other linguistic features that mark it as typically Mappila. Besides the aforementioned kinship system and personal names and titles, there are significant locutions of Arabic or Persian derivation used only by the Mappila community. I have indicated these and other culturally marked locutions through footnotes. Finally, there are a number of phonetic features of the Mappila dialect reflected throughout (e.g., the dropped initial "h" in "Anuman"). Most notable is the frequent substitution of initial "r" by "l" (hence "Lamayana" and "Lavana"). This is most significant in the name of "Lama" itself, particularly in its repetition as litany opening the song's third section. In clear imitation of the opening section of Kerala's standard Malayalam version of *Adhyatma Ramayana,* the phonetic alteration in this context sounds particularly funny. In neutralizing the possible perception of disrespect toward Hindu texts and practices, however, the lines simultaneously invite the self-deprecation of the bard's own linguistic competence. Such were some of the subtleties of comedic method in Hassankutty's "madness." [J.R.F.][3]

Source: M. N. Karassery, *Kurimanam,* 2nd ed. (Calicut, Kerala: Malayalam Publications, 1989), pp. 95–99.

Mappila Ramayana of Hassankutty ("the Mad")
COLLECTED BY M. N. KARASSERY FROM
T. H. KUNHIRAMAN NAMBIAR

Prelude

The song that the bearded saint sang long ago,[4]
The narrative song seen as this, our Lamayana
The song of our squatting idle, in our long wait through [the month of] Karkadakam,
The song we will croon, stopping our ears with our fingertips.
The song of Dasharatha having married three women;[5]
The song of their household confusion, and their childlessness.
The song of the three drinking the milk-offering, and bearing four children;

---

3. I thank Paula Richman for discovering and drafting me into this project, supplying the text in a couple of forms, and putting me in touch with M. N. Karassery. I thank Prof. V. R. P. Nayar for patiently puzzling with me over the idioms and syntax of this text, generously lending his insights and linguist's acuity. And finally, I thank Dr. M. N. Karassery for sharing a delightful afternoon with me in Calicut, providing background information and clearing up certain matters of interpretation. The responsibility for any remaining errors, is, of course, my own.
4. Saint, *auliya* < Arabic [henceforth abbreviated as "Ar."].
5. Married, *nikah* < Ar., here forming a denominative verbal compound with a Malayalam verb.

The song of the one named Lama, most eminent of the four.

The song of his breaking the bow of the god who licks poison [Shiva].

The song of a young child [Sita]whose golden hand he took [in marriage].

The song of the bearded [Parashu] Lama roused to anger and blocking his way;[6]

The song of deflecting that anger, and Lama reaching his own native land.

The song of his aunt's perversity, when she heeded the lies of the hunch-back [maid];[7]

The song of Lama forced to the forest for fourteen years.

The song of the king, tossing in torment, through missing the sight of his sons.

The song of that king of kings, his voice breaking, as he died.[8]

Shurpanakha's Adornment

Rather flustered as she clambered over mountains and hills
 came a beauty, a matron who was the sister of Lavana.[9]

She was Lady Shurpanakha,[10] the jeweled darling of
 the Sultan of great, golden Patalam.[11]

Through misfortune and ruin her Sultan died,[12]
 but depraved as she was, she wanted yet another husband.[13]

She stated her case to her brother, King Lavana,
 who said if she found someone, he would consent.

Her age since birth came to fifty-six,
 but with effort she could seem less than forty.

On each white hair of her greying head
 she put charcoal and honey, to blacken them.

---

6. Anger, *hal* < Ar., with a shift in meaning from a general state of being (as in Hindi), to that of frenzy or anger. Also used to translate the same word in the next line.

7. The kinship term used for "aunt" here is the Mappila dialect form (*elema*) of the Malayalam matrilineal kinship term *ilayamma,* which refers principally to one's mother's younger sister. Here it refers to Kaikeyi, assimilating her as Dasharatha's junior co-wife and, hence, as Rama's "aunt," according to the Mappila matrilineal kinship system. "Hunch-back" refers to Kaikeyi's maid, known by the name of Manthara in most North Indian renditions and Kuni in many South Indian renditions.

8. "Die," *mayyattu* is more regularly *maut* < Ar., again compounded with a Malayalam verb.

9. Matron, *umma* < Ar.

10. "Lady," *bibi* < Persian.

11. The Ar. *Sultan,* "lord," signifies political lordship in this context, but shifts in meaning to the domestic context of "husband" in the next line. The individual referred to is the rakshasa, Vidyutjihva, to whom Shurpanakha was married. Patalam is the multifarious Hindu underworld, the various domains of which rakshasas and other demonic demi-gods ruled. In the process of conquering all of these, Ravana accidentally killed Vidyutjihva with "friendly fire" and thus widowed Shurpanakha.

12. Sultan, *halak* < Ar.

13. The word used is *Mappila,* showing that she sought a member of what is cast here as her own community for a husband.

Then summoning Fatima from the house nearby,[14]
   she settled on a fee and got her hair braided.
Her sunken eyes, like great round wells,
   she encircled with walls of make-up.
She plucked out the long hair growing from her chin,
   and for her disorderly teeth, she hammered her gums.
She dug the rubbish from the hollows of her nostrils with a palm-leaf,
   and chewed palm-sugar with reddener to put a shine on her lips.
She strained to scrub her ears, front and back,
   then donned ivory ear-pendants to make her lobes dance.
She bound stays to her breasts to prop them upright,
   and on top of them mangoes to stand out in her thin blouse.
She opened the strongbox of her long-buried family matriarch,[15]
   and scooped up its gold.
She pleated her fine waist-wrap so that it bunched out behind,
   and bound a waist-chain over it that would hang down below.
Above and below her sets of ten bracelets,
   she had pairs of armlets, beautifully polished and set with gems.
Glittering with gold and glittering with jewels she wore a crisp waist-
   cloth;
   she had a dancing neck-pendant, heavy as a metal mirror.
Colorful and lovely, she gathered around her a gem-blue wrap,
   and a floral drape she let out at length to flutter.
Rather flustered as she clambered over mountains and hills
   came a beauty, a matron who was the sister of Lavana.

Shurpanakha's Overtures of Love

As she saw noble Lama who was wrapped in a hide,
   spreading grass and strewing flowers,[16] desire overtook her.
With entreating eyes Lady Shurpanakha,
   that fair golden matron, crooned to Lama:
"Who are you noble youth, and what's your name?
   Who is the woman I see with you? Is she your wife?
Don't you have any children or nephews?
   Hasn't that ripe maid of yours yet borne fruit?"
"I'm Lama, Sita is my wife, and she hasn't given birth.
   Yonder is my younger brother, Lakshmana, to keep us company.
The land of Kosala, a land racked by intrigues, is my father's realm,[17]

---

14. The Mappila dialect *Pattumma* is used here—from the Ar. *Fatima,* the daughter of the Prophet—showing that Shurpanakha, as a Mappila, has the same for her neighbors.
15. The Mappila dialectal *muttumma,* a nominal compound of Malayalam *mutu,* "old," plus Ar. *umma.*
16. He is dressed like a forest renouncer.
17. Mappila dialectal *bappa,* showing Rama is envisaged as a Malabar Muslim.

And that's the reason we are here in this forest—Who are you?"
"I'm the charming, elegant and fresh young sister
  of King Lavana who holds sway in the land of Lanka.
Oh lovely cuckoo in the blossoming bower! Come along with us to
  Lanka!
  Won't you get a King for your brother-in-law?"
"For a man, there is a woman, and for a woman there is a man: this is
  the law in the Shari'at!
It's calamity indeed, young miss, if one nurses from all and sundry
  breasts.
If the oil you bathe with now suits you, should you change it for some
  other kind?
Lioness of Lanka, you'd better leave, young miss, and tend to your own
  affairs!"
"If a man keeps four or five women, there is no problem with that.
  But that's not allowed for the woman; that's the law in the Shari'at.
My desire! My sweetheart! My gold! My precious pearl!
  My bower-tree in Hades! My flower! My milk and sugar!
Our matriarch has sons, dwelling with fierce grandeur through the ten
  realms,
  and the three of them are here to support us.[18]
And there is an eight-winged, seven-storied mansion for us!
So you need not look askance at all towards preparations for our
  marriage."[19]
"Why should we marry one woman on top of another?
  That flitting parrot, my young brother, desires a woman to wed.
He's suitable, and if he sees you desire will surely blossom in him.
  If he sees your nose, your breasts, your ears, your thighs, will he be
  able to resist?"

Ravana's Overtures of Love

Lama Lama, Lama Lama; Lama Lama, Lama Lama!
  Lama Lama, Lama Lama; Lama Lama, Lama Lama![20]
As King Dasharatha's dear son, Lama, desired,
  he had married the lotus-honeyed Sita.
But one day the ruler of Lanka, ten-nosed King Lavana,

---

18. This line refers to Shurpanakha's immediate grandmother (n. 15). Note that her three sons, Ravana and his two brothers, seem to form a typical matrilineal household with their sister in the traditional Mappila pattern.
19. See n. 5 for this, which also applies to the locutions for marriage in the next two lines.
20. This parodies the opening lines of the Malayalam *Adhyatma Ramayana*, whose use is still prevalent as a kind of domestic litany sung daily during the month of Karkadakam in traditional Hindu households throughout Kerala. The opening lines run, "Shri Rama, Rama, Rama, Shri Ramachandra Jaya! Shri Rama, Rama, Rama, Shri Ramabhadra Jaya!" and continue in this manner over the following lines.

shamelessly intoned to Sita, that jewel of womanhood,
"You pearl of damsels, since we brought you to Lanka,
    so many days have passed, my pearl, my radiant flower garland!
By my two eyes, I swear to you, my golden one,
    that I have had such desire to see you and tell you what I should.
Flower-goddess of my heart! In order to see you,
    I have cast off the renowned wife of my own house.
My heart! Do we not inhabit the same kingdom?
    Isn't this a particular joy for me?
You whose flower body is like a lotus bud,
    so many days has my heart yearned to see you, my pearl![21]
But when such a woman should have entered the bower of bliss
    with me—
    Why, Allah! Why did you come with that pig, Lama?
It wasn't from fear, my gold, that I carried you off in my chariot,
    out of Lama's sight, but rather from desire, young girl.
It has been nearly a year since I brought you here;
    shall we now come to know the pleasures in you?
After the ceremony, shall we not unite in the chamber?
    Though why do you stare like this? Am I not sufficiently handsome?
There will be four elephants, with frontlets bound on each,
    and we will come announced by fireworks and drummers.
Pounding tambours, and double-drums will keep the beat,
    and to receive us, a thousand damsels will gather.
As a sari, they will give you a fine garment, a silver-hemmed drape,
    and the ministers will give you earrings like cembaka blossoms.
Lotus-like bracelets will be made for you, reaching up your arms.
Four measures of gold will be melted and hammered for a chest;
    a fine protective necklace, and dangling pendants for your brow.
Four months previously we got these things here for you.
Two months ago, giving you up and wedding another woman,
    our enemy Lama got on a ship and has sailed away.
By Allah, who brings the monsoon rains! If you hear all this,
    won't your cloudy spirits lift, my little golden parrot?"

Hanuman's Entry to the Flower Grove

While that demon of Death, Black Death,
    Lavana, was getting his ten beards shaved,
The tailed-one, Anuman, leapt over to Lanka,
    and perched on the limbs of a fine tree.
Like chickens trussed up for a sacrifice, five women

---

21. Heart, *khalb* < *qalb*, Ar.

lay listlessly, hands tucked between thighs, asleep.
With ear-pendants and bracelets on her arms,
    one was a dancing girl with a palm-leaf skirt.
One had teeth jutting up like minarets over her cavernous nostrils;[22]
    one stout woman was covered with the scars of leeches.
One, whose teeth poked through her nose, had an angular rump,
    was crawling with vermin like a mongoose, and was quite black.
With eyes on the slant, and a flattened nose,
    one bloated wench had a belly like a rice-bin.
Their skirts had slipped from their loins,
    and he could see their thighs, like black trestles.
With neither blouse nor cover, their breasts
    jutted upright as they panted for air.

Hanuman's Destruction of the Flower Grove

Spying that golden fruit-blossom, Sita,
    as she took her glittering hair ornaments,
When he saw that angelic woman go for her change of clothes,[23]
    the tailed-one made his obeisance.[24]
With the rollicking rhythms of a dancer, he leapt,
    and entered that parrot-maiden's flower grove.
As soon as he entered, those guarding the grove,
    arrived and engaged him in combat.
Taking clods, and blocks, rods, and staves, and spears,
    they hurled them at him again and again.
With blows to their stomachs, blows to their chests, from tail and arms,
    they were beaten and battered.
In circle upon circle, they rushed in to surround him,
    but crushed in his embrace, they got deep, savage bites.
With blows from his tail, kicks from his legs, and blows raining down,
    they received these again and again, and were dying.
Rent by his claws, slashed through the air, faces torn off by the nose,
    suffering these things again and again, they were falling.
Delivering blows with butts of his head, he crushed them in his thighs;
    getting such again and again, they were dying.
With fanning sweeps of legs and arms, his blows rose and crashed,

---

22. Local dialectal *munnar* < Persian, *minar* < Ar. *manar;* whence English "minaret."
23. Angelic, dialectal *malakha* < Syriac *malaka.* This word could be an indication of interaction with Syrian Christians in Kerala, as well as the polyglot trading and cultural connections of Malabari Muslims in the wider Middle East.
24. Here, *nikkaram,* more properly *niskaram,* though historically derived from the Sanskrit *namaskara,* is a dialectal coinage specifically of the Mappila community for signifying Islamic prayer and prostration. So Hanuman seems confirmed as a Muslim as well!

but the tailed-one then had nowhere else to try his strength.
There were no more legs, arms, eyes, nor snouts to go for;
there was not a single man left as guard in that grove.

Translated from Malayalam by [John] Rich[ardson] Freeman

20 Sita Creates Ravana

The play *Chitrapata Ramayana* [Portrait Ramayana] emerged from a unique collaborative endeavor inspired by a folk ballad. *Chitra* can mean a drawing, an illustration, a picture, or a painting. A *pata* is a scroll or single painting. Before mechanical reproduction of images, artisans would work in front of temples, creating quick paintings of the local deity (such as Kalighat paintings called patas) for pilgrims to take home. We know little about the woman to whom the ballad *Portrait Ramayana* has been attributed except her name, Helavanakatte Giriyamma, and that she lived in the late nineteenth or early twentieth century. Jayashree found Giriyamma's idea that a portrait of Ravana would declare love for Sita so intriguing that she wanted to stage it.[1] B. Jayashree, director of Spandana Theatrical Troupe, decided to present the ballad's story in the Bhooteyara Ata drama style of Karnataka, which she had documented.[2] At her request, H. S. Venkatesha Murthy, Kannada poet and university lecturer, composed a script and song lyrics appropriate for the unusual production. Design manager Ananda Raju Krishnappa tackled the practical challenges of presenting a miraculous transformation on stage.[3] The result was a complex, suggestive, multi-layered play about what happens when a painting comes to life.[4]

---

1. I have translated it as "portrait" because the picture is a portrait that comes to life (like an actor creates a character temporarily seen as real).
2. B. Jayashree began acting at the age of three in the Gubbi Channa Basaveshvara Theatrical Company, run by her grandfather Gubbi Veeranna, and went on to graduate from the National School of Drama in New Delhi. A Ford Foundation Grant funded study and documentation of folk drama traditions in Karnataka; the influence of this research is visible in this play.
3. Since the portrait of Ravana plays a central role in *Chitrapata Ramayana*, Jayashree and Ananda Raju staged the creation of the portrait so that it seemed both a picture and a live creature at the same time. In a proscenium theater, Jayashree noticed that the stage curtain had not been fully lowered; it hovered slightly above the floor, allowing her to see an actor's feet. In *Chitrapata Ramayana*, she uses cloth in a similar way. Sita sat on the floor facing the audience and drew. Then the curtain was raised slowly as the rest of Ravana's body appeared. Ananda Raju set up a backlit white sheet with the outline of ten heads and twenty arms. Only the spill light from Ravana illuminated Sita, a visual allusion to the night Ravana came to the Ashoka Grove with a torch and begged Sita to marry him. (Interview, January 11, 2006, Bangalore.)
4. Although Jayashree was told that *Chitrapata Ramayana* circulates in oral Telugu and Kannada renditions, no other printed version has been found that portrays Shurpanakha as a *koravanji*. A Telugu women's song does, however, include many similar elements in its plot. There, Shurpanakha takes the form of a female ascetic in order to cause problems between Sita and Rama. When the ascetic asks Sita to draw a portrait of Ravana, Sita says she only knows what Ravana's big toe looks like. After Sita draws the toe, Shurpanakha completes the rest and convinces Brahma, the Creator God, to bring the picture to life. When Shurpanakha gives the picture to Sita, Ravana starts pulling at her and demanding that she return to Lanka with him. Urmila, Shanta, and other palace women see how worried Sita is and decide to destroy the picture. When they build a fire and throw it in, it does not burn (an echo of Sita's agnipariksha). When they throw the picture into a deep well,

Portrait Ramayana begins after Rama's coronation in Ayodhya. While Valmiki depicts Sita as banished due to the gossip of a washerman, several folk stories portray the story differently: when Sita is tricked into drawing a picture of Ravana, Rama takes it as evidence of Sita's unfaithfulness and banishes her.[5] *Portrait Ramayana* uses this general plot but develops it in particular ways. In the play, Shurpanakha decides to revenge her brother's death by planting doubts in Rama's mind about Sita's chastity. Shurpanakha first disguises herself as Koravanji, a gypsy fortune-teller, to gain entrance to Sita's quarters and then persuades Sita to draw a picture of Ravana. The play follows the ballad's plot to the moment when Ravana escapes from the picture frame. Then the play goes its own way, exploring Sita's feelings as an artist about the picture she has drawn.[6]

The play incorporates ongoing commentary through a chorus that sings in the style of Bhootes. Bhootes dedicate their lives to performing stories of, and praise to, Goddess Tulajapura Bhavani and Goddess Yellamma, traveling from place to place in Karnataka to sing on festive occasions.[7] The Bhoote repertoire is limited to material about the two goddesses, but Jayashree wanted to tell Ramkatha in Bhoote style, so she begins *Portrait Ramayana* by staging a situation in which Bhootes would tell the story. As the play opens, the Bhootes announce to the audience that their guru (religious teacher) asked them to tell a narrative that had not been heard before. They refused, objecting that they only sing about stories in their usual repertoire. He scolded them and urged, "You should adapt to new circumstances!" Eventually he convinced them to be more daring, so they have decided to perform *Portrait Ramayana*.

Venkatesha Murthy relished the opportunity not only to compose the script but also to write lyrics for Bhoote songs. Since *Portrait Ramayana* was based on a folk ballad, he decided to write in the rural dialect spoken in the village where he was born and raised, in western Karnataka. He described how this earthy language gave the dialogue and songs a power appropriate for Giriyamma's story: "Such forms do not present an elitist Rama or an urbanized Rama. This is the Rama of the countryside." He grew up hearing the poetry of local songs, lamentations, and curses, and quoted the saying, "In the village, people even cry

it comes back up again. Rama comes into the bedroom after Sita has hidden the portrait under the bed, and when he sits down, Ravana's picture throws Rama off. Seeing the picture, Rama gets furious and banishes Sita. See Narayana Rao (2001: 126–127).

5. In a North Indian folksong, Sita's sister-in-law entices Sita into drawing a picture of Ravana and then shows the picture to Rama, who banishes her. Even though Sita has been betrayed by her conjugal kin, others give her aid. For example, when Sita gives birth in the forest, female ascetics living nearby assist her and a barber carefully follows Sita's instructions to distribute turmeric, to celebrate the birth of the boys, to Dasharatha, his wife, and Lakshmana but not Rama. See Nilsson (2000: 151–152).

6. In the ballad, the picture starts chasing Sita, enters the border of her sari, and sticks to her chest. With great difficulty, Sita disengages it and hides it under the bed as Rama enters. When the bed breaks, the picture emerges and battles Rama. Although Rama cannot destroy the picture, eventually Lakshmana does. (Interview, January 11, 2006.)

7. The Bhootes accompany their songs with a *dholak* and a traditional musical instrument called the *tun tuni*. For Yellamma, see also #12, p. 138.

in poetry."[8] This poetry gives the play's dialogue its special tonal quality, suitable to the unique way that the Bhootes tell Ramkatha.

The chorus is crucial to *Portrait Ramayana* because the Bhootes divulge the inner feelings of the characters. For example, Jayashree wanted the Bhootes, rather than Sita, to express Sita's feelings that "must usually be kept suppressed." That way Sita maintains the dignity suitable to a royal character, but the audience gains insights into the heroine's yearnings. Venkatesha Murthy did so by giving the Bhootes poetry to sing, which, as he put it, "enables one to say something without saying it." He notes that since "people worship Rama and Sita," he sought to "express things through suggestion and with delicacy," by indicating Sita's inner thoughts without having her voice them.

Venkatesha Murthy, who has been intrigued since childhood by women in Ramkatha, brings a similar subtlety to the character of Ravana's sister.[9] When she first glimpses Rama, she takes on the beautiful form of Chandranakhi, "she with fingernails [lovely] like the moon," in order to win his favor.[10] When mutilated, she returns to her misshapen form of Shurpanakha, "she with fingernails [sharp] like winnowing fans." Then, she becomes the gypsy fortune-teller Koravanji, a stock character in folk theater, who mesmerizes Sita into believing that Koravanji is her childhood friend Parvati (Paroti or Parati in village dialect).[11] Koravanji calls Sita *Akka* (older sister) or "Mother," and Sita calls her *Avva* (younger sister). Using Chandranakhi, Shurpanakha, and Koravanji enables the playwright to represent the shape-shifting nature of rakshasas, while also revealing aspects of Shurpanakha's personality and gendered subjectivity.

The script plays with various notions of representation. Despite her time spent in Lanka, Sita does not know how Ravana looked because, out of modesty, she never raised her eyes above his feet. So Koravanji urges Sita to depict his feet and then use her imagination to draw the rest of his body. As Sita produces the picture, the Bhootes praise Ravana's majestic physique, voicing admiration for his body that Sita would never utter. They also deem fortunate a woman lucky enough to receive so many kisses from so many heads. After the draw-

---

8. This is no mere affectation, since he grew up in the small village of Hodigere, hearing local songs and stories. All quotes from Venkatesha Murthy are from my interview with him in Bangalore, January 11, 2006.

9. A child raised by his schoolteacher mother and two grandmothers, he recalls getting his grandmother to recount Ramkatha night after night as a boy. To date he has composed four plays dealing with Ramkatha, three of which focus primarily on its female characters: Sita, Shurpanakha, Manthara, and Urmila. His play *Manthara* explores the relationship between Kaikeyi, Manthara, and Bharata, while reflecting on the responsibilities of a ruler toward his kingdom. *Urmila* examines how Lakshmana's wife came to terms with the long separation from her husband through caring for her garden of flowers.

10. In Kamban's *Iramavataram*, Shurpanakha also takes on a beautiful form when Rama first sees her, but she does not do so in Valmiki.

11. She would not be allowed into Sita's quarters as either Shurpanakha or Chandranakhi, so she takes on the form of gypsy and asks to see Sita. She explains that she will read Sita's palm and ask her to draw a *chitra* (picture) of Ravana. With the picture of Ravana, the *papi*, "evil-doer," she claims she will teach people to praise Rama for slaying him.

ing is done, Shupanakha asks Sita for milk and, seizing the chance provided by Sita's absence, she gives life to the picture by drawing in its eyes.[12] Then she disappears. Sita returns to a Ravana eager to embrace her. When she rejects his advances, he taunts, "You are the one who drew me / You are the one who invoked me." Suddenly, Sita is confronted with the representation of her own, long denied, desires.

Venkatesha Murthy sought to convey the ambiguity of representation in *Portrait Ramayana* by depicting Rama's response to the picture. Rama is obsessively jealous of any male attention Sita receives. He even makes sure that the palace birds are all female, and Sita wonders why he did not attack Agni for touching her when he lifted her from the fire. Shurpanakha realizes that Ravana's ghost continues to haunt Rama: the portrait of Ravana embodies Rama's deepest fears. Venkatesha Murthy notes, "It demonstrates that the truth is not always what it seems. Rama thought he saw Sita in love with Ravana but he came to a hasty conclusion because of his own perspective. The truth may be something else." Later on, when Rama fights with Ravana, Sita forbids him to kill the portrait, declaring, "Don't defile the relationship between mother and son." Sita feels shocked at Rama's violence since she views the portrait as if it were her child.[13]

The play ends by highlighting the artifice of theater. After Rama and Lakshmana deal Ravana a fatal blow and leave the stage, Sita tears up the picture and collapses. Just then, a Bhoote calls out that the play is over, so Sita gets up and reprises the opening song with the rest of the cast, a cue to the audience that the play has ended. The actress playing Sita, Jayashree, has also produced her own portrait, that of Sita. Indeed *Chitrapata Ramayana* reflects on its own nature as a work of imagination, based on a folk ballad of an ancient story.[14]

Source: H. S. Venkatesha Murthy, *Chitrapata*, pp. 60–74 in *Chitrapata, Agnivarna, Uriya Uyyale (Mooru Natakagalu)*. Bangalore: Ankita Pustaka, 1999.

Portrait Ramayana (excerpt)
BY H. S. VENKATESHA MURTHY

[The excerpt begins after Koravanji convinces Sita that she is Sita's childhood friend named Parvati, which becomes "Paroti" or "Parati" in local dialect.[15]]

---

12. This action parallels that of an artisan who makes an image (*murthy*) of a deity and transforms it into a vessel for the divine presence by painting in its eyes (interview with Venkatesha Murthy).

13. Here Venkatesha Murthy pays homage to his talented predecessor, K. V. Puttappa. In Puttappa's long poem reinterpreting Ramkatha, he has Sita promise that she will hold him close to her in his next birth, and she agrees since he will be reborn then as her son.

14. In the notes from the play's program, Jayashree describes Sita and Shurpanakha as two aspects of the consciousness of modern women.

15. Koravanji says she is Sita's childhood friend, the daughter of King Janaka's charioteer. Since his charioteer stays close by the king, both girls would have grown up together in the palace.

SITA: You've changed so much . . . Come, sit here.

> Avva, tell me, how's the jasmine tree?
>
> Is it still flowering?

(Koravanji takes a handful of flowers from her bag and showers them on Sita.)

KORAVANJI: Where do you think these come from?

SITA: (Sings)

> Avva Paroti, why do you fly?
>
> Take me along while you fly.
>
> The feathers on my wings have fallen off . . .

KORAVANJI: Pretty parrot,

> Perfect one,
>
> Your wings are in your heart
>
> Like rays of a blazing flame.

SITA: Paroti my friend, why do you dance so?

> Take me as your partner while you dance.
>
> The forest tired my dancing feet.

KORAVANJI: My colorful damsel, don't say that!

> Your limbs are in your life. Know that,
>
> Like the feet in the beat of a song . . .

SITA: Go away, my sister . . .

> Why do you rain these flowers on me
>
> Like embers of coal?
>
> I don't want these blazing red flowers in my lap . . .

(Sita is alarmed)

> Oh, dear! I've scattered all these flowers on the bed! If my lord asks me where these flowers came from, what am I to say to him?

(Flustered, Sita starts to gather up the flowers.)

KORAVANJI: Why are you so upset? Won't that man of yours understand if you tell him your childhood friend brought them to you?

SITA: (Somberly)

> A man's mind is like a snake pit. If a worm gets in, it's impossible to get it out.

KORAVANJI: You're the great chaste one who's proven herself through fire. Your Rama doubts you still?

SITA: (With a sad laugh) Agni is a man too. It is my good fortune that my lord didn't ask me why did I leap into another man's arms! Do you know? Even the parrot in this palace is a female parrot!

KORAVANJI: (Stealing up on Sita from behind and affectionately squeezing her shoulders.)

> Even after Ravana's death,
>
> His ghost still haunts your husband, doesn't it?
>
> I want to ask you something. . . .

(Touching her heart)

Open your heart and tell me
(Looking into Sita's eyes)

That Ravana, he gave up his life for you. Why? Have you ever thought about it?

SITA: I sat meditating on Rama. Why would I ever think of Ravana, tell me?

KORAVANJI: He gave up his wife for you, lost his children, lost his brothers, lost his kingdom, lost his dignity and honor, and in the end he even gave up his life! And if only he had had you, it would have been worth losing all this.

He didn't get what he didn't have
What he had, didn't remain.
He didn't win Sita.
He lost Mandodari too.
Poor man, don't you think?

SITA: Poor man? He was a sinner. Shouldn't pity such sinners . . .

KORAVANJI: What sin did he commit? Did he pester you?

Did he force himself on you?
You were a woman, all alone in the Ashoka Grove
With not a soul around.
What a strong man he was.
If he had forced himself on you, what could you have done, tell me?

SITA: (Lost in thought.) He didn't do anything like that.

KORAVANJI: He could have had you out of desire for you.

He could have had you, if only to spite Rama.

SITA: But, he didn't have me like that . . .

KORAVANJI: Shall I tell you why?

He was a real man.
A real man, yes
Real man . . .
A man who knew that a woman is not a plaything of desire.
A man who knew that a woman is not a commodity for sale.
A man who knew that a woman is a woman.

SITA: He . . . if I stood here,

He'd stand over there and talk to me.
If I said to him that he was less than a blade of grass to me
He'd say you are everything to me . . .

KORAVANJI: He didn't touch you . . .

SITA: The lamp was far away—

Only its light fell onto the ground.

KORAVANJI: And in that light what did you see?

At least tell me that, with a truthful heart,
My friend . . .

SITA: Like milk in a tumbler—I can't tilt even a bit, or it will spill—I can't leave it like that on the fire, or it boils over.

KORAVANJI: He stood before a beauty like you, yet he didn't cross the line . . .

What strength he must have had Avva, that man!

If I were you,
I'd have rolled all over his wide chest
Like lighting rolls over dark clouds.
Yes!
A broken man, he was destroyed . . .
At least, draw his picture for me.
I'll worship that instead . . .

SITA: Picture?

KORAVANJI: You are the only one who can draw it. Except for you, there's not a single woman in all this land who's set eyes on him . . .

SITA: Let's go to the durbar hall tomorrow. There's a life-size picture of Ravana there.

KORAVANJI: I don't want Ravana through Rama's eyes, my friend.

I want Ravana through Sita's eyes.

I won't pester you. I won't beg you.

Just one picture.

If you draw that for me, I won't even sleep ever again with my head towards this town.[16]

SITA: That face is all foggy, foggy to me, Avva!

KORAVANJI: Draw me what you see behind the fog.

He'll come tearing through the fog like a hurricane.

SITA: That face is all misty and cloudy to me, Avva!

KORAVANJI: Draw me that very misty cloud that you see, Amma.

That moon will pierce through the clouds!

SITA: What an obstinate woman you are!

If I set out to draw Ravana, and it turns out like a boulder, it's not my fault.

KORAVANJI: You draw a boulder, but let it be a rock like Ravana. Yes!

SONG: She sets out to draw

First, the crescent moons of his fingernails!
And then his legs
She drew.
Then his thighs, his waist,
Her lips trembled . . .
His chest, wide as an ocean
And within, his throbbing heart
The garland around the neck,
Green like the sea coast.
And then the face
Eyes?
Forehead wide as the moon . . .

KORAVANJI: Ahah!

What a magnificent form this man has.

---

16. This phrase means that she will not return in the future.

What is this? A body or the ocean at dawn!
A forehead vast as the horizon
His face a golden platter like the rising sun!
The whiskers of his moustache like rays
His royal blue turban jauntily tilted!
BHOOTE: Arms like waves
Chest decked with a garland of sailing ships
A giggle of froth.
BHOOTE: How impressive!!
Oh, what a fortunate woman is that Mandodari!
Not one, but ten faces!!!
Not two, but twenty arms!
If he came onto you, it'd rain a shower of kisses . . .
BHOOTE: While one hand caresses your chin
One hand curls your tresses into ringlets
While one hand untied the knot
One hand pulls away your sari!
While with one mouth he kisses
Another one bursts into peals of laughter.
KORAVANJI: While one face rests on your bosom
With another face he whispers sweet words,
Oh! What a fortunate woman is that Mandodari.
SITA: Parati, enough. Stop that chatter. This is too much praise of another's husband.
KORAVANJI: Akka, my friend! You've drawn the picture of such a handsome man . . .
But look, there's a flaw in it.
SITA: There's a flaw in the picture that I drew?
KORAVANJI: You've drawn a face. You've drawn a mouth.
You've drawn brows. You've drawn the eyes.
But to those eyes, you have given no sight . . .
SITA: (Shocked) Sight? Can one ever give sight, Paroti? If you give sight to a picture, it would come alive! No, Avva, no . . .
KORAVANJI: Is that so? I didn't know that. Let it be! Avva, oh Sita, . . . I've talked and talked and my throat is dry. Give me at least a mouthful of warm milk, my friend.
SITA: In the midst of all the ado about this picture, I forgot to give you even a tumbler of milk. I'll bring you milk in a bat of an eyelid . . .
(Sita exits.)
KORAVANJI: Aha, this is my chance! I'll give sight to Ravana's eyes! And then I'll vanish in a snap of a finger!
SONG: Oh, Lord of the Island, cross the sea and come!
Step over Sesha's head and come!
Hero of golden Lanka!
Come, brave one!

Come, Love Incarnate!
Ten faces spread like petals of a flower!
Arise like the dawn, my lover!
Bring joy to my eyes!
Lord within my heart!
Break out of bondage and come!
Why hide yourself?

(Koravanji approaches the picture. Koravanji recedes and Shurpanakha appears in her place. Shurpanakha recedes and Chandranakhi comes into view. All three of them dance as if possessed and invoke Ravana into the picture. When Koravanji proceeds to give sight to the picture, the Bhootes try to prevent her but, unable to do so, retreat. The hand in the picture slowly begins to move. Begins to breathe. As Ravana's closed eyes suddenly open, Koravanji swirls like a whirlwind and disappears. Bhootes start to sing the following song, while dancing.)

BHOOTE: I don't know why my right eyebrow flutters
    And the lizard chirps.[17]
  I don't know why my heart pounds.
    The vine trembles.
  I don't know why a storm wind blows.
    The end of my sari slips.
  Dark clouds have gathered above.
    And it's pouring outside.
  Wish her well, wish her well
    Wish this good woman well.
  Let not a false note appear
    In the midst of the melody.

(When this verse is over the Bhootes slip into the dark. At that very moment, Sita enters dancing, carrying a plate with milk, fruits, betel leaves, and nuts. Ravana is watching her, only his eyes moving.)

SITA: Paroti! Hey, Paroti! She was sitting right here! How did she disappear in the bat of an eyelid?

(Ravana laughs. Frightened, Sita looks around to see who is laughing. Ravana freezes like a picture for a moment. Sita goes toward the window, searching.)

RAVANA: Why are you wasting your time, looking for her? She left a long while ago. It's only you and me now . . .

SITA: Is this a dream or what? I'd like to know.
How can a picture come alive like this?
What does it mean for a picture to move its hands?
What does it mean for a picture to move its legs?

---

17. Both the eyebrow fluttering and the chirping of the lizard are omens foretelling misfortune.

What does it mean for a picture to step out of its frame and walk around like this?

Shiva, Shiva! How strange this is!

RAVANA: Sita!

The picture is not a mere picture.

I am your imagination

I am the colors of your dream

I am the beat of your heart.

SITA: Whatever you are,

Please, turn into a picture again.

Don't step out of your frame like this.

My husband is like a blazing fire.

If he sees us, it'll be a disaster

For both of us . . .

RAVANA: What are you talking about, Sita?

You are the one who drew me

You are the one who invoked me—

Now you ask me to go back to where I came from?

Is this fair?

I can't live for even a moment without you.

You are my being

You are my life.

There won't come another moment like this again.

Hold my hand and protect me, my mother!

SITA: I beg you! Don't hold my hand!

He'll slit your throat! My lord husband!

I beg you! Leave me alone!

Why haunt me like this even in death?

RAVANA: I am not haunting you Sita. I am begging you.

SITA: If you beg for what's not right, how can I ever oblige?

RAVANA: You know it for sure

Until you say "Yes"

I'll sit looking at you, without batting an eyelid.

SITA: That means you have to join me.

RAVANA: I have to join you.

SITA: Have to sleep upon my lap.

RAVANA: Have to sleep upon your lap!

SITA: There's only one way to do it. Will you do as I say?

RAVANA: Tell me how. Just say "Yes"

I'll sever each of my ten heads

And place them at your feet.

Tell me, what should I do?

SITA: Instead of pestering me like this even in death

Take birth in my womb and come to life

If you come as my child

I'll feed you milk in a golden tumbler
I'll adorn your cheeks with the black mascara of my eyes
If a conqueror like you is born to me as my son
There'll be none in all the three worlds to stop me . . .
(Saying this, she puts the picture frame around Ravana and pushes him away.)
(Rama standing by the door of the Queen's Chamber.)
RAMA: Sita! Oh, Sita!
The moon hasn't risen yet . . .
You are already asleep?
(Hearing Rama's voice, Sita is filled with fear. She hides Ravana's picture under the bed and quickly opens the door.)
RAMA: I don't know why . . .
You are not your usual self today!
Your golden face is dark and clouded
Your tresses disheveled
Jasmine flowers are scattered on the bed
A milk tumbler lying on the floor . . .
Looks like someone was here
Who was here? Tell me.
SITA: My childhood friend
Paroti had come . . .
Since we were this high
We grew up together playing in the courtyard.
RAMA: (Laughing) So that's what it is!
The guest left with just milk and fruits?
Bad, bad! What have you done?
She could have stayed and left after a meal and dessert.
Open the windows!
The moonlight looks very beautiful tonight!
Moonbeams roll over the sky
Like milk splashed on a blue carpet
The moon god is tumbling across the sky
Come, come!
Let's sit on the bed and watch the pretty moon!
SITA: Not on the bed
I don't know why I'm short of breath . . .
Let's go up to the arbor.
But just wait for a moment.
I'll bring you warm milk.
Sweetened with sugar and
Flavored with saffron.
(When Sita is gone, Rama picks up the jasmine flowers.)
RAMA: Who could have come here when I was away?
There's a smile without a face in the mirror on the wall

There's the warmth of a body on the bed
The milk tumbler was spilt
The jasmine flowers were scattered
Like something untoward has happened
A pair of shadows are playing on the wall
The sandalwood dolls have downcast eyes
The bells on the bed frame are tinkling
The wind sweats
The ground quivers
The parrots stare at each other
If it were her childhood companion . . .
She surely wouldn't have left without meeting me.
Who could have come here?
(Sita enters.)
SITA: Let's go to the arbor, come . . .
RAMA: No, no! The arbor's nice when the sun's shining.
In the moonlight, this carved bronze bed is good.
Come, come. . . .
(In spite of Sita trying to stop him, Rama sits on the bed. With Ravana already on it, unable to hold the weight of two men, it breaks and collapses.)
BHOOTE: Oh dear! What a bad omen this is! If the bed that unites husband and wife breaks; something ominous will surely happen!
BHOOTE: If you sit on it, with all the fourteen worlds within your belly, what else can happen, but the bed break?[18]
BHOOTE: That's why his mother had a bed made of bronze.
It didn't break in all these years.
Then why did it break today?
BHOOTE: Yes, there's surely some riddle here that's not meant to be unraveled!
(Just then Ravana rises from the bed and starts to laugh out loud. Rama sees him.)
RAMA: What! How did this ten-headed evil worm come here? I killed him with my own hands. How did he come alive again?
RAVANA: The deity that protects
Is greater than the deity that kills.
You took my life.
Sita gave it back to me.[19]
RAMA: Sita, what's this Ravana is talking about? How did you bring him back to life, this worm that I killed?
SITA: The Ravana you killed is different from this one.

---

18. Since Rama is a form of the supreme Lord Vishnu, he contains the entire universe.
19. Ravana was killed by Rama but when Sita, an avatara of Goddess Lakshmi (Goddess of Good Fortune) drew Ravana's picture, she can be said to have given him back his life.

This one is a picture that I drew.
Believe me, he's just a picture!
RAMA: Oh, no! Does a picture talk!
Run around!
And it's even capable of dallying with you.
This is a picture that you've drawn!?
SITA: Don't speak such unseemly words.
The picture that I've drawn is my creation.
Don't soil the relation
Between a mother and her son,
I beg of you . . .
RAMA: He is your son?
I am his father?
This is pretty . . .
The son should take care of his father.
That's the way of the world.
But I'll take care of this son of mine.
(Rama and Ravana start to battle. When Ravana gains the upper hand,
Rama calls out aloud to Lakshmana. Lakshmana enters bristling like a
snake. Bhootes start to sing in a fast tempo.)
BHOOTE: Rama wages a war
Against a shadow
Look sister| Look sister|[20]
Take a look at this sister||
Strikes his sworn enemy|
Inside the mirror on the wall|
Look sister| Look sister| Take a look at this||
What rage| What fury|
Like water aboil|
Like water afire|
Look sister| Look sister| Take a look at this||
Yesterday's war has returned
To join battle with today
Like a ghostly shadow of the past|
Look sister| Look sister| Take a look at this||
(Rama and Lakshmana together battle Ravana. When Ravana is fatally
wounded, Sita's maternal heart is wrenched and she comes between Rama
and Lakshmana. She tears up the frame around the picture and throws it
away, and addresses the audience, in an angry sorrowful voice.)
SITA: The picture that I drew—
Mine
Is my conception!

---

20. The translation uses single as well as double lines to indicate where stanzas and refrains of the
songs begin and end.

Don't defile a mother's bond with her son,
I beg of you!
Don't defile a mother's bond with her son.
(She collapses onto the ground. Neither Rama, Lakshmana nor Ravana is on stage. There's no one else. Sita is alone on the stage.)
CAST: The play is over. Get up. Sing the opening song.[21]

Translated from Kannada by Manu Shetty

---

21. Singing the opening song indicates the play has ended, but here it also serves to remind the actress playing Sita that she has only been pretending to be Sita.

K. Satchidanandan (b. 1946), a poet and literary critic who writes in Malayalam and Tamil, completed his Ph.D. in post-structuralist literary theory at the University of Calicut, Kerala. After teaching for twenty-five years as professor of English at Christ College, Kerala, he began serving as editor of *Indian Literature* in 1992 and as secretary of the Sahitya Akademi (the Indian academy of arts and letters), in 1996. He has published more than twenty collections of poetry, many essays on literary theory and comparative literature, and translations of poetry from English to Malayalam.

"Come Unto Me, Janaki" imagines Ravana writing to Sita from heaven after being slain by Rama. Most authoritative tellings of Ramkatha portray death at Rama's hands as the path to religious liberation that ends all desire and pain. In contrast, Satchidanandan's poem depicts Ravana in heaven articulating his longing for Sita and for his beloved Lanka. Ravana presents himself in opposition to Rama, who not only was responsible for Sita's ordeal and banishment, but made the wives of soldiers from Lanka and Kishkindha into widows. Ravana urges Sita to move beyond the past and leave her mother once again to join him, even though she is haunted by nightmares of fire.

Source: K. Satchidanandan. "Janaki, Poru," in *Sakshyangal* (Kottayam: D.C. Books, 2004), p. 61.

Come Unto Me, Janaki
BY K. SATCHIDANANDAN

Twilight, now,
must be leaning over Lanka:
the fragrance of jasmine,
and all the music on earth

merging into the call
of a single nightingale;

the sea melting gold
beneath the soft moon,

and rain in the battlefield
washing the blood away;

my beloved people dreaming
again of white *thumba* flowers.[1]

I sit here lonely and sad;
without you

and with no winds of Lanka
this does not feel like Heaven at all!

———————

Janaki, how I smoulder
as you raise your moon-like face

illumining the clouds over Lanka,
your dense hair falling over your fair shoulders;

my mouth tingles to wet your parted
red lips quivering in love

while those blue oceanic eyes swell
beneath your sweet brow;

like a cool mountain breeze, I long to imbue
your breasts with the camphor of my rapt love

and arouse milk, star, and childhood
with my cardamomed tongue.

My body shivers in wild heat,
the sleepless fever of unbearable love.

———————

Come, Vaidehi, open this door
with fingers slender as the morning waft.

This beckoner is not the heartless one
who, on empty words, condemned you to fire.

Pure One, alone you shall no longer seek
desolate woods to give birth to children,

no more shall Tara's screams
sting your ears

nor Urmila's sighs,
the fierce curse of Shambuka,

———————

1. The *thumba* flower is a symbol of simplicity, peace, and purity. Here it signifies Ravana's aspirations for his people. Seen mostly in South India, it is used as a floral decoration during Onam, a major festival in Kerala connected with King Bali, also considered a demon in brahminical texts.

or the sky-rending shrieks
of the young widows

of our dark heroes your lord had slain,
and those of the she-monkeys;

or the mournful calls
invoking the Earth

of bird, flower, and grove
consumed by the flames from a tail.[2]

Here, the fine whispers of my love
drop softly like dew on the leaves;

only the incessant melody of my golden vina
like a cascade in the distant woods,

and just the wings of our desire
as our passion mounts.

———————

Who has won, and who has lost?
Who is attached, and who, detached?

Who but lovers should make
the rules of love?

Daughter of Earth,
was Rama still the victor

when his extended arms could only hug
the void into which you sank in shame

as I triumph in heaven,
resurrecting myself bit by bit

with a firm dream
even Rama's arrows couldn't kill?

———————

Come unto me, Sita, no more
of your dreadful chastity!

Here I am, the embodiment
of undying love.

———————

2. Here Satchidanandan alludes to Hanuman setting fire to the city of Lanka and, presumably, killing many of its inhabitants.

Confide in your mother
the love you bear for me.

My heart is an expanse
one woman could hardly fill.

Let your laughter fall on my ears
like the anklets of Shiva,

One who has drunk venom,
let me melt into your acid,

and into your dance on the embers
of your dream.
Come, Intense One!

Translated from Malayalam by Rizio Yohannan Raj

Epilogue   *Meta-narrative*

A. K. Ramanujan once noted, "To some extent all later Ramayanas play on the knowledge of previous tellings: they are meta-Ramayanas."[1] The Ramayana tradition has a long history of commenting on Ramkatha from within a particular telling of the story.[2] The most conspicuous example in this volume is Basavalingaiah's re-presentation of *Shudra Tapasvi*, in which the actors relate what Puttappa thought about Ramkatha by Valmiki and Bhavabhuti. By telling Ramkatha in a way that alludes to other tellings, the actors encourage the audience to think about the Ramayana tradition as a whole.

Another kind of meta-narrative occurs in the selection that provides this volume's epilogue. The Telugu women's song "Lakshmana's Laugh" takes a step back from the narrative to consider some of the underlying patterns of the story. Despite the fact that Ramkatha should inculcate dharma, at many junctures characters in the narrative perform deeds of which they feel ashamed. The song refers to incidents from every part of the story and intrudes on the inner thoughts of all sorts of characters: high and low in status, male and female, haughty and humble. In a sense, the song suggests that all creatures have flaws, thereby providing a human perspective on characters expected, at times, to live up to inhumanly high standards of behavior.

Notes

1. Ramanujan 1991: 33.
2. Aklujkar (2001: 83–103) focuses specifically on meta-narrative in *Ananda Ramayana*.

22 Everyone Has Anxieties

"Lakshmana's Laugh" begins just after Rama, Lakshmana, and Sita have returned to Ayodhya after the war in Lanka. Rama has convened his entire court for the first *durbar* (royal assembly) since his exile. He sits surrounded by his newly crowned vassal kings, Vibhishana and Sugriva, and the monkey army. Suddenly, Lakshmana laughs out loud in court, a transgression of proper behavior. The cause of his laugh is innocent. According to a folktale, Lakshmana refuses to sleep during the forest exile because he wants to guard Rama and Sita from danger at all times. When Goddess Sleep first orders him to sleep, he asks her to let Urmila slumber for him: Urmila can sleep day and night so that Lakshmana can keep awake all the time. The goddess agrees to do so until, and only until, Rama returns and holds court in Ayodhya. The minute that Rama calls the court to order, Goddess Sleep appears. Lakshmana laughs at her promptness.

Everyone in the court has some secret action of which to be ashamed, and Lakshmana's laugh brings their insecurities to the surface. One after the other, they imagine that Lakshmana is laughing at them. For example, Shiva is embarrassed at how enamored he is with Ganga, the river goddess, whom he still keeps in his hair as a second wife.[1] Vibhishana feels ashamed that he contributed to the death of his brother, Ravana, by telling Rama that Ravana's source of strength came from the pot of celestial nectar in his belly. Rama shot at Ravana's stomach and killed him. Hanuman felt humiliated because Indrajit, Ravana's son who is much younger than Hanuman, defeated him in battle.[2] In a skillful way, the song suggests that no character in the story is free from blemishes or anxieties about those blemishes.

The song depicts Rama getting easily offended and acting hastily. If Shiva and the women had not dissuaded him, he would have killed his younger brother, without even finding out why he laughed. Rama feels terrible when he hears the real cause of the laugh. Hastily again, he decides to kill himself because he had raised his sword against his brother. Vasishtha counsels him instead to give Lakshmana a foot massage, in order to show his remorse. Lakshmana was sleep deprived, so once he sleeps deeply and then receives a massage from Rama, balance is restored. For fourteen years, Lakshmana sacrificed his

---

1. When the heavenly Ganges River fell to earth, Shiva protected the earth's inhabitants from the impact of her fall by providing his matted hair as a place to land, so Ganga is often depicted as dwelling in Shiva's hair. Some stories portray her as one of his wives.
2. Indrajit used Brahma's divine one-time weapon, which binds anyone against whom it is used, against mighty Hanuman.

life in the palace and the companionship of his wife Urmila in order to guard Rama in the forest. When Rama massages Lakshmana's feet, the gesture affirms that Rama recognizes how precious Lakshmana is to him. Well-being is restored and the song ends auspiciously. [V. N. R.]

Source: Sripada Gopala Krishnamurthy, ed., *Strila Ramayanapu Patalu* [Women's Ramayana Songs] (Hyderabad: Andhra Sarasvata Parishattu, 1955), pp. 225–229, 241.[3]

Lakshmana's Laugh
WOMEN'S FOLKSONG

It was a moonlit night.
The king of Kosala, the great ruler of the entire world,
was holding court out in the open.
Thousands of seats were set up so all the people could sit.
Vibhishana arrived with a bunch of betel leaves and offered them to
    King Rama.
Rama gave betel leaves to the Brahmins that came.
The monkey army sat to the left of Rama, the warrior who killed Vali.
Rama gave Vibhishana lots of gifts, clothing, and jewels.
There were tributes of chariots, horses, and gold
and Rama viewed all seven million of them.
Sugriva sat near Rama's feet serving his lord, who was stronger than
    a lion.

While the court was in full session, Rama's brother, the mighty
    Lakshmana, felt sleepy.
His words were faltering and his head was heavy.
He tried to stay awake but he began to doze.
He stood up straight in his brother's court, shook his head and started
    to laugh.
Right in the middle of Rama's court, Lakshmana laughed, laughed
    aloud.
He laughed and laughed, and the king was upset.
Something seemed to worry them all and the court suddenly fell silent.

Shiva thought that Lakshmana was laughing at him.
Everyone knew he fell for a fisher girl
and carries her on his head even now.

Jambuvan thought that Lakshmana was laughing at him.
Once, when he was invited to Shiva's wedding,

---

3. There seems to have been some confusion in the transcription of this song. "Lakshmana's Laugh" ends with line 17 on p. 229. Another song begins in the 18th line and continues through p. 240. The translation above includes the phalashruti found on p. 241.

he broke his back walking with his short calves.
He felt ashamed and hung his head low.[4]

Adisesha thought Lakshmana was laughing at him.
He had served as the bed of Vishnu all these years
but now he was serving Vishnu's rival, Shiva.
He felt ashamed and bent his head low.

Nila never told anyone why his rocks float on the ocean.
As a child he sank things in the water, so his father cursed that
    everything would float.[5]
Lakshmana surely was laughing at him.

And Angada was sure he was being laughed at.
He was shamelessly enjoying himself
at the victory feast given by his father's killer.

Now Sugriva has something to be ashamed of, too.
He killed his brother and took his brother's wife.
No doubt Lakshmana was laughing at him, and he hung his head in
    shame.

Vibhishana thought that Lakshmana laughed at him.
He was the one who revealed the secret of his brother Ravana's power
    to Rama.[6]
So he caused Ravana's death, and now he rules Ravana's kingdom.

Hanuman thought of his own defeat
at the hands of a young fellow, Indrajit.
He was sure that was why Lakshmana was laughing and bent his head
    in shame.

Bharata and Shatrughna knew too well
that their mother grabbed all the land in the kingdom
by throwing Rama into the dark forest.
Lakshmana must be laughing at them for this, so they bent their heads
    in shame.

Sita thought that Lakshmana was laughing at her:
How could Rama put her on his thighs?
She lived in Ravana's house for six entire months

---

4. Jambuvan is a bear, and since he generally walks on all four limbs, he finds it difficult to stand and walk on just two legs for extended periods of time.
5. Nala supervised the building of the bridge to Lanka. Because Nala had the power to make the rocks that compose the bridge float on the surface of the ocean, the bridge did not need to be anchored in the ocean floor.
6. Ravana swallowed the pot of celestial nectar of immortality when it was discarded after its contents were distributed to the gods. The pot had enough traces of nectar to make Ravana immortal. Ravana would not die until the pot was shattered.

and she spoke so many harsh words about Lakshmana.
Lakshmana must think that women cannot be trusted.
So, Sita felt ashamed and hung her head.

Seeing his wife, Rama felt sad.

Rama has been ruling the monkeys for some time now.
Why is everyone sad today?
He was furious with Lakshmana for laughing in court,
And raised his sword to chop off his head.

But Shiva and the women stopped him.
They protested, "Lakshmana is a little boy
so it is not right to strike him down.
A hero like Rama should not act in haste."

Then Rama asked Lakshmana why he laughed.

"You are a kind man," said Lakshmana.
"You are giver of wishes and king of kings.
Listen, lord, to what I have to say."

"When we were in the forest and I was keeping guard outside your hut, Sleep came to me. I asked her who she was and she said, 'I am Goddess Sleep. I rule the world. All people obey me, even the kings of heaven and the elephants that bear the earth. I move across oceans, and rivers, and move around mountains and trees. Surrender to me,' she said, 'you cannot resist me.'

I walked around her three times, fell at her feet, bowed and begged, 'I am standing guard over my brother and his wife. Go to Ayodhya, where my wife lives. She is lonely, away from me. Hold her, day and night, and leave me alone. One day, my brother will return to the city in full glory and hold court while his armies and ministers serve him and you can visit me then.'

She left me alone all these years and returned now—not one minute late, and that's what amused me, and I laughed."

Rama cried out in grief, thinking of his hasty action and wanted to kill himself to atone for his sin. Vasisththa intervened, saying, "It is not right for you to have such thoughts. Instead, make Lakshmana a bed on which to sleep and then massage his feet."

Rama called all his attendants to sweep the streets, make floor designs
     of pearls,
light lamps of gems, festoon gateways, light lamps on pillars,
set out golden pots, and fetch bunches of jasmine.

They made a bed in the seven storied house,
and put a sheet of golden hues on the bed.

They brought fresh chrysanthemums and abhyanga flowers,[7]
and spread them gently over the bed.
They brought thick jasmines that blossoms after dark,
and spread them gently over the bed.
They brought parijatas right from the vine
and spread them gently over the bed.
They brought kanakaratnas freshly opened
and spread them gently over the bed.
They brought heaps of water lilies
and spread them gently over the bed.
They brought loads of mogali flowers
and spread them gently over the bed.
They brought jaji flowers that opened afresh
and spread them gently over the bed.
They made pillows of mogali petals.

The beauty of the bed was beyond words.
God gave only two eyes to see,
but you need a thousand to take in this sight.
Angada, Hanuman, and Sugriva came;
hand in hand, they came at once.
Lakshmana walked around Rama thrice
and fell at his feet, asking for permission to leave.

They lifted Lakshmana from Rama's feet.
Rama said, "Sleep my brother you are so tired."
Lakshmana bowed to Sita's feet.
Now they put him on the royal elephant.
Musicians followed and singers praised him.
Lakshmana entered the royal gate.

Lakshmana's wife [Urmila] was waiting there.
She had washed her hair and put on a yellow sari.
She wore a necklace worth a thousand and a pendant worth ten
    thousand.
She wore her favorite earrings and jewels studded with precious
    stones.
She walked to the bed with loving glances
and her sari slipped down from her shoulder.

Seeing her mood, Lakshmana said, "woman, this is not the time for you
    to come."

---

7. The flowers enumerated here are of different colors, shapes, and textures. They cover the bed like
a breathtaking mosaic of design and fragrance.

When Urmila left, Lakshmana slept.
He slept for an hour and it felt like several.
He slept several hours and it felt like a day.
Rama was surprised at his brother's slumber.
He sent Hanuman to see what was happening.
Was he sleeping, chatting with his wife, or maybe, playing water games
    with her?

Hanuman took a peek inside and said that no woman was there.
Since there was no woman there, Rama felt eager to see him.
He asked his ministers to stay, and entered there with Shatrughna.
He went in and began to massage his brother's feet.
He took Lakshmana's feet on his lap and began to massage them gently.
Lakshmana was quiet when Rama massaged him once.
When Rama massaged him a second time, he thought he was
    dreaming.
When Rama massaged him a third time, Lakshamana was frightened.
He opened his eyes, stood up, and fell at Rama's feet.

"Brother, you are older, and I should massage your feet.
Your feet gave life to Ahalya,
Your feet adorn Bali's head.
All the gods bow at your feet.
Lord of the World, you should not massage my feet."

Rama raised Lakshmana and made him sit on the golden throne.

"Brother," he said,
"My court without you is like a night without the moon.
My court without you is like a house without lamps.
My court without you is like a wife with no husband.
My court without you is like a pot with no water in it.
My court without you is like a cage without a bird in it.
Come to my court, my little brother."

The king and his brother entered the court.
Rama asked him to sit on the seat of pearls,
and he himself sat on the throne of jewels.

To those who sing this song or hear it—God will give them the highest
worlds.

Translated from Telugu by Velcheru Narayana Rao

Glossary

ADHARMA: deviation from the proper code of conduct; when unchecked, it leads to chaos; an *avatara* descends when adharma is increasing.

ADISESHA (also *Sesha*): the celestial serpent on whose body Lord *Vishnu* rests while floating in the milk ocean; the serpent's hoods provide shade for *Vishnu*.

ADIVASI: "original inhabitant"; term for indigenous peoples who lived in India before the coming of *Aryan* language-speaking peoples.

ADVAITA VEDANTA: Hindu monistic philosophy.

AGASTYA: famous sage; associated with teaching grammar in South India.

AGNI: fire god; when *Sita* entered the fire, Agni lifted her up unburnt due to her purity.

AGNIPARIKSHA: "fire as witness"; the fire ordeal that *Sita* underwent to demonstrate purity.

AHALYA: woman endowed by *Brahma* with unsurpassed beauty; seduced by *Indra* so her husband *Gautama* turned her to stone; vivified by *Rama*; mother of *Sadananda*.

AHIMSA: "non-injury," "non-violence"; refraining from harming living creatures.

AJA: an ancestor in *Rama*'s lineage who died of grief when his wife died.

AMMA: "mother"; a Tamil term used when addressing a respectable older woman.

ANGADA: son of *Vali* and *Tara*.

ANUMAN: *Hanuman*, in the Mappila dialect of Kerala.

APPALAM: deep fried crispy snack that resembles a large potato chip.

ARANYA-KANDA: "forest section" of *Ramkatha* about the forest exile.

ARECA: chopped nut with lime in *betel* leaf.

ARTHA: "worldly"; one of the four human goals; seeking wealth and/or political power.

ARYA VAMSHA: lineage of the *Aryans*.

ARYANS: "nobles"; Aryan language-speaking peoples from Central Asia; dominated society in North India; their priests chanted the *Vedas*.

ASHOKA: tree with red flowers; *Sita* stayed under such a tree in the precincts of *Ravana*'s palace during her imprisonment in *Lanka*.

ASHRAM: hermitage in the forest inhabited by ascetics.

ASHTAVAKRA: an ascetic sage.

ASHVAMEDHA: "horse sacrifice"; royal ritual of universal sovereignty.

ATMAN: the eternal self that does not die when the body perishes.

ATRI: forest sage hospitable to *Rama*, *Sita,* and *Lakshmana* early in their forest exile.

AVATARA: "descent"; a portion of a deity in human form on earth to destroy *adharma*.

AVVA: "younger sister"; a form of address for a woman of younger or inferior status.

AYANA: "journey."

AYODHYA: capital city of *Kosala,* ruled by the *Ikshvaku* dynasty.

AYODHYA-KANDA: "Ayodhya section" of *Ramkatha* about *Rama*'s birth and youth.

BALI: see *Vali.*

BANYAN: a shady tree of the mulberry family with spreading branches that send out secondary sprouts, which root in the soil to form secondary trunks.

BETEL: a leaf in which chopped *areca* nut and lime are wrapped; post-prandial digestive snack; mild intoxicant.

BHARAT: an indigenous name for India.

BHARATA: a brother of *Rama,* son of *Dasharatha* with *Kaikeyi;* regent during *Rama's* exile.

BHARGAVA RAMA: see *Parashurama.*

BHASHA: "language"; refers to authors who write in a regional language; often contrasted with writing in Sanskrit, English, or another translocal language.

BHAVABHUTI: eighth-century Sanskrit playwright who composed *Uttararamacharita,* a play in which *Sita* is banished, raises two sons, and ultimately is reunited with *Rama.*

BHOOTEYARA ATA: a form of folk dance and song performance in rural Karnataka.

BRAHMA: deity who created the world; considered grandfather of all creatures.

BRAHMASTRA: missile created by *Brahma;* once discharged, it cannot be recalled.

BRAHMIN: a member of the highest of the four *varna*s; guardian and preserver of Sanskrit scriptures; qualified to perform Vedic sacrifices.

BRAHMINICAL: beliefs and actions prescribed in authoritative Hindu texts preserved and transmitted by *Brahmins;* often used to mean "orthodox teachings" or orthodoxy.

BUKKA: a perfume for infusing clothes and hair with an appealing fragrance.

CHITRAKUTA: mountain where *Rama* and *Sita* lived and *Bharata* pledged loyalty.

CRORE: a large unit of measure equal to ten million (10,000,000).

DAKSHINA: payment given by the sacrificer (patron) to a priest for performing a ritual.

DALIT: "ground down"; name adopted by ex-Untouchables; refers to their oppression by higher caste people.

DANDAKA: forest where *Rama, Sita,* and *Lakshmana* spent time during their exile.

DASHARATHA: king of *Ayodhya;* father of *Rama* and his brothers; husband of *Kausalya, Sumitra,* and *Kaikeyi.*

DAUGHTER OF THE EARTH: epithet for *Sita,* referring to her mother, Earth.

DEVI: "goddess"; also an honorific suffixed to a woman's name, e.g., *Sita Devi.*

DHARMA: code for conduct determined according to one's *varna,* life-stage, and gender, e.g., *Kshatriyas* protect, students study sacred texts, wives bring blessings to their families.

DHARMA-SHASTRA: treatises that prescribe proper, and proscribe improper, conduct.

DIPAVALI (also Divali): holiday when lamps are lit to welcome *Rama* home from *Lanka* or celebrate *Krishna's* slaying of a demon; a time when Hindus give new clothes.

DRAUPADI: character from *Mahabharata* who dutifully married five brothers.

DRAVIDIAN: language family and its speakers; putatively indigenous to South India.

DURBAR: courtly reception, especially in the audience hall of a ruler.

DUSHANA: general in *Khara's* army, killed by *Rama* after *Shurpanakha's* mutilation.

DWAPARA YUGA: the penultimate of four cosmic ages, when *dharma* becomes increasingly unstable.

ELUTTACCHAN: author of the sixteenth-century Malayalam *Adhyatma Ramayana.*

GANDHARI: queen who blindfolds herself to share her blind husband's disability in the *Mahabharata.*

GANGES (also Ganga): a holy North Indian river worshipped as a Goddess; it is auspicious to submerge the bones of deceased parents in her waters.

GAUTAMA: husband of *Ahalya;* cursed her to become a stone; father of *Sadananda.*

GAYATRI: a Sanskrit prayer from the *Vedas;* recited by orthodox *Brahmins.*

GHEE (also Ghi): clarified butter, used as a sacrificial oblation to the Vedic fire.

GODANTA BOW: bow of Lord *Vishnu.*

GODAVARI: name of a holy river in South India.

GUHA: king of the Nishadas; assisted *Rama, Lakshmana,* and *Sita* as they entered exile.

GURU: religious preceptor; teacher whom disciples venerate.

HAKKULU: plural form of the Telugu transliteration of Arabic "*haq*" meaning "rights," e.g., in "fundamental rights" or "civil rights."

HANUMAN: staunch devotee of *Rama;* courtier of *Sugriva;* visited *Sita* in *Lanka* as *Rama*'s messenger; saved wounded *Lakshmana* by bringing an herbal antidote for poison.

HARIJAN: "children of God"; M. Gandhi's name for ex-Untouchables; call themselves *Dalits.*

HIJRA: community of transvestites; often participate in life cycle and devotional rituals.

IKSHVAKU: family name of the royal house of *Ayodhya.*

INDRA: king of Vedic gods, deity of rain and fertility; cursed for seducing *Ahalya.*

INDRAJIT: son of *Ravana.*

JAJI: name of a flower that grows in Andhra Pradesh.

JAMBUVAN: king of the bears, who allied with *Rama* to battle *Ravana.*

JANAKA: king of *Mithila;* found *Sita* in a furrow and adopted her as his daughter.

JANAKI: name for *Sita* that emphasizes her status as daughter of King *Janaka.*

JATI: "birth"; an endogamous hereditary social group; usually a sub-caste of a *varna.*

JATRA: a folk performance; traditionally connected with a religious festival but today sometimes used as an occasion for activists to spread social reforms.

JOGATI: *Shudra* female or *hijra* devotees of the Goddess *Yarlamma* who have renounced marriage and perform devotional songs in rural Karnataka.

KAIKEYI: youngest wife of *Dasharatha,* mother of *Bharata.*

KAILASA: Himalayan mountain where Goddess *Parvati* grew up.

KAKUTSTHA: an illustrious ancestor of *Rama;* "of the lineage of Kakutstha" is a common epithet for *Rama.*

KALI YUGA: the fourth and most degenerate cosmic age, when *dharma* is in full decline.

KAMADHENU (also Shabala): Sage *Vasishtha*'s wish-granting cow who fulfills all desires.

KAMBAN: author of the twelfth-century Tamil *Iramavataram.*

KANCHANA SITA: a golden statue of *Sita* representing her in *Rama*'s *ashvamedha.*

KANDA: section or canto of a text, e.g., the *Aranya-kanda.*

KANNAGI: selfless heroine of the Tamil epic *Cilappatikaram* who, despite her husband's betrayal, burnt Madurai city when its king unjustly executed him.

KARMA: merits or demerits accumulated by *dharmic* or *adharmic* deeds.

KATHAKALI: form of dance-drama performed in Kerala in which actors wear huge masks.

KAUSALYA: *Dasharatha*'s eldest wife and chief queen; mother of *Rama.*

KHADI: hand-spun and hand-woven cloth; symbol of Indian national self-reliance.

KHARA: brother of *Shurpanakha;* killed by *Rama* after *Shurpanakha* was mutilated.

KISHKINDHA: name of the monkey kingdom; ruled by *Vali* and, subsequently, *Sugriva.*

KISHKINDHA-KANDA: "Kishkindha section" of *Ramkatha* about the monkey kingdom.

KOHL: a cosmetic made of lamp-black used to delineate a woman's eyes, an eye-liner.

KORAVANJI: a gypsy fortune-teller.

KOSALA: the kingdom of which *Ayodhya* is the capital; ruled by the *Ikshvaku* lineage.

KRAUNCHA: bird (probably a crane) killed by a hunter; the cry of its lonely mate inspired *Valmiki* to create the *shloka* meter.

KRISHNA: an *avatara* of *Vishnu.*

KRITA YUGA: the first and purest of the four cosmic ages when *dharma* prevails.

KSHATRIYA: member of the second highest of the four *varnas*; often kings or warriors enjoined to protect and rule.

KUSHA: one of *Sita* and *Rama*'s twin sons, along with *Lava.*

LAKH: a unit of measure equal to one hundred thousand (100,000).

LAKSHMANA: brother of *Rama;* son of *Dasharatha* with *Sumitra;* husband of *Urmila.*

LAKSHMANA REKHA: the protective line drawn by *Lakshmana* around *Sita;* when she stepped over this line to give *Ravana* alms, he abducted her.

LAKSHMI: Goddess of good fortune; consort of Lord *Vishnu; Sita* is her *avatara.*

LAMAYANA: "Ramayana" in the Mappila dialect of Kerala.

LANKA: the capital city of King *Ravana;* usually identified with today's Sri Lanka.

LAVA: one of *Sita* and *Rama*'s twin sons, along with *Kusha.*

LAVANYAKAM: name of a flower cultivated by *Ahalya.*

MANDAVI: wife of *Bharata.*

MANDODARI: favorite wife of *Ravana;* said to be a *pativrata.*

MANTRA: Sanskrit syllables from the *Vedas* imbued with transformative powers.

MANU: traditionally considered the first human and thus father of the human race; the legendary founder of the *Ikshvaku* lineage; a *dharma-shastra* is attributed to him.

MAPPILA PATTU: a genre of domestic, field, and festival songs of Mappila Muslims in Kerala.

MARICHA: son of *Tadaka;* uncle of *Ravana* at whose insistence he disguised himself as a golden deer to lure *Rama* away so *Ravana* could abduct *Sita.*

MATANGA: guru of an *adivasi* woman, *Shabari,* who he foretold would meet *Rama.*

MERU: mountain at the center of the cosmos; heaven of *Indra, Agni,* and other Vedic deities.

MITHILA: the kingdom ruled by *Janaka;* prenuptial home of *Sita.*

MOKSHA: "liberation"; release from the cycle of continuing death and rebirth.

MURTI: "form"; image, icon, statue of a deity in a temple sanctum or domestic shrine.

NALA: the monkey who supervised the building of the bridge to *Lanka.*

NAMBUDRI: a particularly orthodox *Brahmin jati* in Kerala.

NANDIGRAM: forest where *Bharata* slept during *Rama*'s exile.

NARAYANA GURU: a major Hindu religious reformer in Kerala.

NAYAKAR: a *jati* from Andhra Pradesh, whose warriors ruled parts of the Tamil- and Kannada-speaking areas of the South.

PADDY: threshed, unmilled rice.

PALAI: "desert"; in classical Tamil poetry, the wasteland of the separation of lovers or, more abstractly, loss in general.

PANCHAVATI: a forest where *Rama* and *Sita* spent pleasant days during their exile.

PANDIT: teacher; learned, wise, knowledgeable person.

PARAMASHIVA: "ultimate" or "highest *Shiva*"; Lord *Shiva* as Supreme God.

PARASHURAMA: "Rama with an Axe"; a previous avatara of *Vishnu,* defeated by *Rama.*

PARNASALA: modern term for a country retreat; forest cottage.

PARVATI: daughter of the Himalaya mountains; goddess who performed asceticism to win *Shiva* as her husband.

PATALAM: the netherworld; region inhabited by snakes and *rakshasas*.

PATIVRATA: "she with a vow to her Lord/husband"; faithful wife devoted to her husband.

PHALASHRUTI: "fruit of hearing"; a formulaic statement promising merit to hearers of a text.

PRAKRITI: animating force of the natural world, viewed in Samkhya philosophy as female.

PRAYOGAVESHAM: a form of self-sacrifice; fasting unto death.

PUJA: "worship"; acts of devotion with fruit, flame, and water offered to the deity.

PURANA: a major anthology recounting the great deeds performed by the gods.

PURUSHA: spirit or principle of the cosmos, viewed in Samkhya philosophy as male.

RAGHAVA, RAGHUNATHA: epithets for *Rama* that stress the greatness of his lineage.

RAGHU: son of *Kakutstha,* an illustrious ancestor of *Rama;* hence name of *Rama's* lineage.

RAKSHASAS (female, rakshasi): "those who protect"; a class of creatures associated with forests, lust, wealth, and violence; some consider them *Dravidians*.

RAMA (also Ram): *avatara* of Lord *Vishnu;* son of *Dasaratha* with *Kausalya;* husband of *Sita.*

RAMACHANDRA: "*Rama* like the Moon"; epithet stressing his face's radiance and fullness.

RAMKATHA: "the story of *Rama*," the basic skeletal story of *Rama* and *Sita,* as distinct from particular tellings of the story.

RAVANA: *rakshasa* king of *Lanka;* husband of *Mandodari;* father of *Indrajit.*

RISHI: ascetic and learned sage.

RISHYAMUKA: the mountain where *Rama* met *Sugriva.*

RISHYASHRINGA: ascetic who drew rain to *Dasaratha's* drought-ridden kingdom; married *Shanta; Rama's* brother-in-law.

RUDRA-VINA: a stringed instrument said to be modeled after the body of Goddess *Parvati.*

RUMA: wife of *Sugriva.*

SADANANDA: son of *Ahalya* and *Gautama;* attends philosophic debates at *Janaka's* court.

SANDALPASTE: smoothed onto the body as a fragrant unguent on auspicious occasions.

SANDHYA: "twilight"; dawn and dusk.

SANNYASI: person in the fourth stage of life; renouncer who severs his links to family, conventional norms, and social duties.

SANSKRIT: "perfected language"; the language of ancient Hindu texts, including the *Vedas* and *Valmiki's Ramayana.*

SARASVATI: Goddess of learning and arts; patron deity of musicians; wife of Lord *Brahma.*

SARAYU: a river in *Kosala;* when *Rama* completed his time as an *avatara,* he entered the Sarayu and returned to the celestial world.

SARI: six- or eight-yard cloth wound around the waist and then across the upper body; worn by many Hindu women, especially after marriage.

SATYA: "truth."

SESHA (also *Adisesha*): the celestial serpent on whose body Lord *Vishnu* rests while floating in the milk ocean; the serpent's hoods provide shade for *Vishnu.*

SHABALA (also Kamadhenu): Sage *Vasishtha's* wish-granting cow who fulfills all desires.

SHABARI: *adivasi* woman ascetic devoted to *Rama.*

SHAIVITE: devotee of Lord *Shiva* as supreme God.

SHAMBUKA: a *Shudra* who practiced rigorous *tapas.*

SHANKARA: a name for Lord *Shiva.*

SHANTA: adopted daughter of King *Dasharatha;* married *Rishyashringa.*

SHARI'AT: Islamic law.

SHASTRAS: treatises specifying proper ways to pursue *dharma, artha,* and other goals.

SHATRUGHNA: twin brother of *Lakshmana;* son of *Dasharatha* with *Sumitra.*

SHIVA: patron deity of ascetics, husband of *Parvati.*

SHLOKA: *Sanskrit* meter in which *Valmiki* composed his *Ramayana.*

SHRI (also Sree): used alone, refers to Goddess *Lakshmi;* used before another proper name, it refers to an auspicious being who brings good fortune, e.g., *Shri Rama.*

SHRUTI: "that which is heard"; term for religious texts believed to be eternal and intuited by ancient sages; refers generally to the *Vedas* and Upanishads.

SHUDRA: the lowest of the four *varnas;* according to *dharma-shastric* prescriptions, *Shudras* are prohibited from hearing the *Vedas* or practicing asceticism.

SHURPANAKHA: sister of *Ravana;* fell in love with *Rama;* was disfigured by *Lakshmana.*

SITA: *avatara* of Goddess *Lakshmi,* daughter of Mother Earth; found in a furrow by King *Janaka;* sister of *Urmila;* wife of *Rama;* mother of *Lava* and *Kusha.*

SITALA: Smallpox Goddess; a form of the great Goddess.

SMRTI: "that which is remembered"; texts composed by sages; contrasted with *shruti.*

SOMANA KUNITA: form of masked drama performed in rural Karnataka.

SUBAHU: *rakshasa* companion of *Maricha;* slain by *Rama.*

SUGRIVA: monkey king; ally of *Rama;* brother of *Vali;* served by *Hanuman.*

SUMITRA: second wife of *Dasharatha;* mother of *Lakshmana* and *Shatrughna.*

SUNDARA-KANDA: "section on beauty"; the portion of *Ramkatha* where *Hanuman* visits *Sita* in *Lanka;* a section consider especially auspicious for oral recitation.

SURYA VAMSA: "lineage of the Sun"; a major *Kshatriya* lineage.

SWADESHI: "of one's own country"; an item produced in India, e.g., *khadi.*

SWAMI: "Lord"; a form of address or name for a deity or a great ascetic sage.

TADAKA: a *rakshasi* killed by *Rama.*

TAMASA: a river that flows near *Valmiki*'s hermitage.

TAPAS: "heat"; bodily mortification and meditation to burn off fruits of past deeds.

TAPASVI: one who performs *tapas.*

TARA: wife of *Vali* and later *Sugriva;* she cursed *Rama* to lose his wife's company.

TARKA: "logic"; sometimes by modern authors viewed as conflicting with *dharma-shastra.*

THUMBA: white flower in Kerala used on sacred occasions such as the Onam Festival.

TRETA YUGA: the cosmic age when *dharma* starts to become unstable.

TRISHANKU: *Rama*'s ancestor caught between heaven and earth, hence neither here nor there.

TRISHIRAS: a *rakshasa* killed by *Rama.*

TULSIDAS: author of the sixteenth-century *Ramcharitmanas* in Hindi.

TURMERIC: yellow spice ground into powder; smoothed onto the body of a woman in preparation for auspicious ritual occasions.

TWICE-BORN: born into one of the three highest *varnas;* eligible for *brahminical* life-cycle rituals and ascetic practices from which *Shudras* are excluded.

UPANAYANA: rite in which a *twice-born* male is invested with a sacred thread initiating him into the student stage of life.

U RMILA: sister of *Sita;* wife of *Lakshmana;* stayed at the palace while he went into exile.
U TTARA-KANDA: "final section" of *Ramkatha* about *Rama's* reign, *Sita's* banishment, and the origins of *Ravana's* powers.

V AIDEHI: epithet for *Sita* which emphasizes that she grew up in *Mithila.*
V AISHNAVITE: devotee of Lord *Vishnu* as supreme God or of his two most popular *avatara*s, *Rama* and *Krishna.*
V AISHYA: a member of the third of the four *varna*s; those who generate, e.g., merchants and agriculturalists.
V ALI (also Bali, Valin); monkey king; brother of *Sugriva;* warrior who defeated *Ravana* in battle and forced him to go on pilgrimage to holy sites; slain by *Rama.*
V ALMIKI: composer of *Ramayana;* in whose hermitage banished *Sita* took refuge with her sons; creator of the *shloka* meter.
V ARANASI (also Banaras, Benaras): city holy to Lord *Shiva,* where *brahminical* learning flourishes and temples abound.
V ARNA: religiously validated categories of ranking, e.g., Kshatriya, Shudra.
V ARNASHRAMA-DHARMA: code for conduct enjoined for one's social station and life stage.
V ASISHTHA: *Dasharatha's* family guru, adhered strictly to *varnashrama-dharma.*
V EDAS: earliest and most authoritative Hindu texts, believed to be eternal and intuited by ancient sages; transmitted orally from teacher to pupil.
V ERMILLION: a bright red substance worn in the part of the hair by wives in North India, and sometimes in South India.
V IBHISHANA: brother of *Ravana;* joined *Rama* who crowned him king of *Lanka.*
V INA (also veena): a stringed musical instrument with a long fingerboard and a gourd resonator at each end, played beautifully by *Ravana.*
V ISHNU: Supreme God according to *Vaishnavites;* husband of *Lakshmi.*
V ISHVAMITRA: a *Kshatriya*-turned-*Brahmin* through *tapas;* gave divine weapons to *Rama* and *Lakshmana.*

Y AJNA: sacrificial oblations and recitation of *mantra*s presided over by *Brahmin* priests.
Y AKSHAGANA: form of dance-drama performed in Karnataka.
Y AMA: god of death; uses the *karma* people accumulate to determine whether their subsequent rebirth will be in a higher or lower form.
Y ARLAMMA (also Elamma, Yerlamma): in some tellings, the wife of *Parashurama,* who had her beheaded; her son put an untouchable woman's head on her body and revived her.
Y UDDHA-KANDA: "war section" of *Ramkatha* about the battle between *Rama* and *Ravana.*
Y UGA: the four cosmic ages, beginning with creation and ending with destruction of the universe.

Z AMINDAR: large landowner who collected local land taxes, transmitting them to the ruler.

Bibliography

Indian Language Works

Ambai [C. S. Lakshmi]. 2000. "Adavi." In *Kaattil Oru Maan*, pp. 138–168. Nagercoil: Kalachuvadu.

Anonymous [M. Parvati Ammal]. 1918. *Sita Kalyanam: Oru Siru Tamil Natakam*. Madras: S. Murtti and Co.

Arankanayaki Ammal, Vanamalai. 1927. *Iramayanakkummi*. Madras: B. N. Press.

Asan, Kumaran. 1981; rpt. 1986. "Chintavishtayaya Sita." In *Kumaranasante Sampurna Padyakritikal*, pp. 521–563. Kottayam: Sahitya Pravarthaka Cooperative Society.

Bharati, C. Subramania. 1977. "Kutirai Kompu." In *Paratiyar Kataikal*, pp. 285–292. Madras: Poompukar Press.

Bhatta, G. H., ed. 1958; rpt. 1982. *The Balakanda: The First Book of the Valmiki-Ramayana*. Baroda: Oriental Institute.

Chalam, Gudipati Venkata. 1924; rpt. 1993. "Sita Agnipravesam." In *Savitri: Pauranika Natikalu*, pp. 50–58. Vijayawada: Aruna Publishing House.

Chaudari, Tripuraneni Ramasvami. [1920]; rpt. 1966. *Śambuka Vadha* in *Kaviraja Sahitya Sarvasvam*, vol. 2, pp. 1–79. Guntur: Kaviraja Samiti.

Cuppalesksumi Ammal, R. S. 1928. *Kusalava Vakkiyam*. Madras: Hindi Prachar Press.

Dabbe, Vijaya. 1996. *Iti Gitike*. Mysore: Kuvempu Institute of Kannada Studies.

Eluttachan, Thunchattu. 1988; rpt. 1994. *Adhyatma Ramayanam*. Kottayam, Kerala: D.C. Books.

Gowda, Rame, P. K. Rajasekara, and S. Basavaiah, eds. 1973. *Janapada Ramayana*. Mysore: n.p.

Kailasapathy, K. 1970; rpt. 1996. "Ahalikaiyum Karpu Neriyum." In *Atiyum Mutiyum*, pp. 114–195. Madras: Pari Nilayam.

Kane, P. V., ed. 1971. *The Uttara-rama-carita*. Delhi: Motilal Banarsidass.

Karassery, M. N. [Mohiyuddin Nedukandiyil]. 1989. 2nd ed. "Mappila Ramayana." In *Kurimanam*, pp. 95–99. Calicut: Malayalam Publications.

"Kavanasarma" [Kandula Varaha Narasimha Sarma]. 1984; rpt. 1995. "Surpanakha Sokam." In *Kavanasarma Kathalu*. Visakhapatnam: RK Publications.

Kopalakirushnamacariyar, Vai. Mu., ed. 1971. *Kamparamayanam*. Madras: Vai. Mu. Kopalakirushnamacariyar Co.

"Krishnasri" [Sripada Gopala Krishnamurti], ed. 1955. *Strila Ramayanapu Patalu*, 225–229, 241. Hyderabad: Andhra Sarasvata Parishattu.

"Kumudini" [Ranganayaki Thatham]. 1934; rpt. 1948. "Sita Pirattiyin Kataitankal." In *Cillaraic Cankatikal, Limitet*, pp. 75–78. Tricchi: Natesan Books.

"Kuvempu." *See* Puttappa, K[uppalli] V[enkata].

Lenin, Lalitha. 2000. *Namukku Prarthikkam*, pp. 39–41. Tiruvananthapuram: D.C. Books.

Madhavan, N. S. 2006. "Ahalya." *Bhashaposhini* (April): 5–12.

Narasimhachar, "Putina" P. T. 1941; rpt. 1978. *Ahalye*. Mysore: D. V. K. Murthy.

Pudumaippittan [C. Virdhachalam]. 1998. *Annai Itta Ti: Pudumaippittanin Tokukkappatatal Accitappata Pataippukal*. Nagercoil: Kalachuvadu Pathippagam.

———. 2000a. "Ahaliyai." In *Pudumaippithan Kathaikal*, ed. A. R. Venkatachalapathy, I:131–135. Nagercoil: Kalachuvadu Pathippagam.

———. 2000b. "Sabavimosanam." In *Pudumaippithan Kathaikal*, ed. A. R. Venkatacha-lapathy, I:527–540. Nagercoil: Kalachuvadu Pathippagam.

Puttappa, "Kuvempu" Kuppalli Venkata. 1955; rpt. 1990. *Sri Ramayana Darshanam*, 4 vols. Bangalore: Directorate of Kannada Literature and Culture.

———. 2004. *Kuvempu Samagra Nataka Samputa*, ed. K. C. Shivareddy. Hampi, Shi-moga: Kannada University.

Ramavarma, Vayalar. 1988. *Vayalarkavithakal.* Kottayam: Sahitya Pravarthaka Co-operative.

Ranganayakamma, Muppala. 1974–1976. *Ramayana Vishavrksam,* 3 vols. Hyderabad: Sweet Home Publications.

Satchidanandan, K. 2004. "Janaki, Poru." In *Sakshyangal.* Kottayam: D.C. Books.

Satyanarayana, Viswanatha. 1944–1963; rpt. 1992. *Ramayana Kalpavrkshamu,* 6 vols. Vijayawada: Visvanatha Publications.

Shah, Umakant Premanand, ed. 1975. *The Uttarakanda: The Seventh Book of the Valmiki-Ramayana.* Baroda: Oriental Institute.

Sivarudrappa, G. S. 2002. *Rashtrakavi Kuvempuvata Shudra Tapasvi Mattu Smashaana Kurukshetra (Ranga Patya).* Bangalore: Rashtrakvai Kuvempu Vichara Vedike.

Sivasekaram, S. 1995. "Ahalikai." In *Natikkari Munkil.* Madras: National Arts and Liter-ary Association.

Sreedevi, K. B. 1990. "Shilpe-rupini." In *Grihalakshmi.*

Sreekantan Nair, C. N. 1961; rpt. 2001. *Kanchana Sita.* In *Natakathrayam,* pp. 135–186. Tiruvananthanpuram: D. C. Books.

Sripada Gopala Krishnamurti. *See* "Krishnasri."

Thangaraju, Thiruvarur K. 1954. *Ramayana Natakam.* Chennai: The Author.

[Valmiki]. 1969; rpt. 1992. *Srimad Valmiki Ramayana, Uttara Kanda.* Gorakhpur: Gita Press.

Venkatesha Murthy, H. S. 1999. *Chitrapata.* In *Chitrapata, Agnivarna, Uriya Uyyale (Mooru Natakagalu),* pp. 60–74. Bangalore: Ankita Pustaka.

"Volga" [Popuri Lalitha Kumari]. 2003. "Samagamam." *Andhra Jyothi, Sunday Magazine* (4 May), pp. 20–23.

Works in English

Aithal, Parmeswara. 1987. "The Ramayana in Kannada Literature." In *South Asian Digest of Regional Writing,* vol. 12. *Mythology in Modern Indian Literature,* pp. 1–12. South Asia Institute, University of Heidelberg.

Aklujkar, Vidyut. 2001. "Crying Dogs and Laughing Trees in Rama's Kingdom: Self-reflexivity in *Ananda Ramayana.*" In *Questioning Ramayanas, a South Asian Tra-dition,* ed. Paula Richman, pp. 83–103, 370–374. Berkeley: University of California Press.

Antherjanam, Lalithambika. 1988. *Cast Me Out if You Will: Stories and Memoir.* Trans. Gita Krishnankutty. New York: Feminist Press.

Aravindan, G. 1992. "Interview." In *Aravindan and His Films.* Special issue of *Close Look.* Trivandrum: Chalachithra Film Society.

Ashton, Martha, and Bruce Christie. 1977. *Yaksagana: A Dance Drama of India.* New Delhi: Abhinav Publications.

Blackburn, Stuart H. 1991. "Creating Conversations: The Rama Story as Puppet Play in

Kerala." In *Many Ramayanas: The Diversity of a Narrative Tradition in South Asia,* ed. Paula Richman, pp. 156–172. Berkeley: University of California Press.

———. 1996. *Inside the Drama-House: Rama Stories and Shadow Puppets in South India.* Berkeley: University of California Press.

———. 2003. *Print, Folklore, and Nationalism in Colonial South India.* Delhi: Permanent Black.

Burrow, T., and T. B. Emeneau. 1984. *A Dravidian Etymological Dictionary.* New York: Oxford University Press.

Chandrasekhara, B. 1960. "The Plays of K. V. Puttappa." *The Literary Half-Yearly* 1: 2 (January): 24–42.

Chattopadhyaya, Brajadulal. 1998. *Representing the Other? Sanskrit Sources and the Muslims.* New Delhi: Manohar.

Chaudhuri, Shubha, and Purushothama Bilimale, eds. 2000. Special Issue: *Yakshagana. Seagull Theatre Quarterly* 25/26 (March–June).

Coburn, Thomas. 1995. "Sita Fights While Ram Swoons: A Shakta Version of the Ramayan." *Manushi* 90 (September–October): 5–16.

Dharmadasa, K. N. O. 1992. *Language, Religion, and Ethnic Assertiveness: The Growth of Sinhalese Nationalism in Sri Lanka.* Ann Arbor: University of Michigan Press.

Dimmit, Cornelia. 1982. "Sita: Fertility Goddess and *Sakti.*" In *The Divine Consort: Radha and the Goddesses of India,* ed. John Stratton Hawley and Donna Marie Wulff, pp. 210–223. Berkeley: Berkeley Religious Studies Series.

Dineshchandra, S., and Candrakumara De. 1923–1932. *Eastern Bengal Ballads, Mymensing,* 4 vols. Calcutta: University of Calcutta.

Doniger, Wendy. 1991. "Fluid and Fixed Texts in India." In *Boundaries of the Text: Epic Performances in South and Southeast Asia,* ed. Joyce Burkhalter Fluekiger and Laurie J. Sears, pp. 31–41. Ann Arbor: Center for South and Southeast Asian Studies, University of Michigan.

Dumont, Louis. 1980. *Homo Hierarchicus: The Caste System and Its Implications.* Chicago: University of Chicago Press.

Encyclopedia of South India, 2 vols. 1991. Thiruvanmiyur, Madras: Institute of Asian Studies.

Erndl, Kathleen. 1991. "The Mutilation of Śurpanakha." In *Many Ramayanas: The Diversity of a Narrative Tradition in South Asia,* ed. Paula Richman, pp. 67–88. Berkeley: University of California Press.

Freeman, [John] Rich[ardson]. 2006. "Genre and Society: Literary Culture in Premodern Kerala." In *Literary Cultures in History: Reconstructions from South Asia,* ed. Sheldon Pollock, pp. 437–502. Berkeley: University of California Press.

Geetha, V., and S. V. Rajadurai. 1998. *Towards a Non-Brahmin Millennium: From Iyothee Thass to Periyar.* Calcutta: Samya.

George, K. M. 1972. *Kumaran Asan.* New Delhi: Sahitya Akademi.

GoldbergBelle, Jonathan. 1984. "The Performance Poetics of *Tolubommalata:* A South Indian Shadow Puppet Tradition." Ph.D. thesis, Department of South Asian Studies, University of Wisconsin, Madison.

Goldman, Robert P. 2000. "Ravana's Kitchen: A Testimony of Desire and the Other." In *Questioning Ramayanas, a South Asian Tradition,* ed. Paula Richman, pp. 105–116, 374–376. Berkeley: University of California Press.

———. 2004. "Resisting Rama: Dharmic Debates on Gender and Hierarchy and the Work of the Valmiki *Ramayana.*" In *Ramayana Revisited,* ed. Mandakranta Bose, pp. 19–46. New York: Oxford University Press.

——, ed. and trans. 1984. *The Ramayana of Valmiki: An Epic of Ancient India,* vol. 1: *Balakanda.* Princeton: Princeton University Press.

——, and Sally Sutherland Goldman, trans. 1996. *The Ramayana of Valmiki: An Epic of Ancient India,* vol. 5: *Sundara Kanda.* Princeton: Princeton University Press.

Goldman, Sally Sutherland. 2000. "The Voice of Sita in Valmiki's *Sundarakanda.*" In *Questioning Ramayanas, a South Asian Tradition,* ed. Paula Richman, pp. 223–238, 390–395. Berkeley: University of California Press.

Hande, H. V., trans. 1996. *Kamba Ramayanam: An English Prose Rendering.* Mumbai: Bharatiya Vidya Bhavan.

Hart, George L., and Hank Heifetz, trans. 1988. *The Forest Book of the Ramayana of Kamban.* Berkeley: University of California Press.

Hayavadana Rao, C., ed. 1927. *Mysore Gazetteer.* Bangalore: Government Press.

Hess, Linda. 2001. "Lovers' Doubts: Questioning the Tulsi Ramayan." In *Questioning Ramayanas, a South Asian Tradition,* ed. Paula Richman, pp. 25–47, 353–358, 361–366. Berkeley: University of California Press.

Hiriyanna, M. 1993. *Outlines of Indian Philosophy.* Delhi: Motilal Banarsidass.

Holmstrom, Lakshmi. 2000. "Making It New: Pudumaippittan and the Tamil Short Story, 1934–48." *South Asia Research* 20, no. 2: 133–146.

——, trans. 2002. *Pudumaippittan Fictions.* New Delhi: Katha.

Irschick, Eugene F. 1969. *Politics and Social Conflict in South India: The Non-Brahman Movement and Tamil Separatism, 1916–1929.* Berkeley: University of California Press.

Joseph, Salim. 2002. "Mappila Ramayana from the land of Thacholi Othenan." *New Indian Express, Kozhikode* (2 July), p. 3.

Kakar, Sudhir. 1988. "Feminine Identity in India." In *Women in Indian Society: A Reader,* ed. Rehana Ghadially, pp. 44–68. New Delhi: Sage.

Kanaganayakam, Chelva. 1992. "A Breach of Trust: The Poetics of Translation." In *Kilakkum Merkum,* pp. 51–53.

Kishwar, Madhu. 2001. "Yes to Sita, No to Ram: The Continuing Hold of Sita on Popular Imagination in India." In *Questioning Ramayanas, a South Asian Tradition,* ed. Paula Richman, pp. 285–308, 400–401. Berkeley: University of California Press.

Krishnankutty, G., trans. 1988. *Cast Me Out if You Will: Stories and Memoir by Lalithambika Anterjanam.* New York: Feminist Press.

Lal, P., trans. and ed. 1957. "The Later Story of Rama (*Uttara-Rama-Charita*)." In *Great Sanskrit Plays: In Modern Translation,* pp. 289–337. New York: New Directions.

Lamb, Ramdas. 1991. "Personalizing the *Ramayan:* Ramnamis and Their Use of the *Ramcaritmanas.*" In *Many Ramayanas: The Diversity of a Narrative Tradition in South Asia,* ed. Paula Richman, pp. 235–255. Berkeley: University of California Press.

Leslie, Julia. 2003. *Authority and Meaning in Indian Religions: Hinduism and the Case of Valmiki.* Aldershot: Ashgate.

Lutgendorf, Philip. 1991. *The Life of a Text: Performing the Ramcaritmanas of Tulsidas.* Berkeley: University of California Press.

——. 2000. "Dining Out at Lake Pampa: The Shabari Episode in Multiple Ramayanas." In *Questioning Ramayanas, a South Asian Tradition,* ed. Paula Richman, pp. 119–136, 376–379. Berkeley: University of California Press.

Madhavan Kutty, V. K. 1981. "G. Aravindan." In *The New Generation, 1960–1980,* ed. Uma Da Cunha, 42–45. New Delhi: Directorate of Film Festivals.

Mehtha, C. C. 1963. *Bibliography of Stageable Plays in Indian Languages.* M.S. University of Baroda and Bharatiya Natya Sangha.

Menon, A. G., and G. H. Schokker. 1992. "The Conception of Rama-rajya in South and North Indian Literature." In *Ritual, State and History in South Asia*, ed. A. W. Van Den Hoeck et al., pp. 610–636. Leiden: E. J. Brill.

Narayana Rao, Velcheru.1991. "A Ramayana of Their Own: Women's Oral Tradition in Telugu." In *Many Ramayanas: The Diversity of a Narrative Tradition in South Asia*, ed. Paula Richman, pp. 114–136. Berkeley: University of California Press.

———. 2001. "The Politics of Telugu Ramayanas." In *Questioning Ramayanas, a South Asian Tradition*, ed. Paula Richman, pp. 159–185, 382–384. Berkeley: University of California Press.

———. 2004. "When Does Sita Cease to Be Sita? Notes Toward a Cultural Grammar of Indian Narratives." In *Ramayanas Revisited*, ed. Mandakranta Bose, pp. 219–242. New York: Oxford University Press.

———, ed. and trans. 2002. *Twentieth Century Telugu Poetry: An Anthology*. New Delhi: Oxford University Press.

Narayanan, Vasudha. 2001. "The Ramayana and Its Muslim Interpreters." In *Questioning Ramayanas, a South Asian Tradition*, ed. Paula Richman, pp. 265–281, 397–399. Berkeley: University of California Press.

Nath, Lala Baij. 1913. *The Adhyatma Ramayana*. Allahabad: Panini Office.

National School of Drama. 2002. *Bharat Rang Mahotsav* [Indian Theater Festival]: *An Overview*. New Delhi: National School of Drama.

Nilsson, Usha. 2000. "Grinding Millet but Singing of Sita: Power and Domination in Awadhi and Bhojpuri Women's Songs." In *Questioning Ramayanas, a South Asian Tradition*, ed. Paula Richman, pp. 137–158, 379–381. Berkeley: University of California Press.

Niranjana, Tejaswini. 1993. "Whose Culture Is It? Contesting the Modern." *Journal of Arts and Ideas* no. 25–26 (December): 139–151.

Omvedt, Gail. 1995. *Dalit Visions*. Tracts for the Times, 8. Hyderabad: Orient Longman.

Paniker, Ayyappa. 2003. "Theorising about a Theory." In *Interiorization (Antassannivesha): Essays on Literary Theory*, pp. 1–8. Kariavattom: University of Kerala, International Centre for Kerala Studies.

Pollock, Sheldon. 1993. "Ramayana and Political Imagination in India." *Journal of Asian Studies* 52, no. 2: 261–297.

———. 2006. *The Language of the Gods in the World of Men: Sanskrit, Culture, and Power in Premodern India*. Berkeley: University of California Press.

———, trans. 1991. *The Ramayana of Valmiki: An Epic of Ancient India*, vol. 3, *Aranyakanda*, gen. ed. Robert Goldman. Princeton: Princeton University Press.

Ponemballem Pillai, T. 1909. "The Morality of the Ramayana." *Malabar Quarterly Review* 8, no. 2 (June): 83.

Purnalingam Pillai, M. S. 1928. *Ravana the Great: King of Lanka*. Munnirpallam: Bibliotheca.

Raghavan, V. 1998. *Sanskrit Ramayanas Other than Valmiki's: The Adbhuta, Adhyatma and Ananda Ramayanas*. Chennai: V. Raghavan Centre for Performing Arts.

Raghunathan, N. 1982. *Srimad Valmiki Ramayanam*, 3 vols. Madras: Vighneswara.

Raheja, Gloria Goodwin, and Ann Grodzins Gold. 1994. *Listen to the Heron's Words: Reimagining Gender and Kinship in North India*. Berkeley: University of California Press.

Rajadhyaksha, Ashish, and Paul Willemen. 1994. *Encyclopedia of Indian Cinema*. New Delhi: Oxford University Press.

Rajagopalachari, C. 1961. *The Ayodhya Canto of the Ramayana as Told by Kamban*.

UNESCO Collection of Representative Works, Indian Series. New Delhi: Sahitya Akademi.

Ramakrishnan, E. V. 1995. *Making It New: Modernism in Malayalam, Marathi, and Hindi Poetry.* Shimla: Indian Institute of Advanced Study.

Ramanujan, A. K. 1986. "Two Realms of Kannada Folklore." In *Another Harmony: New Essays on the Folklore of India,* ed. Stuart Blackburn and A. K. Ramanujan, pp. 41–75. Berkeley: University of California Press.

————. 1991. "Three Hundred Ramayanas: Five Examples and Three Thoughts on Translation." In *Many Ramayanas: The Diversity of a Narrative Tradition in South Asia,* ed. Paula Richman, pp. 22–49. Berkeley: University of California Press.

Ramesh, S. R. 2000. "The Sociology of Content in Modern Kannada Plays." *Theatre India* 1 (May): 12–19.

Ranganath, H. K. 1982. *The Karnatak Theatre.* Dharwad: Karnatak University.

Ranganayakamma. 2004. *Ramayana: The Poisonous Tree [Stories, Essays and Footnotes].* Trans. B. R. Bapuji et al. Hyderabad: Sweet Home Publications.

Richman, Paula. 1991a. "E. V. Ramasami's Reading of the Ramayana." In *Many Ramayanas: The Diversity of a Narrative Tradition in South Asia,* ed. Paula Richman, pp. 175–201. Berkeley: University of California Press.

————, ed. 1991b. *Many Ramayanas: The Diversity of a Narrative Tradition in South Asia.* Berkeley: University of California Press.

————. 1995. "Epic and State: Contesting Interpretations of the Ramayana." *Public Culture* 7: 631–654.

————. 1997. *Extraordinary Child: Poems from a South Indian Devotional Genre.* SHAPS Library of Translations. Honolulu: University of Hawai'i Press.

————. 2001. "Questioning and Multiplicity within the Ramayana Tradition." In *Questioning Ramayanas, a South Asian Tradition,* ed. Paula Richman, pp. 1–21, 359–361. Berkeley: University of California Press.

————. 2004. "Why Can't a Shudra Perform Asceticism? Śambuka in Three Modern South Indian Plays." In *Ramayana Revisited,* ed. Mandakranta Bose, pp. 125–148. New York: Oxford University Press

————, and V. Geetha. 2006. "A View from the South: E. V. Ramasami's Public Critique of Religion." In *Siting Secularism,* ed. Anuradha Dingwaney Needham and Rajeswari Sunder Rajan. Durham: Duke University Press.

Robinson, David. 1979. "Indian Panorama." *Sight and Sound* 48, no. 2 (Spring): 91–92.

Sahdev, Majula. 1982. "The Portrayal of Rama in Sanskrit Plays." *National Center for the Performing Arts Quarterly Journal* XI (March): 14–24.

Sahitya Akademi. 1990. *Sahitya Akademi Awards: Books and Writers (1955–1978).* New Delhi: Sahitya Akademi.

Satchidanandan, K. 2005. "The *Ramayana* in Kerala." In *Retelling the Ramayana: Voices from Kerala,* trans. Vasanthi Sankaranarayanan, pp. 145–150. New Delhi: Oxford University Press.

Sen, Nabaneeta Dev. 1997. "Rewriting the Ramayana: Chandrabati and Molla." In *Crossing Boundaries,* ed. Geeti Sen, pp. 162–177. Hyderabad: Orient Longman.

Sengupta, Poile. 2003. *Thus Spake Shurpanakha, Thus Said Shakuni.* [Playscript]. Unpublished.

Shastri, Biswanarayan. 1988. "New Light on the Ahalya-Indra Story of the Ramayana." In *Studies in Ancient Indian History: C.C. Sircar Commemoration Volume,* pp. 345–352. Delhi: Sundeep Prakashan.

Shulman, David. 1985. *The King and the Clown in South Indian Myth and Poetry.* Princeton: Princeton University Press.

———. 2001. "Bhavabhuti on Cruelty and Compassion." In *Questioning Ramayanas, a South Asian Tradition,* ed. Paula Richman, pp. 49–82, 366–370. Berkeley: University of California Press.

Sitaramiah, V. 1977. *D. V. Gundappa.* Kannada Writers and Their Work Series. Mysore: Institute of Kannada Studies.

Sivasagar. 2000. "On-going History." Trans. Archana Chowhan. *Indian Literature* (November–December): 108.

Smith, H. Daniel. 1983. *Reading the Ramayana: A Bibliographic Guide for Students and College Teachers.* Syracuse: Maxwell School, South Asian Special Publications, no. 7.

Smith, William L. 1986. "Explaining the Inexplicable: Uses of the Curse in Rama Literature." In *Kalyanamitraraganam: Essays in Honor of Nils Simonsson,* ed. Eivind Kahrs., pp. 261–276. Oslo: Norwegian University Press, Institute for Comparative Research in Human Culture; Distr. Oxford University Press.

———. 1994. *Ramayana Traditions in Eastern India: Assam, Bengal, Orissa.* New Delhi: Munshiram Manoharlal Publishers.

Sreedevi, K. B. 2001. "The Disrupted Coronation." Trans. Jayashree Ramakrishnan Nair. *Samyukta: A Journal of Women's Studies* 1, no. 1 (January): 157–163.

Sreekantan Nair, C. N., and Sarah Joseph. 2005. *Retelling the Ramayana: Voices from Kerala.* Trans. Vasanthi Sankaranarayanan. New Delhi: Oxford University Press.

Sreenivasan, K. 1981. *Kumaran Asan: Profile of a Poet's Vision.* Trivandrum: Jayasree Publications.

Srinivas Iyengar, K. R. 1987. *Sitayana: Epic of the Earth-born.* Madras: Samata Books.

Subrahmania Mudaliyar, V. P. 1908. "A Critical Review of the Story of Ramayana and an Account of South Indian Castes Based on the Views of the Late Prof. P. Sundarama Pillai, M.A." *Tamil Antiquary* 1, no. 2: 1–48.

Subrahmanyam, Sanjay. 2005. *Explorations in Connected History,* 2 vols. New Delhi: Oxford University Press.

Trautmann, Thomas R. 1997. *Aryans and British India.* Berkeley: University of California Press.

Uma, Alladi, and M. Sridhar, eds. and trans. 2001. *Ayoni and Other Stories.* New Delhi: Katha.

Van Buitenen, J. A. B., trans. 1973. *Mahabharata,* vol. 2. Chicago: University of Chicago Press.

Vanita, Ruth. 2005. "The Sita Who Smiles: Wife as Goddess in the *Adbhut Ramayana.*" *Manushi* 148 (May–June): 32–39.

Venkatachalapathy, A. R. 2006. "Consuming Literature: The Contemporary Reputation of Pudumaippithan." In *In Those Days, There Was No Coffee: Writings in Cultural History,* pp. 73–85. New Delhi: Yoda Press.

Zarrilli, Phillip. 2000. *Kathakali Dance-drama: Where Gods and Demons Come to Play.* London: Routledge.

Zelliot, Eleanor. 1976. "The Medieval Bhakti Movement in History—An Essay on the Literature in English." In *Hinduism—New Essays in the History of Religions,* ed. Bardwell L. Smith, pp. 143–168. Leiden: E. J. Brill, 1976.

Zvelebil, Kamil. 1987. *Two Tamil Folktales: The Story of King Matanakama, The Story of Peacock Ravana.* New Delhi: Motilal Banarsidass and Paris: UNESCO.

Websites

http://ccat.sas.upenn.edu/plc/kannada
http://www.censusindia.net/results/eci11_page4.html
http://www.csmonitor.com/2005/0517/p12s01-legn.html
www.hinduonnet.com/fline/fl1809/1809030.htm

Contributors

SHASHI DESHPANDE is a novelist, literary critic, and translator. She has published nine novels, including *A Matter of Time; The Binding Vine; Small Remedies;* and *Moving On.* Among her nine short story collections, one of special interest to Ramayana and Mahabharata fans is *The Stone Woman and Other Stories.* She has also translated the memoirs and a play of Kannada playwright Adya Rangacharya into English. Her *Writing from the Margin and Other Essays* deals with literature, Indian writing in English, feminism, and women's writings. She also wrote the screenplay for the prize-winning Hindi feature film *Drishti,* served on the Advisory Board for English for the Sahitya Akademi, chaired the 2000 Commonwealth Writer's Prize jury, is a trustee of the Centre for the Study of Culture and Society, and advises Sanskriti, which promotes India culture, especially among children.

[JOHN] RICH[ARDSON] FREEMAN holds an M.A. in South Asian studies and a Ph.D. in anthropology from the University of Pennsylvania. His research and publications focus on the interrelation between folklore, classical and regional literatures, and the cultural anthropology of South India, specializing in Kerala. His articles have appeared in *Modern Asian Studies* and *South Asia Research,* and in *Questioning Ramayanas, a South Asian Tradition,* the *Blackwell Companion to Hinduism,* and *Literary Cultures in History: Reconstructions from South Asia.* He has taught cultural anthropology and religious studies at the University of Pennsylvania and the University of Michigan, and will begin teaching at Duke University in 2008.

LAKSHMI HOLMSTROM, translator and literary critic, studied at Madras and received her B.Litt. from Oxford University. Her translations of Tamil short stories include Na. Muthuswamy's *Neermai;* Ambai's *A Purple Sea* and *In a Forest, a Deer; Mauni: A Writer's Writer;* and *Pudumaippittan Fictions.* Her translations of longer works include Ashokamitran's *Water; Karukku,* the autobiography of Bama, a Dalit woman, which won the Crossword Translation Award in 2000; and Bama's *Sangati: Events.* She edited *Clarinda,* an English novel by A. Madhaviah that has been republished by Sahitya Akademi. Her essays have been published in *South Asia Research* and *Nivedini: Journal of Gender Studies.* She was chosen as a Royal Literary Fund Writing Fellow at the University of East Anglia from 2004 to 2006.

GIRISH KARNAD studied at Karnataka University, Dharwad, and at Oxford University, where he was a Rhodes Scholar. His plays include *Hayavadana,* winner of the Sangeet Natak Akademi Prize; *Nagamandala*, which premiered in the United States at the Guthrie Theater, Minneapolis; *The Fire and the Rain*, commissioned by the Guthrie; and *Bali the Sacrifice*, commission by the Leicester Haymarket Theatre. His other plays include *Yayati, Tughlaq, Anjumallige, Taledanda*, and *Tipu Sultan Kanda Kanasu* [The Dreams of Tipu Sultan]. His film *Samskara*, for which he wrote the script and played the lead, was initially banned by censors and when released won the President's Gold Medal. He has appeared in the films of Shyam Benegal as well as television serials of Satyajit Ray and Mrinal Sen. He also served as director of the Film and Television Institute of India (1974–1975), chairman of the Sangeet Natak Akademi (1988–1993), and director of the Nehru Centre in London (2000–2003). He received the Bharatiya Jnanpith Award, India's highest literary award, in 1993.

GITA KRISHNANKUTTY, who received her Ph.D. in English from University of Mysore in 1987, has published many translations from Malayalam into English, including Anand's *Death Certificate; Cast Me Out If You Will: Stories and Memoir by Lalithambika Anterjanam;* V. K. Madhavankutty's *The Village Before Time; A Childhood in Malabar: A Memoir* by Kamala Das; and M. T. Vasudevan Nair, *Master Carpenter*. Her translation of N. P. Mohammed's *The Eye of God* won the 1999 Sahitya Akademi Prize for translation, and her translation of M. Mukundan's *On the Banks of the Mayyazhi* won the Crossword Translation Award in 1999. She has provided subtitles for more than ten Malayalam films and published a historical monograph titled *A Life of Healing: A Biography of P. S. Varier*, about a major figure in the Ayurvedic medicine movement in Kerala.

KRISHNA RAO MADDIPATI, Assistant Professor in the Department of Radiation Oncology at Wayne State University, Detroit, received his Ph.D. in organic chemistry from Indian Institute of Science, Bangalore. He conducts basic research on the design, synthesis, and evaluation of anticancer agents targeting enzymes involved in the biosynthesis of eicosanoids that play a central role in carcinogenesis and metastasis. A founding member of the Detroit Telugu Literary Club, he helped organize the club Yahoo group, http://groups.yahoo.com/group/DTLCgroup, in 1998 to share information among its members and to foster the reading of Telugu literature. The club also arranges meetings with visiting Telugu scholars and publishes Telugu books. Its annual reading list includes poetry, short stories, novels, and literary criticism.

K. MARULASIDDAPPA received his Ph.D. in, and has taught, Kannada literature for over thirty-five years at Bangalore University, advising a large number of Ph.D. students in Kannada literature. Among his many books published by Bangalore University are *Lavanigalu* on Kannada ballads and *Kannada Nataka, Vimarshe* on Kannada drama. His *Adhunika Kannada Nataka* provides a history of Kannada drama, while *Kannada Nataka Samikshe* contains critical essays on Kannada theater from 1971 to 1985. He has translated Sophocles' *Elec-

tra, Euripedes' *Medea,* and Rabindranath Tagore's *Red Oleanders* into Kannada. An active member of many theater associations in Karnataka, including the Rangayana (Mysore) and Natya Sangha Theatre Centre and Samudaya in Bangalore, he has presented lectures on Kannada theater quite widely. He has served as chairman of the Nataka Academy of Karnataka, director of the Centre for Kannada Studies, Bangalore University, and as a fellow of the Karnataka Nataka Academy. He received Bangalore's Kempe Gowda Award and Karnataka State's Rajyotsava Award.

PRATIBHA NANDAKUMAR earned an M.Phil. in Kannada literature at Madras University and currently works as a writer, translator, and journalist. Her Kannada short stories have been collected into two volumes: *Yana* [Voyage] and *Akramana* [Intrusion]. Her Kannada essays came out as a book titled *Mirch Masala* [Chili Masala]. Among her six volumes of poetry, *Kavadeyata* [Game of Cowries] won the Karnataka State Sahitya Academy Award in 2000, and in 2003 she received the Mahadevi Verma poetry award. She has translated the English stories of Shashi Deshpande, as well as Padma Sachdev's Sahitya Akademy prize-winning Dogri poems, into Kannada. English readers will find selected poems by Nandakumar in English translation in the *Chicago Review*'s special issue on *Contemporary Indian Literature; In Their Own Voice: Modern Indian Women Poets* (edited by Arlene Zaid); and several issues of *Indian Literature.* She is senior sub-editor of the *New Indian Express* in Bangalore and directs Kriya Foundation, a cultural forum.

VELCHERU NARAYANA RAO holds the Krishnadevaraya Chair in the Department of Languages and Cultures of Asia at the University of Wisconsin, Madison. One of the foremost scholars of Telugu in the world, his *Classical Telugu Poetry* and *Twentieth Century Telugu Poetry* provide English readers with an overview of the sweep of Telugu poetry. Among his other recent works are *Girls for Sale,* a translation of Gurajada Apparao's classic play *Kanyasulkam* (Indiana University Press, 2007); and, in collaboration with David Shulman, *God on the Hill: Temple Poems from Tirupati,* a translation of the songs of Annamayya; and *The Sound of the Kiss or a Story That Should Never Be Told* and *Demon's Daughter: A Love Story from South India,* both by Pingali Suranna. With Shulman and Sanjay Subrahmanyam, he wrote *Textures of Time: Writing History in South India, 1600–1800.* Among his articles dealing with the Ramayana tradition, the one most relevant to this anthology is "When Does Sita Cease to Be Sita?" in *Ramayanas Revisited.*

SAILAZA EASWARI PAL, a recipient of a Fulbright fellowship, has conducted research on Telugu literature and gender in Andhra Pradesh and taught courses on Indian literature, literatures of the world, and mythology in the Program in Comparative Literature at Rutgers University. Her dissertation, "Sexual Discourse and Telugu Modernity: A Reading of Gudipati Venkata Chalam's *Maidanam,*" examines the works of Chalam in terms of the modern novel and

Telugu feminism. She founded Open Field Media, LLC, an arts and entertainment company that promotes cross-cultural projects in the United States and India, and is at work on a monograph about Chalam.

LEELA PRASAD, Associate Professor of Religion at Duke University, received her Ph.D. in folklore and folklife from the University of Pennsylvania. She published *Poetics of Conduct: Narrative and Moral Being in a South Indian Town,* in which she explores relationships between oral narrative, moral identity, and the poetics of everyday language in Sringeri, South India. As guest curator of an exhibition on Indian American life in Philadelphia, she also edited and contributed to the catalogue of essays, *Live Like the Banyan Tree: Images of the Indian American Experience.* She co-edited and wrote the introduction for *Gender and Story in India,* on women-performed narratives in different cultural and linguistic settings of South India.

PAULA RICHMAN, William H. Danforth Professor of South Asian Religions in the Department of Religion at Oberlin College, has published in the fields of Tamil literature and Ramayana studies. Her most recent monograph on Tamil literature is *Extraordinary Child: Poems from a South Indian Devotional Genre.* She has edited two collections of multi-authored articles: *Many Ramayanas: The Diversity of a Narrative Tradition in South Asia* and *Questioning Ramayanas, a South Asian Tradition,* and co-edited an anthology of translations from Tamil into English titled *A Gift of Tamil.* Her articles on the Ramayana tradition have appeared in *Public Culture, Journal of Asian Studies, Cultural Dynamics,* and *Manushi.*

MANU SHETTY is a Ph.D. candidate of the Committee on Social Thought at the University of Chicago. He was a student of A. K. Ramanujan and collaborated with him on translations of several contemporary Kannada short stories. Shetty won the Katha Prize Stories national award for excellence in translation in 1993. This translation also won the Katha Prize Stories, Best of the 1990s, award in 2002. He has also published an article on the *Bhagavad Gita* in *Journal of the Indian Council of Philosophical Research.*

M. SRIDHAR teaches courses at the M.Phil. and Ph.D. level in the Department of English at the University of Hyderabad, Hyderabad. He has published *Language, Criticism and Culture: Leavis and the Organic Community,* which explores the role of Leavis in developing the field of English studies, and in subsequent criticism and theory. He publishes in the areas of literary criticism, English in India, women's writing, and translation. Among his translations (with A. Uma) from Telugu into English are *Ayoni and Other Stories,* an anthology of Telugu short stories about women and society from 1910 to the present, and *Brothers of Chi Chi Baba,* a children's story about the dangers of nuclear arms in South Asia by D. P. Sen Gupta.

ALLADI UMA teaches courses at the M.Phil. and Ph.D. level in the Department of English at the University of Hyderabad, Hyderabad. Her monograph *Woman and Her Family: Indian and Afro-American: A Literary Perspective* compares the novels of Afro-American and Indian English women writers. She publishes in the areas of African American literature, Indian writing, women's studies, and translation. She has also been active in bringing together translators from Telugu into English for seminars and workshops in Hyderabad. Among her translations (with M. Sridhar) are *Beware, the Cows Are Coming* by Rachakonda Viswanatha Sastry, a mid-twentieth-century novel known for its use of the technique of subversion, and *Antarani Vasantam* [Untouchable Spring] by Kalyan Rao.

RIZIO YOHANNAN RAJ is a novelist, poet, and literary critic. Her novels in Malayalam include *Avinashom,* a work provoked by the suicide of a promising Malayalam writer, and *Yatrikom,* which explores self-exile and return, using a mid-Travancore dialect. *Indian Literature,* the official journal of the Indian Academy of Literature, featured her as one of India's new poets in January 2006, and *Samyukta,* the journal of the Women's Studies Center, University of Kerala, featured her poetry in July 2004. At Navneet Publications India, she pioneered commissioning original works in genres such as horror, adventure, fantasy, and coming-of-age novels for adolescent Indian readers. She edited the three-volume collected poetry of K. Satchidanandan and an issue on Dalit poetry for *Nagarakavitha.* She has also translated two Swedish novels by Torgny Lindgren.

USHA ZACHARIAS works on media, gender, violence, and citizenship in the context of neoliberalism and religious nationalism. She teaches international communication at the Department of Communication, Westfield State College, Westfield, Massachusetts. Her doctoral work focused on the gender and caste politics of the television Ramayana. Most relevant to this anthology is her article "Trial by Fire: Gender, Power, and Citizenship in Narratives of the Nation" in *Social Text.* Other journal articles have appeared in *Critical Studies in Media Communication* and *Cultural Dynamics.* A former journalist in India, her writings have appeared in the *Times of India, Cinema in India,* and *Deccan Herald.* She now writes a monthly column for the Malayalam magazine *Pachakuthira.*

Index